MRS.
PLANSKY
GOES
ROGUE

MRS. PLANSKY GOES ROGUE

SPENCER QUINN

TOR PUBLISHING GROUP

New York

MRS. PLANSKY GOES ROGUE

A Forge Book
Published by Tor Publishing Group / Tom Doherty Associates
120 Broadway
New York, NY 10271

www.torpublishinggroup.com

Forge® is a registered trademark of Macmillan Publishing Group, LLC.

The Library of Congress Cataloging-in-Publication Data is available upon request.

ISBN 978-1-250-33183-0 (hardcover)
ISBN 978-1-250-33184-7 (ebook)

Our books may be purchased in bulk for promotional, educational, or
business use. Please contact your local bookseller or the Macmillan Corporate and
Premium Sales Department at 1-800-221-7945, extension 5442, or by email at
MacmillanSpecialMarkets@macmillan.com.

First Edition: 2025

Printed in the United States of America

0   9   8   7   6   5   4   3   2   1

For Seth, Ben, Lily, and Rosie, who mean so much

MRS.
PLANSKY
GOES
ROGUE

ONE

"What's your favorite sports cliché?" said Kev Dinardo.

"In general?" Mrs. Plansky said. "Or possibly useful at the moment?"

Kev turned to her and smiled, a sweat drop quivering on the end of his chin. They hadn't known each other long, just a few months, mostly getting together on the tennis court, but it was enough for her to have learned he had two smiles: a big one when he was happy about something, which was often, and a small, quickly vanishing one that flashed when he was struck by an unexpected insight. This particular smile was the second.

Mrs. Plansky searched her mind. Her background was not one of those sports-free backgrounds, so she knew many sports clichés, but now she came up empty. That was frustrating. This whole situation, taking place on Court #1 at the New Sunshine Golf and Tennis Club, was frustrating. Her face felt flushed, and not just from the exertion and the heat. Mrs. Plansky loved playing tennis. She liked to win. She did not hate to lose. Her son, Jack, out in Arizona, a gifted player with professional experience on the satellite tour and now a teaching pro, hated to lose. He liked to win. Did he still love or had he ever loved playing tennis? She shied away from that question. What if he'd devoted his whole professional life to something he didn't love? What kind of toll would that take? But this wasn't the slightest bit relevant, not at the moment. What was relevant? The fact that although she didn't hate to lose, she hated to lose like this.

"Here are some," Kev said. They were on a changeover between games, sitting on a courtside bench. The sweat drop wobbled off his chin—a strong, squarish chin that might have been a bit much on some male faces but not his—and fell, somehow landing on her bare knee, cooling a tiny circle of her skin. "It ain't over till it's over. One play at a time. Go down swinging."

Mrs. Plansky was unmoved by any of them, especially the last. Over on the other courtside bench their opponents had set aside their energy drinks and were rising. Changeovers lasted forty-five seconds, but at club level events no one was strict about it, although the umpire in her chair did seem to be glancing down at them. Also the opponents, representing the Old Sunshine Country Club in this North Beaches Sixties and Over Mixed Doubles Championship match, were now on their feet and bouncing a bit, eager to get this—what would you call it? Demolition? Close enough. This demolition over and done. The two clubs were ancient rivals, ancient for this part of the world, going all the way back to the 1995 founding of New Sunshine. Old Sunshine dated from 1989 and had old Florida pretensions. Its members had to wear white on the court. Half white was the rule at New Sunshine: Kev, for example, now in white shorts and a crimson tee, and Mrs. Plansky in a sleeveless peach-colored tennis dress with white trim perhaps making up ten percent of the whole, or not even. She could be something of an outlaw at times.

"Just choose one," Kev said. "I hate to point it out, Loretta, but we're running out of time."

Mrs. Plansky rose and picked up her racket. The opponents were striding onto the court, the woman, Jenna St. Something or Other taking her place at the net and the man, Russell Curtis or possibly Curtis Russell, heading to the baseline to serve. Neither of them looked older than forty-nine. They'd had work done, of course, but still. Mrs. Plansky, too, had had work done, just the once a few years ago, on an afternoon outing with her daughter, Nina, down for a few days from her home in Hilton Head. A nice mother-daughter Botox bonding experience that had resulted in temporary simulacrums of rejuvenation here and there on her face. She was trying to recall some funny remark of Nina's on the subject of needles when Kev said, "Loretta?"

"Right," said Mrs. Plansky. She sipped from her water bottle and took in the here and now. They had an audience, maybe fifty or sixty members of both clubs, sitting in lawn chairs and on the clubhouse patio, some fanning themselves. It was the first hot and humid day of the year. Mrs. Plansky was unsure of Kev's age but probably no more than five or six years less than hers, and she herself was seventy-one. She had an artificial hip, in no way detrimental, and in fact the best joint in her body, a sturdy body that had served her well in many ways, even capable of some foot speed at one time. She'd been a tomboy as a kid, played PeeWee hockey with the boys back home in Rhode Island. But actually irrelevant to the present situation, the headline for which would be: trailing 6–1, 5–love in a best-of-three set match. She didn't have to look to know that some of the spectators were glancing at their watches, planning drinks, dinner, perhaps a quick sail or swim. That was the overview. Mrs. Plansky, going back to her days in business, believed in overviews. Norm had been more about winging it; a bit strange since he'd been the one with the engineering degree.

She put her hand on Kev's shoulder, a thick shoulder, much more muscular than Norm's, Norm being husband, business partner, tennis partner, and love of her life, with whom she'd played countless matches and had looked forward to many more when they retired down to Ponte d'Oro, but one of those quick and merciless cancers had felled him soon after. How she'd loved playing with him! But Kev was the better player. The thought gave her a pang of disloyalty. Was this the time for all that? Certainly not! Overviews yes, but you could overdo the over part and end up with a blurry picture. Focus, Loretta!

"Kev," she said. "You're wrong about running out of time."

"Oh?" he said, an expectant expression crossing his face. For a second or two she could see how he'd looked as a kid.

"There is no clock in tennis. Let's stretch it out, way, way out."

Kev laughed. "Like Einstein's relativity!"

"I don't know about that," said Mrs. Plansky.

And they were both laughing when they took their places on the court to return serve. Puzzled frowns appeared on the faces of their opponents. Who laughs when they're getting their asses kicked?

Late afternoons in April could bring enormous thunderheads looming in off the sea, and somehow those four players—Russell Curtis, Jenna St. Something or Other, Kev, and Mrs. Plansky—were still on Court #1 to see those thunderheads closing in. By that time Mrs. Plansky knew that Russell was the first name, since Jenna had taken to hissing to him after some of the points, as in "Russell! Hit to the open court!" And "Russell! He's getting you with that wide serve every goddam time!" Also, "Her backhand volley, Russell? Hello? How many times do you need to see it?"

Mrs. Plansky and Kev chipped and sliced, lobbed and dinked, came to the net, stayed back, served Australian, used signals, pretended to use signals, went down the middle over and over until Russell and Jenna were squeezing in so close that they whacked each other's rackets trying to make the shot, which Mrs. Plansky and Kev took as an invitation to start hitting down the line. Time expanded beautifully. Mrs. Plansky stopped feeling flushed, her flush perhaps finding its way to Jenna's face. Mrs. Plansky's kick serve even appeared, after an absence of fifteen years. Not a word was spoken, not between Mrs. Plansky and Kev. There was no need. Had she actually patted him on the butt as he pulled off yet one more killer backpedaling overhead? Good grief.

Final score: New Sunshine 1–6, 7–6 (11), 6–4. They'd hugged at the end, pretty standard in mixed doubles. Kev had lifted her right off the ground—which was not standard—somehow making it look easy. She'd been struck by a strange and simple thought at that moment: *More.*

*   *   *

The first raindrops were falling by the time Mrs. Plansky and Kev left the clubhouse. He'd come on his bike, so they stowed it in the back of her SUV—Mrs. Plansky, a mother and grandmother, drove SUVs by long habit—and she took him home, their two trophies bumping together in the backseat.

"Wow," Kev said. "Unreal."

Mrs. Plansky nodded. She tried to think of any other time in her life when the unreal had really happened, and found several right away. For example, there was the camping trip when the kids, Nina and Jack, were small, Norm working at a small engineering firm and making little, Mrs. Plansky a paralegal and making slightly more, when she, fixing sandwiches, said, "Wouldn't it be nice if the knife could toast the bread while you sliced?" An unreality that just popped out. Norm, dozing in his sleeping bag, sat right up. Three years later came the Plansky Toaster Knife, and the small fortune—quite small given the kinds of fortunes that are out there these days—that followed. Or how about Norm on his deathbed—Norm, who couldn't hold the simplest tune—suddenly singing "My Funny Valentine" in a smooth, lovely baritone? And he a tenor to boot? Or take that fairly recent Romanian adventure where after decades of law abidance, she'd purloined—

"Next left," Kev said, gesturing toward a lane lined with silver buttonwoods and paved with sun-bleached seashells. His hand touched down on Mrs. Plansky's hand, resting on the console. He gave a little squeeze. Her hand, acting strictly on its own, rolled over and squeezed back. Rolled over? Rolled over like . . . like some . . . some eager beaver rolling over in bed! Eager beaver? For God's sake! Get a grip. The flush, maybe just on loan to Jenna, returned to her face. What with endorphins and all that, Mrs. Plansky knew she was in a heightened state, just from the length of the match, never mind the triumphant conclusion, but still. Was something about to happen? If so, what? Despite the fact that she was not dating—although she and Kev had had dinner together at the new sushi place by the marina once or twice, which couldn't be called dating—and had never visited any of those apps—Match.com, OkCupid, Mishmash.net,

whatever all those names were—and was perfectly content with
things as they were, deep down Mrs. Plansky knew the answer to
what could happen. It could be . . . anything! Somewhere in the
middle distance thunder boomed.

Kev's hand moved away. He pointed. "Second driveway."

Ah, a baritone. She hadn't realized that until this moment. A full-
time baritone. The rain was pelting down now, the windshield wip-
ers on max, the car steaming up inside. Steaming up would be an
example of that literary technique where nature imitates the moods
of man, the word not coming to her at the moment, although she
could picture Mr. Cabral, tenth-grade English teacher, a little guy
with nicotine fingers and nicotine mustache, explaining the whole
thing. Mrs. Plansky took the second driveway. Thunder boomed
again, closer now, and the sky tried out a rapid color selection, settling on purple.

Kev's house rose at the end of the driveway, an elevated house
with hurricane-resistant curved lines, streamlined and perhaps bigger than it appeared. Through the gun barrel pilings she could see
the ocean, a strip of beach, a white, crimson trimmed boat with a
tall tuna tower, tied to a wooden dock. Perhaps yacht would be the
right word, more precise than boat. How big? Mrs. Plansky was no
expert on yachts—Norm prone to seasickness in anything bigger
than a kayak—but she guessed about fifty feet, although the yacht,
streamlined like the house, also might be bigger than it appeared.

Mrs. Plansky parked in front of the house. "My, my," she said,
"what a lovely—"

Time, which had slowed down so nicely on Court #1 now sped
up in a way that made it hard to keep track of things and was not
nice at all. First came another boom, this one the loudest yet, practically right on top of them. Then—but more accurately at the same
instant—the sleek white yacht with the crimson trim burst into
flames, exploded, was replaced by a ball of fire.

Kev jumped out of the car and ran under the house, toward the
dock. Mrs. Plansky jumped out, too, and ran after him through the
pouring rain, for no reason, just instinctive heart-pounding thought-

lessness on her part, her mind completely empty of thought. Well, not quite true. There was one thought: What about the lightning that always preceded thunder, thunder actually being the sound of lightning, as Norm had explained to the kids on another one of those camping trips? Mrs. Plansky had seen no lightning.

TWO

Too late. There was nothing to be done, the fire already in its roaring midlife stage. Mrs. Plansky realized all that but at the same time she found a hose coiled on the dock, turned on the faucet, and was now sending a limp stream of water into the conflagration, somehow all the more pitiful since it was still raining pretty hard to no effect on the fire. From where she stood she could see the name of the boat, gold-painted on the stern: *Lizette.* The name melted away, slowly at first and then fast. The lines tying the boat burned up and *Lizette* tilted toward the sea and began drifting off. Roaring amped down. Sizzling amped up. Mrs. Plansky glanced at Kev. He stood by a mooring bollard, arms folded across his chest, face impassive, the fire reflected in his eyes. Mrs. Plansky turned off the faucet, recoiled the hose, and moved beside him, putting her arm around his back. They were both soaked through and through.

At first he didn't seem to notice her, might as well have been a statue with a pulse. She thought about saying, *It could have been worse,* but that was stupid. What would be helpful or comforting or at least relevant that wasn't stupid? She still hadn't come up with anything when the rain stopped all at once. Kev suddenly came to life, turned, took her in his arms, and kissed her, a kiss that grew deep, passionate, intimate, and took Mrs. Plansky completely by surprise, but which she returned in kind. Surprise number two, although in kind might not have been accurate, since she'd been out of practice with Norm gone—as long as you didn't count the events of one unplanned night during her Romanian adventure, a sort of sub-adventure. But now the memory of that got mixed in with present-time action, a super-charging combo of mind and body, so who knows what would have come next there on Kev's dock, with *Lizette*, her fire flickering out, now mostly underwater, only the sport tower and the ends of the outrigger rods still showing? Mrs. Plansky's heightened state had heightened some more, so much that she felt like a different person and not a seventy-one-year-old widow with an artificial hip and perhaps—well, no perhaps about it—a few extra pounds on board a body that had always been strongly built, which was how she preferred to look at that whole question. So the truth was that anything could have come next out on Kev's dock despite—or because of!—the end of *Lizette*, but right then sirens sounded, close by and urgent. They let go and backed away from each other. Thunder boomed one more time, distant now and in the west, the storm drifting inland.

A fire truck rolled up the driveway, lights flashing, siren off, seashells crunching under the big wheels. Three firefighters hopped out and hurried toward the dock, two men and a woman. They had numbers on their helmets—27, 99, 133. They took in the remains of the fire and didn't bother unspooling their fire hose. 99 snapped a few photos on his phone and 133 made a call on his. 27, the woman, turned to Kev and Mrs. Plansky, gave them each a quick close look.

"Anyone on board?"

"No, thank God," Kev said.

"This your place?"

"Yes. Well, mine. My name's Dinardo."

27 motioned toward what remained of *Lizette*. "What happened, Mr. Dinardo?"

"We were just driving in and the rain was coming down hard but I got a pretty good look. It was a lightning strike. Toward the stern, I think, but I'm not sure. It was just a big bright flash."

27 glanced at Mrs. Plansky. "Anything to add to that?"

Mrs. Plansky didn't quite know what to add. She would have preferred subtraction, specifically regarding the lightning strike. There had to have been one but that wasn't the same as seeing it. She ended up saying, "I don't think I've ever heard a louder boom." And thus sounding stupid.

27 didn't seem at all surprised by that. She turned back to Kev. "What kind of vessel?"

"Bertram Fifty-S."

"Diesel?" she said.

"Yes."

"Tank capacity?"

"Twelve hundred and some."

"How full?"

"Only about a quarter, maybe less."

27 turned to the other two firefighters, standing on the edge of the dock. "Any slick on the water?"

"Nope," said 99, a short, broadly built guy with a grizzled beard.

"Musta all combusted," said 133, a tall, skinny kid who looked like he might still have been in high school.

"Uh-huh," said 27, her tone discouraging further comment on his part. The kid looked down at his shoes—not shoes, of course, but heavy rubber boots with yellow toe caps. "And get hold of the harbormaster."

"Already done," said 99.

27 turned to Kev. "How's your insurance?"

"Good," said Kev.

"Don't want to jump the gun but the harbormaster will be wanting to short haul what's left down there."

"Should be covered," Kev said.

27 nodded. "Act of God."

"Yeah," said Kev. He shot Mrs. Plansky a quick glance.

"How about we get started on the paperwork?" 27 said.

"Sure." Kev gave Mrs. Plansky a little smile and followed 27 to the fire truck.

The sky began to darken, night moving in fast the way it did down here, down here being how Mrs. Plansky still thought of Florida. A bright light appeared to the south, grew brighter very fast, and soon the harbormaster's patrol boat was gliding into the dock.

133 helped the harbormaster tie up. 99, the short, thickly built guy with the grizzled beard, approached her.

"Mrs. Plansky?" he said.

"Uh, yes?"

"Thought I recognized you."

That was the moment Mrs. Plansky realized she was still wearing her sleeveless peach-colored tennis dress with white trim, not at all a water-repellent garment and still soaked from the rain and therefore on the clingy side. Very clingy, in fact. She could feel just how clingy it was, especially here and there, but dared not look.

"Ah," she said, "I'm sorry but I don't—"

"No, we never met but I've seen you a few times."

"Oh?"

"From out in your parking lot. Picking up Lucrecia when her car was in the shop. I'm her worser half, Joe Santiago."

"Of course, of course." Although she would have preferred to somehow arrange her arms in a body shield position, she shook hands with Joe Santiago. "I don't know what we'd do without Lucrecia."

"Same," said Joe.

Lucrecia was the home health aide who came to Mrs. Plansky's place for four hours every weekday to . . . well, to basically entertain Mrs. Plansky's dad—who despite being ninety-eight had no apparent health problems, although he himself in toto was just about unfailingly problematic—and Mrs. Plansky regretted her last remark immediately. Did it sound patronizing? What could she say to smooth things over? Nothing came to her. Then something sizzled out on the water, actually more of a hiss. They both turned to look but there was nothing to see except dying embers. *Lizette* was gone.

"We were just playing tennis," she said.

Joe sounded very surprised. "You and Lucrecia?"

"No, no, although I'm sure it—" Mrs. Plansky slammed on the brakes before she began a description of the fun she and Lucrecia would have on the tennis court, both she and Joe knowing full well that Lucrecia had no interest in tennis or any other sport. She gestured toward the fire engine, where Kev was saying something and 27 was writing it down on a notepad. "With Kev. Mr. Dinardo. He lives here."

Joe glanced around. "Where's the court?"

"Not here, but earlier, over at—"

Before she could make herself even more ridiculous, the man at the wheel of the patrol boat called over. "Joe? Got a sec?"

"Nice seein' ya," said Joe, walking away.

Mrs. Plansky wanted to call after him: *I'm not even rich! Just comfortable!* In her mind she heard what that would sound like before she could speak.

She stood alone on the dock, watched the harbormaster's crew shine flashlights on the water. Somewhere farther off a piece of wreckage burst into flame. She watched it die down to nothing. Did people still use the word *comfortable* to mean whatever the hell she meant by it? Probably not. Your language gets outdated as you age. You end up becoming like a foreigner. My goodness! What thoughts were these? She heard Norm's voice in her head. *Hook.* Just the one word, his customary signal that it was time for them to leave wherever they were, the hook being the kind that whisked vaudeville performers offstage.

Mrs. Plansky walked off the dock, slowing down when she reached the fire engine. Kev interrupted whatever 27 was telling him and turned to her. "Sorry for all this, Loretta."

"I just hope everything's okay," she said.

"Should take a few days to sort out. I'll be in touch."

"When you have time," said Mrs. Plansky. In her mind—and so brazen!—she thought but absolutely did not say, *To be continued.* Instead she waved what she imagined was a noncommittal goodbye, then got into her car and drove away. The fire engine lights kept flashing in all her mirrors until she made the turn onto the coast road. She dialed up the heat, hoping it would dry out her tennis dress but it only made things clammy. First thing when she got home would be a shower.

As she passed the Green Turtle Club, a Bahamian-style bar with conch fritters Mrs. Plansky craved now and then, she hit a little pothole and the trophies bumped together in the backseat. What remained of her heightened state lowered itself back down to ground zero. Mrs. Plansky's eyesight was kind of marvelous since the cataract surgery, a tiny personal miracle. But she hadn't seen the lightning strike. She probably didn't see a lot of things.

Sometimes Mrs. Plansky pictured abstractions in her mind. She'd been doing it since childhood, had never really thought about it, or wondered if others did the same. For example, she now pictured a door, just a plain simple wooden door, like you'd find in millions of homes. She closed it on the lightning question.

After Norm's death, Mrs. Plansky sold their nice little house on the inland waterway—certainly little compared to the other houses around—and bought a condo on a rise overlooking Little Pine Lake, not far away. Rises were rare in the county and the Little Pine condos, all twelve units, took advantage of the slope, facing away from the entrance and overlooking the lake, a perfectly round spring-fed lake that was refreshing year round, although no one had been swimming in it lately. Mrs. Plansky's condo was number 12, an end unit. She parked and went inside.

Lucrecia was in the front hall, dusting the top surfaces of the picture frames. She didn't have to do that. Cleaning wasn't part of the job but bringing that up was pointless. Lucrecia liked to keep busy. She was in her late fifties, looked something like Carmen Miranda, minus the glamour part, but somehow just as impressive or maybe more, at least in Mrs. Plansky's eyes.

"Lucrecia? You're still here?"

Lucrecia was not one to respond to questions in a traditional manner, if at all. "Oh my God! You look like a drowned rat. Joe just told me all about it. What a scare!" From out of nowhere she produced a towel and tossed it to Mrs. Plansky. "But at least you won. Felicidades."

"Thanks."

"Where's the trophy?"

"Left it in the car."

Lucrecia laughed. "What a cool customer!" she said. "Dry your hair."

Mrs. Plansky, the uncoolest customer Mrs. Plansky knew, dried her hair. "How's he doing?"

"Just fine. Had a nice dinner—spaghetti with that meat sauce he likes, with the anchovies, plus they shared a bottle of red wine—and went to bed."

"They?"

Lucrecia nodded. "She claimed to be suddenly tired. They both claimed to be suddenly tired."

Mrs. Plansky glanced past Lucrecia. The condo had two bedrooms: Mrs. Plansky's on the first floor and a guest room upstairs. There'd also been a small first floor study, but it had been converted into a bedroom for her father when . . . when how to put it? When he got thrown out of Arcadia Gardens? Close enough. Arcadia Gardens was an assisted-living place about forty-five minutes away, where her dad had passed two or three somewhat disruptive and expensive years, the expense borne willingly by Mrs. Plansky and the disruptiveness just borne. He'd had many disagreements with fellow residents and staff, although none violent—with the exception of the beer bottle incident—but the climax, as it were, had come, as it were, on account of his romantic life, of which Mrs. Plansky had been unaware for a long time and was now way too aware. It turned out he'd had a girlfriend, as he put it, or two in Arcadia Gardens, but on different floors and supposedly ignorant of each other's existence. Both were named Polly, a setup for trouble, but in the end trouble had come from somewhere else, much closer to home. One of the Pollys was just a few years younger than Mrs. Plansky's dad, but the other was still in her seventies, meaning not much older than Mrs. Plansky. She'd squirmed, an actual physical squirm, when she first heard that. There was some disagreement among the staff whether the Pollys knew what was going on, or if they even cared. When it was all over Mrs. Plansky had asked her dad about that. "I wouldn't know," he told her. None of that mattered. What blew things up was the appearance of Clara Dominguez de Soto y Camondo, Lucrecia's mother. She'd met Mrs. Plansky's dad when he was staying here at the condo, with Lucrecia hired to watch over him while Mrs. Plansky was in Romania, Arcadia Gardens being closed to him on account of Mrs. Plansky's money difficulties at the time, which turned out to be temporary. Not that she'd made a complete financial recovery but she had more than enough. Those with more than enough, in her opinion, should keep their traps shut about . . . well, practically everything. The point was that the recovery had made it possible for him to return to Arcadia Gardens, reluctantly, and as it had turned out also briefly.

Like a college kid from the fifties—which was what Mrs. Plansky's dad had been, Princeton as he mentioned at every opportunity and even non-opportunity, although people seemed to care about that less and less—smuggling a date back to his dorm room, he'd snuck Clara into Arcadia Gardens on a few or possibly more than a few nights. Clara was her dad's age or even older. That was what finally incensed the Pollys, first the younger and then the older, or possibly the reverse. Things had gotten noisy late one night, first in her dad's room but then spilling out and involving a lot of spectators and kibitzers on several floors. The next day Mrs. Plansky and her dad checked out other assisted livings within a hundred-mile radius. That night he was back at Little Pine Lake.

"Hungry?" Lucrecia said. "I can fix you something."

"Thanks," said Mrs. Plansky. "I'm fine."

"Want me to wake her up, take her home?"

Mrs. Plansky shook her head. "She's no trouble."

"We both know that's a crock," said Lucrecia. "I'll swing by first thing."

After Lucrecia left, Mrs. Plansky took her shower. To get to the master suite she had to pass the former study, now her dad's bedroom, on the way. She slowed down when she came to his closed door. She heard Clara saying something. Although Clara had come penniless from Cuba at the age of nineteen, where she'd been something of a figure on whatever they called their debutante scene, she still didn't seem to speak any English at all. Her dad knew only a few words of Spanish, such as *toro*, which he'd picked up on a long-ago trip to Seville with a cigar club he'd belonged to, and *con hielo*, which he used when ordering his Scotch from any olive-skinned bartender. Nevertheless Mrs. Plansky was pretty sure she heard him chuckle at whatever Clara had just said. A low chuckle, but somehow weighty, as though powered by the lungs of a much younger man. Perhaps there was a much younger man in there, and things were even more off the rails than she thought.

THREE

Mrs. Plansky awoke to find herself in her favorite sleeping position, a sort of twisted *K*. Norm—an engineer, don't forget—had come up with an inverted *C* that fit the twisted *K* perfectly. Once, at a boring party, or maybe even at a not-so-boring one, she'd turned to him and said, "How about some of that old KC?" Perhaps raising her voice a bit over the din. Some nearby guest overheard and jumped in. "Can't beat the barbeque," she'd said. But Norm got the message and they'd skedaddled soon after. Wouldn't a little skedaddling now be just the—

She sat up. The light coming through the curtains wasn't right. Well, it was right, but just for later. Had she slept in? Mrs. Plansky awoke naturally between 6:45 and 7 every single morning. She checked the bedside clock: 8:20. 8:20? Good grief. The day was practically wasted already. Wasting time was a sin in Miss Terrance's book, Miss Terrance having been her ninth-grade home ec teacher, back in a time when there was such a thing as home ec. "God gives us a certain amount of time, girls. Wasting any of that gift is an insult to him." Classroom instruction from another time—and a time Mrs. Plansky was unwilling to say was better than the present—but it still lived inside her as part of her ramshackle philosophy of life. So get up now! That was the point.

Mrs. Plansky got out of bed. There was some bodily resistance, especially from her new hip, the left one. Not a brand-new hip—now in its second year—but it was a big success, had been quiet for months. Of course she'd been on the court yesterday for what must have been almost three hours, so what did she expect? After all . . . At that moment she remembered what had happened at Kev's: storm, explosion, fire. She checked her phone. A bunch of congratulatory texts from New Sunshine members, but nothing from Kev. She gave her head a smack—very light, mostly symbolic—to encourage it to remember faster in future. Then she put on her robe, steadied herself by the dresser, moved her left leg this way and that. Good enough.

Mrs. Plansky went down the hall. The door to the former study— she wasn't ready to call it her dad's room just yet, preferred to think in terms of a visit with no fixed end date—was open, no one inside, and the bed was made, which was a first since he'd arrived. Not that he didn't care whether his bed was made. He cared very much and had specific and detailed beliefs on proper bed making, which he was happy to share with any actual bedmaker.

Mrs. Plansky found her dad on the patio, a nice patio, private and overlooking the lake, where a brown pelican was rising heavily off the water, a squirming crab in its long yellow beak, a beak with a strange red mark near the tip. Her dad was taking no notice of that, instead was sitting at the round glass table, his wheelchair nearby, and polishing off a fine-looking breakfast of bacon and eggs over easy but not too easy, which was how he liked them. Therefore, since neither he nor Clara could cook anything, Lucrecia had already been by.

"Morning, Dad."

He didn't look at her but he did wave a fork in her direction. "Take a seat."

And just like that, she was a guest in her own home. "Don't mind if I do," she said, sending a message he showed no sign of receiving. He dipped a strip of bacon in a marmalade jar and chewed on it slowly. Her dad had once been handsome in a *Mad Men* way but there wasn't much of that left, and from certain angles he even looked a little orc-like, although he did have an almost full head of hair, and not all of it white. He was wearing pressed khakis with a golf-themed belt, polished tassel loafers, and a pajama top.

"Pour me some coffee?" he said "There's a princess. And have some yourself."

Lucrecia had left the Thermos-style carafe on the table, plus an extra mug. Mrs. Plansky poured and sat down, not opposite her dad but sideways to him, partly so she could enjoy the view, but also so she could keep an eye out for Fairbanks. Like many gators in the ponds, lakes, springs, and backwaters of Florida, Fairbanks had been given a harmless-sounding name by the locals, in his—or possibly her—case by Ms. Pietsch of condo #9, a retired professor of film history who'd been the first to encounter Fairbanks on a morning kayak paddle some months before and sold out soon after.

"Too bad I hadn't known about that," her dad said, still at Arcadia Gardens at the time. "Woulda snapped it up."

With what money? Mrs. Plansky hadn't said at the time.

Chandler Wills Banning—Mrs. Plansky's dad—came from a family that, as Mrs. Plansky now understood in retrospect, had been on a descending glide path for a long time, but he was the one who tipped the nose straight down, buying for real into a personal financial image he had to have known, if he simply checked the numbers, was false. First he'd wasted his inheritance, then had a career in various corners of the finance industry where he had to compete against people who'd gotten there by competing, which—again she understood in retrospect—he had no idea how to do. In some ways, maybe all, he was the exact opposite of Norm. Once—this was after it was clear that the Plansky Toaster Knife was a big success, although not crazy big, Mrs. Plansky never under any illusions about that, and around the time her dad requested that first "eeny weeny super short term" loan—she'd said to Norm, "Did he misread the scorecard? Thinking it says he was born on third base when it was actually first?" How Norm had laughed at that! Just delighted. He'd kissed her on the forehead and told her she was the best. To have someone in your life who was delighted by you: who was luckier than she was? Norm himself had never said one bad word about her dad. Neither had Mrs. Plansky's mom, who'd died at forty-nine of breast cancer when Mrs. Plansky and Norm were just starting out, long before the toaster knife. On her deathbed she'd said to Mrs. Plansky, "I just don't understand." Which Mrs. Plansky at the time had assumed was a reference to dying so young, and not her husband.

"What kind of coffee is this?" her dad said.

"Same as always," Mrs. Plansky told him. "The dark roast from Panamanian Moon."

"It tastes different."

Mrs. Plansky had no comment on that. She waited for him to make sure she understood he meant different in a bad way, but that wasn't the direction he took.

"We need a TV out here."

"We've discussed that, Dad."

"Not when I was around. The TVs are better now. Ever heard of pixels? The picture's great outside."

"I like having TVs inside," said Mrs. Plansky.

He gestured at her with a butter knife. "What if there's something good on when you're outside?"

"Like what?" That was unfair and Mrs. Plansky regretted it at once. He had no defense to a comeback like that. Why was she crabby today? Crabbiness was intolerable, meaning in herself. She could tolerate it in others, within limits.

But now he surprised her. "Like a space shot," he said. "When they walk on the moon."

Mrs. Plansky laughed. She reached out and patted his hand. "Next time they walk on the moon we'll have a TV out here, I promise."

Her dad laughed, too. Maybe a little too long and edging into crazy, but it was nice to hear. She was wondering whether her mention of the coffee shop name was somehow twisted into all of this when he dabbed his chin—and then his forehead—with his napkin and said, "Had a nice powwow with Jack yesterday."

"With Jack?"

"A confab. Or maybe the day before."

"You called him?"

"Nope. He calls me."

"He does?" Mrs. Plansky tried to remember the last time Jack had called her. Last Christmas? No, she'd called him, actually waking him up even though it was noon, Arizona time. "How often?" she said.

Her dad shrugged. "That's the trouble these days. All this . . ."

"This what?"

His forehead, already furrowed plenty, furrowed more, deep Vs of annoyance. "You know."

She took a guess. "Quantification?"

"So why'd you ask in the first place?" He buttered a slice of toast, then turned it over and buttered the other side.

"What do you talk about?"

"Huh?"

"You and Jack. When he calls you."

"He's my grandson."

"I know that, Dad."

"Also there's Nina, my granddaughter. Did she end up marrying that asshole?"

Which asshole are you referring to? That was what some devil in Mrs. Plansky wanted to say. She went with, "Who do you mean?"

"That guy, Matt, Matthew, whatever the hell."

"They broke up."

"Any reason?"

A perfect question that seemed to show a brutal but defensible understanding of Nina, but did he mean it that way or was it just some by-product of what was going on in his brain these days, all the firings and misfirings? Mrs. Plansky sipped her coffee. Was he right about that, too? It did taste different, less . . . well, just somehow less. She'd been surprised by the breakup of Nina and Matthew, as Nina liked to call him, or Matt as it seemed he preferred to be called. Mrs. Plansky had heard several explanations for the breakup and didn't know what to believe. She did know that Nina was the marrying type. First had come Zach, father of Emma, Mrs. Plansky's granddaughter, now on a semester abroad. Next in line was Ted, father of Will, her grandson, possibly back in college in Colorado, and if not then a ski tech at Crested Butte, or maybe a chairlift attendant. Then there'd been a second Ted, called Teddy, unless the first Ted had been Teddy. Mrs. Plansky would not have bet money on the answer to that, not a surprise because she'd never in her life bet money on anything.

"Well?" said her dad.

"Well what?"

"I'm waiting for an answer."

For a troubling moment Mrs. Plansky couldn't remember the question. She even considered asking her dad to repeat it. What if he could? That would be worse! But oh, what a nasty, selfish thought! She banished it immediately and as it left the tiny realm of her mind, the question—any reason?—popped up its place.

"I guess Matthew wasn't the marrying type," she said.

"Who is?" said her dad. Then all at once he grew agitated. He shook his finger at her. "I never cheated on your mother while she was alive. Not once! Well, maybe once." He began to deflate. "And that wasn't even . . ."

He left that, whatever the hell it was, hanging. Mrs. Plansky drank more coffee and ignored him. Pointedly? Possibly, but she did nothing to moderate that.

He picked up another bacon strip, dipped it in the marmalade jar, and paused. "Had a nice talk with Jack," he said.

"You were going to tell me what it was about."

"Business." Her dad made a dismissive gesture with the bacon, like business wouldn't interest her, or perhaps would be over her head. Mrs. Plansky had helped build a successful company in a highly competitive space from nothing. She'd been in charge of sales and marketing, done all the hiring and firing, handled the banking relationships. What was there to say?

"In what context?" Mrs. Plansky settled on that, mastered any temptation to be infuriated, disdainful, or even amused. She had been, after all—and maybe still was, except for the lack of an actual paying job—a businesswoman, and had talked more productive business than he'd dreamed—She shut her mental trap.

"Picking my brain, mostly," her dad said, or something like that.

He seemed to be chewing on the whole bacon strip at the same time, a little marmalade blob oozing from the side of his mouth. "Jack values my opinion on various . . ." He thought for some time and added, ". . . . aspects."

"Aspects of what?"

"Business. For example, business opportunities."

"Jack's looking for a job?"

"Wouldn't say that. More in the line of business opportunities. Happy to help. I know something about the subject, of course, stands to reason."

"I thought he was happy at that place."

"Place?"

"The tennis center in Scottsdale. The membership is huge and hasn't he been helping out with the ASU program?" Dark thoughts stirred in Mrs. Plansky, threatening to make inroads into her consciousness. Dark thoughts about her son—like, maybe the ASU thing was actually a suggestion of hers, a suggestion Jack might never have followed up on; like, maybe she had no actual data on the membership numbers at the tennis center in Scottsdale; like, maybe Jack's previous gig, also in Scottsdale, had been a lot better, but he'd left to pursue some sort of start-up that had soon deadended; like, maybe Jack saw himself as a failure, making it even worse than his simply not loving what he did. That was excruciating to her, not because it made her a failure, too, at least partially, which was true, but because she loved him so much he was part of her soul. But last time she'd seen him—two Thanksgivings ago—there'd been failure-knowledge lurking in his eyes, which she realized only now in retrospect. A two-year time lag? Was there a slow-on-the-uptake competition? She had the goods.

"What's ASU?" her dad said.

"Arizona State."

"Never heard of it. And didn't he graduate from college already? I thought Will was the one who . . ." His voice trailed off. His tongue emerged, found the marmalade blob, reeled it in. "Broaden your thinking," he said.

"Excuse me?"

"You gotta broaden your thinking, Loretta. Jack sees what's out there. Wants to be a part. Why don't you get that?"

Mrs. Plansky got that. The year before, Jack had fallen in with a couple of entrepreneurs from Mesa—their names not coming to her—who wanted to partner with him in opening a chain of cold storage facilities coast-to-coast. Through Jack—ah, yes, the last time he'd called her, now filling its box in her disordered mental spreadsheet—they'd invited Mrs. Plansky to be a supporter to the tune of $750K, which she hadn't had the time to decline gracefully before they were indicted on a number of federal charges, luckily regarding an earlier scheme that hadn't involved Jack.

"Tennis is just a game," her dad said. "A fine game." He gave her a big smile. Somehow he still had all his original teeth and they weren't even particularly yellow. "And I know you were always good at games. For God's sake! That's what I liked about you! But Jack's a man, after all. He's looking for bigger things."

All at once, Mrs. Plansky wanted to laugh. She felt an enormous laugh building inside her, just bursting to burst out, her natural self saving her from potential hurt, at least as far as she knew. But her dad wasn't done.

"He was thanking me for putting him in touch with that guy," he said.

"What guy?"

"You know."

"I don't."

"Yeah you do. That tennis partner of yours."

"Kev Dinardo?"

"Sure about that? I thought it was Dev."

FOUR

"Dad?" Mrs. Plansky said. "How do you know him?"

"Who are we talking about?" said her dad.

"Kev Dinardo." Kev had never been to the condo and how could her dad have met him out in the world?

Her dad gazed out at the lake, the surface unruffled as it often was in the morning. "Who says I know him?"

The ruffled one was her. She forced her voice not to show it. "You must," she said, "if you recommended him to Jack."

He thought for a while. "I'm not buying it."

"Not buying what?"

He gestured at the lake. "All that crocodile business." His eyes lit up. "It's a crock!" He laughed and slapped his knee. "Get it?"

Mrs. Plansky got it but she was not in a laughing mood. "It's a gator not a croc."

Now he turned to her and the look in his eyes grew crafty. "So I'm right. There is no croc."

She toyed with the idea of explaining that the Florida crocodile was rare and also not found this far north, that Fairbanks was a gator and had been spotted by a number of people, including she herself, but before she could launch into that—even though she knew it would be headed off some new unforeseen cliff—she was struck by a nasty revelation: her father had needed assisted living, in the broadest sense, his whole life. She shied away from that thought and ended up saying nothing.

Then came a long silence, broken only by the sounds of her dad enjoying his breakfast: buttering toast, stirring coffee, chewing bacon. Mrs. Plansky watched the lake, willing Fairbanks to put in an appearance, but he did not. Finally her dad leaned back, dusting off his hands.

"Kev?" he said. "You sure about that?"

"Yes, Dad."

"Not Dev?"

"No."

"Dev Dinardo sounds better. What's that word?"

"Alliteration. But it's Kev."

"A mover and a shaker."

"Kev? He's retired, Dad." She had Kev's card somewhere, a very simple card with a sketch of a sailboat. There was also his phone number and one line of text: Retired from paying work, but nothing else.

"There's no retiring from success, as they say."

Mrs. Plansky had never heard that one. "What kind of success are you talking about?"

"He made a lot of money." His tone turned angry, not over the top, maybe more like bitter. "What other kind is there? Of success, I mean. Try to keep up, Loretta. The point is I thought he's the kind of guy Jack oughta know. I'm his grandfather. Hello?"

"I'm his mother."

"Your point?"

What was her point, exactly? She couldn't define it but plunged ahead anyway. "This success of Kev's—what sector was it in?"

"He hasn't told you?"

"We never discussed business. We're tennis partners, Dad."

"Is he good?"

"Very."

"Good as Jack?"

"Nothing like Jack. Kev's a fine senior club player. Jack was a touring pro."

"But he never made the big time."

"No."

"How come?"

How come? That was a question she and Norm had discussed many, many times, approaching it from all sorts of angles. Jack was strong, fast, just the right size at 6'2, 175 pounds, crushed the ball from both sides, served 120 with no seeming effort, had 20/15 vision in both eyes. In short, he looked like a top 100 player, but the highest he'd risen—to 319—was nowhere in tennis, the curve at the top being so steep. Three hundred nineteen: why did she have to remember that number so well? But therefore, if the problem wasn't physical didn't it have to be mental or emotional? Perhaps rooted in his upbringing, and thus roping in Norm and Loretta? Not that they'd been pushy parents, their self-image wrapped up in the performance of their kid. They'd actually been more like Roger Federer's parents—if stories about them were true: hands-off, encouraging Jack to play other sports, in all of which he excelled—he was a qualified scuba diving instructor, for example—not attending all of his matches, not close. Should they have taken the opposite approach, been parents of the intense type, even crazed? Mrs. Plansky had made that argument a few times, one of those for sake of argument arguments, unreflective of her true beliefs. Norm loved when she got to the crazed part. He'd lean in and kiss her cheek and say, "How long could we have kept that up? Tennis players are like mathematicians. There are lots of great ones but only a few make a difference."

"The pyramid is very steep at the top," Mrs. Plansky told her dad. "In almost anything else you can think of three nineteen would be fabulous."

"Huh?"

"That's why it's so hard to make it on the tour."

"What tour?"

"The tennis tour, Dad."

"Cry me a river," he said.

An annoying remark but she had no time to deal with it because all at once she had the answer to the riddle: *Oh, Norm! Did we let him forget the most important thing—it's supposed to be fun!*

Silence.

"Did you just say something?" her dad said.

"No."

"Like in a whisper?"

"No." She leaned forward. "Do you know if Jack actually got in touch with Kev?"

"Affirmative."

"Affirmative you know or affirmative he did?"

"All of them."

"How do you know?"

"I know a lot of things."

She searched her mind for some sort of shortcut. "Good to hear," she said. "Among all those things do you know what Kev did or does for a living?"

"Do I look like . . ." He blinked a few times, slow blinks that were somehow more disturbing than fast ones. "A middleman?" Ah, he'd been searching for a word. And found it. There was lots to admire about him. That was something to keep in mind. "So," he finished up, "why don't you go to the horse's mouth."

"Good idea."

Mrs. Plansky walked into the house, searched for her phone, which she thought was by her bed but turned out to be in the kitchen by the coffee machine, and called Kev. Straight to his voicemail, which was not accepting messages. Then she tried Jack, with the same result. She tried Jack again, hoping he'd seen that she called and would now pick up. He did not. She tried once more, just because.

Mrs. Plansky returned to the patio. Fairbanks was gliding along offshore, impossible to miss, but her dad had moved himself to the wheelchair and was dozing, face to the sun and eyes closed. Fairbanks's eye—the only one she could see from her angle—was wide open, glittering in the sunlight.

She addressed Fairbanks, very quietly but aloud for sure, showing Fairbanks a perhaps not so nice side of her not many knew about, only Norm and . . . well, only Norm. And even him just on rare occasions. Her heavy artillery, he called it, locked away in a silo. Mostly she entertained herself with it, not often but going all the way back to childhood.

"I'll be back soon," she told Fairbanks. "Keep an eye on Dad."

"Should take a few days to sort out," Kev had told her. "I'll be in touch."

But this was the next day, and here she was, driving up to his house and parking beside his car, a sports car of a type she didn't know, not a Ferrari or a Maserati but that kind of thing, black with gold trim. Now, on such a bright day, the house looked more beautiful than she'd thought, the curved hurricane-resistant structure not at all alienating, but somehow warm, even homey. Through the pilings that raised it up she could see through to the dock. There was no sign of the fire. Everything looked pristine and just as she'd seen it the first time, except that the Bertram 50S was gone.

Mrs. Plansky got out, opened one of her rear doors. The two trophies, both topped with a tennis figure in the serving position, one male, one female, lay together. She picked up the male, went to the front door and knocked.

The house was quiet. If he wasn't home, she could leave the trophy standing by the door, but this visit was not about the trophy. Nor was it about any post-match . . . exuberance out on the dock as *Lizette* went down but before the arrival of the fire department. What was it about? Answer: the horse's mouth. What she wanted to hear from the horse's mouth was why Kev hadn't told her that her son had contacted him. Twisted into that problem, from the sequence of events if nothing else, like a thread that didn't match, was that passionate moment on the dock, both how it felt at the time and how it had stirred up her future. Mrs. Plansky paused, her fist motionless in the air. Maybe this visit was partly about that after all.

She knocked again and had barely lowered her hand when the obvious answer came to her: Jack had asked Kev not to tell her. Of course! How stupid she could be! Mrs. Plansky had a sudden and disturbing self-sighting in her mental mirror, an image of an interfering mother who couldn't let go, exactly the kind of creature she'd made sure she never was. And now at her age—how ridiculous! She set the trophy on the threshold and began to back away. That was when the door opened.

A man looked out. Not Kev. This was a much bigger man, and younger, perhaps in his late forties. His head was shaved and he had a mustache, an arrangement Mrs. Plansky, for no defensible reason, was biased against, but he was actually pleasant looking, like an assistant football coach who was good at recruiting. Then she noticed that one of his ears was cauliflowered and switched out football for wrestling.

"Can I help you, ma'am?" he said. She heard friendly traces of the southwest in his voice, somehow confirming her suppositions.

FIVE

"Is Kev here?" Mrs. Plansky said.

"Mr. Dinardo?" said the man. "'Fraid not."

"Ah," said Mrs. Plansky. "Do you know when he'll be back?"

"'Fraid not. Mr. Dinardo's away at the moment."

"Ah," said Mrs. Plansky again, the reply popping out before she could change it to something more intelligent. She'd never been inside Kev's house but now she caught a glimpse of the front hall. In the center stood a fountain with a big bronze fish as the centerpiece, the bronze scales reflecting the light in a lifelike way, as though a real fish were leaping. But it wasn't showy, just really nice. Water dribbled from its mouth and splashed into the pool, a tile pool in muted colors, allowing the bronze to be the star of the color show, and on the floor by the side of the pool lay a tennis bag.

"Any message I can relay?" said the man.

Uh-oh. Mrs. Plansky turned to him. Had she gotten offtrack, distracted by the fountain? She didn't know. But conversations have a rhythm. She sensed that she was off the beat. "Well," she said, "You could give him—" She held out the trophy.

He looked at it and blinked, like he didn't know what it was. But surely there were trophies in wrestling? "What's this?" He made no move to take the trophy.

"A trophy," she said. "A tennis trophy." She motioned with her chin at the tennis bag, the big kind capable of holding three or four rackets, a towel or two, even a change of clothes and an extra pair of sneaks. He didn't turn to look. "We—" She was on the verge of saying they'd won, but stopped herself in time. "Just tell him I dropped it off."

"And you are . . . ?"

"Loretta. Nice to meet you, Mr. . . . ?"

"Mitch," he said. "From the insurance company." He took the trophy, put his other hand on the door, getting ready to close it.

"Oh, dear. Was there damage to the house?"

"That's what I'm investigating, ma'am."

"I'll leave you to it." She had a sudden mental image of a busy man and a dithering oldster, as seen from high above.

"You have a nice day now."

"You as well," said Mrs. Plansky, her polite little response not quite done before the door closed.

Mrs. Plansky drove away from Kev's house in what Norm called one of her vaguely discontented moods. The term came from a song, or maybe a poem. "It'll come to me," she said aloud, more of a mutter, really. She found she was gripping the steering wheel much too tight and tried to relax. Her vaguely discontented moods, which were very infrequent, drifted in out of nowhere and hung in some corner of her mind like dark balloons. Among his many gifts, Norm had a way of popping those balloons. First of all, he was aware of their arrival as soon as she was, or sometimes even earlier! How was that possible? How could one person know another so well? How lucky she'd been! And just like that, this new balloon of vague discontentment went pop. Somehow Norm was still doing it. How lucky she still was.

Mrs. Plansky pulled to the side of the road at the first safe place. She was in tears. No driving in tears, that was basic. Not a flood of tears: Mrs. Plansky was not a crier. This was more just a welling up and a brief overflow. Norm had been their crier. For example, at movies, when things turned out well for a deserving character. She took a tissue from the glove box, dabbed at her eyes, checked her face in the rearview, stretched her lips this way and that. Her lipstick—a high-end faint pink satin, Mrs. Plansky not one to pinch pennies when it came to important minor things—had gotten smeared. She tried to unsmear it but only made it worse. Had she been attempting to get back to bliss out there on Kev's dock? Certainly not. Bliss round two was off the table. If there was such a thing as bliss round two then bliss did not exist. But did that mean there couldn't be something good, even loving, as a possibility?

She wiped her lips clear with the tissue, took out her lipstick, reapplied it, doing a neat, precise job. All sorts of random things could drift through her mind during those ten or fifteen seconds of lipstick application. Take, for example, the tennis bag on the floor by Kev's bronze fish fountain. It wasn't his normal bag. His normal bag was just a basic single racket type that he fixed with a bungee cord to the carrier over the back wheel of his bike. Did he have another bag? Or was Mitch a tennis player, the bag belonging to him? But what sort of insurance adjuster brings his—She went still, the lipstick poised in midair. There'd been embroidered initials on that bag. With these sharp-sighted, cataract-free eyes of hers, she'd actually been able to make them out. *KD*? Or had it been something with an *M*? Her memory, so balky, refused to deliver. Well, it made a partial delivery. There'd been three initials, blue against the white of the bag. She could see that, although not what they were. But a big bag, for sure. You might even say comprehensive. Did she know a single club-type player with a bag like that? A brand-new dark balloon rose up in the back of her mind.

Back home, her dad was asleep and snoring in his room. He had his own way of snoring, a three-parter that began with a long loud inhale broken by rhythmic beats as though on a loosely tightened snare drum, followed by a silence that lasted long enough to induce anxiety every single time, and ended with a high-pitched but barely audible wheeze. Through the partly open door she could see his feet, one bare and white as bone, the other still wearing a tassel loafer.

He'd left a note taped with a Band-Aid to the fridge. His notes were printed, not written, although she knew he could still write because now and then she needed his signature. This one, in shaky block caps, and on three lines read:

> **REPORT**
> **ER SWUNG**
> **BY**

This was a report from him to her? The report being *er swung*, and *by* was the closing, as in *good-bye*? What about *er swung*? She could make no sense of that at all. But what about the *er* part? *Er* as in *the ER*? Was it possible he'd had some sort of medical episode, been desperate to get treatment but hadn't figured out how to call her although he'd called her countless times, and ended up taping his frantic note to the fridge and collapsing on his bed?

She hurried back to his room. Everything was as before: snoring in three acts, one shoe on, one shoe off. He didn't seem desperate. Of course, as someone said—it would come to her—some people, or possibly most or even all, those differences obviously crucial, led lives of quiet desperation. Mrs. Plansky watched him for a while. If there was any desperation in him it wasn't quiet. As for his inner life in general, at this stage of their relationship, he ninety-eight and she seventy-one, she still had no clue.

Mrs. Plansky called Jack and was directed to his voicemail, which was still full. She began to feel restless, and yes, even vaguely discontented again. You might even call it worry or anxiety. Exercise had always been her remedy for that kind of thing. She called Melanie, her regular tennis partner at the club.

"Loretta! What a match! It should have been on ESPN. Honestly."

"Well, I wouldn't . . . but thanks. Any chance you're up for hitting for an hour or so?"

"Today?"

"I was thinking maybe this afternoon."

"My God! So soon? Shouldn't you be resting?"

"I guess." But how could you rest if you were restless?

"Anyway I can't today. I'm taking Larry in for tests."

"Oh. I hope . . ."

"Thank you. But I'd love to hit sometime soon. I'll call."

Melanie and Larry were a few years younger than she and Norm, or rather what Norm would have been now if he'd kept going. They, too, were a long-married couple. Larry—a former homebuilder from Knoxville—had lost the last two fingers of his left hand in a long-ago nail gun accident and wore his wedding ring on his right hand. A big burly guy, although less and less burly these days, now that she thought about it, he'd visited Norm many times at the hospital. Mrs. Plansky would often arrive and there he'd be at Norm's bedside, the two of them laughing over an anecdote about batteries or rebar or something like that. But it wasn't always about laughs. Once she'd come upon Larry—who'd gone to work straight out of eleventh grade—reciting Lincoln's Second Inaugural Address in a soft undertone, almost like he was making it up for the first time. And Norm's face, quite skeletal by that time: simply rapt.

Mrs. Plansky called Jack and was directed to—oops. She'd already done that. She laid the phone down, went into her bedroom, and opened her swimsuit drawer. There were three: one floral with a skirt, another, also skirted but with a pattern that turned out to resemble horizontal stripes, and was worn just the once, and the third, by far the best for actual swimming, black and skirtless but not at all immodest, as long as she got everything just so. She put it on, checked herself in the mirror despite telling herself not to, and then went out onto the patio and down the slope toward Little Pine Lake, the dense Zoysia grass—Norm's favorite of all the Florida grasses and he'd made a careful study—feeling so pleasant under her bare feet.

Between the grass and the water lay a narrow strip of sand, not the beach kind but swampier, dark and spongy. Her feet liked the feel of that, too. She was up to her thighs in the warm still water, hands outstretched in preparation for a headfirst launching into the lake, when she remembered Fairbanks.

She paused, looked all around and then straight down, where she should have checked first. And there were her legs and feet, highly visible in a sunshine beam. Visible and possibly tasty-looking to reptilian eyes. Mrs. Plansky had been something of a risk taker in her younger days—knew how to ride a motorcycle, for example, had done some free-diving spearfishing on a spring vacation in the Grenadines with a college sort-of boyfriend, where it turned out she was the superior free diver, dooming the relationship, as she'd figured out later, her misery over the breakup ending at the very moment—but these were not her younger days. Sometimes she had to remind herself of that fact!

"You really must be crazy," she told herself as she started to back out of the water. But right then was when she spotted Fairbanks, sunning himself on the far side of the lake. The lake, an almost perfect circle, had a diameter of what? A quarter of a mile? A little more? What was an alligator's average swimming speed? Norm could have come up with all the data and crunched it in seconds. Instead of even trying for a ballpark estimate, Mrs. Plansky said, "What the hell," and dove in.

She swam back and forth parallel to the beach, perhaps somewhat faster than usual but trying to do it quietly. Her restlessness, her vague discontentment began to vanish, like the lake—or Mother Nature!—was absorbing her toxins. When they were all gone—in surely not much time at all, making this a perfectly safe undertaking on her part—she swam to shore, walked up on the grass, gave her head a quick shake, water drops glinting in the sun, and only then, as though she'd established control, glanced over at the far shore. There was no sign of Fairbanks.

Mrs. Plansky felt good. Odd, the way using energy made you energetic. Her mind was empty in a soothing way. She checked on her dad—still asleep—then got in her car and drove to Kev's house. It was almost as though the car drove her there on its own. That was what she told herself as she pulled up beside Kev's sports car. Had there been another car here before? There must have been, unless Mitch, or Mr. Mitch, had come by boat, always a possibility in these parts. She walked out on the dock. No boat tied to it, no boat moored nearby. She gazed at the water where *Lizette* had gone down. For a moment she thought she saw a tiny gleam from the bottom but a second look and a third revealed nothing.

Mrs. Plansky went around to the front of the house and raised her hand to knock. What exactly was she doing here? Could she put it in words? Yes, she could. That oversized tennis bag: she wanted a closer look. Mrs. Plansky knocked on the door.

"Kev?" she called. She was about to call his name again when a white van drove up. Mrs. Plansky turned to it. A man dressed in paint-spattered white overalls got out.

"Hey," he said. "Sorry about Tuesday."

"Tuesday?"

"I was supposed to come Tuesday but I got hung up." He fished a crumpled sheet of paper from his pocket and squinted at it. "You Mrs. Dinardo?"

Mrs. Plansky inclined her head in a general way, open to interpretation.

"So it's okay to do it now?" he said.

She advanced a little deeper into wild country. "Remind me of what."

"Oh, the boat thing."

She waited for more.

"Changing the name."

"The name?"

He glanced at the paper. "*Lizette*, right? He said to white it out and paint in a new one." He held up his phone and gave it a little shake. "Got some fonts you can check out."

"What's the new name?" said Mrs. Plansky, advancing deeper still. But why? Sometimes, after all these years, she was still a puzzle to herself, maybe even more so as time passed.

"He didn't tell you?"

She shook her head.

"Uh-oh. He was going to tell me when I got here. Maybe it's like a surprise."

"For sure," said Mrs. Plansky. "But since he's not home right now and I don't know, I'm afraid you'll have to come back another time. I'll have him call you."

"No problem." The painter started to get in his van, then paused. "What's your name? Just so's I can think about the spacing."

"Let's not jinx it," said Mrs. Plansky.

"Ha! Too true." He drove off.

Mrs. Plansky made a complete circle of the house. She saw no sign of damage whatsoever.

Six

On her way home, Mrs. Plansky took a little detour through the town center, a fancied-up block on one side of the state highway and a fancied-up block-and-a-half on the other, and picked up a slice of mille-feuille at a bakery called Pie Face, where the staff seemed to be having a tattoo competition. Mrs. Plansky was not at all put off by tattoos. She herself had none, which she saw as her contribution to the tattoo phenomenon. Didn't some people have to remain un-tattooed for the whole thing to make sense? The mille-feuille was for her dad, a recently discovered treat he called "mill fillers" and consumed pretty much every day. He was also planning on getting a tattoo himself, and every so often ran an idea by her, such as a tugboat or something that would look good on his butt—did she have any suggestions?

Next door to Pie Face stood Ponte d'Oro Insurance. Sherry Rabineau, her agent for home and auto, spotted her through the front window and waved. Mrs. Plansky waved back. Sherry raised a finger in a wait-a-moment gesture, rose from her desk, and came outside.

"Loretta! Word is you're quite the tennis player!"

"Good grief. Well, thanks, Sherry. I'm just a hacker really."

"Not what I hear. How's things?"

"No complaints." Mrs. Plansky paused. How had she—they—found Sherry? Something to do with a distant cousin of Norm's back in Rhode Island? Sherry was short, round, energetic, pleasant. "I've got a question," Mrs. Plansky said.

"Shoot."

"Do you have anyone named Mitch in the office? Or possibly Mr. Mitch?"

"No. We're actually completely manless at the moment."

"Is that good or bad?"

"Both," said Sherry. "Why do you ask?"

Why indeed? Could she find a short, simple, concrete answer? If not then this was the moment to slam on the brakes, say no reason, and be on her way. But right then an image of *Lizette* rose in her mind, the flash, the boom, the inferno, small-scale and brief, but violent just the same. It was like a shove in the back, pushing her into action.

"Well, this is a bit . . . indelicate, but I'm not sure an acquaint . . . a friend of mine is getting the kind of insurance support he needs. I don't want to interfere, of course . . ."

Sherry nodded. "But you thought that if it was us you might put in a word."

"That kind of thing."

"And if it wasn't?"

"I'd have a recommendation for him."

Sherry smiled. A businesslike smile but not fake. Mrs. Plansky, a longtime business person herself, knew that smile: friendly, although they weren't and never would be friends. "Do you know the address?"

"Ninety-two Seaside Way."

"Ah," said Sherry. An *ah* that told Mrs. Plansky that Sherry knew the house, its current value, the ownership history. Very few of the citizens of Ponte d'Oro had been born there, but it was still a small town of sorts. "I'll give you a call."

"Got the mill filler?" her dad called from somewhere in the condo as Mrs. Plansky came through the door.

She went into the kitchen. He wasn't there. She put the pastry on a plate, grabbed a fork, and went into the little bar area off the dining room. He was in his wheelchair by a side table, watching one of those shows about real estate in the Caribbean.

"You know what they say about the islands," he said, not turning to look at her. "It's all one big slum when the sun don't shine."

Then why are you watching? she wanted to say. But of course she didn't. "That's not true, Dad." She set the pastry on the side table. "Remember all those years you went to Saint Lucia?"

"Sure. I climbed the goddam Pitons. The easy one, anyways. Coulda done the hard one if what's her name hadn't been so chickenshit."

"What's her name?" said Mrs. Plansky. If he was referring to her mother she didn't know what she'd do.

"One of those girlfriends. With the red hair. After your mother . . ." His voice got so quiet she almost couldn't hear the next word. "Passed." Then he sighed a long sigh that had a bit of a whimper in it.

"Here's your mille-feuille, Dad."

"Later." He made a waving-away motion.

She'd taken a few steps toward the kitchen when he said, "Know what we need around here?"

She waited.

"A gun."

"A gun, Dad?"

"Come on! A firearm, a weapon, a blaster. Like a Winchester 73, the gun that won the west."

"What for?"

"What for? Look around."

"The west is already won," Mrs. Plansky said.

Now he turned to her. "You were always a good athlete," he said. "Can't have everything."

Not looking, he reached toward the side table, his fingers wriggling like insect antennae. They found the mille-feuille, wrapped themselves around the whole thing. Mrs. Plansky proceeded on to the kitchen.

Her phone beeped.

"Loretta? Sherry. It's Silver Sands Realty up in Port Clemens. It's a reputable firm. But we're always happy to compete, of course."

"Thank you. I'll . . . I'll follow up." Which was true in a way, if a bit misleading. *Telling the truth is always best in the end, girls.* That was Miss Terrance's advice. Was a partial truth better than an outright lie? None of the girls had known to ask that kind of question. Wouldn't it be nice if Miss Terrance could come strolling in this very minute? Mrs. Plansky was an optimist by nature, perhaps too stupid to admit realities, but she was pretty sure that the Miss Terrances of the world had gone extinct.

"Silver Sands Realty. How can I direct your call?"

"May I speak to Mitch?"

"Mitch?"

"Or possibly it's Mr. Mitch. I believe he's one of your agents."

"We have no one here of that name."

"Maybe he's employed in some other capacity?"

"I'm sorry, no."

"Possibly a temp?"

Silence.

"A big guy, like a former—" Mrs. Plansky, on the road to self-embarrassment, stopped, maybe, or almost certainly, on the late side.

"We have a number of agents on duty. Would you like me to transfer you to one of them?"

"Um," said Mrs. Plansky. "Maybe some other time." She clicked off.

"Some other time what?" said her dad.

She whirled around, startled. He'd wheeled himself into the kitchen doorway where he now sat, looking highly alert, a custard smear on his upper lip.

"It's nothing," she told him.

"What kind of nothing?"

Was he glaring at her? "Is something wrong, Dad?"

"You're giving me the boot. Right or wrong?"

"The boot?"

"The boot. You know what that means. Don't play dumb. Just one more thing you can't pull off."

Was that an insult or a compliment? Mrs. Plansky didn't know. Did he? Yes, for sure. The tone said it all. He knew. Insult, 100 percent.

"You're not going back to Arcadia Gardens. That's settled."

"Crafty."

"Excuse me?"

"What about all those other places? Like Peasant Grove Estates? You didn't rule those out. Think you can slide that by me?"

"Pleasant Grove, Dad. Not Peasant."

He glared at her again, had never looked more orcish, genuinely menacing despite everything. Then he blinked a few times and said, "Ha."

"What's funny?"

"One of those Freudian slips. You didn't catch it?"

Mrs. Plansky laughed. Then they were both laughing together. She came close to walking over and kissing his deeply wrinkled forehead, and would have done it if she hadn't been pretty sure he'd have some negative reaction, like a lip curl, for example.

"What do you think about him?" he said.

"Who?"

"For God sake. Freud. Aren't you listening? Was he a Jew, by the way?"

Another one of those eruptions from that same old fault line deep down in him. "What difference would that make?"

"None to me myself, Chandler Wills Banning. Some of my best friends were Jewish."

"For example?"

He nodded like that was going to be easy-peasy. Then came a long, long silence, which was no surprise to Mrs. Plansky. She had memories, none particularly uplifting, of a few of his golfing buddies and drinking buddies, but were they friends? She doubted that. Meanwhile she was well aware that lack of friends was a commonality they shared. Norm had filled the friend space as well as the love space, and all the other spaces. Although it was only fair to mention that she'd had a great childhood and early adulthood friend, Tilly Leandro. They'd been three-year-olds together, never stopped calling each other—to the annoyance of others—Tee-Tee and Lo-Lo. Tee-Tee had been maid of honor at her wedding, delivering a speech that was funny and sweet at the same time, and, most importantly, short, and later danced up a wonderful storm. Mrs. Plansky could still see that dance so clearly, somehow more clearly as the years went by, so now the image was clearer than the original.

"Norm," her father said at last.

"Norm?"

"Hello? Former husband of yours?"

Mrs. Plansky had never struck another human being—with the exception of a single incident in PeeWee hockey, when she'd spent two minutes in the penalty box for high-sticking—and not even felt the desire. But now? She took a deep breath.

"You thought of Norm as a friend?" she said.

"Why wouldn't I?"

If there was a heaven then Norm was looking down now and laughing his head off. Please let there be a heaven, if only for that. Mrs. Plansky made her decision. Deep down she'd still been leaning the other way, but—

"Dad? You can stay here."

His eyebrows, two bristly outcrops, rose. "Forever?"

What a question! Didn't Shakespeare have some line about how old age circles back to babyhood?

"Yes, Dad."

"Good enough," he said, and started to back away. His gaze went to the fridge. "You saw my note?"

In fact Mrs. Plansky had forgotten all about it. She peeled the note—*REPORT/ER SWUNG/BY*—off the fridge door and brought it over to him. "Is it about the ER, Dad?"

"ER?"

"Emergency room."

"Why would you think that?" He stabbed at the note with a scaly finger. "She didn't say anything about the ER."

"Who are we talking about?"

"For chrissake." He stabbed again. "The reporter. The reporter who swung by. Jeez. Plain English."

"A reporter came here?"

"Swung by. Slang. Cool slang. You know. Hip. I'm up to date. Don't underestimate my . . . my . . ." He couldn't think of whatever it was.

"What did she say?"

"'Hello, sir.'"

"And after that?"

"'Is Loretta Plansky here?'"

"And then?"

"You weren't here. Finito."

"Did she leave a card?"

"No siree Bob."

It came to her. "Oh."

"Oh?"

"She must be a sports reporter. It's about the tennis match."

"Well, well. You're gonna be famous." He backed away, started rolling down the hall. "On a real small stage," he added. And then, from farther away, "There's this new thing. Like Viagra but no prescription. On the computer, if you don't mind looking into it." Or something like that.

Mrs. Plansky called Kev and then Jack, with the same results as before, but somehow now more unsettling. She found herself considering another swim. Out on the pond there was no sign of Fairbanks. He could be down below. He could have packed up and headed for some better spot. But were there better spots than Little Pine Lake? Was it possible that what interested Fairbanks most of all were the Little Pine condos themselves? In that moment Mrs. Plansky understood Fairbanks through and through. He was down below all right, making reptilian plans and keeping reptilian time.

She called Nina.

"Hi, Mom!"

And right away knew something was up.

"How are things in Hilton Head?"

"I'm actually in New York right now."

"Oh?"

"In fact, Mom, I've been meaning to call you."

"Here I am."

Nina laughed. "That's just what I was saying the other night. It's not just that she—meaning you—hasn't lost a step. She's gained one! If that's even an expression, gaining a step."

"Saying to who?" said Mrs. Plansky. By now she knew what was up. Nina was high on something, and Mrs. Plansky knew what it was. Nothing illegal or physically harmful, invisible to any kind of medical test, and not even for sale, not the real thing.

"That's exactly the topic!" Nina laughed.

Mrs. Plansky heard, or thought she heard, at least traces of the sound of the laugher laughing at herself. She adored Nina, simple as that.

"You'll never guess, Mom. I've met someone."

"I'm all ears," said Mrs. Plansky, who by then had guessed everything but the name. Well, not true. Ahead lay news of this someone's age, a potential minefield, marital status, same, marital history and present entanglements, same and same.

"You know what I read the other day?" Nina went on. "Someone in my cohort can expect to live to the age of her oldest living relative, plus five years, six months. Think about that. What if Grandpa makes it to a hundred and ten?"

"There's a thought," said Mrs. Plansky, not adding that just the concept might kill her then and there. Meanwhile, she said a silent prayer to whatever power was in charge: Please make this new boyfriend not an actual boy. Over thirty-five would be a lovely bonus.

"How is he, by the way?" Nina said.

"The same."

"Does he really have a girlfriend?"

"Yes."

"Do they—I don't even want to say it."

"Good."

Nina laughed again. "His name's Hamish. He's Scottish. Well, of extraction. Partly. His ancestors came over on the *Mayflower*."

"I didn't realize there were Scots on the *Mayflower*."

"Maybe it was the *Arbella*. He doesn't wear a kilt or anything like that. Although he has one. But he doesn't wear it in public."

Only in private then. Mrs. Plansky got the picture. Soon she had the details. Hamish was thirty-three, never married, worked in health care, loved country music, had played rugby in college. And those weren't all the details, but they rushed by so fast Mrs. Plansky couldn't hold on to every one.

"I can't wait for you to meet him," Nina said.

"Anytime."

"You're the best."

"What does he do in health care, by the way?"

"Gotta run now, Mom. The driver's here."

"Where are you going?"

"I don't know! It's a surprise!"

Mrs. Plansky felt a bit high herself at that moment. But at last she came to the point of the call. "One quick question—have you spoken to Jack recently?"

"I've been meaning to. Just so busy. Tell him I said hi. Bye, Mom. Love you."

"Love you, too," said Mrs. Plansky to the silence, which had replaced dial tones. She gazed through the kitchen window at Little Pine Lake. Ripples appeared on the surface, not far away, and then vanished. A pelican—yes, her pelican, with the strange red mark on its beak—came circling down, almost touched the water, and then rose back in the sky, maybe changing its mind.

SEVEN

Water got into her dreams. Mrs. Plansky knew quotes from two famous writers about dreams. One was *tell a dream and lose a reader.* The other was *in dreams begin responsibilities.* How to reconcile them? She had no idea, didn't have that kind of mind. But in the morning when she awoke she felt like she was ascending from the depths, and as she hit the surface an idea popped into her mind, an idea that brought with it a responsibility, and if that was a little highfalutin then just call it something to do.

Lucrecia arrived in time to handle breakfast. Clara was with her. Clara looked peppy, wore deep red lipstick, emerald green eye shadow, and a really nice embroidered shawl that looked a lot like a shawl of Mrs. Plansky's. In fact, on closer inspection, it was.

"Buenos dias, jovencita!"

She was always jovencita to Clara, spoken without a trace of irony that Mrs. Plansky could detect, and therefore endearing. Clara gave her a little wave, just the merest movement of the hand—like an aristocrat who did a lot of waving from balconies—and headed down the hall to her dad's bedroom, where the door was still closed. In her free hand she held what looked like a small brown plastic pill bottle.

"I'll be back soon," Mrs. Plansky said.

"No rush," said Lucrecia, turning on the oven.

Mrs. Plansky was already wearing her black one-piece swimsuit, concealed under a collarless sky-blue shirt and khaki skirt, and had her mesh bag packed and ready to go. She slid it onto the passenger seat of her car and drove to 92 Seaside Way.

Kev's sports car—not a Ferrari or Maserati but that kind of thing—was still out front. Mrs. Plansky parked beside it, and then, in the mood to nail down facts, walked over and examined the badge on the hood. Lamborghini, in gold caps, accompanied by a swaggering and probably snorting gold bull, the gold matching the car's gold trim. This was the kind of moment when Tee-Tee would shake her head and say "Men!" Norm was not the only person who went on living in her head. Soon it would be SRO.

She knocked on the door. The house remained silent. She took the mesh bag around to the dock. The breeze was gentle and seas were light. In the distance, a cream-colored sloop with a creamy sail was coming about, leaving a thin sun-colored keel track on the blue. Mrs. Plansky kicked off her sandals, stripped off her shirt and khaki skirt, opened the mesh bag, and took out her mask, fins, and snorkel. Not a high-end set with the superlong fins they had now, but far better than what she'd had as a girl.

She squatted down on the dock, a bit mesmerized by the sight of her gear. Mrs. Plansky hadn't used it since Norm got sick, but she'd snorkeled pretty much all her life. Tee-Tee's grandfather was a lobsterman who'd been born in Cape Verde and had a small house—more of a shack, really—within walking distance of Second Beach, the shack long gone now of course, the whole area developed and redeveloped. He hardly ever spoke, but he'd taught them how to make one seamless creature out of you and the gear, how to free dive, how to use the Hawaiian sling and the speargun, how to be confident in the water, how to not scare the fish. "Don't scare the fish, little ladies, else there's no supper." That was one of the few things he said, usually with a stinky cigar bobbing out the side of his mouth. "Those girls turn into mermaids every summer," Tee-Tee's grandmother said. That's what Tee-Tee used for the start of her maid-of-honor speech. "Here's something you don't know about the girl in the white gown. She's a mermaid."

The mermaid, now much changed, spat in her mask, leaned over the edge of the dock, rinsed out the mask, donned her gear, and slipped feetfirst into the water. The mermaid felt a twinge in her new hip as her butt cleared the dock.

Ah. The sea—temp today about seventy-five, like some protected Rhode Island cove at the end of July—had a personality so much bigger than Little Pine Lake or any other freshwater body she'd swum in. Her own body composed itself for getting along with this big personality, her legs already in a rhythm that wasted nothing, but sent all the force of each stroke to the tips of her fins, her hands still and relaxed by her sides, her head straight, eyes on the bottom, her movements minimal and quiet. Right away she felt a lot younger, or at least somewhat, or a tiny bit, please. Her hip seemed to be arguing the other side of the case. Had that match on Court #1 been a little too long and intense? She wouldn't change a thing.

Mrs. Plansky swam parallel to the dock, the pilings sunk in white sand at a depth of what looked like twelve or fifteen feet. Water clarity was pretty good, better than Rhode Island, nothing like the Grenadines, meaning how the Grenadines were on that long-ago spring vacation with a college boyfriend. Please let the water down there still be just as it was.

A hogfish, deep red with a stringy yellow dorsal fin, emerged from behind one of those pilings, came quite close to her, and veered away, out to sea. Mrs. Plansky swam back and forth in lines parallel to the dock, moving farther and farther from shore. The harbormaster had done a good job, not much remaining of *Lizette*. She spotted a toilet seat partly buried in the sand, a small length of heavy chain twisted through some mossy rocks, a bent length of pipe with a few tiny fish nibbling at one end. *Lizette* must have left a depression on the bottom and surely the sand had been blackened or charred here and there, but the tide had already cleaned up. The tide being tidy! Mrs. Plansky was chuckling into her snorkel at that stupid little joke when she spotted something shiny in a patch of eelgrass somewhat farther out.

Mrs. Plansky swam toward the eelgrass. A wave, bigger than the rest, splashed over her, sending water down her snorkel. Without thinking she blew it back up and out. Was it true there were some things you never forgot? She tried to think of another and couldn't. Mrs. Plansky chuckled again.

She hovered over the eelgrass, waving slightly, like a slow-motion breeze was blowing down there. The eelgrass grew on a slope, its highest point about twenty or twenty-five feet down, the bottom vanishing in shadows. Although she'd kept up with snorkeling, it had been some time, possibly decades, since she'd done any free diving, but back in the day she'd been able to pull seventy feet or even more. So if she was still even half as good? The math was on her side!

Tee-Tee's grandfather had taught a multi-part method for free diving. One: close your eyes. Two: close your mind. Three: take three deep breaths. Four: a no-splash, duck dive—the duck dive itself a two parter he taught separately—splashing scaring the fish. Five: straight down like a plumb line, moving only what must be moved, no vibration—vibrations attracting the sharks. "Keeping our eyes closed the whole time, Vô?" Tilly had said, *Vô* meaning *grandpa* in Cape Verdean. "Like till we come back up?" He'd pretended to swat her, pretending as close as he ever came to actual swatting.

Mrs. Plansky's eyes didn't want to close. Despite the success of the cataract surgery, they didn't seem to be doing their best work in a watery medium. She made an attempt to close her mind, something she'd had a knack for in her free-diving days, a knack now lost, her mind preferring to stay wide open and restless. She managed the three breaths, perhaps not as deep as in the past, when at the very end of the last one her chest would rise and her spine would straighten right out, as though she were morphing into some sort of formidable amphibian. And now for the duck dive, which she managed but in a way guaranteed to warn any fish on the east coast. Mrs. Plansky followed that with a descent like a dinner bell to the shark community.

But she was on her way down, hands at her sides, legs kicking in a way that didn't feel powerless, and she felt good, in fact better and better the deeper she went, although this descent seemed to be taking longer than she'd imagined. Had she underestimated the depth? She glanced at her wrist. Good grief! As though she were wearing a depth gauge. Did she even have one anymore? She tried to think where it could be and was still rummaging around in her mind when her fingertips encountered something slimy.

Eelgrass. Ah-ha! She was there, on the bottom of the sea. Well, look at you, Lo-Lo! She flattened out her dive, kicked once or twice, her chest skimming a tall blade of eelgrass, and almost at once, the shiny object appeared: a beer can. A somewhat disappointing result, but all-too predictable. Had it drifted off the wreck of *Lizette*? Mrs. Plansky couldn't imagine Kev tossing empty beer cans over the side. That just wasn't him. She picked it up, read the label. 40–Love Hazy IPA, it said, accompanied by two stick-figure lovers with tennis-ball heads in a passionate kiss. She held on to the beer can, intending to dispose of it properly, and began to kick her way up, but she'd hardly begun when she spotted another shiny thing in the eelgrass, although this one lay farther down the slope, too far to make out any detail or even its contours. But it wasn't shiny like the beer can. It was shiny more like gold.

Meanwhile didn't the surface seem farther away than it should? The ocean was another world, of course. We have two worlds on earth, land and sea, a wonderful gift really. Mrs. Plansky kicked a little harder. She began to feel the urge to breathe. So soon? The urge to breathe was just a side effect of carbon dioxide buildup in the lungs and could be controlled, at least for a bit, with willpower. She now applied her willpower, and still had the upper hand on CO2 when she broke the surface. Mrs. Plansky exhaled, kind of a feeble exhale but enough to clear her snorkel, and sucked in a huge breath and then some more normal ones. The smell or taste or whatever you'd call it of those first few breaths of air was delicious. When had she last felt this good? Mrs. Plansky couldn't remember. She treaded water, just breathing and feeling the sun on her face. Wouldn't it be nice to be . . . what? A seal? Well, maybe not a seal, on account of how avid sharks were about them. But what about an orca, with nuttin' to fear from no-body? Yes, being an orca would be nice.

Mrs. Plansky swam over to the dock, with the intention of climbing out and tossing the beer can into the trash barrel under the house. But . . . but she happened to glance back at the eelgrass. No sign of that golden whatever it was from this distance or angle, plus golden shininess could come from so many things, chocolate wrappers, to name just one. Still, could it hurt to take another look? She was retired, after all. Time was not a factor! These were her golden years. Ha! Mrs. Plansky, shamefully amused by herself, tossed the beer can onto the dock and turned back to sea. At that very moment she felt an urge to yawn. How crazy was that! She wasn't the least bit tired.

Mrs. Plansky swam back out to the eelgrass growing on a slope or . . . or knoll as it might be called if on land. A grassy knoll? Best not to think of that. She glanced all around, a prudent move from time to time in waters where sharks could be, and saw no sharks, only her hogfish and a few sea urchins in the sand, one black and alive and the others dead and white. A few more kicks and she was hovering over the slope again, her gaze sweeping back and forth in search of that golden glint and not spotting it. Maybe she'd imagined it, or it had been a brightly colored fish, a yellow tang, for example, or some kind of goldfish. They weren't called goldfish for nothing, so that's what must—

A beam of sunlight, as though switched on by a stage director, suddenly shone down from above, probing through the sea and finding the shiny gold object. From this distance—certainly more than twenty-five feet, possibly thirty-five or even more—Mrs. Plansky couldn't make out what it was, but certainly not a fish or a chocolate wrapper.

A slight swell started up, rocking her in a gentle way, almost like the sea wanted to ease her into sleep. She floated horizontally, hands at her sides, fins seeming to make all the little adjustments by themselves, buoyant in a way that only happens in salt water. That buoyancy made the descents more difficult, of course, as did, for example, a wet suit on the outside of your body or too much fat on the inside. Mrs. Plansky weighed herself every Sunday morning, almost like a religious act, as Norm had pointed out. The number was nobody's business but hers, and that included Norm.

"Come back," she muttered into her snorkel, "and I'll tell you the goddam number."

Her gaze went down to the gold thing, perhaps a rectangle of some sort. The day they'd moved down permanently to Florida, Norm had bought a metal detector and begun patrolling various beaches, sweeping the detector back and forth, a quest that went on fruitlessly for months, until a big storm coughed up an old Spanish silver coin, now on a wall plaque in the front hall of the condo. Her dad had showed some interest in it before discovering coins just like it could be had for $175 on eBay.

A rectangle, but maybe with a rounded end. A gold rectangle with a rounded end could be . . . what? She had no idea. But also the thing might be brass, not gold, some fitting from *Lizette*, for example. The harbormaster and the tide had taken care of the wreckage, leaving little behind: toilet seat, beer can, and this thing down there in water that looked a little too deep. So this adventure, quite pleasant so far, was over, unless she was mistaken. But, you dummy! You are mistaken. How could it be over? What are you doing out here? Not nosing around or checking out—it was more like . . . investigating. That was it. You're investigating *Lizette*. Kaboom! Remember?

Mrs. Plansky remembered. She remembered everything, including—or maybe starting with—that kiss. Some people kissed with open eyes. She herself was a closed-eyed kisser. Now Mrs. Plansky closed her eyes. She closed her mind. It opened by itself with a question: What did they call that thing that sometimes happened to free divers on the ascent from a deep one? She, who'd just remembered everything, couldn't remember that. She reclosed her mind and took three deep breaths, and then a fourth for luck. A feeling of total peace and calm flowed through her, an amphibian in her soul, no doubt about it. The next thing she knew she was halfway down.

Halfway down and descending quite fast, surprisingly so, her legs getting the timing just right, sending a little extra oomph down to the tips of her fins. She entered a colder layer of water, meaning she'd already gone deeper than on the beer can dive. Practice makes perfect, which is not something Miss Terrance had ever said, Mrs. Plansky realizing at that moment that Miss Terrance never resorted to clichés. Had Miss Terrance ever married or had—

Mrs. Plansky's attention was suddenly attracted to the slope, gliding by beside her. She was already a considerable way below the summit, and had perhaps entered another yet-colder layer. Also the slope itself seemed to have steepened quite a bit. Perhaps it might be prudent to—

But then, with prudence now on the table, she was there! The gold rectangular object with the rounded end stood right in front of her eyes, leaning against a twisted clump of seagrass. She could reach out and touch it, which she did. It felt like metal, which she expected and was not particularly interesting, but how it looked? Oh, my. It was dazzling. What was the word? Figurine? Didn't that mean a small sculpture of a person? If so then this was a figurine, a figurine of a standing woman, about eight inches high, wearing a skirt that fell just above her knees and sandals on her broad, sturdy feet. She had a somewhat broad nose and wore hoop earrings. Her golden eyes were prominent and fixed on Mrs. Plansky and her hands were extended in a gesture that seemed friendly, even welcoming.

"Tee-Tee," Mrs. Plansky thought, or maybe even murmured into the mouthpiece of her snorkel. She picked up the figurine. It had a lot of heft for its size. Well, same with poor Tee-Tee. There was a bit of seaweed around the neck of the figurine and some sand stuck in the tiny spaces between her toes, but not much of either. She hadn't been down here for very long at all and cleaning her up would be a matter of only a minute or two. But that would have to wait, Mrs. Plansky thought, quite sensibly. She glanced up at the surface. So far away? Really? But perhaps one of those optical tricks the sea could play. She started kicking her way up.

"Long and strong." That was Vô's advice on ascents. "And no panicky button, little ladies. Not ever the panicky button."

Mrs. Plansky kicked long and strong, off to an excellent start in her opinion, body straight to the vertical, hands at her sides, one of them holding the figurine, nothing moving except her legs. There was only one little problem: her left leg, the one connected to her with the new hip, didn't seem to want to do its job. She forced it to step up. The new hip did not like being forced. She forced it anyway. The effort made her grunt, grunting not a good thing when free diving, the grunt taking the shape of an air bubble escaping from the top of the snorkel. Mrs. Plansky glanced up to see that stupid air bubble, air she needed inside her, and noticed a couple of things. For example, she was no longer on a straight ninety-degree path to the surface but had veered off to something more like seventy-five degrees. Also the surface, shining in the sun, still seemed rather far away. Mrs. Plansky altered course to ninety degrees and began kicking longer and harder and faster, if pretty much a solo effort on the part of her right leg. A furious, out-of-control sort of kicking, in fact, just as though she were hitting the panicky button, something she absolutely refused to do.

Then came a bright golden flash, followed by a soothing and quite lovely high that reminded her of the anesthetic kicking in before the hip surgeon made his first cut. And after that, just as in the OR, total blackness.

Well, perhaps not totally total. Instead she was transported back to a long-ago Wellfleet vacation, Nina seven and Jack five. The two kids had gotten caught in a rip and begun screaming. She'd plunged in, calling, "Don't fight it! Ride it out!" Which Nina had done, the rip dissipating about twenty yards out and leaving her bobbing in the swell, but Jack had fought the rip and gone under. She'd grabbed him, yanked him to the surface, and swum him to safety, swimming on her back with Jack facing up, and one of her hands on his chest. How his little heart had beat, like a hummingbird! Mrs. Plansky remembered like it was happening now. And she was Jack.

EIGHT

Splish-splash and another golden flash. Mrs. Plansky opened her eyes, or perhaps realized they were open, and found herself bobbing on a calm sea, sort of on her back with her face above water and an endless blue sky overhead, without a doubt the most beautiful sight she'd seen in her whole life, just heavenly.

Heavenly? Uh-oh.

She lowered her gaze, turned her head a bit. It felt disconnected somehow, like her inner wiring had loosened. All she saw was the sea, going on and on, in constant motion but not at all aggressive, like an enormous engine on idle. She turned her head a little more and a sailboat entered the picture, a cream-colored sloop with a cream-colored sail. Ah. Hadn't she seen this already? Just closer. Now it was farther. She realized she was breathing, filling her lungs with air and letting it out. How lovely! She remembered something she'd been trying to remember, a term. Shallow water blackout. Ah-ha!

Right away she realized something else, namely that she'd been wearing a mask and snorkel and now she was not. She fluttered her feet. They fluttered not like bare feet but like feet wearing fins. So there was that. She finned herself around in a complete 360, except she paused at 180 when Kev's place came into view, his aerodynamic-looking house on pilings and his dock with something small and shiny lying on it, all of that farther away than it should have been but not worrisomely so. In fact she was worry-free, felt pretty damn good, except for the way something hard and metallic was pressing against one of her breasts. She reached down the front of her swimsuit, felt the hard and metallic something, pulled it out, and held it so she could see.

The figurine. There in the sunshine she looked not like the representation of some deity but the god herself. Well, a rather highfalutin thought that Mrs. Plansky made a mental note to keep to herself. Meanwhile the details of this aquatic adventure came tumbling into her mind where there was lots of space for them, her mind pretty much empty at the moment, and those details trailed ripples of fear in their wake. That made Mrs. Plansky angry. The danger—perhaps exaggerated in retrospect, considering how comfortable she was and had always been in the water—was passed. There was nothing to be afraid of.

"Get a grip," she told herself.

She forced that fear wave to shrink down in submission. Was she shaking a little? That had to be because of the water temp. Even seventy-five degrees will kill eventually, just ask all those sailors from the Battle of the Coral Sea. Mrs. Plansky swam to the dock, not as quickly as she wanted on account of the balkiness of her new hip. No need to use the word pain. Pain was a word reserved for . . . for others in pain? What an odd thought! Her free hand—the other holding the figurine—touched the dock, which stood on pilings on the shore side but floated on the seaside, meaning pulling yourself out of the water was easy, nothing to it.

But in the here and now there was nothing easy about it. Mrs. Plansky struggled and grunted and flopped around like some fat-bodied pinniped. What a disgrace if anyone was around to see, or even if not! She rolled over, boosted herself into a sitting position, got hold of a bollard with her free hand, hauled herself erect. A bird's-eye view of herself at that moment was not something she wanted to see or even imagine.

The shiny object she'd tossed on the dock was the beer can, of course, 40–Love Hazy IPA. She took it and the figurine to her car, got in, pressed start, and then noticed her blue shirt, khaki skirt, and sandals lying on the dock. She retrieved all that, and then, concealing herself behind one of the pilings holding up the house, peeled off her swimsuit and got dressed. She couldn't help but see a bruise already developing on her thigh and another on her shoulder, their causes unknown, lost at sea. That lost-at-sea idea, so cartoonishly self-aggrandizing, was pretty funny, at least to her at that moment, and closed the door to any self-pitying rooms she might have entered, or even any simply labeled "self." She got back in the car and drove home, the beer can and the figurine on the passenger seat, but not together, like they had some beef going on. She left them there when she got back to the condo.

Clara was at the kitchen table wearing magnifiers on her nose and painting her nails, and Lucrecia was loading the dishwasher. There was no sign of her dad.

"Jovencita!" Clara peered at Mrs. Plansky—her eyes huge and watery through the thick lenses—very happy to see her, like they'd been parted for eons.

Mrs. Plansky was not in the mood for watery, but she smiled the most convincing smile she could. "Hi, Clara."

Clara said something to Lucrecia in Spanish, too rapid for Mrs. Plansky to catch. Lucrecia turned. "Been for a swim?" She patted her hair. Mrs. Plansky realized her own hair was still wet, and no doubt matted and twisted in some sort of drowned rat arrangement. She resisted the urge to pat things into place.

"Yes," she said.

"*Brrr*," said Clara, hugging herself but carefully, to keep the nail polish, a shade of red more assertive than any Mrs. Plansky had ever seen, unsmeared.

"The ocean's seventy-five goddam degrees." Mrs. Plansky kept that totally rude and unnecessary outburst to herself. How loud and angry that sounded in her head! Had some of it leaked out? But no. Clara and Lucrecia went on behaving normally.

Lucrecia closed the dishwasher and started it up. "We'll be leaving now unless there's something else."

"No, see you tomorrow. Thanks for everything."

"De nada." Lucrecia made a chin gesture toward the hall. "He's resting."

"Contentamente," said Clara.

After they left, Mrs. Plansky brought the beer can and the figurine inside and set them on the kitchen table. Old and new, the figurine being old and the beer can new, although she had no way of knowing the age of the figurine, or anything about it. In some ways the beer can looked older than the figurine. It was dented and scratched down to bare aluminum in a couple of places, while the figurine was pristine except for a few strands of sandy seaweed. She picked them off. Was it possible the figurine and the beer can had nothing to do with *Lizette*, were already on the bottom when the boat went down? The beer can: yes, it was possible, but she doubted it, based just on the name of the beer and how any tennis player, coming upon it on a store shelf would want to give it a try. The figurine: also yes, but only if it was worthless. If not, if valuable, then it had been aboard when *Lizette* went down. Was she making an indefensible mental leap? If so, who was going to argue the other side? At that moment she thought of Jack, another mental leap, this one into thin air.

She gazed at the figurine. Here indoors the figurine didn't shine. It glowed. That was one of the classy attributes of gold, the way it glowed rather than shone. But was it gold? She hefted the thing. Heavy for its size, but so was lead. Was she looking at gold-painted lead, perhaps with no real gold even in the paint? Maybe this was some trinket for tourists, like an Eiffel Tower or a Big Ben.

Mrs. Plansky went into her bedroom, opened the safe, took out her jewelry box, and brought it to the kitchen. She didn't have a lot of jewelry but what she had was nice, although not at all grand or anything like that, nothing anyone would look at twice, which was fine with her. For example, take this bracelet, which Norm had given her the day they sold their one hundred thousandth Plansky Toaster Knife. She held it up: a fairly narrow and not particularly thick gold band from which hung, on braided gold threads, a few small gold nuggets, not many at all. Had she ever even counted them? She counted them now. Hmm. A dozen. That was a bit of a surprise.

But not the point. She'd gotten sidetracked, in fact sidetracked herself. She resolved to keep an eye on that in the future. Meanwhile . . . meanwhile she'd lost the thread. Her gaze went to the beer can, the figurine, the bracelet. Ah, right. Those nuggets—found in Australia, if she remembered right—were 22 karat. Wasn't that the point of nuggets? For a scary moment she realized that that last bit sounded, in her mind, like something her dad would say. Please God, no.

She set the bracelet next to the figurine and stared at them. Then she got one of the nuggets between finger and thumb and hefted it in a mini way, at the same time hefting the figurine again in her other hand. Based on those two not-very-scientific tests, she concluded that the figurine was gold. It was too beautiful not to be gold. Gold wasn't even the point of the thing. Beauty was the point. Just look at those sturdy feet. So like Tee-Tee's! She might have posed for the artist.

Mrs. Plansky turned to the beer can. She sniffed at the opening and smelled nothing of beer, simply the sea. She checked the name again—40–Love Hazy IPA—and studied the artwork: two stick figures, one in shorts, the other in a tennis dress, their tennis-ball heads together in a passionate kiss. Well, perhaps it was more complicated than that. The male kisser seemed to be winking at the viewer. The female had her eyes closed. The ABV was 6.9, the IBU, whatever that was, 38, and the company, Drop Shot Brewers, was out of Macdee, Florida, which she might have heard of and thought was inland somewhere.

At that moment her skin sent a message that it was feeling salty. She pictured the hose coiled on Kev's dock. Why hadn't she hosed herself off? Hosing yourself off on a dock after a saltwater swim was one of those tiny pleasures in life. She couldn't allow herself to skip those. What if the secret to happiness was simply to string together all available tiny pleasures you could from birth to death?

God in heaven. She was losing it. She went into her bathroom and took a long shower. Mrs. Plansky liked to end every shower with a blast of cold but skipped that this time. She dried herself off, checked those new bruises in the mirror, discovering one more, and headed to her closet to pick out something to wear. But she didn't quite make it, instead sat on the edge of the bed on her way, taking an absurd sort of break. Even worse, she was soon lying down. Not only that but lying down and getting comfy with the pillows and the quilt! Mrs. Plansky had never been and would never be a napper. A sleeper during proper sleeping hours? Certainly. But a napper? Never.

Mrs. Plansky awoke with her mind in complete disarray, the remnants of disturbing but instantly forgotten dreams zooming off like fragments of some flywheel mishap. She sat up, glimpsed her face in a wall mirror, the personification of her inner state. And the time on the bedside clock? Shameful. As for naps, never again.

She rose, ignoring the seeming fact that she ached all over, and got dressed—a plain short-sleeve white tee with a turquoise collar, the turquoise quite subdued, and lemon-colored linen slacks that went well with the turquoise, the slacks not baggy but formfitting although not too much so—and barefoot went into the kitchen. The beer can and the figurine were gone.

"Dad?"

She hurried down the hall. The door to his room was open and he wasn't there.

"Dad?"

"Relax," he called from the other end of the condo. "I'm fine."

She found him, whiskey in hand, in the little bar off the dining room, gazing out the slider at the lake, the surface reddish in the late-afternoon light.

"Dad? Was anyone—"

The beer can and the figurine were on the bar, the can straight up, the figurine lying down.

Her dad tried to turn his head around to see her, couldn't manage that much rotation. He wheeled himself into position.

"Was anyone what?" he said.

"How did those get there?" She pointed at the bar.

"How the hell should I know?"

"They were on the kitchen table."

"Check."

"So you brought them here?"

"Duh."

"Why didn't you just say so?"

"Not all questions have answers. You collecting beer cans now?"

"Excuse me?"

"For getting back the deposits."

"There are no deposits in Florida."

"Huh? When did that happen?"

"It never happened."

"You're not making sense. Care for a drink?"

"I'm fine for the moment."

"Think so?"

Mrs. Plansky went over to the bar and stood up the figurine.

"You know your problem?" her dad said. "You should drink more. Loosen you up."

Mrs. Plansky ignored that. Her father—a mediocrity in many ways, if she was willing to voice a harsh truth, just to herself, of course—was a world champion when it came to zingers. Did he zing Clara? She had her doubts about that.

"What's that ugly thing?" he said.

"Ugly thing?"

"That brass thing. You're lookin' right at it."

"You think it's brass?"

"Gotta be. Copper's more red. From the flea market?"

She said nothing.

"Come on. The flea market, you know, in town, across from the library."

"It's not from the flea market."

"Hope you didn't pay a lot for it. Not more than five bucks. It's a copy. You're aware of that?"

"A copy of what?

"You can tell it's a copy because it's brass. They didn't do brass."

"Who?"

"The Navajo, the Hopi, none of them. No alloys. They did silver." He pointed. "So that's a copy, proof positive. What did you pay for it?"

"Nothing."

"Smart." His eyes narrowed into a shrewd expression, not becoming on him. "A gift from some cheapo boyfriend?"

"I don't have a boyfriend, as you know."

"There's such a thing as secret boyfriends."

"What are you talking about, Dad?"

"For example, if he's already married."

"Do you really think I'd do that?"

He shrugged. "People get desperate."

Mrs. Plansky was not the kind to glare at anyone. She'd probably done it in her life, although she couldn't think when. But she was glaring now, glaring at her dad with what she was sure was one of those if-looks-could-kill looks.

He raised his glass. "Cheers!" And downed the contents.

Mrs. Plansky swept up the beer can and the figurine and swept out of the room.

A drink right now sounded like just the thing. Only not with him. True they'd ruled out all the assisted-living places within reasonable driving range, but what about unreasonable driving ranges? Even out-of-the-question ones? Mrs. Plansky happened to notice the speedometer, registering eighty in a fifty zone. She ramped right down just as she was approaching the Green Turtle Club sign, a laughing turtle mounted up above the palms, martini glass in one flipper. It was a nice spot for a drink and the conch fritters were tasty, but she drove on, another idea forming in her mind. Half a mile down the road she pulled into the parking lot of Bevo's, a brew pub she'd never been to.

In fact, she'd never been to any brew pub at all, although beer sometimes hit the spot, especially on a boat or after tennis. Bevo's was a weathered wooden affair, with tables on an outside deck, maybe half of them occupied and filling up, and a musician dressed Jimmy Buffett–style setting up on a low dais. Inside things were nautical, as though she'd boarded Old Ironsides, except for the absence of cannons. Oops, it turned out there was one: a miniature, mounted on the bar at the far end. That's where Mrs. Plansky sat, even if she could have chosen anywhere, the bar pretty much deserted. There was a long row of beer taps, a couple of dozen at least, each with a highly individualized handle: a red parrot, for example, or a skull and crossbones. She'd come to the right place, although she hadn't spotted a handle with kissing tennis balls before the bartender came over.

He was a skinny little kid, maybe of college age—the age of youngsters getting harder to nail down precisely—with a dominating and ill-conceived Vandyke beard and vague eyes gazing a couple of inches above her head.

"Hey, there. What can I getcha?"

"A 40–Love Hazy IPA, please."

Now he managed to look her in the eye, if only a second or two. In that very brief time Mrs. Plansky realized something incredible. She was barefoot. She'd left home wearing her white short-sleeve shirt with the muted turquoise collar, the lemony linen slacks that matched perfectly, but nothing on her feet. Incredible in the true meaning of the word. She barely resisted the temptation to glance down and confirm what her feet already felt. The truth was that her feet were feeling happy about the situation. What did they call those longtime inhabitants of the Keys? Conchs? That was it. In just a few years in Florida she'd somehow turned into a conch.

The bartender opened his mouth to speak. She half expected he was going to say, "No shoes, no service," and bum-rush her out of the joint. Instead he said, "Sorry, ma'am, don't have that one. I can fix you up with something pretty close."

"That'd be fine."

"Sixteen ounces, twenty-four, or our best value, thirty-two?"

"Sixteen, please."

He went to one of the taps, returned with a frosted pint glass filled to the brim, and then just stood there. Ah, waiting for her to try it. She tried it.

"Very nice. Do you have anything else by the 40–Love people? Drop Shot Brewers, I think they're called."

"We did, but not lately."

"Any idea why?"

He shook his head. "Depends on the distributor, mostly. But it's cool, you liking it and all. They had a party here awhile back, introducing us to the brand. A local dude's one of the investors."

"Oh?"

"That's where the branding comes in."

"Branding?"

"Forty–love, drop shot—that's tennis, um, terminology. This investor dude's something to do with tennis."

"What's his name?" she said, at the same time fearing that tooblurty question needed a little watering down. She watered it down. "I play tennis!" Watered it down stupidly, as she heard with her own ears.

But it didn't matter. "Couldn't tell you."

He turned to go. Mrs. Plansky had a brain wave.

"Are there any pictures of the party?"

"Pictures?"

"Photos. Maybe on your phone. I like parties."

I like parties? Really? She couldn't do better than that?

But again it didn't matter. "Cool," the bartender said, the vagueness suddenly clearing from his eyes, leaving behind an intelligent look, like he'd had the phone idea himself.

He got busy with his phone, then turned it so she could see. It was one of those too-small photos. Three men seemed to be raising foaming glasses in a toast. They stood by the miniature cannon, close to where she sat now, but she couldn't really make out their faces. The bartender expanded the photo with a quick motion of his finger and thumb, a move at which Mrs. Plansky was still not adept.

"That's the investor dude, in the middle."

The investor dude was Kev Dinardo.

Somewhat of a surprise, but not totally unexpected. She'd never seen the man on the left, who looked like a golfer, not the weekend nineteenth-holer type but the kind you see on TV. The man on the right was Mitch or Mr. Mitch. That was the big surprise.

She pointed to him. "Is that Mitch? Or Mr. Mitch?"

"Doesn't ring a bell," the bartender said. "But I'm bad with names."

NINE

The next day was the weekly OT day for Mrs. Plansky's dad. She delivered him to Surfside Wellness Center, where they were working on his unaided walking. He did very little unaided walking these days at home, so she'd assumed he was getting worse before finding out he did much better at the wellness center. There'd been a meeting at the center about this very issue, involving Mrs. Plansky, her dad, and the OT lady. Her dad admitted he walked better at the center because "I just don't feel like it" at the condo. So what was the point of OT, especially after the OT lady shot Mrs. Plansky an accusatory look, like his enthusiasm gap was her fault? It was good to have the condo to herself, if only for a day. That was the point.

So, coming home after dropping him off, she was surprised to see Lucrecia sitting in Joe's car in one of the parking spots, Joe behind the wheel. Lucrecia climbed out.

"Sorry to bother you," she said.

"You couldn't," said Mrs. Plansky.

"Got a moment?"

"C'mon in." She looked over at Joe. "Joe?"

He smiled and shook his head.

Inside Mrs. Plansky sat Lucrecia down and poured out coffee.

"I've been thinking," Lucrecia said. "About the assisted-living problem."

"You have my attention."

"My mom's not against it, not the way she can get when she's deep-down against."

"Oh," said Mrs. Plansky. "I thought you were talking about my dad."

"I am, partly." Lucrecia took some cheerfully colored brochures from her purse. "There's a few assisted livings that take couples. In the same quarters, I mean, a kind of suite. My mom would be okay with that."

"With him, you mean?"

"Si."

"Do you think he'd do it?"

"We'd leave that in her . . . in her hands."

They both thought about that for a few moments.

"Just one catch," Lucrecia said.

"What's that?"

"They'd have to be married. That's the rule."

"An assisted-living company rule?"

Lucrecia shook her head. "Her rule."

"But they're having—they're together now."

"Not living together, under the same roof." Lucrecia glanced at Mrs. Plansky over the rim of her mug. "My rule too, actually."

Mrs. Plansky nodded, her instincts possibly in agreement even if her rational mind was not. "But will he do it? Get married?"

"Again, that will be up to her."

"Meaning she'll pop the question?"

"Clara Dominguez de Soto y Camondo—and those aren't even all of her names—pop the question? Nunca en el vida. She will persuade him to pop the question."

"What if he says no?"

"Is he the type to say no?"

"Lucrecia! It's his go-to."

"Ha!" said Lucrecia. "Not to worry." But right then her face darkened. "As for the expense, naturally these places cost. Of course, Joe and I will cover half. We expect—since there will be paperwork for signing and all the rest—that you will want to see our financing for this, which starts with a second—"

Mrs. Plansky held up her hand in the stop sign. "Since we're in old-fashioned mode on this project, the husband pays for the marital home. He wouldn't have it any other way."

Lucrecia sat back. "But—but he's broke, no? Forgive me for knowing."

Mrs. Plansky, not a liar by nature, now unleashed a whopper on Lucrecia. "He'd be embarrassed not to pay."

"You think so?"

"I know him." There. A clever evasion, in some twisted way making up for the lie.

"Well," said Lucrecia, "I don't know. How about we go over it again? Maybe with Joe?"

"Sometime in the future," said Mrs. Plansky, in her mind closing the deal. She'd closed many deals in her business career—what a negotiator she was, as Norm often said—but had any of them been more satisfying than this? Absent the bottom-line aspect. But money wasn't everything. Easy for her to say, of course.

She walked Lucrecia out to her car, went around to the driver's side.

"Hi, Joe."

"Hey." The sunlight gilded his grizzled beard. All at once, and completely irrationally, Mrs. Plansky knew why Lucrecia loved him so much. "Did she tell you this crazy idea?" he said.

"Here comes the bride," Mrs. Plansky said. "Start working on your toast."

Joe laughed, and was still laughing when Lucrecia said something very quick to him in Spanish. His face softened—had she just told him the result of the financing discussion?—and he turned to Mrs. Plansky.

"All recovered from the other night?"

"Oh, yes."

"Is Mr. Dinardo back yet?"

"Back?" One of those dark, uneasy balloons took shape in her mind: the Kev balloon. Perhaps it was there all the time now and she only noticed periodically. There was also the Jack balloon. The two balloons drifted around, sometimes together, even bumping into each other, at other times far apart.

"He mentioned he'd be gone for a few days in case FD had any questions," Joe was saying. "Turns out we do, on account of these new EPA regs."

"I haven't heard," Mrs. Plansky said. Did he say where? she wondered, but kept to herself, on account of, well, the sin of pride, might as well admit it. Luckily for her some part of her mind chipped in with an actual idea. She tried to frame it in a cagey way. "In terms of all that, EPA and such, what happened to the boat? What was left of it. The wreckage."

"Got hauled by salvage."

"Ah. Where to?"

"Not sure. There's a few yards up and down the coast, but Force Ten Marine Salvage in Fort Prince been doing most of the business lately."

"Interesting," said Mrs. Plansky. She couldn't imagine sounding any stupider.

Joe patted her arm with his hand, a strong, wide, rough hand but the touch was gentle. "See you in church," he said.

The balloons vanished at once, as though in the aftermath of a medieval miracle. That turned out to be unsettling. Was nothing off the table right now? It was like realizing your backyard was a potential sinkhole—a not so rare occurrence in these parts—and not being able to move past the thought.

Mrs. Plansky had never been to Fort Prince. It turned out to be downscale from Ponte d'Oro, and Force Ten Marine Salvage was downscale from that. There were two single-story concrete block buildings—one an office, the other a warehouse lined with floor-to-ceiling shelves stacked with propellers, winches, outriggers, cables, anchors, and lots of stuff she didn't know the names of—the doors to the buildings open but both unoccupied. On the water side was a yard surrounded by a chain-link razor-wire-topped fence and packed with boats in various states of ruination. Mrs. Plansky scanned them all. *Lizette* wasn't there.

Beyond the yard a wide cement pier extended thirty or forty feet into the ocean, and on that pier stood a mobile crane. Two men were busy hauling a yacht with a stoved-in bow out of the water, the crane operator, an older guy—well, possibly younger than she was—with sun-blemished forearms, a problem she'd dodged so far—and a younger assistant with dreads, standing on the stern of the boat and making hand gestures. They'd bound the wreck with two or three cables, connected at the top to a thick steel eye, and now the operator swung his hook right into the eye, dead center, rather speedily for such a delicate maneuver, then lifted the boat clear of the water, backed the crane up, drove it off the pier over to the fenced-in yard. The assistant, still on the boat, made some more hand gestures. The operator lowered the boat inside, then parked the crane behind the concrete block buildings. The assistant jumped down off the boat and walked out of the yard, locking the gate behind him. Mrs. Plansky, just a few steps away, had never been interested in work like this. Now it was mesmerizing her. If she'd been a man, this was the kind of—

"Uh, help you?" said the assistant.

She snapped out of it. "Why, yes. At least I hope so. I'm looking for a boat you might have salvaged recently."

"Here's all the recents." He gestured toward the boats in the yard.

"Ah," said Mrs. Plansky. "I don't see it."

The assistant shrugged. She noticed that all his movements—not just the jumping off the boat, but every little thing—were graceful, like a dancer's. Meanwhile the crane operator had come over.

"Odell? What's up?"

"Lady's looking for a boat."

"What boat?"

"*Lizette.*"

"You see it in there?"

"No," Mrs. Plansky said.

"Then we don't got it."

"*Lizette*?" Odell said. "From the lightning strike down in Ponte d'Oro?"

"That's right," Mrs. Plansky said. "Basically." That last little addition a feeble gesture to the fact she hadn't seen any lightning herself.

"We did the job," Odell said. "Now she's gone."

"Where?"

"Laos, Cambodia, some such," the crane operator said.

"I don't understand."

"Cause China's not takin' no scrap no more." The crane operator looked like he was about to spit but he did not. "That's what this country's coming to."

"Hey, Errol," Odell said.

"Well, it's the truth," said Errol, but he sounded apologetic.

"So the boat got . . . got crushed already?"

"You wouldn't believe how small," said Odell.

"And put on a container ship?"

"Outta Savannah," Errol said. "You the owner?"

"A friend. I saw it happen."

"The lightning strike?" said Odell.

She nodded but remained silent. Some next step needed taking but she didn't know what it was.

"No one got hurt, right?" said Errol.

"Right."

"That's the main thing. Sorry we couldn't—"

"What I was wondering is if you search the boat before the crushing and all that."

"Weren't much to search. All burnt up and scraped off the bottom type of situation."

"Do you . . . comb through it all anyway?"

"Comb through?" Errol said.

"In case there are any valuables."

"You lost something?"

Mrs. Plansky tried another silent nod.

"What?" said Errol.

She went with the first thing that came to mind. "A watch."

"What kind?" Odell said.

At that moment she couldn't think of the brand name of one single solitary luxury watch, or even a cheapo off a drug store rack. "It had sentimental value."

"The way this works," Errol said, "we got salvage rights, law of the sea since time immaterial."

"But," said Odell, "you can contact your insurance."

"Make a claim," Errol said. "Like we told the other fella."

"Other fella? Fellow?"

"Come here also askin' about valuables on that same vessel."

"And also," said Odell, now giving Mrs. Plansky a new look, quick but searching, "friends with the owner."

"A big man?" Mrs. Plansky stretched her arms in a sort of Mitch-or-Mr. Mitch-shaped big man illustration in the air.

"Wouldn't say big," Errol said.

"But in good shape," said Odell.

"Lean, like," Errol said.

"Short hair, clean-cut," Odell said. "Ring a bell?"

Maybe, but too faint to summon anything useful. Mrs. Plansky shook her head. "Well, uh, I appreciate the information."

"No problem," Odell said. "But we didn't find any watches, any jewelry, nothing like that."

"Thank you."

"Goes to the bottom, stuff like that," Errol said. Now he, too, was giving her a searching look. "Whole different MO with drugs. Your drugs is buoyant. Your drugs floats right up and the tide takes 'em far and gone. That's the story on your drugs."

What was this? Could it possibly be? They suspected she was some kind of drug smuggler? The proper reaction would have been to laugh in their faces, but she couldn't manage that. Instead she turned bright red. This had nothing to do with drugs. It was about . . . what would you call them? Clues, that was it. Something not good was going on.

Mrs. Plansky could feel it. Tee-Tee was a clue to whatever it was. And also the beer can. Had other clues gone down with the ship, now squished to practically nothing and en route to Cambodia? She had no idea. But one thing was sure. She wasn't the only one asking that question.

TEN

On her way back, Mrs. Plansky swung by 92 Seaside Way, just to have a little look-see. Swung by? Look-see? Her mind seemed to be adopting some sort of slangy way of talking that wasn't at all how she herself talked. Where was that going to lead? Meanwhile the swung-by part reminded her of the sports reporter, whom she probably wouldn't be hearing from again, the New Sunshine/Old Sunshine Ancient Folks mixed doubles championship story being not very newsy even when fresh. As for the purpose of this detour, it was all about two dark balloons. And let's not forget the kiss. Two dark balloons and a kiss. What about that kiss, a kiss that came right after the fireball, almost like cause and effect? The kiss had stayed with her, like an overture to something big. But . . . but had there been a hint of goodbye in it? Had Kev been kissing goodbye to well, to who knows what? Or was that just retrospect talking? The universe of what she didn't know kept growing.

Mrs. Plansky stopped the car in front of Kev's house. Everything looked the same as before, except the Lambo was gone. Lambo? The slang term for Lamborghini, never used by her, even in thought. But now there it was, the word, front and center in her mind, even if the object itself was gone, like she was part of some balancing act, and not by choice. Mrs. Plansky felt a bit breathless. Nothing to worry about, just a momentary glitch, as though she were passing through a very narrow airless zone. She got out of the car, took in a lungful of sea air, emerged at once from this vacuum or whatever it was. After all, she was healthy as a horse, had always been that way. Mrs. Plansky knew she was one lucky lady.

She walked up to Kev's front door and listened. The house was silent. She gave the door—somewhat oversized, made of dark wood, perhaps mahogany—a close look. Below the heavy wrought-iron handle was a keyless touch pad lock, one through nine plus zero. She touched nine and then two, but only because she knew that wouldn't work. The little light at the bottom of the pad flashed red. Mrs. Plansky was not the B&E type, although guessing a touch pad combo might not qualify as B. She knocked on the door, something she'd already done at least once, but now she sensed something about it she'd missed. She ran her fingers along it. Not mahogany or any other wood. Kev's door was made of steel.

Meanwhile no "who is it?" or "coming!" from inside, no footsteps. Mrs. Plansky moved toward the nearest window, small and oval, which she guessed would have a view of the entrance hall. A high window: she had to stand on her tiptoes to see inside.

Yes, the entrance hall, with the bronze-fish fountain, not running, pool dry, and the tennis bag with the initials she hadn't been able to read before and still could not, the bag at the wrong angle. But Mrs. Plansky did spot one change from before, namely Kev's tennis trophy, last seen in the big hands of Mitch or Mr. Mitch. Now it lay in the fountain pool just under the tail of the bronze fish and no longer whole but in pieces, the serving tennis player separated from the base and the base itself separated into its component pieces.

Mrs. Plansky couldn't see beyond the fountain. She knocked some more, harder this time, unmissable. The house was silent. She hit nine and two again on the touch pad, and had there been letters she would have added S-E-A-S-I-D-E, but there were not. The light flashed red. She got back in her car.

Her dad must have heard her coming into the condo. He came wheeling fast from somewhere inside.

"Where have you been?"

He was agitated. His agitation was always accompanied by lots of hard-to-miss signals, like a supporting cast of over-the-top actors. For example, like now, his head was extended at almost a 180-degree angle, closing in on whomever he was facing, in this case her.

"Here I am, Dad. Is there a problem?"

"Here I am. Golly gee. Yes, there's a problem. If there wasn't would I be . . . ?" His voice, perhaps waiting for ammo that got delayed, trailed off.

"What's the problem?"

He blinked a few times and his mood changed. His head rose up closer to normal, not really all that high these days. For a moment he almost looked sweet. Then his shrewd look took over.

"I wouldn't say that. No, not a problem. Only paperwork. That's it. Dumbass paperwork. No more, no less."

"Specifically?"

"Huh?"

"What sort of paperwork?"

Her dad thought about that. "Simple. Not even paperwork. Just one line."

"Which is?"

"Your John Hancock. Ha! Johanna Hancock! Ha-ha! Who'da thunk I'd end up as a feminist?" He grinned, a grin that was charming, a relic of his *Mad Men* days. A stranger might have taken him for a big success in his prime.

"You want my signature?"

"Bingo."

"Why?"

"Formalities."

"What formalities?"

"Cosigning. Just need you to cosign this loan thing."

"You want to borrow money?"

The furrows in his brow, already deep, deepened more. "What I want to do is lend. Make interest work for me. Not against. But you need capital for that. Do I have to explain capitalism now?"

"You need to borrow money to get capital?"

"What I need, goddam it to hell, is financial independence."

He glared at her. Like it was her fault. Mrs. Plansky understood what was going on. Clara was a fast mover. That made sense. And even though he knew that everything—the wedding and all the living arrangements—were covered, he wanted to cover them himself. Not making it look that way, but for real, real in this case meaning money that would not and could not be paid back and might not even be used for the supposed purpose. The answer to that plan was no. She didn't even feel bad about it.

"We're doing all right, Dad."

He seemed to inflate, some outburst on the way, but then quickly shrank down, like his temper had sprung a leak.

That night Mrs. Plansky went to bed with her window open, the full-time-AC part of the year still a month or so away. A southwest breeze was blowing, slight but enough to ripple the surface of the lake. She loved that rippling sound. It wafted her to sleep and at the same time made her want to stay awake and listen. The wafting always won but there was something delicious about the battle, and Mrs. Plansky was luxuriating in it—talk about the small pleasures in life, even teeny-weeny in this case—when something splashed out there. Not a little something. It jolted her back up to complete consciousness, and somehow that jolt sparked an idea. She sat up.

This idea was all about touch pads. You could punch 92 but not Seaside on a touch pad since there were numbers but no letters. This was all supposing you would use your address for the code— maybe not the most secure level of security, but what she would have done if the condos had touch pads, which they did not. After all, were we going to make an endless fetish of codes and passwords and two-step, three-step, infinity-step verification? But that was a detour. The open road—the road to the opening—was all about the revelation that had come to her: Numbers could substitute for letters! For example, one was *A*. Two was *B*. And so on to twenty-six for *Z*. So you could put—you could numerify, as Norm would say—Seaside into numbers! She corrected herself: would have said.

But meanwhile she was now at her desk, light on, notepad in front of her, pen in hand. Seaside. Two *E*'s, two *S*'s; this wasn't going to be hard. *S* would be . . ." She began counting on her fingers. Well, perhaps a bit harder than she'd thought, but in the end this was 92 Seaside in number code. Ninety-two, of course, followed by 19-5-1-19-9-4-5. The nineteens and ninety-two would have to be separated to work on the one-through-nine-plus-zero touch pad, making the number string rather long and complicated, a top-notch code after all. She tried to imagine a different life where she'd ended up running the CIA, or perhaps just the Moscow office or station or whatever they called it, and couldn't quite get there.

Mrs. Plansky, obviously reminded by "Moscow," thought for the first time in years of Brad Mosto. Brad was a big kid with the face of a full-grown man, who'd played number two on the boy's high school tennis team where Jack was number one from the first day of freshman practice right through senior year. Jack, even as an eighteen-year-old, still had a hint of baby in his own face. He and Brad had been pals at first but that had cooled off. Mrs. Plansky hadn't thought much of it but she did have a clear memory of sitting in the stands at a match where only Jack and his opponent were still on the court when she happened to notice Brad, one row down, a towel around his neck, doing a quick, surreptitious fist pump after a Jack double fault.

For a graduation present Jack wanted a Corvette Stingray. He wanted it badly; it didn't have to be new; he'd be grateful forever; he'd pay them back. It was out of the question. To Mrs. Plansky. But not to Norm. He'd hunted around, found a used one in good shape, taken out a loan, arranged a good deal, then cajoled and charmed a yes out of Mrs. Plansky. The look on Jack's face when he woke up and saw the shiny thing parked in the driveway!

There were strict rules. No drinking, obviously, complete obedience to all traffic signs, and only Jack could be behind the wheel. The Friday night after graduation Jack had gone out with Brad and totaled the Stingray on a twisty back road in Little Compton. Neither boy was hurt and Jack swore he hadn't been speeding, simply hadn't seen the curve in the road. But the police, investigating the crash, turned up an eyewitness—in fact, a nun—who swore that the car had indeed been going very fast and that Brad, not Jack, had been at the wheel. That had led to all sorts of nasty complications, but the nastiest part came when the boys were confronted: the brazen look on Brad's face, the lost look on Jack's.

And now—was he lost for real? Mrs. Plansky's heart began to beat a little too fast. Sleep was out of the question. She walked into her walk-in closet, stripped off her nightie, actually flinging it on the floor, and pulled on her only pair of yoga pants, worn the last time she'd been to yoga, several months ago. Or maybe a year. They were black. That was the point. She put on a long-sleeve black tee and red sneakers, since she didn't have black and red would do just as well at night. To be unseen! That was the point.

Mrs. Plansky turned to leave the closet, paused, picked up the nightie, and hung it on its proper hook. After that she opened the slider and stepped out on the patio. Then she paused again, went back inside and took the pencil flashlight from the bedside table drawer. A plan was taking shape in her mind but not in an orderly way. Orderly would have been nice, yet Mrs. Plansky didn't let that bother her, convinced that as long as she kept her mantra in mind—to be unseen, surely at the top of the list of don'ts governing B&E's—she'd be all right. At that moment it hit her that you couldn't simply drive up and park in front of the venue, or whatever the venue was called in B&E speak. You turned yourself into a shadow, a piece of the night.

The two end condos came with boat racks on the side, and on Mrs. Plansky's boat rack rested an ultralight kayak, left by the previous owners. She'd taken it out on the lake several times, but gotten bored with that long before the arrival of Fairbanks, and once she'd carried it—with several rest stops even though it weighed only thirty pounds—along a path that led under the highway to an arm of the inland waterway, a distance of a few hundred yards. The waterway connected to the sea by a little canal just south of Seaside Way, almost five miles by land but two—or even less!—by water. Just an estimate of course but now the plan was really coming together, taking shape in the very act of execution. Just imagine! She thought of Lewis and Clark and Buzz Aldrin and folks like that.

Mrs. Plansky made sure the paddle was inside the kayak, then got the kayak under one arm and headed for the path, which began just past the lawn equipment shed. She was so jazzed she was sure that this time she wouldn't need any rest stops at all, although that wasn't how it played out. In fact she might have taken one or two more than the last time. Why would that have been? Had the kayak somehow put on weight? She had no other ideas. The moon appeared from behind a cloud, a crescent moon, like it was giving her a sideways grin. Things got a little brighter, violating rule one on the B&E list, but there was no controlling the moon.

Up ahead the lane curved slightly and there was the arm of the waterway, quite narrow along this stretch, the water itself silvery from the moon, everything else a collection of shadows and smelling swampy. It crossed her mind that Fairbanks might have buddies, but then she remembered reading that gators weren't active at night.

Mrs. Plansky lowered the kayak into the water.

Or was it manatees?

She clambered into the kayak—well, no. It turned out that her left leg preferred not to go first; this after a whole lifetime of going first. She raised her right foot, but tentatively, the rest of her body unsure about how to proceed from here. Mrs. Plansky waded around to the other side of the kayak in the hope of somehow fooling her body into getting it done. Her sneakers sank into the mushy bottom, swamp-smelling air bubbles popping to the surface. Would tossing them aboard while still on land have been a good move?

"Hard to argue against," she said aloud, but very softly.

Meanwhile she somehow found herself properly seated in the kayak, paddle in her hands. She lowered a blade, pushed off, and glided away, the faint whisper of the gliding hull along the water a lovely sound, somehow like a message from real life. For the first time since the move to Florida she felt at home. Maybe she could start a nighttime kayaking support group for retired widows.

"Only one rule for the kayak, young ladies," Vô told them. "No lily dipping. Don't let me ever see no lily dipping."

"So it's okay to tip?" Tee-Tee said.

They were out off Second Beach on a hot August afternoon, no wind, no waves, the three kayaks all scavenged by Vô after the storms of the winter before—and nobody in life vests, now that Mrs. Plansky thought about it. With a few powerful strokes he glided up to them and using just one strong hand tipped Tee-Tee's kayak and then Lo-Lo's.

"Okay to tip," he called over his shoulder, paddling away toward shore.

That was the day the girls learned—taught themselves, really— how to right overturned kayaks and get back in. "Okay to tip" be- came a sort of catchphrase or private handshake; Mrs. Plansky didn't know the name that fit. It was the last thing Tee-Tee ever said to her.

Mrs. Plansky paddled down this narrow arm of the waterway, a kind of bayou. The moonlight, the quiet, being all alone—it was like going back in time. Had there been a female equivalent of the Swamp Fox? If not, why not, goddam it! She came to the waterway proper, with houses, condo developments, marinas, lights, meaning back to present time, and stayed on the near side, close to shore. A man fishing from a dock said, "Hey, cutie-pie," in a low voice, pos- sibly meant to be seductive.

"That'll bring the fish," she said as she glided by. She said that out loud! Wow! Lady Swamp Fox!

"Hey," he said again, although this time with a very different tone, like he was actually interested.

Waterway to the canal, canal to the sea, no slipups at all. Mrs. Plan- sky settled into an easy rhythm, maybe not the most powerful stroke but with good torso rotation and lots of muscles taking part, certainly no lily dipping. Vô was a good teacher. He'd seemed ancient at the time but had probably been thirty or forty years younger than her dad was now—and in fact younger than she was. This sort of mulling wasn't going to lead anywhere, but Mrs. Plansky kept mulling anyway, her body carrying on solo style. What made a good teacher? First, you had to want to do it. But why wouldn't you, when confronted by any halfway normal kid?

Out at sea, to her right, a cruise ship was headed for the islands, all lit up and not looking quite so obtrusive as it did up close. To her left, twenty yards away or so, the shoreline unreeled, one big waterfront house after another, some raised, some not, but none of them aerodynamic like Kev's. She steered toward his dock, swept wide with her right-hand blade, and glided in, the kayak's momentum zeroing out at the exact right second. Mrs. Plansky got hold of the bowline and climbed onto the dock, the first unsmooth—call it clumsy—move of the whole journey. She tied up with a proper cleat hitch, checked the well of the kayak for her pencil flash, didn't see it, patted the pocket of her yoga pants, found it.

The house was quiet, no lights showing. She made her way underneath without using the flash and walked around to the front door. The whole neighborhood was quiet. She could hear distant traffic but nothing close by. Mrs. Plansky shone her light on the touch pad. It was just as she remembered it, no curve balls. She took the cheat sheet from her pocket, unfolded it, and began typing in the secret code.

9-2-1-9-5-1-1-9-9-4-5

Now was the moment for the little round light at the bottom of the pad to flash green. It flashed red.

Easy to make a mistake with all those numbers, of course. Mrs. Plansky tried again. Red. She bent closer to the touch pad and gave it another go. Red. She tried once more, real slow, taking what seemed like ten seconds between each number. Red. She blew on her index fingertip, in case it was too damp or had some other flaw the touch pad didn't like. Red. She tried with her left index finger, an idea that struck her as inspired. Red.

Mrs. Plansky switched off the flash, backed away, took a few deep breaths. The address, 92 Seaside, was not the code. How could she have imagined it would be? Kev was smart. Using your address—even with the clever twist of subbing in numbers for letters—was maybe not smart, although that would have been her approach. Not now. Now she would use something else, something unpredictable, so off-the-wall that no one would ever guess. At the same time this wonder code would have to come from her real life, so she herself would never forget it and get redded out of her own home. Something like, for example, like . . . like . . . like 40–love! 40–Love! Tennis! Beer! Beating the crap out of those snooty Old Sunshiners! Unforgettable.

So let's see. 40 was 4-0. Love was going to take work. Ha! Mrs. Plansky touched 4 and then zero, and started counting on her fingers. *L* was 12, meaning 1-2. She typed 1 and 2. *O* was 15. 1 and 5. *V,* so late in the alphabet, was a problem. She lost her way several times but at last settled on 22. 2 and 2. *E* was easy, just a simple 5.

Nothing.

Well, it was worth a—

Green.

Eleven

Mrs. Plansky pressed down on the heavy, wrought-iron handle. She heard a click. The door opened. She stepped into Kev's house.

So dark. She closed the door softly behind her. What if someone was inside? Kev, for example, fast asleep in his bedroom, wherever in this huge place it happened to be. Some people slept with a firearm under the bed in case of situations just like this. These thoughts seemed to be arriving a little late. Norm was—had been—persnickety about nothing, but he came close to persnicketiness on the subject of doing things in the right order.

So what now? How about knocking loudly again, although this time on the inside of the door? Or finding light switches and turning them on? Or calling out, "Hey! Anyone home? Don't be alarmed! It's me, a friend! Or possibly more!"

None of those ideas appealed to her and she couldn't think of others. Well, there was one: she could step back outside and simply walk away, forgetting the whole thing. But wouldn't that be on the wobbly side? Like . . . like if Julius Caesar had crossed back over the Rubicon? She could see the looks on the faces of his legions when he tried to pull that stunt. She was no Caesar, in no way at all grand, but she really hadn't done much wobbling in life and didn't want to start now. Mrs. Plansky switched on her pencil flash.

She shone the light here and there, pausing on different images: down feathers spilled across the marble floor in the next room, the bronze fish, Kev's tennis trophy, now in pieces.

Mrs. Plansky walked over to the fountain and picked up the

pieces of the trophy. What if, in a way, way over-the-top display of sore-loserness, the Old Sunshiners, Jenna and Russell, had gone berserk, broken in, taken revenge? She could almost believe it of Jenna. Well, no. A ridiculous idea.

She examined the trophy pieces. The man had lost his serving arm, the tiny metal hand still gripping the tiny racket, and had also come loose from the wooden base. The base was made of two parts, a platform for the tennis player, and a bottom piece, just a flat round disc with a hole for a small screw. She didn't see the screw but the flat round disc was undamaged, as though the base hadn't been disassembled forcefully, instead taken apart with . . . with what? Some care? Forethought? But why? Mrs. Plansky had no answer.

She moved around the fountain, crouched before the tennis bag. It was the big kind, with room for three or four rackets, plus a towel or two, water bottle, spare socks, a cap. *Babolat* was written on one side and on the other, in much smaller print, were the embroidered letters she'd seen before but hadn't been able to make out. Now she could. No *KD*, but instead *JMP*.

JMP rang only one bell: Jack Miles Plansky, her son. Coincidence? Jack was indeed a tennis player, although many, many rungs up the ladder from anyone Kev would be hitting with. But since there were only twenty-six letters in the alphabet, a fact that she'd been dealing with only a few minutes before, wouldn't the same combos turn up over and over when it came to the initials of people's names? That seemed right, mathematical, scientific, rational. Except there was the one other odd fact, if it was a fact, that her dad had recommended Kev to Jack.

Mrs. Plansky unzipped the bag. There were three rackets inside, identical Babolats, all with freshly wrapped grips. Wasn't Jack sponsored by Wilson? Or was it Yonex? One or the other, of that she was sure. She rummaged around, found a half dozen used tennis balls, an empty plastic water bottle with no markings, and a plain white towel, not folded. Mrs. Plansky picked up the towel and sniffed it. She smelled maybe a tiny hint of sweat. Male? Female? Recent?

Old? She had no clue. Any random dog would be ahead of her right now. She checked the side pockets, all empty.

Mrs. Plansky shone her light on the bronze fish. It really was beautiful, a work of art with a hypnotic effect, at least on her. She realized that Kev was a deep person, with lots of subsurface activity going on, which she knew nothing about. It struck her right then that he might have security cameras tucked away all over the place. She probed the shadowy walls with her light, saw no cameras, but despite that now had the feeling she was being watched. And with it came the urge to flee, and if not flee than simply leave the house in an orderly manner.

Mrs. Plansky mastered that urge, maybe not obliterating it but at least squashing it down. She walked out of the entrance hall and into the next room, a large living room with sliders all along the sea-side, expensive looking but minimalist furniture, art on the walls. But the cost of the furniture was missing the point about it, which was that every piece was upside down, slashed, torn apart. And the art, despite how her mind had cleaned up what her eyes were seeing, was not on the walls, but also on the floor, frames broken, canvases ripped out. Who would do something like this? Someone very angry? Someone looking for something? She couldn't think of any other category.

Mrs. Plansky walked softly through the whole house, walked in fear, but did not miss a room, all of them in the same violent disarray. The master bedroom, at the top level of the house and reached by a spiral staircase, came last. She understood the source of her fear, which was all about the thing she dreaded to see, the kind of thing an angry person would leave behind when it was all over, but she shied away from even admitting that to herself, and most certainly from picturing it in her mind.

The master bedroom was the biggest she'd ever been in. The whole ceiling was made of some transparent material, a sort of giant skylight. Through it she could see the night sky, starry and with that crescent moon, its light strong enough to at least partially illumi-nate the room. A shambles: drawers pulled from the desk and overturned, with papers scattered over the floor; the king-sized mattress, perhaps bigger than king-sized, if there was such a thing, leaning, slashed open, against the far wall; clothes all over the place. Nothing was undisturbed except for the heavy curtains drawn over the entire length of the seaside wall. Her heart, already beating too fast, ramped up some more. What a cliché, the bad guy hiding behind a curtain! But had any bad guy ever said to himself, "Hide behind a curtain? Not me. I'm no hack"? Mrs. Plansky ran her light along the curtain at floor level, watching for the telltale toe caps of a pair of wing tips, or scuffed-up sneaks, or simply bare feet. Hairy ones, for example, which would have sparked a heart attack on the spot. She saw none of those things. She checked the walls for some button that would open the curtains, but saw none. So the next move, if she was going to be a perfectionist about it, was to get behind the curtain and walk its entire length. Mrs. Plansky decided not to be a perfectionist. Why start now?

But not to let herself off too easily, she next went over to the bed, got down on her knees—which didn't bother the knees at all, although her left hip wasn't happy about it—and swept the flashlight beam back and forth. There was nothing to see except a pair of bedroom slippers, the backless kind. She slid them out. Size eleven. Mrs. Plansky picked one up and took her second investigative sniff of the night. She knew she was acting strangely and also futilely, but did it anyway. Kev had a pleasant smell—you couldn't be someone's tennis partner and not get to know his smell—but her only reaction to the smell of the slipper was that it wasn't too bad and could have been the foot smell of any fungal-free human.

Mrs. Plansky lined up the slippers neatly and stuck them back under the bed. She'd sidetracked herself. The slippers weren't the point. There was no body under the bed. Yes, a bit on the melodramatic side, but that was the point. She put her hands on Kev's bed, pushed herself up to her feet, felt a little dizzy. An unopened bottle of water lay on the floor. She opened it and drank almost half. For a moment she felt like one coolheaded gal.

She went into the bathroom, a big open-concept bathroom,

mostly undamaged. There was plenty that an angry person could have damaged—the shower fixtures could have been ripped out, for example, or the mirrors shattered—but someone searching for something wouldn't have bothered. There wasn't much in the way of hiding places. The only sign of intrusion was the top of the toilet cistern, lifted off and resting on the toilet seat, and a framed photo hanging askew on one wall, the glass broken. Mrs. Plansky moved in for a closer look.

It was a black-and-white photo of *Lizette*—the name visible—out on the open sea, probably taken from another boat close by. A man and woman stood in the stern, laughing with their arms around each other. The man was Kev, looking maybe ten years younger. He turned out to be the type who'd gotten leaner with the passing years. The woman, looking to be about the same age as Kev, wore a naval captain's hat askew, and also a striped blouse and white slacks, both vaguely nautical and beautifully tailored, probably bespoke. Mrs. Plansky had never worn bespoke in her life but she knew it when she saw it. But there she went again, sidetracking herself. What was the first thing anyone would have noticed about the woman on the boat, their spur of the moment impression? She was a bombshell, that's what. A blond bombshell. A knockout. There were lots of pleasant-looking people out there—the majority, in her opinion—and plenty of pretty ones, plus a few actual beauties, and then at the tippy top came this. Mrs. Plansky reached for the photo and—

"Ow."

—cut her finger on a shard of glass.

Blood spurted out, landing on the photo itself and reddening Kev and the bombshell. Mrs. Plansky grabbed a towel off a nearby rack and pressed it against her finger, in the process losing the pencil flash which rolled away somewhere. For a moment or two she couldn't see a thing. Then her eyes adjusted—very slowly, despite the bang-up cataract surgery—to the much weaker light coming down through the skylight from that sideways grinning moon. Mrs. Plansky didn't like what she was seeing: blood seeping through the towel, blood dripping on the floor, Kev and the bomb-shell still visible, but now reddening. She went to the sink, ran her finger under cold water. A tiny pinkish whirlpool started circling the drain. With her other hand she opened the medicine cabinet, glimpsing her face in the mirror as it swung out, another sight she could have done without. Her eyes, so dark and scared? What an embarrassment! Where was her composure? True, this was her first B&E experience, but she had lots of experience in countless other life activities. She'd once delivered a complete stranger's baby, for God's sake, in a taxi on the Cross Bronx Expressway. No time now for all that, but the point was made.

"Get a grip."

Mrs. Plansky came close to throwing the F-word in there, but re-sisted the temptation. That would have been an admission of defeat, allowing her emotions to get the better of her. She stood up straight, found a box of Band-Aids, applied several over the cut, kept adding Band-Aids until no blood seeped through.

"Voilà," she said, her mind wandering off to some French crime movie she'd seen decades before. Meanwhile she found the pencil flash—which had fallen into the wastebasket, perhaps the kind of oddity B&E'ers got used to in time—and began mopping up every single trace of blood, missing none. There was no mopping up the blood on the photo. Mrs. Plansky removed it from what remained of the frame, rolled it up carefully, and slipped it into the pocket of her yoga pants. In the act of doing that, she felt a shift in her mind, as though thoughts were clicking together, like Lego pieces. What had gone down in Kev's house was not about rage or anger. It was about finding something. She tapped the top of the rolled-up photo, making sure it was secure. The photo wasn't the object of the search—obviously, since it hadn't been taken—but: that kind of thing, Loretta! Her mind was humming.

Mrs. Plansky left the bathroom, walked through Kev's bedroom, descended the spiral staircase, first facing backward as though she'd forgotten how to go down a spiral staircase. When was the last time she'd been on one? She was still trying to remember when she found herself back in the entrance hall. The moonlight was much dimmer here, but somehow the bronze fish seemed to be shining.

Mrs. Plansky stepped into the empty pool, reached out, and touched the fish. It . . . it was like touching art itself, directly, without an intervening object. How weird was that! The fish was good, not great, nothing like a Vermeer or any of those guys. She realized she was in a heightened state. Was that the true attraction in the B&E world? It got you high?

But . . . but was it possible that the fish itself was the object her B&E predecessor had been seeking? No, because here it was and who could miss it? She patted the fish's head, which was at her own head level.

"You're just an innocent bystander, sweetie," she said.

Then it occurred to her that turning on the fountain might be a good idea. Sort of her calling card! A James Bond type of move. She spotted a faucet, mostly hidden under the fish's tail, and turned it.

Nothing happened. Maybe the fountain didn't work, was only decorative. She reached into its mouth, feeling for some sort of pipe or small showerhead. Mrs. Plansky felt both of those things, and also something else.

TWELVE

This something else was at the back of the fish's throat, or where the fish's throat would have been, had Mrs. Plansky been dealing with a real fish. And did real fish even have anything you'd call a throat? She didn't know. Her ignorance of fish anatomy was pretty much uniform from head to tail. The truth was her ignorance in general was vast and getting vaster with age. How was that possible? Easy. Everything you'd learned in the past was warping beneath you. Mrs. Plansky suddenly saw herself from the outside, a woman of a certain age, let's say old, but still strong in many ways and in decent shape, certainly no bombshell although perhaps not unpleasant viewing for those who liked the somewhat broad-faced type. A la Kate Winslet! As Kate would look many, many years from now, and scaled way, way down beauty-wise—let's be realistic. And to keep up with the realism, she had to admit that the above-described character seemed to have blanked out at the very moment she was discovering something interesting. Why? Because it was late at night and she was exhausted? In truth, she was tired and wired at the same time. The wired part kick-started her back into action. Her fingers began exploring whatever this was, hidden in the mouth of the bronze fish.

She felt a plastic square, maybe three inches across, and at the edges something of a rougher texture, possibly tape. A baggie taped to the metallic innards of the fish? Could there be a fishhook in that baggie? Was this some elaborate joke or artistic statement? She pricked the edges of the baggie with her fingertips, slow and cautious, giving little tugs here and there, and pulled the thing out. Yes, a sandwich baggie with white adhesive tape at the edges. Inside was a folded sheet of paper.

Mrs. Plansky removed the sheet of paper, crouched down, unfolded it on the floor, shone her light. She saw a pencil drawing. A tree stood near the center of a roughly triangular shape with a deep notch in the hypotenuse. At first she thought this might be a child's drawing, but the tree—a palm—seemed too well rendered for that. Hard to tell because there was nothing else—a person, for example, even a stick figure—to scale it with, but she saw it as a tall palm, perhaps one of those royals. Here and there, both within the triangle and outside it, were tiny X's, plus some lines and numbers, maybe half a dozen. Mrs. Plansky had no idea what she was looking at. But point one: someone had been looking for something in Kev's house. Point two: this sheet of paper had been carefully hidden. Had that someone found what he—or she, but lifting that mattress off Kev's size-one-up-from king bed had to mean a he—was searching for? Or was this it? Mrs. Plansky refolded it and stuck it in her pocket, crowded it in, really, with the rolled-up photo. She felt like she'd accomplished something, an unjustifiable feeling at this stage, but what the hell?

Mrs. Plansky switched off the flash. She went outside, closing Kev's door carefully behind her. The night was quiet, almost no breeze now, and all the shadows were motionless, the way she liked them. How about calling the police? She went through some scenarios, more than one ending with her, Mrs. B&E, as a suspect. What would Norm advise? *More data!* Mrs. Plansky walked under the house to the dock, climbed into the kayak—very far from smoothly but at least not ending up in the drink—unhitched her line, coiled it in the bow, and paddled away.

"Hey! I need a woman's opinion. Wakey wakey. Haven't got all day. Up and at 'em, lazybones."

Mrs. Plansky opened her eyes. She was in her bed. The bedside clock read 11:27 AM. Her dad had rolled up to the head of the bed, was pretty much in her face, and not figuratively. But 11:27 a.m. was impossible. She'd never in her life—at least since babyhood—awakened so late or even close. Maybe her dad wasn't really here, and this was all a bad dream, the uneasy kind rather than an all-out nightmare. Then she smelled his bacon-and-eggy breath, plus a whiff of tooth decay, and knew it was real.

He poked her shoulder. "One too many?"

She sat up. That turned out to be surprisingly painful, but she managed not to wince, or at least tried.

"That's a ridiculous idea, Dad."

"Oh, yeah? Then how come you're still in bed?"

The events of the night before began unreeling in her mind, but not in an organized storytelling way, more like a movie edited by a maniac.

"There was no drinking involved," she said.

His eyes narrowed. "Involved in what?"

"Nothing."

"Ah, sweet mystery of life! Don't worry about me. My lips are like this." He zipped them. "Speaking of that kind of thing, which is why I'm here, what's the percentage? I always thought ten but now I'm hearing twenty-five. That sounds outrageous but what isn't these days? So which is it? Ten or twenty-five? This is up your alley."

"Percentage of what, Dad?"

"Oh for God's sake! Didn't I just explain? You're a woman. You should know these things."

Mrs. Plansky moved to get out of bed, then paused to feel under the covers, making sure her nightie was covering her properly. She found she wasn't wearing her nightie, instead still had on her long-sleeve tee and yoga pants. The tide or the wind or something else had been against her on the way back. It had been a long, long paddle. Had she had the strength to carry the kayak back to the boat rack? She didn't think so.

"Is Lucrecia here?"

"Been and gone. Otherwise why would I be asking you?"

In a moment of sudden weakness, Mrs. Plansky felt a strong desire to stay in bed all day, though not with him in the room. At the same time, getting out of bed dressed as she was would expose her to God only knew what line of questioning.

"Take it from the top, Dad."

"Huh?"

"I'm a little slow today. Just . . . just give me more details on this percentage thing."

"Slow?"

She shrugged. "It happens."

He looked alarmed. "Whoa!"

"What does that mean?"

"Jesus, why didn't I think of this?"

"Of what?"

"Of what? Of what shoulda been obvious, that's what."

"It's not obvious to me."

"Then I'll spell it out for ya. What happens if you kick the bucket ahead of yours truly?"

No, she'd never thought of that, either. She began thinking about it now.

"Don't worry," he said.

"Thanks, Dad."

"We caught this in plenty of time."

"Plenty of time for what?"

"Why, to change your will, of course. Assuming I'm not already there. As a . . . what's the word? Starts with *B*?"

Some devil in her wanted to reply, *Bastard. Selfish old bastard.* "Beneficiary," she said.

"Bingo! Hey! Bingo starts with *B*!" He laughed and laughed, pleased with himself. "Funny how the mind works."

"It is," said Mrs. Plansky.

He wiped his brow with the back of his mottled hand. "Whew," he said, now looking tranquil. "That should do it, then. I'm going with ten percent, damn the torpedoes. Twenty-five's wacko."

"Ten percent of what?"

"Annual income. I'm assuming pretax. It's the way you calculate how much to spend on the engagement ring. A tradition, Loretta, like turkey on Thanksgiving. I thought you'd know that."

He backed away, wheeled around, headed for the door—but braked as he came to her makeup table, his attention caught by what lay on it, which turned out to be the bloodstained photo of Kev and the bombshell on the deck of *Lizette*. He stared at it for what seemed like a full thirty seconds or so, then said, "Hmm," and rolled out of the room.

"Dad?" she called, getting out of bed. "What does that mean, that hmm?"

"Nada."

"Nada?"

"I'm learning Spanish. It means zilch. *Besame mucho* is *kiss me a lot.*"

"Right, but that hmm?"

Nada.

Ten percent—even twenty-five percent—of zero was zero.

Mrs. Plansky called Lucrecia. While the phone was still she went over to the makeup table, a table that Norm had built for her, copying Greta Garbo's from a picture in *Life* magazine, a table she loved because he'd done it and never used, preferring to do all that fussing in front of the bathroom mirror, much simpler. She had no memory of putting the photo there, no memory of coming into the house. All she remembered was paddling and paddling, moony silver crescents making patterns on the water, like embroidery on the move. She picked up the photo. Underneath lay that odd drawing of the triangle with the deep notch cutting into the longest side, and the royal palm.

"Loretta?" Lucrecia said.

"Uh," said Mrs. Plansky, quickly shutting away the photo and the drawing in the makeup table drawer, like she'd been caught with contraband, "about these, um, nuptials."

"I know, I know. I apologize."

"Nothing to apologize about." She opened the slider, went out, walked over to the side of the condo. The kayak lay in its place on the boat rack, lined up just so. "It's only that, well, an engagement? Really?"

"She's gone insane," Lucrecia said. "She's always been a bit insane—I hate to say that about my own mother—but never like this. I just don't understand. Can you explain it to me?"

"No."

Mrs. Plansky heard splashing on the lake. She turned and saw some ripples petering out on the far side.

"It's a mystery," Lucrecia said. "But maybe we can get them to skip the engagement part. To speed things along, sabes? You know? Except maybe putting it some other way. It's like walking through—what's that thing?"

"A minefield."

"Ha!"

Mrs. Plansky leaned against the boat rack. The sun was way too high in the sky for the amount of time she'd been awake. Some people, rock stars, for example, probably felt like this every single day, maybe even thrived on it. What would Mick Jagger, for example, make of last night's events, supposing he'd been in her shoes? She had no idea, no clue at all. Maybe he'd have been inspired by the bronze fish to come up with a bluesy tune about being hooked on a woman, or more probably a gal, and can't let go.

"Can't let go, can't let go," she sang, off-key or in several keys at the same time, musical keys just one more area of her ignorance. Was her dad currently hooked on Clara? Was she hooked on him? Or were they both simply hooked on . . . well, life, and saw one another as lifeboats? That seemed a little too dark for Mrs. Plansky. She settled on true love instead.

Mrs. Plansky called Jack and got sent right to voicemail, which was full and not accepting messages. She gave the phone a little shake, like a loose part was at fault, and tried again with the same result. Then she went inside, finding her dad in the little bar off the living room, gazing at the TV. Her dad liked watching sports and old westerns, but this seemed to be a reality show about a bride and her bridesmaids.

"Dad?"

He made an impatient gesture, not taking his eyes off the screen. "They're just at the good part."

Mrs. Plansky took a closer look. The women, all in their twenties, seemed to be trying out different face creams.

"When was the last time you spoke to Jack?"

"Couldn't tell you." His gaze didn't leave the screen.

"Was it recently?"

"You're badgering the witness."

"Witness to what?"

Now she had his attention. Slowly he turned his head toward her and gave her a down-the-nose look. "You're smarter than you—" He cut himself off. "I know, I know, that's not fair. Hell, it's not even true. You do look smart in a certain way, like from the side. Your face, I'm talking about. Did you ever consider law school?"

"No."

"Is that one of your biggest regrets?"

"It's not a regret at all. Have you spoken to Jack in the last day or two?"

"No siree Bob! But I'd like to. We have nice talks. Grandpas are advisers. Goes way back. Take the Bible."

"What do you advise him about?"

"Anything that comes down the pike."

"Like what?"

"Business things. You wouldn't understand."

"For example."

"What did I just say?"

Mrs. Plansky did not reply. The light in his eyes dimmed. He licked his lips. She knew he was trying to remember what he'd just said and couldn't. Was she in a mood to give him a prompt, let him off the hook? Far from it. Instead she exploited his weakness. She could be a bad person at times.

"What kind of business things do you and Jack talk about?"

He nodded and even seemed to cheer up a little. "Freezers. Thousands and thousands of freezers, all around the country, maybe even in China. Or millions. Mighta been millions."

"What was your advice on that?"

"Full speed ahead! I mean, come on! Global warming? Freezers! Like if you build roads people are going to need cars. Exactly the same. Nothing's changed since Henry Ford."

"Any news on the freezers?"

"Waiting to hear. I'm in line for a finder's fee."

"You are?"

"Why not?"

"Did Jack agree?"

"We haven't discussed it yet, not in words. But he'll agree. He's an agreeable type. Comes by it honestly. From that husband of yours."

This bad version of Mrs. Plansky found herself wishing she was much, much worse: Cruella de Vil with a toothache. Jack's freezer idea, a chain of cold storage facilities, came from his involvement with two entrepreneurs from Mesa who, according to her information, were up on charges, regarding some earlier, pre-Jack idea. Their names, possibly both beginning with *R,* were right on the tip of her mental tongue, but that was where they got stuck.

"You can forget about the finder's fee." Oh, my goodness! She'd said that aloud.

"Huh? What was that?"

"Nothing."

"Something about finder's fees? I'll tell you this, young—ha!—lady. Jack's big on finder's fees."

"I didn't know that."

"Surprise, surprise. It's all about putting people together. Lubricating the machine. That's all business comes down to. Lubricate." His eyes got an inward look, like he'd gone somewhere else. "Lube," he said softly.

Wherever he'd gone, she was staying right here. "Dad? Did you put people together on the freezer deal?"

"Nope."

"Then why would you expect a finder's fee?"

"Didn't I just explain?" He turned back to the TV, watched for a few moments, and then pointed at the screen. "Do you use that kind?"

The bride was holding up a jar of face cream. The camera zoomed in, showing the name and the logo, a bright pink rose.

"No."

"Why not? It's the best."

"What makes you think that?"

"She just said so. Try to follow along. And I want some."

"You want face cream?"

"Not just any. That one. Today would be good. Gift wrapped."

"Ah. For Clara?"

"Let's not spell it out."

"Okay, Dad. I can do that. But before I go, can we talk about Kev Dinardo?"

"Fire away."

"Do you know him?"

"Huh? Personally?"

"Yes."

"What a crazy idea! Do I get around much these days? Use the old beano."

"But you know of him."

"Guilty as charged."

"What do you know?"

"He's your tennis buddy."

"What else?"

"You won a trophy. Didn't I congratulate you? You were always a fine athlete. That's what I—" The bridal party suddenly grew raucous, with two bridesmaids wrestling on the floor and the others cheering them on. Her dad got distracted. She left the room.

*   *   *

Mrs. Plansky bought her face cream, shampoo, conditioner, and soap at the drugstore where the prices were reasonable, but for lipstick and nail polish she went to Beauty By Design, where they were not. She tried the drugstore first, with no result, then drove three blocks to the nicest part of Main Street, and parked in front of Beauty By Design. A sign painter in white overalls was at work on the big front window, lettering JUST IN! ÉTOILE DE PARIS!, with a two-inch roller and a tray of silvery paint. How quickly and smoothly he worked! She got out of the car. The painter leaned in a little and using just the edge of the roller and a tiny scraper turned the O in *Étoile* into a face that reminded her of a Toulouse-Lautrec dancer. She came close to saying bravo.

The painter stepped away to give himself another angle, and noticed her.

"Oh, hi," he said, as though he knew her. "Your husband back yet?"

Ah. He'd come to white out LIZETTE and paint the new name, not knowing then and seemingly now that the boat was gone.

"No," she said, which couldn't have been truer. Inside she was thinking "I wish."

"Just have him call me when he gets back."

"Will do." She pointed to the window. "That's so good, what you did with the *O*."

He shrugged, looked a bit embarrassed, but also pleased. She started toward the door.

"Can I ask you a question?" he said.

"Sure."

"Does you name begin with *L*?"

"It does. Why do you ask?"

"He said I could leave the *L* for now. When whiting out the name, if you see what I mean."

She did and she didn't.

THIRTEEN

TWO parking spaces came with each unit at the Little Pine Lake condos, Mrs. Plansky's closer to the path leading to the front door, and the other vacant unless Lucrecia was around. Lucrecia's ride was an ancient but pristine Caddy that ran smooth and looked like a relic from some fabulous era. A small sedan sat in it now. Mrs. Plansky pulled into her spot and got out. The driver's side door of the sedan opened and a woman stepped out and approached.

"Loretta Plansky?" she said.

"Yes?"

"Hi. My name's Valencia Sims. That's my byline but everyone calls me Val. I'm a reporter for the *Caribbean Tribune*."

Ah, the sports reporter who'd swung by. Mrs. Plansky had trouble believing that New Sunshine/Old Sunshine tennis was newsworthy, but Val Sims looked like a tennis player, even somewhat resembling Venus Williams.

Val held out her hand. They shook.

"I'm a bit surprised a local seniors match could make the news," Mrs. Plansky said.

"Excuse me?"

"Unless it's one of those 'oldsters keeping active under the warm sun' type of things."

"I'm not sure I understand," Val said.

"This isn't about New Sunshine/Old Sunshine tennis?"

"No."

Of course it wouldn't be. *The Caribbean Tribune*? Mrs. Plansky hadn't heard of it but how could her tennis match be of any interest to a Caribbean readership? Unless one of the players, meaning Jenna or Russell, had some Caribbean connection? Or Kev? But no point thinking about that since Val had just said she wasn't here about tennis. Sharpen up!

But before any sharpening got done, Val smiled—a very nice smile, big and bright—and added, "Why would you think that?"

"I haven't done anything newsworthy recently." Or ever, she thought, not upset at all by the realization, although what about the Plansky Toaster Knife? Hadn't there been a brief mention at the bottom of an inside page in *The Wall Street Journal* Business section? While all that was meandering through her mind, Mrs. Plansky grew aware of Val's gaze—penetrating but not impolite—on her face. "So I naturally thought of this tennis match from a few days ago."

"What tennis match was that?"

"A very unimportant one in the scheme of things—the North Beaches Sixties and Over Mixed Doubles Championship match, the New Sunshine tennis club, that's mine, against Old Sunshine."

"And you won?"

"Barely."

"Congratulations."

"It really was nothing."

"But always nice to win, is it not? Who was your partner?"

"One of the senior men," Mrs. Plansky said. Well, that went without saying. Couldn't she sound at least halfway intelligent? "A fine player," she went on. "His name's Kev Dinardo."

"Owner of a Bertram 50S yacht called *Lizette*?" Val said.

Mrs. Plansky paused, trying to guess where this was going. Was there a road map? If so, she didn't have it.

"That's right," she said.

"Then maybe you could help me," said Val. "I'd like to talk to Mr. Dinardo about a story I'm working on but I'm having trouble reaching him."

Same, thought Mrs. Plansky. But she said, "What's the story?"

"Excellent question. Is there somewhere we can go for a little talk?"

Sure, come inside. That was the obvious answer, but inside would probably involve an encounter with her dad and possibly Clara, too. A lively human-interest story, perhaps, but best left unpublished, from her point of view.

"How about we go for a walk?"

"Lovely."

Val had a bit of an accent, a mix of British and the islands, with a middle-American overlay, making Mrs. Plansky feel she was hearing something fresh and pleasing, worthwhile on its own and never mind the meaning. Guarding against that would be prudent. She underlined that idea in her mind.

"There's a gazebo on the south side of the lake."

"Lead the way."

Mrs. Plansky led Val around the side of her condo, past the boat rack, and onto a hard-packed dirt path that one faction of the association wanted to improve for biking, requiring an assessment, and another faction opposed. Mrs. Plansky was in neither faction and had developed an arsenal of deflections for when the subject came up. The path began in a grove of pond cypress hung with Spanish moss, which could get spooky on cloudy days, but right now the sun was beaming down here and there, lighting up little alcoves of beauty.

"So nice," Val said. "How long have you lived here?"

"Coming up on two years."

"Are you from Florida originally?"

"Rhode Island," said Mrs. Plansky. "And you?"

"Originally? Atlanta. But I'm based out of Miami now."

Mrs. Plansky didn't probe. They stepped around a rotting tree trunk that she was sure Val could have vaulted easily, mounted a rise, and then, through a screen of flowering myrtle the lake appeared, skyblue and calm. Val glanced at Mrs. Plansky at the same moment Mrs. Plansky was glancing at her.

"Most people find a way to ask about my background," Val said. "The accent and all."

"What are some of the ways?" said Mrs. Plansky.

Val's eyebrows rose. "Well, for example, 'have you spent a lot of time abroad?' That's one of my favorites. Then there's, 'Yeah, but where are you from, really?' More toward the bottom of the list."

Mrs. Plansky laughed but said nothing. The path rose up a slight slope and at the top, off to one side, stood the gazebo. It predated the condos, seemed to be owned and cared for by no one, and could have used a paint job, but there was something tranquil about it, like it had been built for meditation. Which maybe was why Mrs. Plansky had found she couldn't sit in it for more than three minutes without getting restless.

There was a simple bench inside, with a clear view of the lake, the condos off to one side and nothing else human in view except for a distant cell tower.

"One of those old Florida remnants," Val said. She turned toward the condos. "You've got a great spot."

"Thanks."

"Who's that?"

"Where?"

"There." Val pointed. "Isn't that your patio?"

"Yes, but I don't see—" And then her eyes, which had gone a bit cloudy for some odd reason, cleared and she saw her dad. At this distance she couldn't be sure but he seemed to be practicing his golf swing. Then something splashed in the lake and she realized he'd found his ball bucket, which she'd put away in the storage closet—locked away, if she remembered right—and was now driving golf balls into the water. He wore a Sam Snead style fedora and that was all. Splash.

"My dad," she said.

They watched him. It was hard not to.

"Is he visiting?"

"For an extended period."

"I play golf myself. He has a nice swing."

"I'll tell him you said so."

"How old is he?"

"Ninety-eight."

Val was silent for a few moments. "Lucky you."

At first Mrs. Plansky didn't get it, and she wasn't sure until Val added, "I lost my dad when he was thirty-nine."

"I'm sorry."

"He was St. Lucian. My mom was a Brit. To answer the question you didn't ask."

Mrs. Plansky, aware that something tricky was coming and not knowing whether to trust this person—a journalist, after all!—nevertheless felt an unguarded connection. "Was?" she said.

Val nodded. She gazed out at the lake where the golf ball ripples were petering out. Mrs. Plansky's dad had gone inside, leaving the slider open, which was against house rules on account of the insects. He hated when insects got indoors, complained every time he encountered any, and was also responsible for the problem. A haze of tiny bugs was on the move, a few feet over the water and headed toward the condos.

Val turned to Mrs. Plansky and smiled, a subdued smile this time. "But we're not here to talk about me."

"So what's the agenda?"

Val gave her a close look. "Can I ask what you did before retiring?"

"Is that the agenda?"

Val laughed. "No. Getting sidetracked seems to be my MO in this profession."

"How's it working so far?"

"There you go again."

"I don't understand."

"Making me curious about your background. Were you a lawyer?"

"Absolutely not. My husband and I had a small kitchen products company."

"Is he still . . . ?"

"He died a couple of years ago."

"My condolences."

"Thank you."

Val was silent for fifteen seconds or so. Mrs. Plansky had the odd feeling she was observing a moment of silence for Norm.

"What sort of kitchen products?" Val said.

So—not a moment of silence, but for dreaming up the next question. "Only one was what you'd call a success."

"Which one was that?"

Over the years Mrs. Plansky had grown a bit weary of telling the toaster knife story but it hadn't come up in some time and now she didn't feel quite so weary.

"The Plansky Toaster Knife," she said. "It's—"

"Oh, my God! For real? You're *the* Plansky? I love that damn thing. I recommend it all time. Please send royalties."

Mrs. Plansky laughed. "You'll have to take that up with the new ownership. We sold out."

She expected some sign of amusement, but Val's mood had changed. She gazed at her fingernails, long and red. A muted red, called Audrey H, available only from a Scandinavian company. Mrs. Plansky had a tube on the lipstick shelf of her medicine cabinet.

"Did you make any enemies in business?" Val said.

"Enemies? We had some difficult negotiations, and competitors came along—the usual business friction, which can get emotional. But enemies? No. Why do you ask?"

"I'm just gathering facts at this stage."

"For your story?"

"That's right."

"It involves enemies I might have made in business?"

"No, not at all. Almost certainly not."

Mrs. Plansky folded her arms across her chest.

"The problem is I don't know nearly enough about what's involved," Val said. "What can you tell me about *Lizette*? I'm talking about the boat."

"Not much," said Mrs. Plansky.

"It belongs to Mr. Dinardo?"

"Yes." But did she know that for a fact? There was no time to sort through any relevant memories.

"Did he operate it himself or was there a hired captain?"

"I don't know."

"So you never went anywhere on it? To the Bahamas, for instance?"

"No."

"According to the Ponte d'Oro Fire Department, you were a witness to its destruction."

"I was."

"What happened?"

"It was after the tennis match. I drove Kev home because it was raining and he was on his bike. It was one of those late in the day thunderstorms. We'd barely gotten out of the car before there was this boom and the boat went up in flames. It was pretty much destroyed by the time the fire truck arrived."

Mrs. Plansky was rather pleased with that summary. The kiss, edited out, was nobody's business. Meanwhile Val had taken out a notepad and was writing quickly, her red-tipped fingers darting across the page. "So *Lizette* was struck by lightning?" she said without looking up.

"I believe it's not uncommon around here."

"Did you see the lightning yourself?"

Val's eyes remained on the notepad, her pen poised and waiting. Finally she turned toward Mrs. Plansky.

"I think that was the fire department's conclusion," Mrs. Plansky said. "You'd know more than me if you've seen their report."

"Yes, that's what it says. I'm just asking if you saw the lightning."

"I definitely heard the boom. More than one."

The pen moved on. "What about Mr. Dinardo? Did he see the lightning?"

Good question. Mrs. Plansky thought back. She was pretty sure Kev had seen it, but mostly remembered the reflection of the flames burning in his eyes. "You'd have to ask him."

"I've tried. Voice, texts, emails, knocking on his door. I can't reach him."

Val went silent. Mrs. Plansky knew this silence, the silence that demands to be filled by the other party. She'd had it used on her in her business days and had used it herself. Now she sat quietly. The silence ballooned, a sort of invisible but intrusive question mark. Val folded first.

"When was the last time you saw Mr. Dinardo?"

"That night. On the dock."

"What about the last time you spoke?"

"Same. Are you . . . concerned about him in some way?"

"If it really was a lightning strike, no, probably not. If it was something else, then yes."

"Something else like what?"

"Like *Lizette* getting blown up."

Val's pen reached the end of sentence and stabbed an emphatic period.

"Have you talked to the police about this?" Mrs. Plansky said.

Val shook her head. "All I've got is speculation."

"Let's hear it. Maybe start, if you don't mind, with what got you interested in *Lizette*."

Val smiled at her, a smile that looked pretty close to fondness. At that moment her phone beeped. She halftook it from her pocket, glanced at the screen, shoved it back in. "Are you afraid of flying?"

"No."

"Ever been in a small plane, say, a four-seater?"

"Once or twice."

"You were okay with that?"

"Yes."

"The company leases a couple of Cessna 172s. I've got a private pilot's license and nine hundred hours of flight time. Are you free tomorrow morning at nine?"

"Where are we going?"

Val rose. "How about I explain en route? It'll all seem more real. Do you know Storybook Ranch Airfield, off of 17?"

"I'll find it."

"See you there. I've got to run."

They shook hands. Val ran.

"Do I need my passport?"

Val, now screened by Spanish moss, didn't hear.

Mrs. Plansky stayed where she was, seated in the gazebo, trying to organize her thoughts. They didn't want to be organized. Out on the lake a pelican appeared, her pelican, the one with the red-tipped beak. It dove in with almost no splash, like an NCAA champ, disappeared for what seemed like a long time, emerged with another wriggling crab, and then rose heavily above the water, wings straining for the first five feet or so. Her pelican wasn't great at liftoff but it knew how to fish. Mrs. Plansky was feeling proud of it when the water ruffled up, right where her pelican had just been, and Fairbanks glided into view.

FOURTEEN

"And one more thing," said Mrs. Plansky, now with no expectation of being heard, "can I see your business card? To make sure you are who you say you are? Just a routine precaution. Remember Mitch or Mr. Mitch? That kind of thing."

But too late. Was it possible that there was a sort of uniform speed for human interaction, like say the speed of sound, which is what again, Norm? A thousand feet per second? Something like that? Call it a thousand feet per second. Suppose the uniform speed of human interaction is one thousand thought particles per second, unchangeable. Where relativity comes in is this curveball, the speed too slow when you're young, frustratingly so, followed by decades when it's just right, and then comes the decline, when the speed of interaction is too fast and getting faster. How does that grab you? Isn't it right in your swing zone? How about we lie down and discuss it? Norm?

Meanwhile Fairbanks was on the move, not simply gliding now, too fast to be called gliding. Whatever it was, Mrs. Plansky didn't have the word, but it did seem purposeful, and somewhat unsettling, perhaps since the means of propulsion was out of sight, so different from a human swimmer. Also—and maybe this was the unsettling part—he was coming her way. Well, not her way. There was nothing personal involved. It was just that he seemed to be aimed toward the part of the shoreline where the gazebo sat, a quite safe twenty or thirty overgrown feet from the water, or even more.

Closer and closer he came, only the top of his head visible, the skin bumpy, like he wasn't quite a finished product. But of course his kind had been around a lot longer than her kind. Was there something comical about him, like he was one of those rough-edged funnymen, the John Belushi type? She was entertaining that notion when she caught the look in his eyes and dropped it right away. And was he really at the water's edge? In fact, were his scaly front feet already planted in the mud, or even the damp greenery beyond the mud? His head rose. Their eyes met. But surely that was her imagination. Didn't alligators have poor vision?

"You're not fooling me," she said aloud.

Fairbanks stayed where he was, doing nothing. Mrs. Plansky considered getting up, leaving the gazebo, taking the path back to the condo. But in the end she did just what he was doing, namely nothing. After a while, Fairbanks's throat bobbed—maybe a burp?—and he slid backward, vanishing into the lake.

"I win," said Mrs. Plansky, which she didn't mean and wished she could take back, just in case there was some being out there in charge of punishing the hubristic. She considered an apology, settled for a quiet, "Fairbanks? Let's call it a draw."

Back in the condo—closing the patio slider on her way and checking on her dad, quiet behind his closed door—Mrs. Plansky opened her laptop and went to the *Caribbean Tribune* site. Valencia Sims was a staff reporter specializing in maritime affairs, shipping, tourism, and resort development. Mrs. Plansky read an entertaining piece she'd written about a bribe paid to the wrong man, a pineapple vendor with the same name as an island cabinet member. There was a photo of Val at her desk, which didn't capture the force of her presence, and below that a bio. She'd been born on St. Lucia, grown up in Atlanta, graduated from Emory where she'd been captain of the women's golf team, and lived in Miami.

Mrs. Plansky closed her laptop and opened her desk drawer. The golden Tee-Tee lay in a padded envelope under all the usual desk drawer things. She took her out and stood her up. Those feet, wide and strong. Everything about her was superb but those feet were the best. Tee-Tee was built to last. Not the real Tee-Tee, which was another story.

Meanwhile part of her mind was occupied with duty, meaning hers. What had Val said? The subject was whether to worry about Kev. And then: if it really was a lightning strike, no, probably not. If it was something else, then yes. Probably not word for word, what with her memory these days, but close enough. Was the right move now to give Val a tour of Kev's house? Was it deceitful not to? Something menacing had happened inside 92 Seaside Way. Some menace—if that wasn't being too dramatic—was on the loose. Mrs. Plansky had little experience with deceit, possibly zero. Her heart wasn't in it.

But not zero, because at this very moment of deciding about the house tour, she was forming a deceitful sub-plan. The problem was blood, her blood, left on a towel in Kev's bathroom, with possible traces elsewhere. Was there any way Val would miss it? No. Would Val believe her explanation? Maybe, but what if she thought it was time to call in the police? Mrs. Plansky peered into that murky future where she herself became a suspect in the trashing of the house and God knows what else. She shrank away from the obvious answer to this problem, the deceitful sub-plan that involved reentering 92 Seaside Way before guiding Val's tour and . . . rearranging things slightly. But only in the interest of clarification! Anything that turned her into a suspect was misleading—because she was innocent!—and misleading Val or the police was wrong, and might even be a crime itself, when it came to the police. Once she and Norm had hired a CFO who, after getting the job, revealed a tendency to use the term "nonzero chance" and others of what Norm called McKinsey speak and regarded as a firing offense. The CFO had move onward and upward before anything like that could happen, but the point Mrs. Plansky was trying to come to in her mind was all about a nonzero chance she could end up in prison. What were the levels in the prison system? Max, medium, country club? Something like that. She knew she would not do well in any of them. In fact, there was a 100 percent chance she would no longer be her, but someone else, lost and debased. She returned Tee-Tee to her padded home and closed the drawer.

Mrs. Plansky was shrinking away from prison thoughts as she walked away from Little Pine Lake and around the condo to the parking lot. She hit the road, sticking to the speed limit like glue and checking the rearview in a way that was close to bobbleheaded, the most obedient citizen in the land.

Ninety-two Seaside looked unchanged, at least from the outside. No Lambo out front, no vehicles of any kind. Instead of going to the front door, Mrs. Plansky found herself walking between the pilings under the house and onto the dock. No *Lizette*, of course, no craft of any kind tied to the dock, not much action out to sea—a tugboat chugging north, a sport fisherman headed south at high speed, a freighter on the horizon. Her gaze moved closer, settled on the patch of sea with the eelgrass slope underneath, too deep to be visible even though it was a calm day. Was it worth another little ex-pedition, more organized this time? Mrs. Plansky had taken a scuba certification long ago, but except for mask, fins, and snorkel had none of the gear. Plus the gear she'd learned on was obsolete by now, and also she no longer had her mask and snorkel. And could you even rent a tank without a current certification?

"The small things can hem you in," she said to nobody.

Like Gulliver, she thought as she went to the front door. She glanced around, seeing no one. She heard a leaf blower not far away, and could make out the low hum of traffic, but the coast was clear. A plan formed in her mind. First, the bloody towel. That would have to be removed, taken off-site, disposed of later. Second, the Band-Aid wrappers, same procedure. Third, any other bloodstains eradicated, and the eradicating materials also removed. Eradication turned out to be vital if you chose the criminal path.

"For that reason alone," she said, and turned her attention to the touch pad.

40–love. Forty was simple. Four zero. And then? Hadn't she

written out the code? She must have. Mrs. Plansky patted her pockets. Where was her bag? Not hanging from her shoulder, where it
belonged. She returned to the car. Aha, on the passenger seat. She
searched her bag. If she'd written out the code, it wasn't there. Mrs.
Plansky opened the glove box, took out a pen, and on the inside of the
warranty book cover worked out the code all over again. She walked
back to the front door, went over the three-step plan, and reached out
to the touch pad.

4-0-1-2-1-5-2-2-5

Green.

She opened the door.

And just stood on the threshold, frozen. The front hall looked
exactly like before, not the last before, but the first one, when she'd
met Mitch or Mr. Mitch. No mess at all, cleanliness, neatness, and
tidiness as far as she could see. Water was gurgling from the mouth
of the bronze fish and splashing in the pool, the sound somehow
taunting.

She shrank back. But what good would leaving do? Was that
what Caesar said to himself when he decided not to cross back over
the Rubicon? It would probably look better in Latin, inscribed on
some pediment. *But* was *sed*, *what* was *quid*, *good* was *bonum*, and
that was pretty much all she remembered from ninth grade, her one
encounter with Latin, verb tenses, mood, and voice proving impen-
etrable, at least to her. Mrs. Plansky remembered her frustration,
could still even feel it a little bit. She stepped up and rapped on the
open door, good and hard, like a gladiator in a no-nonsense mood.

"Hello? Anybody home? Hello?"

The house was silent. But someone had obviously been inside
since her midnight visit, someone who'd cleaned up the entrance
hall and . . . and also removed the tennis bag with JMP embroidered on the outside.

Mrs. Plansky entered the house. The bronze fish seemed to be
gazing at her, and not just that, but in a knowing way, like they
shared a secret. Which they did. She paused for a moment, trying to

remember where she'd put the strange drawing. The answer came to her quickly, locking into place with a little chunk-chunk she could almost hear—in the top drawer of her makeup table together with the pinkened photo of Kev and the bombshell. She started off into the house, revisiting every room she'd visited before.

Every single one of them, every single inch, was pristine. Not a trace of damage, vandalism, or however you would characterize the violence that had gone down in this house. Had the wrecked furniture been repaired? Surely not. All of it must have been replaced. And what about the art on the walls? Hadn't some of it been ripped and torn? Not anymore. Was it new art? Either because the light had been dim before or because she'd been inattentive, she didn't know how closely it resembled what had hung on the walls before, if at all.

Mrs. Plansky climbed the spiral staircase to the master bedroom, now sunny under the enormous skylight. Everything was perfect, as though awaiting the team from *Architectural Digest*. Or, looking more closely, maybe the team from *IKEA Digest*, if it existed. She went into the bathroom. No sign of the bloody towel, not a trace of blood anywhere, no Band-Aid wrappers, empty wastebasket. On the wall where the photo of Kev and the bombshell aboard *Lizette* had hung, there now was a framed painting of a lighthouse in a storm.

She just stood there, motionless. Inside Mrs. Plansky, her whole plan—taking Val on a tour, possibly getting the police involved—disintegrated. Just imagine! *Well, um, you see, it wasn't like this before and, uh, my gosh the code turned out to, ah, and I have this bloody photo that I swear to God I, blah, blah, blah.* Then came an annoying thought. She might have been able to sell this pitiful story when she was younger, not because she'd been smarter then—although that was probably true—but because people would have listened in a way they wouldn't now, on account of her age and nothing else!

"Damn them all!" she said aloud, regretting it at once because she didn't care for outbursts like that, and also because it backed up their assumption, namely that she was a batty old lady. She found herself damning them once more. Did she even make a fist? Yes, batshit crazy—perhaps a weapon in some jiujitsu way.

She made her way down the spiral staircase, which she remembered as not being easy the last time but now was like nothing. Batshit crazy was working already!

The staircase stood in a corner of the living room. Taking the last step, Mrs. Plansky noticed something she'd missed before: a pocket door in the back wall, the street-side one, if her orientation was right. She slid it open. On the other side was a small room that seemed to be devoted to sports equipment.

Well, not sports equipment in general, but more like just for water sports. And even more limited than that, in fact. This small room was all about scuba diving. A compressor stood by a water trough containing a few scuba tanks. More tanks were lined up on the floor, and on the wall hung regulators, buoyancy compensating vests, wet suits, masks, fins, underwater cameras, spearguns. She remembered from somewhere that the water trough was for keeping the tanks cool while the compressor was filling them. Mrs. Plansky dipped her hand in it, stirred up a few little waves, and found herself connecting to the heart of the thought machine deep down inside her. A powerful feeling, although no thoughts were being generated at the moment. Maybe the thought machine was simply filing away facts for the future. She didn't know. Did a human being ever arrive at a complete and correct understanding of herself or himself? Mrs. Plansky didn't know that, either. Norm said that we would never figure out all the secrets of outer space because we just weren't smart enough. What about inner space, Norm? What she would have given to hear his answer to that, but really just to hear his voice.

She headed back to the front door, her mind in a jumble. If only she'd taken a picture of what she'd seen on her midnight visit! Everybody else on earth seemed to whip out their phones and snap photos of every stupid darn thing nowadays. Why not her?

Mrs. Plansky crossed the entrance hall, opened the door, and stepped outside. For no reason at all, she remembered how a lock of Jack's hair was forever drooping over his eyes when he was a kid, and even later. How many times had she smoothed it back in place! She took out her phone, called him, got sent to voicemail, still not accepting messages. Meanwhile a car was turning off Seaside and coming up the driveway. Not just any car, but a Lambo, black with gold trim.

FIFTEEN

Springtime in Florida: when the days begin with clear blue skies, clouding over later as ocean evaporation gets going. On this particular day it was still too early for that, the sun nice and bright, meaning the glare off the Lambo's windshield was so dazzling it hurt Mrs. Plansky's eyes just to look, never mind seeing who was inside. Whoever was in the driver's seat banged the stick—she assumed Lambos had sticks—into reverse and peeled backward out of the drive with tires smoking, an effect she'd seen only in movies.

She raised her hand in a gesture of stop or wait or simply hello. Her hand seemed to lower itself, like it was more realistic than she was, quickly realizing that the Lambo spoke some other language, devoid of polite gestures. The Lambo did a backward three-point turn, squealing and growling at the same time, and roared off on Seaside Way. Her mouth hung open. That turned out to be a real thing, not just some potboiler cliché. Mrs. Plansky clamped it shut, and then, maybe a little late in the game, thought: the license plate! Get the number!

She ran out to the road. The Lambo had come to the first cross street, a stop sign intersection, but was blowing right through. A Florida plate for sure, the juicy orange at the center amazingly clear. But the numbers and letters, the actual identifying features, were a blur. The Lambo came to the next street, Harbor Road, turned left, away from the water, and vanished.

Mrs. Plansky spun around—a rapid movement of the instinctive kind she'd been making all her life, except now her hip had its doubts—hurried to her car, and jumped in, jumping being the idea although the result was something more clumsy. That prompted a thought in some corner of her mind: car chases? Really? She squashed it at once and the next thing she knew she was barreling down Seaside. But only to the stop sign. Mrs. Plansky came to a full stop at stop signs. She'd been doing that for decades. Why? Because of Tee-Tee. Every single stop sign was a reminder.

Mrs. Plansky drove on, picking up speed, catching the light at Harbor, turning left. Harbor ran straight all the way to the interstate and beyond, slightly gaining elevation so she had a pretty good view of the traffic, not too heavy, with no sign of the Lambo. She switched to the passing lane, caught a few lights along the way, then stopped for a red. What if the Lambo had turned down this street or any of the others? She glanced both ways, saw all kinds of cars and trucks but not the one she wanted. What was this called? Tailing someone? Lots of folks—Eddie Murphy, Sylvester Stallone, Nick Nolte—made it look like a snap, but it was not.

Someone honked behind her, one of those angry honks. The light was green.

"Concentrate, for Pete's sake!" she said, and rolled forward. Traffic thickened near the interstate and she had trouble getting into the passing lane, but when she did she got a clear view of the underpass where Harbor continued west, the interstate running north/south. It was shadowy in the underpass, but in those shadows she glimpsed flashes of black and gold, no doubt about it. Mrs. Plansky stepped on the gas.

Beyond the interstate traffic in the passing lane thinned out and her accelerator foot stomped down, like it was not even her foot, but, say, Nick Nolte's. Up ahead those black-and-gold flashes stabilized, taking the shape of the Lambo. Look at her, tailing like a pro! She—who'd never been a natural at anything—turned out to be a natural at this! Mrs. Plansky leaned forward, a feeling of tremendous power flowing through her, a feeling unlike any she'd ever had, almost masculine.

"Oh, baby," she whispered, and might have gone on along those lines, when a siren sounded behind her. Not sounded but shrieked, and not simply behind her but right behind, like in the backseat. She looked in the rearview mirror and saw only her terrified face. Her hand trembling, Mrs. Plansky adjusted the mirror. A blue-and-white police car loomed up, almost touching her rear bumper, lights flashing. An amplified voice spoke, loud and in some sort of surround sound, like it was broadcasting from heaven. She didn't understand a word but she got the idea. Mrs. Plansky pulled over and stopped by the side of the road.

The police car parked behind her. She'd never been stopped by the police in her whole life. What was the drill? Were you supposed to put your hands on the wheel to show you weren't armed? Mrs. Plansky remembered that from somewhere. She gripped the wheel. What was armed again? Carrying? She had to get the lingo right. Cars on both sides slowed for a peek and moved on. The Lambo was gone.

Mrs. Plansky gazed straight ahead, a model citizen, and was considering patting her hair in place when someone rapped on her window, startling her. She turned to look. Not just someone but a police officer, of course. She stared at him. He frowned and rapped on the window again. What the hell did he want? She'd pulled over, hadn't she? Some long-slumbering—possibly lifelong—belligerence within her began to stir.

The officer said something she couldn't make out. Was that her fault? She gave him a blank look. He made an impatient twisting or perhaps rolling gesture with his hand. Ah, rolling. He wanted her to roll down the window. Did he realize that meant taking one of her hands off the wheel? She raised her eyebrows at him, sending that message. He spoke again, whatever he was saying still incomprehensible but much louder this time. Mrs. Plansky took her left hand off the wheel and pressed the window button on the door panel. One of the rear windows slid down.

The officer had been wearing aviator style shades. Now he took them off. Mrs. Plansky preferred him with them on. Would it be rude to say, "Shades back on, if you don't mind?" or something to that effect? Had she ever made that request of anyone? This was turning out to be an unprecedented situation in many ways.

"The window, please," he said, his voice coming clearly now through one of the backseat windows, more likely on her side, although she didn't turn to look, a tricky move what with her right hand on the wheel and her left on the door panel buttons.

"Open," he said. "I won't say it twice."

Fine with me, thought Mrs. Plansky, but then she realized he was making a threat. That awoke her fight-or-flight reflex. All at once she understood every TV traffic-stop scene she'd ever seen, especially the messy ones. She stabbed all the buttons on the control panel, one two three four five. Five? How could there be five, the car having only four windows? Well, five with the rear, but it couldn't go up and down. But meanwhile all the other windows were in motion. Through that transparent blur she noticed that the officer now had his hand on his gun butt. She whisked her hand off the control panel, held it motionless in midair, then surreptitiously allowed it to slide back over to its proper traffic-stop position, on the steering wheel. Meanwhile her window was down, somewhere inside the door—how did that work, anyway?—and no longer a disruption.

"License and registration." He held out his left hand, his right still on the gun butt. Ah, a married man, I see.

She kept that reassuring observation to herself. What she said was, "I'm not carrying."

"Beg your pardon?"

"As it relates to the hands issue." She raised her hands an inch off the wheel and lowered them back down.

"Something wrong with your hands?"

"No, no, it's not that. I've still got good use of my—" Something in his small, dark, and unreadable eyes made her close the door on wherever she'd been going. "The license is in my bag and the registration's in the glove box."

"So hand them over."

"Right. Sure thing. But in order to do that, I'll have to take my hands off the wheel."

He raised his head slightly, looked down his nose. Were the nostrils quivering, like the nostrils of a sniffing dog? "Have you had anything to drink?"

"Today, you mean?"

"You getting smart with me?"

"No, no, officer. Certainly not! Me? Smart? Ha! Ask anybody. And the answer to your question is one cup of coffee, black, and a glass of orange juice, the kind with pulp."

"Alcohol," he said. "Anything alcoholic."

"It's the middle of the afternoon."

His face flushed. A horrible insight flashed through her mind. He was about to say *step out of the car*, and the next minute she'd be by the side of the road, hands on the car roof—or even handcuffed!—and on the six o'clock news, even the lead on a slow news day. Somehow she rounded up her license and registration in one speedy movement and thrust them through the open window.

He took them. No "thanks," or anything like that. Mrs. Plansky was not one of those old folks who lamented the level of civil discourse nowadays, but sometimes it was hard not to.

"You on any medication?"

Whoa! How could that possibly be any of his business? She scrolled through the Bill of Rights in her mind. Was it an unreasonable search and seizure type thing? Connie Malhouf, her lawyer back in Rhode Island, would know. Connie was smart, incisive, no pushover. How to get Connie on the phone with this officer, cutting out the middleman, namely her?

"I asked you a question."

"Statins," she said. And there was one other, a little yellow oblong every day or every second day, hard to remember which. Also she couldn't remember the name, so she stopped at statins.

"Wait here."

He walked back to his cruiser and got in. The lights kept flashing. In the rearview mirror she could see him busy with what looked like office-type tasks. She picked up her phone, called Connie Malhouf, got put right through. Connie had been the lawyer on their—hers and Norm's—incorporation, and everything that had followed. Mrs. Plansky liked her a lot, but they hadn't spoken since the Romanian adventure, or misadventure, the accurate label probably somewhere in between.

"Loretta! Good to hear from you! How's life?"

"No complaints. And you?"

"Complaints, but no audience. Anything I can help you with?"

Yes, the Bill of Rights and traffic stop etiquette in general. But Mrs. Plansky found herself too embarrassed to go there. Instead she blurted out, "Do people ever blow up their own boats?" The question, which hadn't even occurred to her until that moment, right away seemed important, even primary, the big bang—ha!—that had started this whole strange universe she was now partly living in.

"Practically every frickin' day," Connie said. "Scams and boats are a couple, like the Macbeths. Don't tell me you're contemplating something along those lines."

"All I've got is a kayak, so it would be dumb as well as illegal. But suppose you had a situation during a thunderstorm where—"

The officer was standing by her open window.

"Connie? I'll call you back."

"Holding my breath."

She turned to the officer, perhaps giving him a too-bright smile. How much had he overheard? The word *illegal*, for example?

"Mrs. Plansky?"

"Yes, officer?"

"Any idea why I pulled you over?"

Ah-ha! She knew the answer to this one. No. Period. No was the answer, God bless the right to dodge self-incrimination. What could be more basic? Thank you, Madison or Jefferson or whoever.

"Speeding?" she said.

"How fast?"

"Way too fast."

He nodded, handed back her papers. "Drive safe." He put his shades back on and tapped her roof.

*   *   *

Mrs. Plansky drove on, heading west but on the alert for a good spot to pull a U-ee. Well, not pull a U-ee, more like finding some side street, going around a block, doing it all by the book. She'd never been this far down Harbor Road, now called something else on the occasional road sign that went by, too quickly to read. She slowed down at the next cross street, hoping to read the sign, the name of the cross street visible first: Macdee Road. Macdee Road? That rang a bell, but for no reason she could think of. Was that happening more and more these days, bells ringing, their sound waves flowing through her mind, finding no harbor, silence? Should she eat more walnuts? Or was it pumpkin seeds? She preferred walnuts but couldn't get excited about either. But when the kids were little what fun they'd had carving the pumpkin and roasting the pumpkin seeds. Norm did the carving. He was so good at it, always doing the face of one of the presidents, his own little orange Rushmore. Nixon was his pièce de résistance, but his LBJ was pretty great, too, and his Bill Clinton, such a wily pumpkin! The trick with the pumpkin seeds, her responsibility, was to roast a little more and salt a little less. That way—

Mrs. Plansky noticed that she'd turned onto Macdee Road, heading north and soon northwest, and narrowing up ahead to a two laner. Also up ahead she spotted a food truck parked on a flat unpaved patch by the roadside, a good spot for turning around. She was slowing down when the Macdee Road sound wave made landfall: 40–Love Hazy IPA! Drop Shot Brewers! Macdee, Florida! She remembered those tennis-ball heads, of course, the passionate kiss, the wink. But also the ABV—6.9—and the IBU, even though she had no clue what it was—38. How amazing what the mind could do! She was still in the game, a player. Mrs. Plansky glanced around for any wood to knock on, even a crummy fake strip of console paneling, but there was none. She pulled onto the unpaved patch, took out her phone, tapped the map image, typed in **Macdee FL**. Only twenty-seven miles away. Mrs. Plansky stepped on it. But prudently.

She hadn't done much driving in inland Florida. Most people she came across didn't have much to say for it, and she certainly didn't know it well enough to disagree, but she did disagree, silently, to herself. Flat, hot, humid, waterlogged, buggy, no ocean, no beaches, and visibly poorer than the coast: all of that added up to something appealing to her. Despite the fact that she knew finding the picturesque in rural poverty was a character flaw!

But how delightfully soggy it all was! So many ponds, lakes, slow moving streams, watery ditches: this was the mother earth of the dinosaur age, here long before humans and sure to endure long after. Although perhaps the entire state was a recent development, geologically speaking. And she didn't like the idea of earth without humans, and missed the entertainment value of movies about the last few surviving humans wandering through hellscapes. But at that moment, dystopian thoughts darkening her mind, Mrs. Plansky smelled something nice. What was it? She lowered all the windows, switched off the AC, sniffed the air—and then noticed the strawberry fields on both sides of the road as far as she could see, mostly dark green but with bright red highlights here and there, more and more of them the longer she looked. Just up ahead stood a fruit stand, a small girl standing by. Mrs. Plansky stopped the car and got out.

"Hi, there."

"Hi."

The girl wore a wide-brimmed straw hat that kept her face in shadow, but otherwise was dressed like any kid—flip-flops, shorts, a T-shirt with the picture of a cartoon character that Mrs. Plansky didn't recognize.

"These look good." She gestured toward the quart boxes of strawberries on the table, glistening, as red as it gets, intense. Life itself, if you allowed yourself that sort of grandiosity. Which Mrs. Plansky did not. These were just strawberries. She wanted some.

"How much?"

The girl tilted up her face. My God! This was Tee-Tee at the same age, so, so close, at least physically.

"Six dollars and fifty cents for each."

For a moment Mrs. Plansky couldn't speak. She cleared her throat. "Two, please."

The girl nodded. "Also we have strawberry cookies, ten dollars a box."

"Sounds good."

The girl reached into a basket behind the table, grace in every movement. Tee-Tee had been the same.

"And there's strawberry bread, seven fifty a loaf."

"Bring it on."

"Fourteen for two."

"I'm in."

Mrs. Plansky paid. The girl produced a cash box and made change. Mrs. Plansky could have watched her making change forever.

Macdee had once been a little something, now reduced to half a block at the town center occupied by two old brick buildings side by side, one now housing a gift shop on the first floor and the second a café. The rest of downtown seemed to be a dollar store, a gas station, a bar with dust-covered or possibly mold-covered windows, and a neon sign advertising Jax Beer, which Mrs. Plansky thought was now defunct. Plus there was a market—Food, Ice-Cold Drinks, Ice—a post office with a CLOSED sign on the door, and another dollar store.

She turned into the gas station and filled up. The station had a single bay, the door raised, a car on the lift, a mechanic working underneath. Mrs. Plansky went over.

"Excuse me. I'm looking for Drop Shot Brewers."

The mechanic turned. A gum chewing mechanic, and also a woman. You didn't see that every day. The woman part, not the gum. She had a streak of grease on one cheek and was also quite bosomy, a heartwarming combo to Mrs. Plansky for some reason.

The mechanic pointed. "Second right, end of the road." She went back to work.

* * *

Mrs. Plansky took the second right onto a road that was paved at first and then hard-packed dirt, somewhat reddish, like Georgia clay. The setting went from wood-framed residential to trailers spaced farther and farther apart to rural. She passed through a small oak forest and reached the end of the road, or rather a white gravel driveway leading to what looked like an old two-story farmhouse with a porch and a weather vane. An old farmhouse, yes, but freshly painted skyblue with orange trim, probably not the original color scheme. Also the weather vane was unweathered copper and in the shape of a tennis racket. The sign on the door read DROP SHOT BREWERS. Two pickups were parked in front of the house. No Lambo, which snuffed out one little idea, but by now Mrs. Plansky had a bigger idea in mind. She climbed the porch stairs and went inside.

She found herself in a big shadowy room, dust motes drifting in the unshadowy parts, aluminum and copper vats and other brewing equipment at the back, kegs stacked along one wall, some unoccupied tables and chairs in front of her, and a tasting counter at the other side. A tubby old man—well, probably her age—in denim overalls but shirtless was mopping the floor.

"Hi," Mrs. Plansky said. "Is Kev Dinardo here?"

The tubby man stopped mopping and squinted at her. He wore a belt, kind of unusual with overalls, and on that belt hung a knife holster, rather long and thick, with a leather knife handle sticking out. The tubby man, armpit sweat dampening his bare sides, didn't appear to be customer interface material but, not knowing a thing about the beer business, it wasn't her place to judge.

The man turned toward the back of the room and called, "Rudy?"

SIXTEEN

A lean, fit-looking man stepped out from behind one of the copper vats. Tan, clean-shaven, nicely cut short hair, in his forties. He wore a polo shirt, chinos, and boat shoes, looked like a golfer, except for the wrench in his hand, which seemed incongruous to Mrs. Plansky, although why? Sometimes things needed fixing no matter what you wore. She tried to imagine Tiger Woods busy in his basement workshop but couldn't quite get there.

"Hey, Rudy," the tubby man said. "Lady here's askin' for Mr. Dinardo."

Rudy turned to her. There was the briefest little flash in his eyes, perhaps a trick of the light, and then he said, "Mr. Dinardo," his tone close to making it a question, but not quite.

"That's right," Mrs. Plansky said. "Kev Dinardo. Is he here by any chance?"

"And you are?"

"Loretta."

"Loretta what?"

He smiled. His teeth were white and even, actually a little too white, a common sight nowadays. Mrs. Plansky had made that mistake herself quite a few years back, allowing her dentist at the time to talk her into it. She'd put a stop to that the day she checked out her new smile in the mirror. What was she selling again? The Plansky Toaster Knife, yes. Herself, no. Now her teeth were clean, cavity-free, and a fine shade of off-white, off-off-white in the case of some of them.

"Rudy what?" she said, just popping that out like she was a quick thinker, which she most certainly was not.

Rudy kept smiling, perhaps not so forcefully. Mrs. Plansky, without quite looking to see, was aware that the old man was watching Rudy with interest.

"Rudy Mesa," he said. "Like table in Spanish."

Mesa? That triggered something in Mrs. Plansky's mind, but just out of reach. And what about Rudy, his first name? Did that trigger something, too? Whether because of all the triggering, or because of what had happened to Kev's house—first trashed and then cleaned up, which she suddenly saw as an act of gaslighting—or because of the way the old man was watching, she introduced herself as she hadn't in a long, long time: without actually lying. Lying had never come easy to her, and as with many things that don't come easy she'd finally given up on even trying.

"Banning," she said, going with her maiden name. "Loretta Banning."

"Nice to meet you," he said, sticking the wrench in his pocket and offering his hand.

She shook it, a strong hand although he didn't do anything to demonstrate it. Also it felt warm to her, possibly meaning she was cold. Maybe because her northern-bred mind worked better when things were on the chilly side, she now realized she'd seen Rudy before. But where?

"Welcome to Drop Shot," he said. "Retooling, so we're not really open, but what can I do for you? How about a sample?" He turned to the old man. "Ducky? Rustle up a tasting flight for Loretta here."

"That's not—" she began.

"Yes, boss," said Ducky.

"And check the computer."

"The computer?"

"To see the freshest kegs we've got up."

"Yes, boss." Ducky went off.

"Very nice of you," Mrs. Plansky said, "but I'm looking for Kev Dinardo, as I mentioned."

"That you did," said Rudy. "But Mr. Dinardo and I work together and he's not here. So is there anything I can help you with?"

They worked together? The weight of that little fact was enough to tip a balance in her mind, and she remembered where she'd seen Rudy before—not live but in a photo on a phone. The phone belonged to the skinny little kid bartender at Bevo's, the brewpub, and the photo was from the party that Drop Shot Brewers had sponsored there. Rudy was the man on the left, with Kev in the middle, and Mitch or Mr. Mitch on the right. Solid information! They said that information is power. Mrs. Plansky hoped to feel some of that and soon, if possible; she didn't trust Mitch or Mr. Mitch and therefore how could she trust Rudy?

"It's not important, really," she said. "I was passing through and just thought I'd say hi."

My God! Could she have come up with anything dumber, more pathetic? What was wrong with her? Well, plenty, but no time for that now. Or possibly ever, time no longer on her side in life, something she knew intellectually although it hadn't seemed to make the slightest impression on the inner her.

Rudy smiled his dazzling smile like he was having fun and said, "Passing through Macdee?"

If he was having fun, then she was the object of it. Now she had to play the hand she'd been dealt, a lousy one, and dealt by herself. Mrs. Plansky made a terrible joke, but silently: couldn't she have at least shuffled first? "On my way to Tampa," she said. "I like back roads."

Rudy nodded. "Where are you from?"

"Originally?" Mrs. Plansky was rather proud of the nifty sidestep. "Up north. And yourself?"

My goodness! Was this a bit like tennis? You put some spin on the ball and hit it to somewhere unexpected? Perhaps she could get by in situations like this, despite not actually understanding what was going on in the least.

"Out west," Rudy said.

Which Mrs. Plansky already knew. For some reason she wasn't

half-bad with regional accents, had figured Rudy for somewhere west of west Texas but east of California, where the twang was fading but not quite gone.

"What brought you to Florida?" she said. How about that! Taking the offensive? Like she was the Serena Williams of tricky conversations!

"Business," Rudy said. He'd started to tap one of his feet lightly on the worn wooden floor. The sole of the boat shoe made soft slapping sounds.

"The beer business?"

"Correct." The foot tapping sped up. "What's your interest in—" Rudy stopped himself and started over. "How do you know Mr. Dinardo?"

Right away Mrs. Plansky thought of that kiss. A kiss with a flaming yacht in the background. It was like a scene in a movie. And seeing it like that she caught a new angle. There'd been something desperate about it, not at all on her part, but on his. As for her it had been . . . wonderful. She admitted that to herself. Wonderful like being young and in love, or falling in love, or knowing that falling in love was possible. Or even sex! Yes, or even that sex was about to happen, sex with a decent man who cared about you and maybe was on the exact same track. Except for the desperation part. That was mysterious. Meanwhile Rudy's foot was going slap, slap, slap. What was the question? How did she know Kev? She needed a clever answer, even if it involved an outright lie. What about this?

"I really don't know him well. We met at a restaurant and he told me about this . . . endeavor of his. Drop Shot, et cetera. I thought, on my trip to Tampa and all, I'd swing by and take a gander."

Gander: a nice touch if she said so herself. Mrs. Plansky smiled her off-white smile. Was she coming across as one of those Sunshine State clichés, the late in life divorcée or widow on the prowl? That could work. She would masquerade as a cougar. One small glitch: she'd probably aged out of cougardom. What was another big cat? Saber-tooth tiger. Extinct, as she recalled. It didn't get any older than that.

As for Rudy, his head was now tilted to one side, like another angle would make things clearer to him. Didn't that have to be good? All the same, she was well aware that things were far from clear in her own mind, not just the big picture but her own recent actions. She gathered up the facts and herded them into order. She'd been following the Lambo. Then she'd lost it. And, completely on spec driven out here to Drop Shot Brewers, based only on the facts that Kev was an investor in the company and when last seen the Lambo could have been headed this way. At least it hadn't been going in the opposite direction.

"So you're interested in beer?" Rudy said.

"In moderation," she said. Telling the truth—she didn't mind beer but perhaps downed a case a year on average—would lead by default to Kev alone being the reason she was here, and after that unknowns, likely to be awkward.

"What kind—" he began, but then Ducky arrived, bearing a beer flight board with four little glasses on it, all of them filled to the brim with beers ranging from pale gold to mahogany. Ducky and Rudy exchanged a quick glance. Ducky shook his head, a tiny movement, hardly noticeable, but she noticed.

Rudy checked his watch. "Why don't you take Loretta here over to the bar and run through the tasting, Ducky?"

"Sure thing."

Rudy turned to her. "Nice meeting you." In his eyes she saw he'd lost interest. She'd ended up boring him, was now just a little old lady like all the others, although not little in her case, more what you'd call sturdy. He walked away and out through a side door.

"This way, ma'am," said Ducky.

He led her over to the bar, motioned to a stool, set down the flight, walked around to the other side. Outside there was some opening and closing of car doors and then a car started up and drove away.

"This here's our pilsener." He pointed. His hands had had a rough life, and not the cleanest. "Light and crisp. We always start with the pilsener. Czech style, got a little zip at the finish."

Mrs. Plansky drank. She found she couldn't taste a thing. Her mind was on that quick glance she'd seen, and Ducky's tiny head-shake. A headshake meant no. But no to what? She tried to remember Rudy's instructions before Ducky went off to pour the flight. Had there been confusion on Ducky's part? Something about checking the kegs? Checking them on the computer? Would the brewing times be recorded on the computer? Why not? Lots of things could be recorded on the computer. Why, you could look up practically anything. Just enter anything, like someone's name or—

"Whaddya think?" Ducky said.

What I think is that Rudy told you to look me up on the com-puter. But because you looked up Loretta Banning you got noth-ing, other than hits on other Loretta Bannings. If you'd looked up Loretta Plansky, the New Sunshine blog would pop up, and there I'd be with Kev. Maybe that wouldn't have been quite so boring for Rudy.

She said none of that, just smiled and said, "Very nice."

"Our biggest summertime seller. Next we got two IPAs, hazy and clear. This is the hazy. We call it 40–Love. The name comes from tennis."

"Really?"

"Yeah." He handed her the glass. "It's how they score."

"I had no idea." Perhaps that was laying it on a little too thick. Was that a common temptation in the spy and counterspy world? "Do you play yourself?" She didn't seem to be able to stop.

"Ha!" Ducky said. "Tennis? Where I grew up?"

"Where was that?"

"Huh? Right here."

"What about the others?" She took a nice long drink, making that question as casual as possible. The 40–Love IPA was tasty, no doubt about it.

"Others?"

"Where they're from. Mr. Dinardo. Rudy."

Ducky scratched his head, first in puzzlement but developing into something more intense, the kind of scratching dogs like. "All over the place," he said at last. "How's that IPA?"

"Delicious. Is Mr. Dinardo a tennis player?"

Ducky's eyes shifted one way and then the other. He was nervous. She could feel it. Nervous and unsure. The smell of fresh sweat was always said to be not unpleasant. With Ducky we had the exception.

"Wouldn't know about that," Ducky said. "Could be."

Mrs. Plansky drained the rest of the 40–Love, picked up the clear IPA, and sipped it. "This is nice, too. What's the name?"

"First Serve."

She laughed, part genuine, part not, but with a slight musical gurgle in it that came from who knows where. She was feeling very alive right now. No wonder actors fell in love with acting!

"What's funny?" Ducky said, suddenly sounding a bit churlish.

"Just that first serve is tennis talk, too, isn't it? You should get some former player to be the spokesman."

Ducky thought about that. "Like Tom Brady?"

"Exactly! Except from tennis. Does Mr. Dinardo have connections in that world?"

"What world you talkin' about?"

"The tennis world."

"Maybe. Maybe not." Ducky slid the beer flight an inch or two closer her way. "That there's the porter, number four. Chocolate porter. The ladies love it." He handed her the porter glass, even though she wasn't quite done with the First Serve. Mrs. Plansky got the message. She put down the clear IPA and tried the porter.

"Mmm. The ladies are right."

No response from Ducky. Some folks lacked a sense of humor, although perhaps that was unfair to Ducky. Perhaps she just wasn't funny. Although she felt funny. Right then was when Mrs. Plansky realized she might have had a sip too many.

Ducky brushed his hands together, like a worker after the job was done. "What's your favorite?"

"The porter, I think. Can I buy a six-pack?"

"Sorry. We're kinda retooling, like the boss said."

"Rudy's the boss?"

"Yeah. Sure." Ducky looked a little puzzled.

"Not Mr. Dinardo?"

Ducky's eyes narrowed. "Where'd you get an idea like that?"

"I must have misinterpreted." Mrs. Plansky drained the rest of the porter. She recalled from somewhere that porter got its name from being the favorite drink of porters, the guys who lugged stuff around. They believed it gave them strength. That part was feeling 100 percent true to her. "But where does Mitch fit in?"

"Mitch?"

"In the C-Suite."

"Huh?"

"Or possibly Mr. Mitch."

"Don't know what you're talking about." He gathered up the empty glasses. "Thanks for dropping by."

"The pleasure was mine." She rose from her stool, prepared to shake hands, but Ducky didn't offer. "Is there a restroom?"

He pointed.

She crossed the floor, feeling his eyes on her the whole way. Up to now she'd thought that was a melodramatic fiction. Now she knew it was real. The organ that did the feeling was right between the shoulder blades.

There were two restrooms, Roosters and Hens. Mrs. Plansky chose Hens. Not spotless, but she'd seen far worse. Still, her preference would have been to sit on the seat without quite touching. Her new hip, such a wonderful success, wasn't quite up to it today.

There was a small, dusty window over the sink. Washing her hands, Mrs. Plansky gazed out and glimpsed an old red barn behind a screen of scrub oaks, the red faded almost all away in some spots. A white bird of a kind she didn't know came circling down and landed on the roof of the barn.

Mrs. Plansky walked out of Hens. No sign of Ducky or anyone else. She went outside, took a few steps toward her car, then changed direction and headed around the side of the building. Would anyone watching take her for a wandering touristy type with time on her hands, maybe looking to snap a Spanish mossy landscape photo or two? She tried to impersonate that being.

Mrs. Plansky passed through the screen of scrub oaks and came to the barn door, the wide, sliding kind. There was a rusty hasp with a rusty loop, but no padlock hanging from it. She stood motionless and listened. It was so quiet she could hear the flapping of the white bird's wings as it rose off the roof and took to the sky. She pushed the door open about a foot and peered inside.

It was shadowy, with a few dusty sunbeams crisscrossing here and there. She saw two broken down tractors, a stack of rotting pallets, hoes, scythes, and pitchforks. And the Lambo.

SEVENTEEN

Mrs. Plansky walked around the Lambo. She peered through the windows. She ran her fingers over the gold badge with the snorting bull. She learned nothing. All she had were questions: had Kev been at the wheel of the Lambo? She had the strangest feeling that he was close by. Was he hiding from her? Was he afraid she suspected he'd blown up *Lizette*? She was starting to. Scams and boats, a couple like the Macbeths. And then the Jack balloon floated into mental view. Could he have played a role? Knowingly? Unknowingly? She tried to picture Kev as a sort of Brad Mosto figure, but grown-up and sophisticated, a sleek new Lambo to a secondhand Stingray, and couldn't quite make it work. But where the hell was Jack?

Something rustled in a dark corner of the barn. Snakes liked dark corners. Mrs. Plansky was not terrified of snakes—unless one suddenly appeared close by—and knew that most were harmless, even had a pretty good idea of how to identify the ones that weren't, and appreciated their importance in the ecological scheme of things. But she was not a fan. She hurried out of the barn in what she believed was a controlled manner, passed through the scrub oaks, and came to the parking area in front of the brewery. Ducky, his back turned, was moving away from her car and toward the remaining pickup. She improvised a quick half circle, making it look like she was coming from the brewery. A long time in the restroom, perhaps? Ah, women. Just one of their many foibles.

Ducky heard her and turned. She adjusted her skirt slightly, as though getting all her mysterious female undergarments arranged just so. But not to worry. Ducky didn't seem at all suspicious. If anything, there was a furtive look in his own eyes.

She waved, a slow, sustained gesture, stolen from Elizabeth II. "Thanks for everything."

"Uh-huh."

Mrs. Plansky got in her car. Nothing looked out of place, strawberries, strawberry cookies, and strawberry bread on the passenger seat just as she'd left them. She drove away. In the rearview mirror she saw Ducky climbing into the pickup. She spotted him once or twice as she followed the red clay road but by the time she reached pavement he was gone.

Sometimes Mrs. Plansky needed a little think. The phrase came from Tee-Tee. Even when no more than a second or third grader, Tee-Tee would need a little think, after falling off her bike, for example. Mrs. Plansky parked in front of one of the dollar stores in Macdee, sat up straight, and tried to compose her mind. First she went over everything that had been done and said at Drop Shot Brewers, searching for . . . for what? A narrative of what was going on? Close enough. But it just would not take shape. She came to Ducky at the very end, that furtive look. He'd been walking away from her car. Well, not necessarily true. He might have been doing something outside that made it look like that, her car simply in his path. Plus everything in the car seemed the same, all the strawberry purchases. Almost unconsciously she opened the package of strawberry cookies and started munching on one, and as she munched she opened the glove box.

There were two shelves in the glove box. The bottom one was for the car manual, never opened, a box of tissues, and a Swiss Army knife, never used although it had seemed like a handy idea at the time. The top shelf was for the registration. Only now it wasn't there. Instead the registration was now on the bottom shelf, lying on the box of tissues.

Mrs. Plansky reached for another cookie. The problem was the traffic stop. The officer had handed back her license and registration. "Drive safe." And then what?

She opened her bag: nice enough, fine-grain leather, although not a famous brand imported from some European country where cow skin was even finer, upper-mid range at most, and bought on a post-Christmas sale. Her license was in its proper place, zipped in the side compartment. The registration was not in its proper place, but maybe she'd been too flustered to get that right. She tried to remember and could not. The registration, which she'd never actually read or even given a second look to, was a typical government-issue form, of no intrinsic interest. Plate number, VIN number, expiration date, etc., etc., with her name and address at the bottom left.

Loretta Plansky.

Not Loretta Banning.

Right there in black and white, but that didn't mean Ducky had seen it. And if he had, then what? She had no idea. In place of an idea she found herself picturing the knife on Ducky's belt. Then she revisited the question of going to the police and got stuck in the same muddle as before. What about Val? She was seeing Val in the morning. Perhaps she'd try running everything by her, but in a cautious, exploratory way. She'd get Val's take and have another little think based on that. There! A plan!

Mrs. Plansky realized she'd eaten two strawberry cookies and had no idea what they tasted like. That made a third obligatory, simply for scientific purposes.

Night was falling when Mrs. Plansky got home. No one was there. A note on the kitchen counter read: *Took them to Zarelli's. Fresh empanadas in the fridge. Back Later, Lucrecia.*

Zarelli's, a few miles away in a swamp drained back in Flagler's day, was one of the oldest drive-in theaters in the country. She checked their website. Tonight was the weekly senior special, a "black-and-white WW2 double dip" featuring *Mrs. Miniver* and *Casablanca*. Her dad had never mentioned Zarelli's. Also he was not a movie lover. He watched golf, football, and cooking shows.

What was the seating arrangement? Lucrecia in front, Clara and her dad in the back? The reverse? Or Lucrecia and Clara in the front and—no, that one was a nonstarter. The reverse, maybe? Didn't Rick say, somewhere toward the end of *Casablanca*, that the problems of three little people didn't amount to a hill of beans in this crazy world? Mrs. Plansky had always believed he was wrong about that and here was one more proof. On the other hand Rick was Humphrey Bogart in evening dress talking to Ingrid Bergman and she was just, well, who she was, thinking to herself. No contest.

Mrs. Plansky went into her bedroom, opened her desk drawer, and took Tee-Tee out of the padded envelope. She thought of another Bogart movie, *The Maltese Falcon*, specifically the scene where Sidney Greenstreet hacks away at the black-coated falcon statuette, hoping for gold underneath. Would hacking away at Tee-Tee reveal a worthless core? She gazed at Tee-Tee. The look in those prominent eyes said *Don't be an idiot.*

Good advice. Going forward, she would resist idiocy every chance she got. What, for example, would a non-idiot do right this minute? Maybe something to eat—even a proper meal—and a glass of wine? Aside from the strawberry cookies, when had she last eaten? Mrs. Plansky poured herself some red, warmed the empanadas, and dined at her desk, Tee-Tee standing by the glass and the laptop open.

She typed in gold figurines and then images. Endless rows of shiny objects showed up, page after page, but nothing that looked like Tee-Tee. She revised the search this way and that, eventually recalling the term pre-Columbian and trying that.

Ah-ha! Eight or nine images. No more Tee-Tees, but some of them could have been relatives, especially one slightly bowlegged fellow. She clicked on him. He was 22.08-karat gold, Incan, dated from the 1400s, and belonged to the Metropolitan Museum of Art. He was beautiful but not as beautiful as Tee-Tee. Her inner life was much richer. As for value, Mrs. Plansky had no idea. Gold was what? Two thousand dollars an ounce, or something like that? She hefted Tee-Tee, feeling crass as she did so. A pound and a half? Two pounds? Somewhere in the condo she had a pair of two-pound pink dumbbells, which she'd carried on a walk once and once only. Two pounds or just under felt right for Tee-Tee, meaning the material value alone was whatever it was. Substantial. That was the point. What about the artistic value? That was far greater, at least in Mrs. Plansky's eyes. And the rarity value? She knew nothing about that. It would be nice to know, although not in any personal sense. Tee-Tee was not hers. Whose was she? The artist and the artist's people and the artist's culture were long gone.

"You're mine in quotation marks for now," Mrs. Plansky said. She gazed at Tee-Tee. "So what's your story? Start with the most recent part—how you came to be on *Lizette*—and work back from there."

Tee-Tee was silent. Her eyes were not. Was there something impatient in them? Like, what's with you? Get on the stick!

"I'm trying," Mrs. Plansky said. She tucked Tee-Tee back in the padded envelope and put her away.

She went to bed, fell asleep, woke up when her dad came home. It sounded like he was alone. She slipped back into sleep, but as she did she heard him talking to himself, maybe passing by in the hall.

"Here's looking at you, kid," he said.

At first she thought he meant her, and was touched. Then she realized it had to be Clara, and was touched again but in a different way. Finally she wondered if in fact it was Ingrid Bergman, so she ended up confused. That was him.

Mrs. Plansky wriggled into her twisted K, all set for knitting up the raveled sleeve of care, as Shakespeare put it somewhere or other. But as she sank down dreams rose up, dreams with their own agenda. Golden Tee-Tee was in them, saying something too soft to hear, and there was a giant strawberry, which Ducky sliced to bits with his knife, and after that a stop sign emerged from all the red and Tee-Tee, the flesh and blood Tee-Tee, came blasting right through on her bike. Then came a honk or a scream or both at once, like some brand-new horrible sound, just invented.

Mrs. Plansky sat up, damp with sweat. The condo was silent, but was it the silence that sometimes follows a loud noise—a scream, for example—or just normal silence? Screaming in the night wasn't her, had never been her, and wasn't going to be her. She checked the time: 2:49. Not good because she was wide awake. She rose, changed from her nightie into a robe, opened the slider, and took a glass of water out to the patio.

A slight breeze, Mars over the horizon, an airliner headed south, its lights faint. Meaning it was way up there, probably not Miami bound but en route to Rio or Bogotá or Peru.

Strange about the stop sign—so vivid—since she hadn't been there, living in their East Providence rental at the time, hers and Norm's, and Tee-Tee down in Charlottesville, working on her PhD. The crash hadn't killed her, not directly. It had concussed her, broken her clavicle and some ribs, and given her a bad compound right leg fracture, multiple fractures, in fact, compounded in multiple places. Compound fractures were high risk for infections and there'd been some delay in treatment, the reasons never clear. But Norm had been worried about infection from the start, and that was what finally got Tee-Tee, not long after the amputation. An hour after, in the recovery room, Tee-Tee shifted her oxygen mask to one side and said, "Why do they say you should go down swinging?"

"You're not going down," Lo-Lo told her, the only time she'd ever lied to Tee-Tee.

Mrs. Plansky had never cried around Tee-Tee, and she didn't cry when she spoke at the funeral, keeping her crying for later. She'd cried plenty then. She was crying now. But silently. Meanwhile her mind was preparing a nightmare where it was Jack, not Tee-Tee, blowing through the stop sign. She kept herself awake for the longest time to keep nightmares at bay, but finally slipped into a sleep that turned out to be dreamless, all her resources perhaps focused on recovering her strength for tomorrow.

"Should I get in the back?" said Mrs. Plansky.

"Up front beside me," Val said. "You can slide over if I'm incapacitated."

Mrs. Plansky laughed, but not full-throatedly.

They buckled in. Val got busy with the instrument panel. Mrs. Plansky's thoughts went to the window buttons on her car. Val put on a headset and handed her one. A short clipped conversation got going between Val and the Storybook Ranch Airfield flight controller—Mrs. Plansky could see him out her side window, a guy in a backward baseball cap in the not very tall tower—of which she understood nothing, as though they were speaking a language that sounded like English but was not.

They took off, a smooth, nonviolent uplift, unlike those rocket launches down the coast, for example, where the force required was so evident. This was more like magic. She was tempted to think technology always goes too far, but she wasn't qualified for thoughts like that. She took in Val's profile, posture, hands: a montage of confidence-inspiring snapshots. She folded her own hands and sat back.

Mrs. Plansky was one of those people who can't fall asleep on airplanes even though it's so obviously the best use of the time. Even on the one and only first-class flight of her life—a perc from a happy corporate customer—where the seats folded down perfectly flat, her eyes had snapped open at once and stayed that way. Norm was the opposite, falling asleep on takeoff and often having to be nudged awake after they'd taxied to a full stop.

"Why you and not me?" Mrs. Plansky had said.

"I'm in touch with the collective unconscious," he'd told her.

She'd smacked him on the back of his hand, but lightly.

But now in this little Cessna, so unlike an airliner, more like a Spitfire or even a bird, and flying at . . . at what? Ten thousand feet? Fifteen? She peered at the instrument panel where the information had to be but couldn't find it. The point: there was plenty to see at this altitude but her eyelids were growing heavy.

Mrs. Plansky heard the hum of the engine and knew Val was watching her, even thought she could read Val's mind: some version of *sleepy old lady*. She opened her eyes.

Val wasn't watching her, instead was looking out her side window. "Ever been to the Bahamas?"

"No."

"Any of the islands?"

"The Grenadines, but long ago."

"Not dissimilar, at least this part."

Val dipped the wing on Mrs. Plansky's side, giving her a better view.

"The Jarndyce Cays," she said. "The most northerly part of the Bahamian archipelago. Coral islands with reef protections, as you can see. No cruise ships, no casinos, no happy hour, no Junkanoo, no people."

Mrs. Plansky gazed down at a sort of living map unscrolling beneath them. There were a dozen or so cays, crescent shaped, peanut shaped, a few basically round with lumpy extensions, one triangular, none of them very big, and all bony-colored with a dull green overlay. Not beautiful, but the beaches were perfect and the water dazzling, a transparent green just offshore changing abruptly into translucent turquoise with no intermediary shading, and finally to deep opaque blue. Under the surface, mostly in the turquoise parts, lay reddish formations.

"The reefs," Val said. "Some of the best in the world. That's why we're here."

"Oh?"

Val leveled out the wings, tilted the nose up a little, began turning toward what Mrs. Plansky thought was the east.

"See those islands, due west?"

Ah. Totally wrong on her part. And just when she'd been thinking that flying lessons might be a fun activity.

"Those are the Abacos." The plane kept circling. "Now we're looking east. Open water all the way to Spain. The dangerous part is over."

"The dangerous part?"

"Of the journey," Val said. "I'm talking about the old days. The pre-chronometer days of sail, when maps were full of blanks. I shouldn't have said the dangerous part was over. I just meant that blue water sailing was safer than being inshore, the opposite of what you might think."

Mrs. Plansky didn't know what to think. Early in her business career she'd learned that when you didn't know what to think you kept your mouth shut. She watched a tiny black freighter tracing a tiny white line on distant deep blue. The plane tilted and the Jarndyce Cays appeared again, first smaller than they'd been before, then bigger.

Val pointed. "See that one?"

"Like a skinny guy with a potbelly?"

Val laughed. "Jack O' Hearts Cay."

Mrs. Plansky sat up straight. "Jack?"

"O' Hearts," Val said. "The knave. Place names can be whimsical in these parts but this is the only one in the chain with fresh water. Maybe that has something to do with it. Fishermen camp here sometimes. Can you make out that stone hut on the potbelly?"

"Yes," said Mrs. Plansky, her mind stuck for a moment on *knave.*

"It goes way back, maybe not to Columbus's time but far."

"You've done some research."

"I'm writing a book."

"Congratulations."

"Thanks, but I'm far from finished. Not even close."

"Just setting out on something like that always seemed like a big deal to me," Mrs. Plansky said. "Have you got a title?"

Val gave her a smile. It seemed so genuine, like Val was enjoying her company. Still, she was a journalist, so you had to be careful, plus she was working on a story that involved Kev, so you had to be super careful. But how nice to have another human being enjoying your company! Did it happen every day? It did not. Well, there'd been a period of her life—decades, for the love of God!—when it had happened every single day. What a lucky gal! She decided to take Val at face value, and simply be enjoyed.

"Yes and no," Val said. "Publishers have a lot to say about titles. Quote: titles are a marketing tool, first and foremost. End quote."

"So don't get upset if the publisher changes yours?"

"You got it."

"But at least, none of my business, you seem to have landed a publisher."

Val laughed. "Got one to take the bait!" She pressed gently down on . . . what was it called? The stick? It looked more like a squared-off steering wheel. The plane eased lower, like sinking into a pillow. Down below everything reeled by faster.

Val gave her a sideways glance, like she was a little unsure about something. It couldn't have been her flying ability. Mrs. Plansky had never felt safer.

"The title—the working title—is *Rogue Waters*."

"I love it," said Mrs. Plansky. A partial truth. She did love the *Rogue* part. The *Waters* part was a bit confusing. But that was probably just her. "Can I ask what it's about?"

"Do you want the elevator pitch or the full Monty?"

"Both."

"Ha! We're peas in a pod."

What a lovely thing to say! Totally untrue: what pod could hold someone like Val, a knockout beauty in the prime of life, and her?

"Ha!" she said.

"I'll start with the full Monty," Val said, a bit of a surprise to Mrs. Plansky, but she knew nothing about the book business or the art of storytelling in general. "I was working on a Weekend Travel section type piece on seventeenth, eighteenth, and nineteenth century wreckers in the Bahamas. Familiar with wrecking?"

"No."

"Basically marine salvage, where islanders plundered goods from ships wrecked at sea. Lots of that went on in the Bahamas and the Keys, going all the way back to the first Spanish treasure galleons returning to Spain. There are stories about the wreckers luring ships onto the reefs by shining lights on land but that almost certainly didn't happen. Any idea why?"

"Because of what you said before? About blue water sailing being safer than close to land? So lights would be a warning, not an attraction?"

"Bingo!" Val said. "The creator of the Plansky Toaster Knife strikes again!"

"Well, now," said Mrs. Plansky.

"That's the main reason," Val went on, "but also why bother if you were a wrecker? These waters are so dangerous anyway, then throw in the hurricanes, inaccurate charts, sketchy navigation, and you get plenty of supply. So that's where I started—a brief potted history of wrecking on the Bahamian Out Islands. Pretty soon I learned that it wasn't one of those stories with a beginning, middle, and end."

"Because you haven't reached the end yet?" Mrs. Plansky said.

Val gave her a quick glance. "What makes you say that?"

"I don't know." The truth was it just popped out thoughtlessly, a fact best kept to herself. "It just popped out thoughtlessly," she said.

Val laughed, one of those delighted laughs, so nice to hear. "Here's an idea. I should do a piece on you and the toaster knife. I'd need a hook of some sort but that shouldn't—"

"Forget it," said Mrs. Plansky. "I want to hear about the wrecks that are still undiscovered."

"I didn't quite say that."

"But weren't you going there?"

Val nodded. "Sure you were never a lawyer?"

"We've been through this."

"Or a detective? The kind that snares the bad guy on his own petard?"

"Oh, brother," said Mrs. Plansky.

"But yes, that's where I was headed," Val went on. "One of my problems is when I start looking into something I can't stop, so I keep going long after I've gathered enough material for the story. You know the business expression about talking past the sale? It's like that. I ended up in a naval museum in Peru at one point. On my own dime! Same with a couple of Spanish maritime museums. I wish I had your head for business."

"You do," said Mrs. Plansky.

Val didn't get it at first. Then she laughed that delighted laugh again.

Mrs. Plansky noticed something. "Is that a coral reef? Sticking right up on the surface?"

"Not uncommon around here, especially at low tide."

Val swung the plane down in a long slow curve. The reef went on and on, reddish when submerged, golden when close to the surface, a glinting light brown above. It stretched away on the west side of the Jarndyces as far as Mrs. Plansky could see, from Jack O' Hearts to the triangular cay and beyond.

"That's what the mariners feared the most, especially during a nighttime blow," Val said. "But even by day the submerged reefs were dangerous. A fully loaded galleon could draw eighteen feet and those sailors weren't great at reading these waters—still true of some boating types you see around here. Not all. There's an Abaco fisherman, Basil Nottage, kind of a contact of mine, who can see the bottom like the water's not even there. But the point I'm making is that thousands and thousands of wrecks are still waiting to be found. There's one in particular I'm interested in."

"For your book?" said Mrs. Plansky.

Val glanced over. "For the book but also, well, I've caught the bug, I admit it. But not for the loot. Anything like that in these waters belongs to the Bahamian government. And it's a long shot in any case. The ship I'm talking about—can I trust you with the name?"

"Of course." And why would you even ask, thought Mrs. Plansky. She kept that to herself.

"Nuestra Señora de las Aguas," Val said. "Our Lady of the Waters."

"I'm liking your title more and more."

Val smiled a big smile, steered the plane past the triangular cay— Mrs. Plansky noticed a tall palm tree growing at its highest point— turned east and then back up the chain, flying low. Two dolphins leaped out of the water, almost close enough to touch.

"Our Lady sailed out of Havana in July or August of 1601, but most of her cargo originated in Peru, back in the days when the plundering was still good," Val continued. "She was seen by a Spanish naval caravel coming the other way sometime in late August, the exact date unknown since the caravel's logbook has been lost, but I was able to confirm——" Val took one hand off the wheel and made an impatient backhand gesture. "I'll spare you all the boring stuff. The bullet points are that this sighting, most likely somewhere off North Abaco, was the last one, and a few days later a big hurricane came barreling through."

"You think she sank somewhere out here?"

Val nodded. "And although Our Lady has stayed under the radar—kind of fitting—all these years, I may not be the only one. Which is fine, by the way. But if someone else is looking I need to know. Part of the story, if you see what I mean."

"I do," said Mrs. Plansky. She saw that, and maybe more.

"Basil—my fisherman friend?—called me a couple of weeks ago. He said a Bertram 50S he's seen before has been poking around again. Basil kept his distance but with binoculars he spotted two scuba divers on the platform. He could even make out the name on the stern."

"*Lizette*?" said Mrs. Plansky.

"Yup," said Val. "You weren't one of those divers, by any chance?"

"You must know that."

"I apologize. My fault. Sometimes I get so locked into the interrogative. I'm sorry."

"It's all right."

"Thank you." Val brought the nose up, at the same time tilting the plane to maybe a thirty-degree angle or so, Val's wing down, Mrs. Plansky's up, turning west, like they were headed home. She heard a tiny pop, somewhere beneath her.

"One last question?" Val went on.

"Shoot."

"Is there anything you can tell me about *Lizette*?"

"Yes and no," said Mrs. Plansky.

"Go on."

And Mrs. Plansky was all set to go on, to tell her whole tale, the break-in, the second break-in, Tee-Tee, all of it, but before she could—

BANG!

A big bang, underneath or behind or both. Val's hands moved—fast, controlled, without the slightest sign of panic. Mrs. Plansky glanced back. The cabin was on fire. When she turned toward the front she saw that Val's hands were still on the squared-off wheel, still looking controlled and unpanicked, but the wheel itself was no longer attached to anything. Then they were upside down.

EIGHTEEN

Even at her best—some years ago, certainly in double digits—when she was pretty good at absorbing information no matter how fast it was coming in, Mrs. Plansky never could have processed what came next. Such as the blood rushing into her head and the wind screaming by, and gentle ocean waves where the sky should have been, somehow—and maddeningly!—gentle when all this chaos was going on, and the propeller coming loose and shooting by, so very close, and those dolphins leaping up again, almost landing in what was left of the cockpit, and Val shouting, "Seat belt!" Followed by a crashing blue deceleration with no give in it at all, as though water had turned to steel, and then a noisy kind of internal blanking out, not a loss of consciousness, exactly, like a boxer getting KO'd, but more an internal disconnection, like the neurons in her brain were suddenly all speaking different languages.

And now a waterfall was plunging her down, an earsplitting waterfall where the sound was muffled just the same, and she got twisted and pummeled this way and that, and suddenly Val's seat went zooming past, followed by Val, her mouth wide open, air bubbles streaming out, and Mrs. Plansky's hands, operating independently, unfastened her seat belt with not the slightest difficulty, and she began tumbling, first down, then sideways, and finally up.

Up, up, and into the air. She floundered around, swallowing water, choking, gagging, gasping, and at last sucked in a lungful of air, and then another and another. Was she treading water? She seemed to be, but in a wild, frenetic way, like she could launch herself into the air, an impossibility, of course, so she dialed back the water treading, tried to calm herself, tried to take stock. Was she hurt? She didn't feel any pain. Was she bleeding? She glanced around, saw no blood in the water. Facing her was endless ocean, on and on as far as she could see. That couldn't be good. She tried to kick herself just a bit higher to get a better view, but could only manage an inch or so. Mrs. Plansky craned her neck. Water, water everywhere. No, not good. She got stuck on that thought until a wave, stronger than the rest, slapped her face good and hard and turned her around. And there, not far away, was land, bony-colored land with a white sand beach, low scrub, some trees. Plus, over to the right, a stone hut. Also it was a beautiful day, the kind you see in travel advertising.

But Loretta! Back to the stone hut. She was looking at one of the Jarndyce Cays. She even knew the name. It would come to her. Right now her best move would probably be to swim over to this cay and haul herself out of the water. She laid flat, reaching out for the first crawl stroke—and her hand hit something solid. Solid, big, alive. Right away Mrs. Plansky thought shark, and her heart lost all control of its beating. But the solid, big, alive thing was not a shark. It was Val.

Val, face down, bobbing in the swell but making no motion of her own.

"Val! Val!"

No response. Mrs. Plansky grabbed Val, tried to flip her over onto her back, couldn't do it. She did manage to turn Val's head sideways, lifting her face out of the water. Val's eyes were closed and her mouth was open.

"Val! Val!"

No response. Was she breathing? Mrs. Plansky pulled Val closer, so their faces almost touched. She didn't feel Val's breath on her skin, not the tiniest little breeze of breath. Was her heart beating? Mrs. Plansky reached down, put her hand on Val's chest, felt no heartbeat. Maybe she was doing it wrong. She placed her fingertips on the side of Val's neck, where some artery lay just below the surface, as she knew from countless movies and TV shows. No pulse. But maybe she was doing that wrong, too.

"Val! Val!"

Nothing from Val. The swell seemed to be gathering strength, taking control, raising them up, lowering them down. Gently rocking in the swell—wasn't that an expression? But there was nothing gentle about this swell. It had something in mind. The ocean—the whole earth—had a mind of some sort. That brought her right back to the hill of beans conversation. This was not the time.

"Val! Wake up!"

Mrs. Plansky took Val's head in her hands and pleaded with her. Val's eyes stayed closed, her mouth stayed open. Mrs. Plansky realized what she probably should have done first thing. She placed her own mouth on Val's and breathed in.

Nothing.

But wasn't there a first step to this? Didn't you have to somehow squeeze out any water that had seeped into the lungs before getting to the breathing part? Mrs. Plansky, kicking hard to keep both of them afloat, wrapped her arms around Val and squeezed her tight, as forcefully as she could, even savagely, again and again. Finally Val gasped, or maybe there'd been a few gasps already. Mrs. Plansky couldn't be sure. Her arms were strangely weary. Meanwhile Val had vomited up something liquidy that ran all over Mrs. Plansky's face. Mrs. Plansky leaned in, lips to lips, and gave Val another breath. Then she turned on her back, took hold of Val with one arm under her jaw, and began towing her to Jack O' Hearts Cay. The name—a kind of destiny—came to her.

Scissor-kicking was the way to go if she had any chance to get this done. Otherwise she'd lose her grip on Val, which did happen once or maybe more than once, or find herself heading in the wrong direction, which had also happened but only once for sure. The sight of endless ocean—all the way to frickin' Spain!—when she'd been expecting the beach on Jack O' Hearts Cay? Who could forget something like that? Or allow it to happen again?

Therefore scissor-kicking, her left arm helping out now and then, her right maintaining that hold under Val's jaw, except for that time or times when Val had slipped away and Mrs. Plansky had had to reel her back in. But—and maybe a bit Pollyannaish on her part—things were looking up, or at least not worsening. Fact one, as Norm would have said, although in truth he wasn't at home in the water: Val's heart was beating, maybe not as strongly as Mrs. Plansky would have liked, but Val's heartbeat—which Mrs. Plansky felt on the inside of her elbow because of how their bodies were arranged on this little trip—was very encouraging. As for her own heart, it was pounding like a drum, a drum mic'd up close and the drummer on speed. Not that Mrs. Plansky had experience with speed or any other drugs, with the rare and long-ago exception of pot, which had triggered a temporary addiction to ice cream but had also muted the joy inside her. Mocha chip by the pint! Good grief. But how lucky—as she kicked and kicked and kicked again—that she had no heart problems. The statin pills, about which she'd had that conversation, rather lively in retrospect, with the state trooper or perhaps sheriff's deputy or even local cop—my God, how many supposed certainties in her life were unestablished when you got right down to it! But back to the statins, which were blue and had nothing to do with the heart, if she'd understood her GP correctly, a Florida GP, his name never really solid in her mind and now he'd retired, leaving her GP-less and quite unbothered by that, emotionally if not intellectually. As for those one-a-day yellow pills, what were they called? What were they for? Surely not the heart? Mrs. Plansky was still trying to recall anything at all about the yellow pills when her left shoulder ground into sand.

Sand? She twisted around, saw beach, some scrubby sea grape bushes, a few other trees, and not too far away that old stone hut, dating back to Columbus or even earlier if she was remembering right.

"It doesn't matter," she told Val. "The whole history of the world don't matter! We made it! Jack O' Hearts!"

No response from Val. Her eyes were closed but she was breathing and her heart was beating. Mrs. Plansky let go of her and scrambled up the beach. Scrambled in her mind, meaning the command to scramble went out to all the relevant body parts. What actually happened was a laborious crawl on all fours, her hip reacting in a way she came very close to admitting could be called pain, followed by several attempts to stand, all of them failures. She crawled on, came to a rock, or rather a rock-shaped lump of coral, bleached by the sun, got a grip on that, changed her grip to a bumpy outcrop lower down that wasn't so sharp, and pulled herself to her feet. The loud grunt that accompanied that was the only human sound within hearing, the soundscape on Jack O' Hearts Cay all natural. Also there were no other humans in sight, just her and Val. Not a boat on the sea or a plane in the sky. A cloudless sky with a powerful, dominating sun right overhead. Mrs. Plansky owned a nice beach chair with an awning and a drink holder. Comfortable, the seat higher than the seat of most beach chairs, with straps for carrying on your back, and only eight pounds! A gift from Nina, so thoughtful. This new boyfriend was what? Old enough to drive? Perhaps he was mature for his age, although she had yet to meet a man who fit that description, of any age.

Oh, dear. A nasty thought. And untrue. There was Norm, of course. And what about Kev? Yes, what about him? And Jack? How mature was he? She'd been avoiding that question for far too long.

Mrs. Plansky looked toward the water. The tide was going out, exposing more of Val. There was no apparent damage, no blood, no limbs at wrong angles.

"Val?"

No response. A seagull came out of nowhere and dove in Val's direction.

"Hey! Hey!" Mrs. Plansky clapped her hands as loudly as she could. "Hey! Hey!" The bird pulled out of its dive and flew away. Mrs. Plansky hurried across the sand, meaning she went as fast as she could, although the very short journey seemed to take a surprisingly long time.

She stood over Val. Still breathing. And now Mrs. Plansky could see a pulse in her neck, not close to where she'd been feeling for it. Clumps of wet sand had gotten into Val's braided hair. Mrs. Plansky didn't like that. It made her angry, like the sea was trying to take possession of her friend.

She knelt and carefully brushed those sandy clumps away. A mini-clump or two was enmeshed in one of Val's long, thick eyebrows. Mrs. Plansky was extra careful getting rid of that. Val's eyelid quivered against her fingertip. Was it a signal, a deliberate signal, some kind of Morse code? That didn't seem likely. Still, it had to be a good sign.

"Val?"

No answer.

"The question is—now what?"

The tide was still falling, Val now fully out of the water. Mrs. Plansky placed a hand under one of Val's shoulders and raised it slightly, trying to test Val's weight. Val was about her own height and somewhat slimmer. Say 140 pounds or so. Was there something called the fireman's carry, a sort of lift that would end with Val up on her shoulders? Mrs. Plansky knew she couldn't have managed that on the strongest day of her life. She rose, made a bullhorn with her hands, and shouted, "Hello! Hello!" in various directions. Perhaps shouting *Help! Help!* would have made more sense but she'd never liked asking for help. It didn't matter. No one answered and any answer would have been a surprise. They'd flown over Jack O' Hearts Cay not long ago and—

Mrs. Plansky checked her watch. It was gone.

"Never mind. The point is we were flying low enough to see people and there weren't any. So that's off the table." She gazed down at Val, hoping she'd pitch in with a suggestion. An energetic tongue of water slid up the sand and covered Val up to the knees. Mrs. Plansky felt the sun on her shoulders. The tropical sun had a bite to it that the northern one did not, even in midsummer.

"Val? Time to get out of the sun."

No sign that Val was in a hurry to do that.

"Dehydration's going to be a problem. I don't mean to pester but we've got to think ahead. Also the tide seems to be—"

Whoa! It hit her—but so late!—the thought that would have come first to anyone younger, even the dullest. Was there cell service on Jack O' Hearts Cay? Mrs. Plansky felt in her pocket for her phone. No phone. Also no pocket. No slacks, no blouse, no shoes. She was dressed in bra and panties and that was it. A bit of a shock. She came close to covering up by crossing her arms over her breasts, which would have been ridiculous. Meanwhile Val was fully clothed, all except one shoe.

"What sense does that make?"

No sense at all. Nothing was making sense. That was infuriating. Mrs. Plansky hardly ever felt anger—maybe to the point of it becoming a character flaw—but when she did the same thing followed every time. The silo within her opened and out rolled the heavy artillery.

That was what happened now. She bent down, turned Val fully onto her back, hunched a bit, and gripped Val under the shoulders. Then, backing up, she began dragging Val across the beach as gently as she could while still getting it done, which was probably not gentle at all. Mrs. Plansky was very angry, not at Val, of course, not at anyone in particular.

"That's part of the whole damn problem!"

An outburst? There were outbursts all over the place these days. Her position had always been not to contribute, but now she did it again.

"The whole damn problem!"

Her hip hurt. Mrs. Plansky hated to have to put it so unequivocally. She cursed that hip, her language just terrible.

"Excuse me," she said to Val.

Nineteen

One Love.

The faded letters were written in alternating colors, green and yellow, on the eastern wall of the old stone hut. Narrow beams of sunlight shone through chinks in the western wall, lighting them up in a way that reminded Mrs. Plansky of some scene from the Bible, although she couldn't summon up any of the details.

It was shadowy in the hut, not in any way cool, but at least they were protected from the biting tropical sun, they being Val, lying asleep faceup at the back, and Mrs. Plansky, sitting at the other end by the opening. The builder of the hut hadn't used any mortar and yet had been able to form a roof—a slightly domed roof, to boot. Where had these rocks, grayish and quite uniform, come from? They didn't look like the kind of rocks you'd find on a coral island, although she couldn't be sure. Ballast, perhaps? Ballast off some ancient wreck? Didn't they use cannonballs for that? The only cannonballs she knew about were the ones Norm performed as the first entry into every pool they swam in. He just couldn't get over the fun of cannonballs. Jack had been the same as a kid and for a few years he and Norm had cannonballed together. Then Jack had grown out of it. Norm never did.

But maybe the hut wasn't made from ancient ballast, was much more recent. It had certainly been used recently, which she knew from an unbroken Coke bottle in the dirt, cigarette butts, and some empty sardine cans wrapped in a newsprint page of the *Nassau Guardian* dated November 10 of last year. The page had been

soaked or smeared with something greasy so the content of both
sides was illegible except for the beginning of a letter to the editor:
What's to become of the middle class? Mrs. Plansky didn't know the
answer. She did know that she would have preferred that the paper
was today's edition, and the sardine eater would be back soon to
clear up the litter.

Meanwhile she was thirsty. Well, not thirsty but getting thirsty.
And Val would be thirsty, too. What had Val said about fresh water?
That Jack O' Hearts was the only one of the Jarndyces with fresh
water? Or was it one of the other cays?

Musing was not going to get it done. The next step was obvious.
"Get up, Loretta. On your feet." She told herself that several times
but her body remained inert. It wasn't that she was tired from what
it had taken to get the two of them from the beach to the hut, a
much longer distance than she'd imagined at the beginning, a slog
that would have been impossible except for the appearance of a path
flattened through the scrub. Nor was it that she'd been emotionally
worn out from the crash, or paralyzed by fear of what was to come.
Mrs. Plansky denied all those things.

"So don't be a hypocrite. On your feet."

But standing up? The hut didn't have the height for that. The
realization amused her. And somehow her amusement propelled
her into a half crouch. She went over to Val, took the only vitals
she knew how to take—pulse and respiration, existence of, both
unchanged—then picked up the empty Coke bottle.

"Back soon," she said, and went outside.

Was that too breezy, maybe not inspiring confidence that she
would in fact be back? Was something stronger needed, like . . .
like one love?

"One love," she said.

Fresh water. You found it in streams and rivers, lakes and ponds,
those kinds of places, of which Mrs. Plansky could see none. She
followed the somewhat beaten path that had led from the beach

to the hut and seemed to continue toward the center of Jack O' Hearts Cay, the highest point of the cay although probably no more than twenty or thirty feet above sea level. Was fresh water likely to be found at the highest point of any place? She turned off the path, stepping carefully through scrub that proved to be thorny and in an unpredictable way, the thorns too small to be seen—at least by her—until they were stuck in her bare feet. Each time that happened Mrs. Plansky had to stop and balance on one foot while picking the thorn out of the other. Not so easy, but the alternative— sitting down to do it—was out of the question for obvious reasons. And then, when she came to a non-scrubby stretch, it always turned out to be sharp-tipped coral. Before bloodying her feet—actually not quite before—she made her way back to the beaten path. Meanwhile the sun was biting, she was sweating and thirsty, and she'd hardly gotten anywhere, the hut so disappointingly close by.

Her gaze fell on a stunted-looking sea grape tree a few steps away. She'd never eaten a sea grape. Were they edible? Grapes of any kind had to be mostly water. Water was what she needed. She plucked a sea grape, sniffed it, bit into it. A tiny jet of liquid spurted onto her tongue, somehow sweet and salty at the same time. The rest of the sea grape, meaning most of it, turned out to be the pit, which she took from between her lips with her fingers and tossed away. Mrs. Plansky was not a spitter, except when brushing her teeth.

She got to work, stripping sea grapes off the tree and one by one squeezing the juice out of them and into the Coke bottle, one of those slow, mindless tasks that required concentration but couldn't be hurried, this one taking even longer than it should have because both her hands seemed to be trembling a bit. Mrs. Plansky, a good worker, didn't mind that. She could take care of herself, for God's sake. What she minded was the fact that she wasn't taking good care of Val. She sped up the process even knowing that the idea was irrational. But it turned out the process could be sped up after all! She knew there was a lesson in there somewhere, and would pursue it on a later day.

Mrs. Plansky returned to the stone hut with about three inches of sea grape juice in the Coke bottle. Very well, call it two. Or a hair less. She knelt beside Val.

"Grape juice," she said. "Sort of. I know you're thirsty."

No reaction from Val.

"Just open up. I'll do the rest."

Val did not open up. Mrs. Plansky took those two vitals again, with the same results as before, except that now Val's skin seemed to feel a little hot.

"You need liquid. C'mon now. You know you do."

She held up the Coke bottle, gave it an encouraging shake in Val's field of vision, had her eyes been open, hoping to reverse engineer the eye-opening mechanism. No go. Then she touched the tip of the Coke bottle to Val's lips. Also no go.

Mrs. Plansky sat down beside Val. "Boy oh boy." Meanwhile she was pretty thirsty herself. Why hadn't she brought back clumps and clumps of sea grapes for squeezing out here in the shade of the hut? How about just one little sip from the Coke bottle now?

"Nope."

What a terrible thought! You start down that road and where does it end? *Lord of the Flies*, that's where.

"Val? A little cooperation?"

Val kept breathing. Her heart kept beating.

"I know," Mrs. Plansky said. "You're doing your best."

She stuck her finger in the Coke bottle, tilted it, got her fingertip good and moistened with sea grape juice.

"Here you go," she said and touched her finger to Val's lips.

They parted. Slowly and not very wide but wide enough. The tip of Val's tongue emerged and made contact.

"Attagirl," Mrs. Plansky said. "Everything's going to be just—"

Right at that moment, not a triumphant moment but at least encouraging, a hideous noise came from above.

WHAP! WHAP! WHAP!

And not that far above. It shook the whole hut, knocking loose a rock or two from the domed roof. Mrs. Plansky cried out, sprang to her feet, striking her head on that same roof, so low, after all, falling to the ground, dropping the Coke bottle, scrambling—so slowly and awkwardly—back up, and running, hunched over, out of the hut.

Whap! Whap! Whap! But not so loud now. Mrs. Plansky turned toward the sound, saw a red-and-white helicopter rising fast and headed away to the west. She ran after it, waving her arms. "Hey! Hey! We're here! Turn around! We're here! Come back! Tilt the wings!"

The helicopter got smaller and smaller, went from red-and-white to black, shrank to a dot, and vanished. Mrs. Plansky stopped waving her arms. Red and white? *The* Coast Guard? Meaning her coast guard? Maybe the Bahamas had no coast guard. There was so much she didn't know. But she was pretty sure of one thing: someone was searching for them. Had Val filed a flight plan? And now the tower guy in the backward baseball cap knew they were overdue back at Storybook Ranch Airfield? Or some other sequence like that? It didn't matter. The hut had hidden them from view. That was what mattered. But why hadn't the helicopter people spotted the wreckage of the Cessna?

Mrs. Plansky hurried down to the beach. The tide was going out again. Also the sun was low in the sky, and the western world was turning red. There was no sign of any wreckage, not the least little scrap of Cessna, not even a seat cushion or something you might expect like that. The waves lapped unhurriedly up the sand and slid back down.

Mrs. Plansky followed the beaten path back up to the hut. The hut was what? Fifteen feet above sea level? And the grade was gradual. Why didn't her legs want to perform such a simple task? She forced them.

"But don't go making this a habit," she said.

Back in the hut the light was fading. She had to pat-pat over the floor with her hands to find the Coke bottle. It was empty.

Val was mostly just a jumble of shadows now, except for her one bare foot. She'd painted her toenails an ivory color and now they seemed to be catching all the remaining light. Mrs. Plansky took that for a good sign.

"I'm back." She added, "Just like I said." That was to keep Val from losing confidence in her. "But I have to go out again. Not for long. The hydration issue." She leaned in, close enough to make out Val's face. Unchanged. She took the vitals. Also unchanged. "Keep it up." She patted Val's shoulder. But what was this? Her shirt was damp? Oh, no! Val had been lying in damp clothes the whole time? Those clothes should have been removed hours ago, laid outside to dry in the sun, then put back on to ward off the chill of the night. Was there any point in doing all that now, with the sun gone? Mrs. Plansky felt Val's clothing. Damp, certainly not what you'd call wet, and bordering on dry in a few places. All right. Just one place. But Val's vitals were good and the air inside the hut wasn't cool in the slightest, warmer than in the day, if anything.

"We dodged a bullet."

She picked up the Coke bottle and went out to gather sea grapes.

Night fell quickly in the tropics, just one of those things that made it alluring. It had already fallen in the short time she'd been in the hut, but Mrs. Plansky wasn't worried. Soon the moon would be up and she could see fine by moonlight. Hadn't she proved just that on her recent kayak excursion? She walked quite quickly along the beaten path toward the center of the island and the sea grapes.

Meanwhile the moon was taking its sweet time. As were the stars. Mrs. Plansky gazed up at the sky. Uniformly dark. What was up with that? She closed her eyes tight, opened them, and saw what she'd just seen. Therefore it was the sky and not her.

"Moon, stars, let's go."

She walked on, but slower now. That didn't keep her from stepping on one of those tiny thorns with her right foot. And then another with her left. She bent down to pluck out one, lost her balance, and almost fell. She steadied herself against a bare tree trunk—although she didn't remember any tree trunks on the beaten track—and got rid of those thorns.

"Back to square one."

But what was wrong with that? Square one meant you were still on the board, damn it. Mrs. Plansky moved on. Perhaps no longer quite on the beaten path—her bare feet told her that—but at least in the right direction, which she knew instinctively, although it would be thoughtful of the moon and stars if they could simply get with the program. She checked the sky once more, at the same time taking another step. Not a complete step, since she stubbed her toe on a rock and pitched forward, plunging into warm water. But while still in midair Mrs. Plansky realized the obvious: it was a cloudy night.

Down she went, deeper and deeper into dark water. She couldn't see, didn't know which way was up. Mrs. Plansky remembered that air bubbles rose in water, a totally useless fact because she couldn't have seen bubbles even if there'd been any. She floundered. But there remained some tiny non-floundering sliver of her mind, and that non-floundering sliver came up with a scrap of an idea: how about breathing out a little breath, just a few bubbles, and then feeling for the direction they went? She tried it, letting out a puff of air with her hand a foot or so from her mouth, feeling for where the bubbles went—which turned out to be into her palm, then up her fingers, and away. She swam in the same direction. In just a few strokes she hit the surface, took a nice breath of warm night air, calmed down.

Were there gators in the Bahamas? Mrs. Plansky thought not, but she stopped calming down. Caimans lived on some of the islands. She was pretty sure of that. Were caimans just another kind of gator? Were they gators at heart? She started swimming, not in a panic, but just this side of it. Mrs. Plansky had always been a good swimmer, although something seemed to be off. Ah. She was clutching the Coke bottle in one hand. How odd! She was about to let it go when she was struck by a sudden realization. This water tasted fresh! Whoever had said there was fresh water on Jack O' Hearts Cay was right. It was true and she had found it! Her free hand touched mud.

Mrs. Plansky climbed out of this hole or pond or whatever it was, a hole or pond full of fresh water. This, she wanted to tell Norm—oh, how he would have enjoyed the story—was the very definition of serendipity, which didn't mean lucky in general, but only the kind of lucky that begins with something very unlucky. She filled the Coke bottle, drank it down, did that a few more times, finally acknowledging that it was far from the best water she'd ever tasted, although still fresh. The best water she'd ever tasted? That had been on a night they'd been invited to a water tasting—like a wine tasting, but artisanal water.

"This'll be a hip crowd," Norm said. "That's why I'm dressed like this."

"You're wearing what you always wear." Button-down shirt, khakis with cuffs, etc.

"Exactly."

Back in the hut, after a return journey that turned out to be a series of frustrations until she stumbled—not a figure of speech—onto the beaten path, she crouched before Val's dark and undefined form.

"We're in business," she said. "Just need to figure out how . . ."

She felt for Val's face, then placed the Coke bottle gently against her cheek.

"Water. Can you open your mouth?"

Val's mouth remained closed. Mrs. Plansky moved the Coke bottle slightly, touching the opening to Val's lips. They didn't open. She tried what she'd done before, wetting her finger and touching Val's lips. They parted slightly and her tongue touched Mrs. Plansky's finger. Did it make any kind of licking motion? She couldn't be sure, but in any case this method was much too cumbersome, needed speeding up. What about simply pouring the water into her mouth? Could people drink safely like that? Mrs. Plansky didn't think so, but then she remembered nursing Nina and Jack, holding them in the crook of her arm, therefore basically on their backs just the way Val was lying now. The kids had loved it! And so had she.

Well, Nina hadn't loved it, no sense fooling herself about that. With Nina they'd moved onto formula quite soon. But Jack? He'd loved it for sure, had been unwilling for the longest time to give it up. She'd been unwilling, too, not taking it to any extreme, of course. What had Miss Terrance said? "Girls—whatever you do, don't make an example of yourself." Tee-Tee had raised her hand. "What about an example of something good?" Tee-Tee and Miss Terrance had not gotten along.

Meanwhile she'd maneuvered Val into a sitting position, supporting her with one hand behind her back. Mrs. Plansky held the Coke bottle to Val's mouth. At first nothing happened. Then Val's mouth opened, slowly and slackly, like it wasn't in touch with central command. But maybe good enough.

"There's a girl."

She tilted up the Coke bottle, just a little. Water flowed out, also just a little. She could hear it and even feel it through the glass. *Gurgle-gurgle.* The water did not come back; Val did not choke or gag. Taking her time, oodles of it, Mrs. Plansky got that whole bottleful into Val.

"How was that?"

No response.

Mrs. Plansky eased her back down, took those two vitals. Stable or even slightly improved. She rose, went to the opening of the hut, and lay down just inside. Had she ever felt this worn out? Not that she remembered. But crazily enough, at least for a while, her eyes refused to close.

"Jack. Where the hell are you?"

Right overhead she saw those daubed green-and-yellow letters: *One Love.* But that was impossible in the pitch-black.

TWENTY

Someone was whistling "A Kiss to Build a Dream On," a Louis Armstrong number Mrs. Plansky had always liked. The whistler came to the trumpet solo part and whistled right through it, hitting the high notes no problem. Dreams were like movies. Hadn't some famous director said he just filmed his dreams and cashed the checks? Not the point, which was that movies had soundtracks, so there was no reason a whistling version of "A Kiss to Build a Dream On" couldn't turn up in one of your—

She opened her eyes. The song continued. For a moment she had no idea where she was. It all came back to her in a jumble. She sat up, an involuntary groan or grunt or something in between escaping her. What was happening to her self-control? Mrs. Plansky was not in the mood for slipups on that score.

There was daylight in the hut, lots of it. Val lay in her place at the far end, unmoving, eyes closed. Mrs. Plansky stood up, not all the way up, remembering the low ceiling just in time. That bit of mental acuity was countered by the realization that she ached all over. She deleted that part and held on to the acuity half.

"Val?"

No response. She went over and took the vitals. Unchanged. Now what about that whistling? She cocked her head. There was no whistling.

Mrs. Plansky went outside. A bright sunny day, westerly breeze, a contrail high in the sky, nothing flying low, no helicopters. Something splashed. She remembered those two dolphins, witnesses to the whole thing. Maybe one day we'd be able to communicate with them. A lot of good might come of that. A dolphin in the White House, for example. She heard another splash.

"Back soon," Mrs. Plansky said, and set off toward the beach on the beaten path.

"A Kiss to Build a Dream On" started up again, louder and louder. Mrs. Plansky picked up the pace.

She stepped out of the scrub and onto the sand. A nineteen-or twenty-foot Boston Whaler—the air was so clear she could read the red lettering on the white hull, but she was familiar with Whalers, a common sight in Rhode Island waters—rode at anchor, twenty or thirty yards away. A man wearing shorts and a sleeveless tee, his back to her, was fishing off the starboard side.

"Excuse me?" Mrs. Plansky said. No reaction. She raised her voice and tried again.

The whistling stopped at once. The fisherman turned quickly, more like a half turn, his right hand still plying the rod. His hat had one of those long fisherman-type bills and he wore gold-tinted sunglasses. He actually resembled Louis Armstrong a bit, the Louis Armstrong of early middle age, the image maybe Photoshopped to make him look less mid-twentieth century.

Mrs. Plansky didn't know where to begin. She gave him a little wave.

"Mornin', Miss," he said, his voice deep and pleasant.

At that moment Mrs. Plansky remembered what she was wearing, bra and panties. True, bra and panties of high quality, French, not cheap. Mrs. Plansky did not stint on intimates. Stinting on the intimate parts of life? What sense would that make? Still, she was in her underwear and he was a strange man. What would he think?

"Loretta," she said. "Loretta Plansky. Mrs. That's me."

"Pleased to be meeting you," he said. "Basil Nottage. Mr."

"Basil Nottage?"

"That's right."

"You know Val Sims?"

"Val? Most certainly."

"We crashed! She's—" Mrs. Plansky gestured in the direction of the stone hut.

Basil Nottage started the outboard, weighed anchor, and glided into the beach, all in less than a minute. He also snagged a nice-sized grouper somewhere in the middle of all that, which he unhooked and deposited in a cooler.

"In case you feel a chill, Miss," he said, tossing her an oversized hoodie. Oversized for her, not him. It came down to midthigh, good enough. There was artwork on the front: one of those marijuana leaves, with smoke rising around it.

In the next few hours, Mrs. Plansky got an inkling of how Robinson Crusoe felt on being reintroduced to human society. Just an inkling, and of course she kept it private. This was not the time for self-dramatization. The self-dramatizing years of life, if ever justifiable, were long gone. But to go so abruptly from primitive and isolated existence back into the modern world was a little destabilizing. She left it at that. Well, there was this twist, just a touch of fondness in her heart for those primitive hours. An idiotic reaction, no doubt about that, which was where Mrs. Plansky left it in the end.

Basil Nottage called in the cavalry on his ship-to-shore. That was how he put it, and when that was done he followed Mrs. Plansky to the hut, handing her a baloney sandwich and an Orange Crush on the way. He gazed at Val, placed his hand gently on her forehead.

"She's not hot."

"No."

"And she breathes."

"Yes."

"What about drinking with straws? I have straws in the boat."

"We could try." Mrs. Plansky explained about the Coke bottle.

"She drank Coke?"

"No, no." She explained again, this time better.

"You found Lusca Pool?"

"A pool. If there was a sign I didn't see it."

Basil laughed, a deep, pleasing laugh, not unlike a bassoon. "Only the one, Miss, only the one in this whole string. Lusca Pool."

"Was Lusca a pirate?"

"Oh, we had pirates in these islands, pirates for sure. But Lusca, he's a sea monster."

"A legend, then."

"Lots of legends here, true and not." Basil looked like he might go on, but then came a *whap, whap, whap*. Mrs. Plansky devoured the baloney sandwich and drained the Orange Crush.

"Bread okay?" Basil said.

"Delicious."

"She bakes. The wife."

Two helicopters—one from the Coast Guard, one from the NTSB or FAA or possibly both—landed on Jack O' Hearts Cay. A Bahamian naval patrol boat and a Coast Guard cutter arrived, lowered tenders, and sent in a dozen or more people, some in uniform, some not. Medics went into the hut, came out with Val on a stretcher, an oxygen mask on her face and an IV needle in her arm. They loaded her into the Coast Guard helicopter and flew her away. Mrs. Plansky stood on the beach, watching the activity and wondering whether a second baloney sandwich was available. And another Orange Crush to wash it down would be nice.

A man in a blazer with shiny brass buttons approached her. "I'm—" he said his name but Mrs. Plansky didn't catch it. "Business manager of the *Caribbean Tribune.*"

She was slow to get that.

"Where we're very proud to publish Valencia's work," he went on.

"Right, of course." She offered her hand. "Loretta Plansky."

"A pleasure to meet you. From what Mr. Nottage says I gather you saved Val's life."

Mrs. Plansky didn't know what to say. She just shook her head.

"Anything you need or want, just give me the word," he said.

"Very nice of you but I can't think of anything," said Mrs. Plansky, unable to raise the subject of the baloney sandwich and the Orange Crush. "How is she?"

The business manager glanced in the direction the Coast Guard helicopter had gone, the sky now empty. "Beyond the fact that she's in a coma, they didn't say."

"What about her vitals?"

The expression on the business manager's face changed, a change you see sometimes see when a man—it's usually a man—realized he had to up his game. "They didn't mention anything about that, either. They're taking her to UF Health in Jacksonville. I'll let you know the moment I hear anything." He took out his phone. "What's your number?"

That was often a difficult question because everyone's phone captured your number so you didn't have all those chances to commit it to memory, like in the old days. But now Mrs. Plansky surprised herself and rattled it right off.

"Got it," said the business manager, putting his phone away.

Only then did Mrs. Plansky recall a relevant fact. "But it's gone to the bottom."

"Ah."

"Maybe they'll find it."

They both turned to the sea, where one of the tenders was motoring slowly back and forth, crew members gazing down over the side.

"In the meantime, would you like to use mine?" the business manager said. "To call your people? I don't believe this is on the news yet, but it's only a matter of time. A short time."

"My people?"

"To hear from you first. So they won't be alarmed." He smiled. "Or too alarmed."

Mrs. Plansky took the phone, moved off to the side. Her people. That would be her dad; her kids, Nina and Jack; her grandkids, Emma and Will. The one she wanted to speak to the most was Jack, not so much to convey her news as to hear his voice, to find out he was all right. But she didn't know his number. She didn't know any of their numbers! That left the landline in the condo, used by no one, but locked in her mind. She entered the number. Maybe some-one would pick up, preferably Lucrecia.

"Hi, there," said her dad.

"Hi, Dad. It's me."

"What up?"

"What up, Dad?"

"That's what they say on the street. Real life. Gotta get with the program, Loretta."

"I just wanted to let you know I'm fine."

"Lucky you."

"What do you mean?"

"Do I have to spell it out? I'm not fine."

"What's wrong?"

"We're out of marmalade, that's what."

"There's a jar in the right-hand cupboard, top shelf."

"That's not the kind I like. I like the kind with the royal crest. How many times?"

"Is Lucrecia there, Dad?"

"She left. Wait a minute! Whoa! Were you out all night?"

"In a way."

"In a way? Like with that guy?"

"What guy are you talking about?"

"The tennis guy. Wheeler-dealer. The one Jack told me about."

"Kev Dinardo?"

"Yeah. And what the hell kind of name is that?"

"But I thought you told Jack about him."

"So?"

"Not the other way around."

"Let's not argue. When will you be back?"

"Later today."

"Don't forget the marmalade."

"Wait! Don't hang up! I need Lucrecia's—"

Too late.

She walked over to the business manager and returned the phone.

"My pleasure," he said.

Had he overheard the conversation? He glanced quickly at her hoodie and then away. But from that very brief look she could tell he was dialing his game back down.

A man from the FAA and a woman from the NTSB came over and introduced themselves. The three of them sat on some worn coral rocks at the back of the beach.

"Okay if we record this?" the woman said.

"Sure," said Mrs. Plansky.

"Just take us through what happened."

"Starting when?"

"Whenever you like."

She began with her and Val on the plane talking about Spanish galleons, and went from there. The FAA man and the NTSB woman didn't say a word. They were both young, with professional faces that didn't give much away, but at the beginning she thought she could tell that their expectations were low. You saw a lot of that when you got older. But by the time she reached the part about hauling Val onto the beach all that had changed. It wasn't that Mrs. Plansky wanted to impress them or anything like that. And she had no complaints. Still, it was nice to be treated like a normal person.

The FAA man and the NTSB woman exchanged a glance. Was this a good-cop, bad-cop situation? Was that even a real thing? But how ridiculous! Good cop, bad cop was for use on perps, not witnesses. Perps! Just listen to her! Mrs. Plansky wondered if she was in one of those heightened states again. Did great artists—the really greats, like Chekhov—live their whole lives like that?

Before Mrs. Plansky could take one more step down that surely irrelevant road, the FAA man said, "Do you have any piloting experience yourself?"

"No."

"How about as a passenger in small planes?"

"This was my second or third time."

"Were you uneasy about it?"

"Not when I realized how competent Val was."

"What gave you that impression?"

"She was relaxed and alert at the same time."

"Going back to those final moments," the FAA man said, "can you describe the bang you heard?"

"It wasn't enormous, like . . ." Like another explosion I've heard recently, but so complicated to go into that now. ". . . just not enormous. It came from the stern. The tail. And then the wind was blowing through and we were upside down. The steering wheel came loose."

"How do you mean?"

"Val had it in her hands but it wasn't connected to . . . to whatever it's supposed to connect to."

"Did you see any other flying object that could have struck the plane?"

"Like what?"

"We've had incidents with drones," the FAA man said. "Or birds—usually a flock but a single large one might have done it."

"I didn't see anything like that."

"Did the pilot say anything after you heard the bang?"

"I don't think so. But if she did won't it be on the black box?" Mrs. Plansky looked from one to the other, saw no reaction she could put a name on. "Or in the black box? Have you found it yet?"

"Technically speaking," the FAA man said, "there's no such thing as a black box. There are two devices, CVR and FDR—a cockpit voice recorder and a flight data recorder—which are not required in Cessna 172s and other similar craft and were not aboard this one."

"But you'll still be able to . . . to re-create whatever happened when you bring up all the pieces? The water was pretty shallow. It was right over there." She looked out and pointed. Both tenders were going back and forth, but no longer close to the crash site, instead off to the south, half a mile or more away, the sound of their engines growing faint. "They should be . . ." Mrs. Plansky made a gesture, like she was motioning the tenders back in.

The FAA man and the NSTB woman glanced out at the ocean, but not with much interest.

"Anything else you'd like to say, Mrs. Plansky?" the FAA man said.

"Well, this is not my area," she said, her area—her former area—being one tiny corner of the kitchen supplies business, "but what if you don't find the wreckage?"

"In terms of reconstructing the event?" said the FAA man.

"That's right."

"Given the lack of any last-minute communication with the pilot, any reconstruction will be problematic. That doesn't take away from your exemplary conduct following the event."

He started to rise, meaning this interview was over. Mrs. Plansky found that word—*event*—a bit inadequate as a description of what had happened. There was a whole sub-class of that sort of language, and a whole population of officials who spoke it. She didn't want to make a fuss and if you got irritated by things like that you'd live out your life in a state of unhappiness. Just the same Mrs. Plansky was a little bit irritated.

"What about a bomb?" she said.

There was a silence. Then the NTSB woman spoke for the first time. "And your reason for asking that?"

Ah. Perhaps a good-cop, bad-cop routine after all. And she'd missed it just because the woman was the bad cop! Mrs. Plansky felt shamed by that, outdated and out of touch.

"A bang, after all," she said, and shrugged her shoulder, a gesture they might have missed on account of the size of Basil's hoodie.

"Do you have much experience with explosives?" the NTSB woman said.

"Me?" said Mrs. Plansky, putting her hand to her chest, right in the middle of that smoke-ringed pot leaf.

"Maybe your family's in the construction business, or mining."

"Nothing like that."

"What about enemies?" the NTSB woman said. "Got any?"

Mrs. Plansky came close to going through her pot-leaf routine for the second time. "Not that I know of," she said.

"What about Ms. Sims? Does she have enemies?"

"Not that I'm aware of. But I really don't know her that well."

The NTSB woman nodded. "Let's circle back to how the two of you got together for this trip. Something about Spanish galleons?"

"Val's writing a book. There were lots of wrecks in the Bahamas in those days, especially in hurricane season."

"And what do you bring to that subject, Mrs. Plansky?"

"Nothing at all."

"Are you friends, then? You were just along for the ride?"

"Pretty much."

"Pretty much meaning . . . ?"

"Yes. We're friends. Well, maybe more accurate to say we met recently and hit it off."

"How recent?"

"Very. Just days ago."

"How did you meet?"

"Through Val's work."

"She was doing a story on you?"

Mrs. Plansky was sitting out in the open on an islet in the vast sea, but she was feeling more and more enclosed. The NTSB woman had maneuvered her—effortlessly, no doubt about that—into a corner, and now she had nowhere to turn. The true answer was all about witnessing the flaming destruction of *Lizette*, officially caused by a lightning strike, and the fact that some time earlier *Lizette* had been sighted in these waters. Then there was golden Tee-Tee. Plus Val probably had suspicions regarding the lightning strike determination and—Mrs. Plansky just arriving now at the obvious—was hoping to probe her on that subject on this very trip. Did she now have to cough that all up?

Mrs. Plansky didn't want to do that. She had her reasons but there was no time to sort them out. She just knew. Not that she knew what was right. This was something else. Call it woman's intuition, if that was still a thing.

"I won a mixed doubles senior tennis tournament," she said. "A very small deal but Val sensed one of the Florida retirees stories, the human-interest kind." What a wretched lie! Mrs. Plansky knew right then she was going to pay for it. The only question was when.

They gazed at her. If she'd had to bet money—which would have been a first in her life—she'd have gone all in on the FAA man buying her story and the NTSB woman not.

"And that led to this hitting it off, as you put it?" the NTSB woman said.

"Stranger things have happened," said Mrs. Plansky.

Did she notice a flicker of doubt in the eyes of the NTSB woman, like she was buying the story after all? Mrs. Plansky almost said "stranger things have happened" again.

TWENTY-ONE

"Here's the plan for getting you back home the quickest," the *Caribbean Tribune* business manager said. "Subject to your approval, of course."

Then came a lot of details that breezed by Mrs. Plansky as soon as he mentioned home. Home was where she wanted to be, lying under the covers in her twisted K. Anything that got her back home fast would do just fine.

"And one of the Coast Guard crew women is about your size." He handed her a shopping bag.

She gazed into the bag, a bit confused.

"That's called tropical blue. Dress whites were also available, but she thought you'd prefer these."

Mrs. Plansky got it.

There was nowhere private to change except for the stone hut and she didn't want to go back in. But changing in the open? Out of the question. She walked back up the beaten path. The stone hut was physically unchanged yet very different. The aura was gone. Not quite the same thing inside, where that daubed green-and-yellow *One Love* held on to its power. Mrs. Plansky went to the back where Val had lain and saw no sign that she'd ever been there. In fact, the whole place had been cleaned up—sardine cans, cigarette butts, newsprint scrap, Coke bottle, all gone. People could be so good in small ways. Then she remembered how 92 Seaside Way had been cleaned up and even doubted that last little observation.

She emptied the shopping bag: navy-blue trousers with a black web belt, a sky-blue short-sleeve shirt, a navy-blue baseball cap with USCG on the front in big red letters, a pair of flip-flops—probably not official—still in its plastic wrapper, plus a package of scent-free cleansing wipes. One thing for sure: our coast was in good hands.

Mrs. Plansky stripped off the hoodie and fancy French lingerie, dropped all that in the bag, then took out the bra and panties and put them back on. Yes, they needed laundering ASAP, but whatever had she been thinking? After that she donned a uniform for the first time in her life, and remembering not to bump her head, strode out into the sunshine, right away in the mood to give orders, if she could have thought of any.

Basil was standing nearby. The moment he saw her he brought his heels together, straightened up, and saluted. The sight of him saluting the way he was—barefoot, in shorts and sleeveless tee, both sun-faded almost white and with threadbare patches—might have seemed satiric or ridiculous but it very much wasn't, not to her. In fact, it almost brought tears.

"All set, Miss?" he said.

"For . . . ?"

"For getting you back to the mainland, back home. Mr. Blyden, he didn't explain?"

"The man from the *Tribune*?"

"That's right. He's got you flying out of Marsh Harbor at five. I'll run you over. Plenty of time. And here's one of them what they call burner phones. Mr. Blyden says just to throw away when you're done."

"That's so nice. I'd like to thank him."

Basil shook his head. "He's gone. Most of them's gone."

Mrs. Plansky looked around. She didn't see the remaining helicopter, the tenders, the Bahamian patrol boat, the Coast Guard cutter.

"But what about the search? Did they find any wreckage?"

Basil shook his head. "Still searchin'. Searchin' and searchin'." He made a broad backhanded wave into the distance. "But don't be holding on too tight to hope."

"Why not?"

"I can show you, if you have a mind for a little detour."

"That's fine."

Basil saluted again.

Basil's Whaler was called *Tangs For The Mem'ries*. Mrs. Plansky didn't get it until they were under way, Basil at the console amidship and she facing him on the bow seat. Then she remembered that tangs were beautiful little tropical fish and she fell in love with the name at once.

Basil steered slowly south about ten or fifteen yards offshore, the outboard chug-chugging quietly. "Miss?" he said. "Uh, Mrs.?"

"Call me Loretta. Please."

"Loretta," he said, and repeated it, maybe assessing its appeal. He nodded to himself and said, "Where was the tide?"

"When we crashed?" She had to think.

"That's all right." He waited patiently. "Many, many land people don't watch the tides."

"I'm from Rhode Island. I watch the tides."

"Ah, it's an island! Like Hawaii! I never thought!"

Basil beamed at her. Now the pressure was on, as though the reputation of the whole state—yes, the Ocean State, and insular in so many ways, but not a geographic island—was in her hands. She remembered the clumps of sand in Val's braided hair. "The tide was going out."

Basil nodded like that made sense. "Makes two falling tides since," he said. "The falling tides this time of year? That's the story."

"I don't understand."

"Show-and-tell," said Basil.

They rounded the southern tip of Jack O' Hearts Cay. Mrs. Plansky hadn't realized how close the next cay was, the channel between them twenty yards wide at the most.

"This here is No-Name Cay, baby of the chain," Basil said. "Now we ride for free."

He cut the engine, and then there was no sound except what the ocean made. Basil grinned and raised his hands in the look-ma-no-hands gesture. Meanwhile *Tangs For The Mem'ries* was surging forward like a surfer on a powerful wave.

"You dig?" he said.

"There's a current? The tide swept the wreckage around the tip and through here?"

"You dig," Basil said. "You surely dig."

"Meaning the wreckage is out there somewhere?" She turned and pointed east toward the open sea.

"Yes and no, yes and no," said Basil. He switched the engine back on and they motored east, the ocean's surface now ruffling in a light chop, although it retained that lovely emerald color. Then, maybe half a mile from the cays, the green darkened rapidly and all at once turned deep blue. Basil backed the engine into neutral. The boat made one last surge and settled back down.

"Do you ever fall seasick?" he said.

"No."

"A natural mermaid!"

Confirmation of Tee-Tee's point! And from an expert waterman! Mrs. Plansky smiled. She was liking Basil Nottage a whole lot. Meanwhile he was rummaging around in the console cabinet, coming up with a dented aluminum bucket, one end open, the other glassed-in.

"Know what is this?" he said.

"A viewing bucket." She held out her hands to catch it but Basil walked around the console and gave it to her instead. "Take a . . . what is it? Not goose but . . ."

"Gander."

"Gander." He laughed. "Take yourself a gander."

Mrs. Plansky moved to the port side, knelt, and leaned over the gunwale, lowered the bucket, submerging the glassed-in end to a depth of a few inches. At first she had no idea what she was seeing. She saw but couldn't make sense of the sight. To the west, on the emerald green side, was deep water, maybe eighty or ninety feet, partly sandy and partly covered with seagrass, seagrass that leaned over sideways, as though in a strong westerly breeze. And then, just one more inch to the east, came nothing, no sand, no seagrass, no bottom, just darkness, down and down. This was awesome in the true meaning of the word, and also scary, like reaching the end of the known world.

"Continental shelf, Loretta," Basil said. "Drops from ninety feet to six, seven thousand, just like that." He snapped his fingers.

Meanwhile down below something was rising up from the blackness.

"Oh, my God. A big shark, really big! I think it's a great white."

"Could be, but not so usual in our waters. Can I see?"

Basil knelt beside her, gazed through the bucket, their heads touching. "Mako," he said right away. "Great white's cousin. But big for a mako, so you're right about that, the bigness. Do you want to catch him?"

"Catch him?"

"One of the best sport fishes in the sea. I charge a client a thousand a day U.S. for mako fishing. For you—on the house. Better with my big boat, for sure, with the fighting chairs and deep-sea tackle, but we could venture."

"Thank you," Mrs. Plansky said. "Maybe some other time."

Basil nodded. "He ain't goin' no place."

As if to make a liar of Basil, the mako rolled sideways—graceful and predatory at the same time—and headed back down, vanishing from sight at once. Basil didn't seem at all upset by that, if anything looked thoughtful.

"Maybe he's finding it already," he said.

"Finding what?" said Mrs. Plansky.

"The pieces."

She didn't understand. He read that on her face. In the shadow of the outsized bill of his cap, his eyes were gentle.

"Of the plane, Loretta." He motioned back, toward the channel between Jack O' Hearts and No-Name. "What I'm trying to pass along, the ground rules out here, this current of ours. It picks things up and carries them east. Everything you can think. Didn't Columbus find coconuts in the middle of the ocean? How he knew where to go, you with me? But coconuts, they float."

She was with him. "The plane's down on the bottom?"

"Somewheres."

"Did you tell them? The navy, the Coast Guard, all the rest?"

"Oh, they know. Or will real soon from all their measuring."

"And they'll come back?"

"For the *Titanic*, oh yeah, bet your sweet—" Basil put a stop to that one and went on. "But a little small Cessna? Down there but who knows where? Could be still on the move. A little small Cessna with no iceberg, no movie, no dead bodies?"

Yet. No dead bodies yet. But Mrs. Plansky didn't want to even think that thought, let alone voice it. Basil turned the boat around, gripped the control lever to throttle up, and paused.

"You know about this treasure galleon of Val's?" he said.

"A little."

"How we got together, Val and me. She booked cruises all around these cays, snorkeling and snorkeling, searchin', searchin'. She musta made hundreds of dives even with me tellin' her right from the start same as I'm tellin' you."

"That it got swept over the drop-off?" Mrs. Plansky said.

"Sure as sure can be, but she don't want to hear. The bottom out there in the deep ocean ain't like the bottom under us right now. It's more like a desert—a desert under miles of water. Thousands of wrecks out there all over the oceans of this world. We ain't never goin' to know." Basil smiled. "She didn't want to hear. The searchin'—that's what Val likes."

They bobbed on the water. The sun shone down. The sea sparkled. Basil was speaking of Val in the present tense. All that was nice. For a moment Mrs. Plansky was living in the moment, which didn't happen often, and this was the kind of moment that deserved to be lived in.

But it passed. Something in her brain resisted living in the moment, always wanted to move on, to deal with any lurking problems. For example, Val wasn't the only one searching in these waters, as she'd discovered. Kev had been here, too. What about Tee-Tee? Had he found her somewhere in these cays? She had no proof of that. Kev could have bought her from an art dealer, or acquired her in other ways. It was all speculation. She needed facts. *Nuestra Señora de las Aguas* had carried a cargo originating in Peru. That was a fact. The Metropolitan Museum of Art had a solid gold Incan figurine that looked a lot like Tee-Tee, but not quite so beautiful. That was another fact. Things were actually not so speculative after all.

Basil was gazing at a distant flock of birds, poised like a haze over the water.

"Basil?"

He turned.

"Have you ever seen *Lizette* around here?"

"Oh, yes."

"When was the last time?"

"Have to think," he said, taking off his cap and knuckling his forehead. "Been awhile, that's for sure. Maybe a year, maybe two. She moved to Arizona."

"Excuse me? Can you say that again?"

"What part?"

"The whole thing."

He looked surprised, maybe hearing something new, something off, in her tone. Then he shrugged. "I haven't laid these eyes on Lizette in a long time. Can't say exactly how long. She moved to Arizona and if she's been back in the Bahamas I ain't seen her."

"You're talking about the person, not the yacht?" Mrs. Plansky said.

Basil's face lit up. "Ha ha! Now I see the confusion! Not the yacht, no, no, no. I mean the person, Lizette Dinardo."

He chuckled at the humor of it all. Mrs. Plansky, never once seasick in her life, began feeling queasy.

TWENTY-TWO

"But you were meaning the Bertram?" Basil said. "The Fifty-S?"

"I was," said Mrs. Plansky.

"The Bertram, a very beautiful craft. I've seen it a number of times, but the last one?" He thought for a few moments, then nodded to himself. "Two weeks ago? At some distance, too far for hailing." He made a gesture toward the southeast, then grew thoughtful again. "Val was asking this same thing."

"About the boat or the person?"

"The boat. She was never mentioning the person."

"Lizette."

"That's right. When Lizette left, Mr. Dinardo asked if I knew any good boat names. He likes this one." Basil patted the gunwale the way you might pat a dog.

"So do I," Mrs. Plansky said. "Can I ask how well you know him?"

"Mr. Dinardo? Oh, not well, not well. A fine gentleman. Not the kind for putting on airs, if you know what I mean. They stop by Maybelle's for a drink or two sometimes. Not so many visitors come to Maybelle's. More of a locals place. But everyone welcome, of course."

"Where's Maybelle's?" Mrs. Plansky said.

"Near Marsh Harbor, airport side."

"And by *they* you mean Kev and—you mean the Dinardos?"

Basil checked the position of the sun in the sky and throttled up, but just a little, keeping the engine noise down. "Don't mean to have a wagging tongue," he said, "but they's divorced. You, uh, know him?"

"Not well." Had she ever spoken truer? She thought right away of the kiss just after the explosion, not just the fact of it but how it felt, and even what it might have promised. Her memory of all that was clear but she just didn't understand. And why after the explosion and not before? She didn't understand that, either. Plus there was now the almost certain fact that Kev had some sort of relationship with Jack by that night, and hadn't told her. "We belong to the same tennis club," she said.

"You're a tennis player?"

"Yes."

"You play with Mr. Dinardo?"

"I have."

"You must be good."

"Why?"

"Mr. Dinardo is good."

"Do you play, Basil?"

He put his hand to his chest and laughed. Then he throttled up some more. "But I saw him play. The two of them were playing. You can tell when someone's good." He took off his gold-tinted sunglasses. "And not just tennis. Am I right, Loretta?"

"I don't know," she said. "You can fool yourself about things. I don't mean you personally. I mean . . . me."

"Naw," Basil said, and put his sunglasses back on.

They cruised back through the channel between Jack O' Hearts and No-Name and Basil pushed the throttle down all the way. *Tangs For The Mem'ries* surged forward, proving to be much faster than she would have expected. She looked past him to the outboards, hadn't realized there were two. They were massive, but the horsepower numbers were on the back, and not visible.

"I know what you think," he said, raising his voice over the roar. "We're overpowered. Am I right?"

"Oh, no, not at all," she shouted back.

"Sure we are! Sure we are! But just enough. You get what I'm saying?"

Mrs. Plansky glanced around, saw the ocean reeling past, a blue blur, almost like it was on the move and *Tangs For The Mem'ries* still. "I get it," she said.

Basil put his hand to his ear, although she was certain he'd heard perfectly well and just wanted to hear her say it again. She realized there wasn't a fish in the sea that stood a chance against him.

Meanwhile her queasiness had vanished, kind of counterintuitive, and she was hungry again. She was even wondering if there was another baloney sandwich on board when she noticed the next cay down in the chain, maybe a half mile or so south of No-Name. It had a longer shoreline than No-Name, but shorter than Jack O' Hearts, and a single tall palm grew in the middle.

She pointed and raised her voice again. "What's that one?"

Basil glanced behind him and yelled back, "Lady Cay. No water. No nothin'. Current between them two's just as bad, maybe worse."

"I'm home!" called Mrs. Plansky, feeling like a sitcom dad in the black-and-white era. It was early evening—the exact time unavailable, what with her smart phone on the bottom of the sea, although she did have the burner, still untried in her pocket due to a totally unjustifiable premonition that any call made on it would connect to a drug dealer. The condo was silent but the lights were on.

"Hello? It's me."

Then came running footsteps down the hall.

"Mom?"

It was Nina.

"Oh my God, we've been so worried about you." Nina threw her arms around her and held her tight. Mrs. Plansky did the same to her daughter, but not so tight. An over-the-top release of all sorts of emotions? What would be the point? And also she was a bit too tired for all that.

Nina held her at arm's length. "Are you all right? We called you and called you."

"My phone's no longer in service."

"Of course! Of course! But are you okay? Are you hurt?"

"I'm fine."

"You were on the news! Not your name. Just a local Ponte d'Oro woman in a plane crash in the Bahamas. Plane crash! But that nice man—Mr. Blyden, with some magazine?—called the landline. Grandpa answered so I'm not sure of . . . but what's that you're wearing?"

Mrs. Plansky stepped back to give Nina a better view. "Tropical blues," she said.

"Oh, my God! From the navy?"

"USCG."

"What's that?"

"The Coast Guard, darling."

"Oh, my God!" Nina hugged her again.

Mrs. Plansky patted her back. "Did Mr. Blyden say anything about Val?"

"Val?"

"Valencia Sims, the pilot. She works for him."

"Right, right. He did say something. A coma? Was that it?" Nina turned and called over her shoulder. "Hamish! Hamish! My mom's home! Come meet her." She turned back to Mrs. Plansky. "We flew down the moment his shift was done."

Hamish. The details came back: the *Mayflower* or possibly the *Arbella*, Scottish extraction, owned a kilt but didn't wear it publicly, never married, worked in healthcare, played rugby in college, was on the youngish side, but not in his twenties, so that was a blessing.

Enter Hamish. Had Nina qualified his Scottishness with a "partly"? Mrs. Plansky thought so and it would certainly have made sense, since although Hamish had the size and powerful build she associated with Scottish males—going back to the Picts and the Scots versus the Romans and all that—his complexion was not conventionally Scottish, having plenty of the Indian subcontinent in the mix. He had an open, friendly gaze and was dressed as a hospital orderly.

"Hamish? Say hi to my mom. Mom, meet Hamish."

"Pleased to meet you, Mrs. Plansky."

"Loretta, please. And the pleasure's mine."

They shook hands. His was big and dry, with lots of power he kept on the back burner. During the handshake, she was able to make out the stitching on his chest. HAMISH BANERJEE, M.D., EMERGENCY. She told herself to sharpen up.

"Where's Grandpa?" she said, which was what she called her dad when the kids were around. He'd told the great grandkids, Emma and Will, to call him Big G, but Will called him Biggie and Emma had settled on Chandler, his given name. He blinked the exact same way every time she did it, a rapid one, two, three.

"At the drive-in," Nina said.

Normally that would have rolled right off Mrs. Plansky, even amused her, but she wasn't feeling normal. Maybe Nina saw something on her face.

"This was after word came that you were okay, Mom," she said.

"What's playing?" said Mrs. Plansky.

For a moment, Nina didn't get it, but Hamish laughed immediately, a delighted laugh, quite boyish. The look he gave Mrs. Plansky right then was very nice to see.

"I can't wait to find out," he said.

Hamish got busy in the kitchen, lovely smells soon in the air. Mrs. Plansky went into her bedroom to change. She hung her tropical blues in the closet. Not hers, of course, but was there some way to keep them? Even wear them on occasion? That idea, wearing them, was probably ridiculous. She would happily settle for keeping them, if only for a while, their presence in the closet like an ace in the hole.

As for her bra and panties, she tossed them in the wastebasket, then lay down for a brief rest before dinner. After a minute or so, she got up, transferred the bra and panties to the laundry basket, and lay down again, resuming her brief rest.

*   *   *

When Mrs. Plansky woke up, her room was full of early morning light and she was lying in a heavenly twisted K. Heaven was for when you were dead. She bounced out of bed—at least in her mind, the actual movement protracted, graceless, and not without hip discomfort, not just in the new hip but in both. That was new, most likely a product of her imagination, maybe brought on by hunger. She was starving! And what she craved was a baloney sandwich on Mrs. Nottage's homemade bread. Even two of them.

She took a shower, scrubbing off any remains of Jack O' Hearts Cay, towel dried her hair, and brushed it straight back still damp, then got dressed—calf-length pearl-colored capris and a tee shirt, the color almost indistinguishable from tropical blue—and went out to the patio.

Nina was sitting at the table, an avocado-green cream smeared all over her face and neck, busy on her phone. She looked up and smiled, her teeth like a flash of light in all that green. "Morning, Mom! It was a double feature—*Stagecoach* and *Red River.*"

Mrs. Plansky laughed. "Is he up yet? Or . . . or should I say they?"

"He, and no, not up yet." Nina poured coffee for the two of them. "Hamish has gone for his run—five miles every day, without fail. And guess what he can bench press?"

"Three hundred pounds."

Nina's eyes—the most beautiful dark eyes she'd ever seen—opened wide. "Mom! How did you know?"

Mrs. Plansky shrugged.

"You're such a jock, Mom. But before he left he checked on your friend."

"My friend?"

"Val, isn't it?"

"Yes. How did he do that?"

"Hamish has buddies at UF Health. He said to tell you that she's still in a coma but stable. There's no prognosis yet but he's satisfied with the care she's getting. Also—" Nina took a slip of paper from the pocket of her robe—"here's someone you can text for updates, a neurologist who's working on the case."

Mrs. Plansky read the name, folded the paper carefully, and slipped it in her pocket. "This is so thoughtful."

They exchanged a glance, mother and green-faced daughter, the connection deep and basically healthy.

"I can't believe my luck, Mom."

"Does he play the bagpipes?"

"Yes."

"No one's perfect," said Mrs. Plansky.

Nina laughed. Also there were tears in her eyes. "All those other men, Mom—what did you think of them? Honestly?"

This was a rabbit hole Mrs. Plansky had no intention of entering. Was it Emerson who said the unexamined life was not worth living? Or Thoreau? No matter. But whoever it was, he'd meant your own life, not rooting around in the lives of others.

"That's a head-scratcher," she said.

"You got that right. Here's what I'm just realizing. I sold myself on all of them, every single one. You never sold yourself on Dad, did you?"

"You know the answer to that."

"I do. And not him on you, either. Not for one second."

Mrs. Plansky showed no reaction. The only selling had come at the end. She'd sold herself on the idea that one of the treatments would work and normal life would resume. And he'd done the same, at least in the beginning stages of the disease, although he'd given up eventually. Who wouldn't, in a similar situation? Well, maybe her, but what did that say?

"I miss him," Nina said. "You must miss him terribly."

Mrs. Plansky, dry-eyed, nodded a curt nod. This was no time for any sort of group cry. She had an agenda to get to, even if the bullet points on it were unclear.

"Has Jack been in touch?" she said.

"No. We were wondering about that. Hamish's guess is that Jack hasn't heard. Apparently the story was only on local news and they didn't have your name."

"Have you spoken to him lately?"

Nina shook her head. "But I've been calling. His voicemail's full. What about trying him at work?"

A brilliant idea. Why hadn't she thought of it? "Do you have the number?"

"No."

"What's the name of that tennis center?"

Neither of them knew.

"But it must be in my phone somewhere," Mrs. Plansky said, remembering, half a beat too late, God help her, all about her phone. "Or in an email." She rose.

"Wait, Mom. You missed dinner. Here's some leftover dessert. It makes a nice breakfast." Nina handed her a plate.

"What is it?"

"Miguelitos. Well, a variant, I think, that Hamish came up with. He can be quite creative in the kitchen. And, um."

Mrs. Plansky took the Miguelitos—which turned out to be a pair of finely made puff pastries stuffed with something that smelled of cream and dark chocolate, with a hint of blackberry—and sat at her desk, laptop open. Scrolling through her emails, she tried one of the Miguelitos. Oh, boy. Simple and complex at the same time, not too sweet, surprisingly tangy, and then just sweet enough. Hamish! Creative in the kitchen, and Nina had been about to move onto other rooms as well, but left all that unsaid, as she wouldn't have done for a friend. No matter how much you loved your kids, they were never really friends.

Meanwhile she hadn't come across the tennis center in Scottsdale and had polished off the first Miguelito. She bit into the second. Surprise! Hamish had substituted a different berry, the same color as the blackberry but smaller and smooth skinned. Acai, perhaps?

She didn't know. But it changed everything, like a completely new experience. That was enough to convince Mrs. Plansky that Nina wasn't selling herself on Hamish. He was the real deal. Picasso, a real deal if ever there was, had said, "I sell myself nothing." Mrs. Plansky knew that because she'd once had to give a talk on marketing and sales at a kitchen designer convention. Marketing was in her swing zone, but she had no feel for sales. The Picasso quote gave her a theme and no one walked out on her, and if they did it was unobtrusive. As for the age difference, there was something sensible, even sweet, about an older woman and a younger man, very much not the case with the reverse, at least to her way of thinking.

She chewed thoughtfully on the second Miguelito, her mind actually blank. And then, as though a thoughtful demeanor could induce thought, she remembered you could narrow this sort of email search, in this case simply by typing Jack in that little box.

Voilà! Or viola, as Tee-Tee liked to say. Emails from Jack appeared, not many. She looked at the most recent, many months old, with a subject line that read: Cold Storage Follow-up.

Hey, Mom, thanks for at least "giving an ear" to the cold storage proposal. I know $750K is not peanuts but my partners will draft an agreement guaranteeing payback dates of your choosing and they will—we will—be generous re interest rate terms. Plans are to be in Tampa for meeting suppliers next month and hope we can swing by later. Ray and Rudy are excited to meet you! Love, Jack.

Rudy?

Reading the email had triggered an uneasiness in Mrs. Plansky's mind from the beginning but when she got to that name—Rudy!— her heart started beating much too fast, not pounding, much too light for that. And then came—she hardly knew what to call it—a chest pain? She'd never had a chest pain in her life. She rose at once, pushing herself up from her desk, pushing away that chest pain, rendering it imaginary. And it worked, although it made her dizzy.

She sat back down, perhaps a little abruptly, and composed herself. Then she read the email again, word by word, seeing how the meaning had changed from when she'd first received it to today.

Mrs. Plansky had forgotten all but the bare bones of this proposal, first broached around the time of her Romanian problems. Jack had gotten involved with a couple of entrepreneurs from Scottsdale—or was it Mesa?—Arizona who believed cold storage was the next big thing and had a plan to open a whole chain of cold storage places, with Jack in the role of . . . Mrs. Plansky hadn't known the answer to that one. Before she'd had to figure out how to couch her "no" the two entrepreneurs got indicted on federal charges regarding some earlier scheme, her information on the indictment not in the emails, so Jack must have told her that over the phone.

But: Rudy!

Not an uncommon name, but . . . Her mind drifted back to her Rudy and his first appearance, when he'd stepped out from behind a copper vat at Drop Shot Brewing, looking like a clean-cut golfer, not the weekend duffer model but the modern-day fit touring pro. She'd been a bit shifty during the introduction, when "Loretta" on its own hadn't done the job so she'd added "Banning." How clever she'd thought at the time, a rather short time, concluding with her discovery of her automobile registration in the wrong place, with PLANSKY in block letters in the surname box. But had there been some tit-for-tat shiftiness on his part, too? Hadn't Rudy offered "Mesa" as his last name? Maybe the first thing that came to his mind under pressure? Not proof. She had no proof of anything! But what if Jack's Rudy and her Rudy were one and the same? Mrs. Plansky tried to shape all that into some narrative and ended up with nothing except a bad feeling.

She went back to Jack's emails, a dozen or so in all. One of the earliest, from over two years ago, had "Look who dropped by today!" in the subject line, with a photo attached. In the photo Jack and Martina Navratilova stood side by side, with big smiles on their faces. In fact, Martina looked like she was laughing at something Jack had just said. Mrs. Plansky had no memory of having seen this photo before. How odd, especially since she was a big admirer of Martina and the thought of Jack amusing her would have been very pleasant and was pleasant now. Then she checked the date: two days before Norm's death. That explained it. She hadn't been herself. She still wasn't really, not back to being her old self. Instead she was some new self, formed from Lorettan clay and remolded.

But enough of that! What mattered now about the photo wasn't Jack or Martina, but the sign to Martina's left. It was shaped like an upright person-sized tennis racket and had an oval sign where the strings would have been: DESERT RANCH TENNIS CENTER.

A minute later Mrs. Plansky was calling the number on her burner phone.

"Desert Ranch Tennis. How can I help you?"

"May I speak to Jack Plansky?"

Silence. And then, "Jack Plansky?"

"I believe he's the director."

"Mr. Plansky is no longer with us. Can I connect you to someone else?"

"Do you know how I can get in touch with him?"

"Excuse me?"

"Some forwarding address. Or a number. For Jack, I mean. Jack Plansky."

"Mr. Plansky didn't bo—We have no information on any of that. Is there anything else I can help you with?"

Mrs. Plansky was about to say, "No, thank you," and her mouth opened to say just that, but what came out was, "Is Lizette Dinardo around?"

"Lizette? Let me check."

TWENTY-THREE

While Mrs. Plansky waited, the burner phone clutched much too tightly in her hand, she had two thoughts. Thought one: whatever this is I'm not cut out for it. Thought two was about Basil. Val had told her he could see the bottom of the ocean like the water wasn't even there. That was what she needed now, to see clearly down into some sort of human deeps. Did she have it in her? Mrs. Plansky banished that question at once. Doubts about this or that in the objective world were fine, but self-doubt was paralyzing. No one had taught her that. She just knew, maybe from all the way back in childhood.

Through the wall came the sound of her dad groaning as he got out of bed. That wasn't a new thing coming in old age. He'd always done it, at least since she'd known him.

The woman from Desert Ranch got back on the line. "Lizette's not here yet. Her court's at eleven. Any message?"

"Not just now, thanks," said Mrs. Plansky, hanging up.

Not just now? What had she meant by that? Was the speaking part of her brain ahead of her, making plans on its own?

She turned back to her laptop, found a map of the Bahamas, zoomed in on the Jarndyce Cays, and zoomed in some more, scrolling down from Jack O' Hearts to No-Name, to Lady, trying to make these images click into place with the real living and breathing thing. Seen from above, in this map-style view, the shape of Lady Cay was—

"What the hell?" her dad called from somewhere in the condo. Mrs. Plansky closed the laptop.

MRS. PLANSKY GOES ROGUE 199

She found him in the kitchen, standing in front of the open fridge, his back to her. He wore his terry robe from the Gritti Palace, now somewhat threadbare, and tassel loafers, and also had his cane, a sign he was doing well. He was using it to poke around in the vegetable drawer.

"Dad?"

"It's a simple thing," he said. "How come there's always problems with the simplest thing?"

"What's the problem, Dad?"

"I told you already. I'm blue in the face."

She put her hand on his back, turned him gently away from the fridge. A red pepper got loose and rolled across the floor. He waved the cane at it, trying to do who-knew-what but almost hitting her leg. Mrs. Plansky took the cane, got him seated at the table, put the pepper back in the fridge, closed the door.

"How about some breakfast?" she said.

He pounded his fist on the table. "That's the whole goddam issue!"

Mrs. Plansky was not in the mood for this. There was only one thing to do. She pretended she was in the mood. The right mood came settling in.

"Can you just put it in a few words?" she said.

"I can put it in one word! Marmalade!"

"Dad? Didn't I tell you it was in the right-hand cupboard, top shelf?"

He twisted around and glared at her. "And didn't I tell you it's the wrong kind? I need the kind with the royal crest."

Mrs. Plansky went to the cupboard and found the marmalade. The royal crest was right there.

"Look, Dad." She took the marmalade to the table, pointed to the crest, read it aloud. "Royal warrant by appointment to His Majesty the King."

There was a silence. "I mean the one with the queen," he said.

But not aggressively. The fight had gone out of him. Mrs. Plansky even tried a little joke. "You wouldn't want to hurt the king's feelings, would you, Dad?"

He nodded like that made sense.

Not long after that, he was chowing down on bacon and poached eggs on toasted English muffins thickly spread with marmalade.

"A feast fit for a king, huh, Dad?" She was unable to restrain herself.

He chewed silently for a few moments, like he was thinking that over. But it turned out he wasn't. "What does *guapo* mean?" he said.

"Did Clara call you that?"

"Uh-huh. Guapo. Muy guapo."

"It means *handsome.*"

"It's not *bird poop*?"

"That's *guano. Guapo* is *handsome. Muy* is *very.* So—*very handsome.*"

He smiled, a simple, uncomplicated, happy smile. Mrs. Plansky pulled up a chair.

"Jack is also muy guapo. There's some physical resemblance."

"Between me and him?"

"I've always thought so."

He nodded. "That can't be bad."

"No, it can't," said Mrs. Plansky. "We need to talk about him."

"Who?"

"Jack," she said.

"What about him?"

"You tell me." She poured herself a cup of coffee, watching him over the rim as she sipped.

"No milk and sugar?" he said.

"You know that, Dad. We've been through it."

"Let's go through it again."

"I like my coffee black."

"But why? That's the heart of the matter. I like my coffee with milk and sugar. What makes you so different?"

A reprehensible something in her makeup wanted to kick him under the table. Instead she said, "I'll have to think about it. But right now can you tell me the story of Jack, Kev Dinardo, and you?"

"What story is that?"

"Your relationship. Take it from the top."

"The top," he said, poking the yolk of a poached egg with his fork, "is that the same as the beginning?"

"Sure. The beginning will be fine."

"We talk business from time to time."

"You and Jack or you and Kev?"

"Me and Kev? What sense would that make? He's not my grandson."

"But you know him?"

He pointed at her with a strip of bacon. He preferred his bacon extra-crisp, so this strip didn't go all floppy but stayed stiff and accusatory. "I know of him. It's not the same."

"You're right. So did you hear about him from Jack?"

He got a crafty smile on his face. Was there something called the circle of love, with everyone you loved inside it? Norm was dead center in hers, and Jack and Nina orbited close by, Emma and Will not too far beyond that, but there were others, like Tee-Tee, long gone, and her own mother, even longer gone. Her dad was inside the circle, too, out where the comets roam, but still within, barely. Mrs. Plansky's heart couldn't keep itself from including him.

He lowered the bacon strip and said, "Yes and no."

"What does that mean, Dad?"

"Ha! Simple minds need simple answers."

She let that go by and waited.

"Here's the deal," her dad said. "I've got a lot of experience in the corporate world. Who wouldn't want to pick my brain?"

"Jack got in touch for advice on the corporate world?"

"Many times."

"Like how many?"

He thought. "Three. But—I got in touch with him, too. Make it six all together."

"And one of those calls was about Kev Dinardo?"

"More than one, less than six. So between two and five if you're doing the math. My money's on three."

"How about we start with the first call about Jack?"

He gazed at her. "You're deep."

"Excuse me?"

He bit off half the bacon strip, chewing while he talked. "That's what your mother said, when you were this high. 'Loretta's deep, Chan. She's going to do big things.'"

Mrs. Plansky was wholly unready for that. It stunned her. Why was she just learning it now? Why did she have to learn it all, to find out at this late date that she'd failed her poor mom? Because she had not done big things. She had just . . . lived.

"And," her dad went on, still chewing, "she was right! Hit the target dead center!"

"What are you talking about?"

"Huh? The toaster knife, of course. Dammit, Loretta, try to keep up. The Plansky Toaster Knife. Did you ever consider naming it the Banning Toaster Knife, by the way?"

"No."

"Wasn't it your idea?"

"It was a joint idea, Norm and me."

"But the inspiration! The lightning strike! Like Einstein—how about I split the atom and drop that bejeezus bomb? Wasn't that you?"

She had no idea what to say. She went with, "My name was Loretta Plansky by then."

He glared at her, but just for a split second. "My point is the toaster knife is deep."

"You think so?"

"Hell, yeah. How many millions did you make off it?"

"We did all right."

"But how many? Just to the nearest million. I won't tell."

Mrs. Plansky knew for sure he'd tell Clara the moment he saw her, but she wouldn't have told him anyway. She didn't even know the number. Well, that was a lie.

"I'm curious, that's all," he said. "I don't want your money."

Maybe so, but he had the use of it anyway. Her dad had no money of his own. He didn't even get social security, on account of some long-ago tax razzle-dazzle. His long stay at Arcadia Gardens, his living expenses for years before that, all paid for by her. Of course she didn't mention any of that. She'd done it, and was still doing it, willingly. At that moment she realized there might be Cuban musicians—perhaps even dancers as well—at the wedding, and factored that in.

"Curious to see," he said, "whether Jack was right."

"About what?"

"Huh? About revenue from the toaster knife. What we've just been discussing, for cryin' out loud. His guess was seven mill."

"That's ridiculous. How did the subject even come up?"

He dabbed at the corners of his mouth with his napkin, not how a normal person would, but more like an actor making a show of it. "You've got to remember the psychology, Loretta. Everything starts with—" He paused, folded his napkin carefully and placed it on the table. "With psicologia."

For God's sake. The double features at the drive-in and the discussions with Clara before, during, and after, were changing him right before her eyes. Was he sliding very late in life into the role of a Cuban intellectual? Would she be burying him in a beret? A nasty thought, which she suppressed at once.

"Go on, Dad," she said.

"The psicologia of Jack. That's what I'm talking about. Men have inner . . . what would you call it? Like John Wayne in *Red River*. He wants to drive those cattle up the Old Chisholm Trail. That's his . . . oh, hell, you know."

"Motivation?"

"Yeah, motivation. What's the motivation of a loser?"

"You're saying Jack is a loser?"

He looked alarmed. Maybe her tone had gotten away from her. "Not in so many words," he said. "But you said yourself that three nineteen was nowhere."

Three nineteen? That was Jack's high water ranking in the tennis world, which, yes, she had mentioned recently but he hadn't been following that conversation at all, had been at his most obtuse—this involuntary obtuseness that had its grip on him—and now he was throwing the exact number out there, like some data master?

"That doesn't make him a loser," she said.

"Maybe not in your world."

"What world is that?"

"The woman's—" He stopped himself, got a clever look on his face, but wasn't clever enough to hide it. "A mother's world. How's that?"

She made sure to lower her voice, all the way down to blandness. "You're out of your lane, Dad."

He burped. "It happens," he said. "What's your point?"

"My point is that Jack's not a loser. Running a big tennis program—" She cut herself off and started over. "Teaching tennis doesn't make you a loser. The opposite."

"Yeah? Then how come you didn't do it?"

There was something wrong with him and always had been. That was the plain truth. It changed nothing now. She searched for the best way to trick him out of this and get him back on track.

"I'm not good enough at tennis to teach. Not even close."

"Gotcha," he said.

"But Jack is. Anyone would be lucky to learn from him."

"Not the way he sees it. That's why he consults me on business." He waved his finger at her. "The business of America is business, Loretta. Not tennis."

Mrs. Plansky took a deep breath.

"Cold storage—now that's business. All fell apart. Goddam government. Frustrating for the kid but give him credit. He kept digging. Gotta dig in the business world, gotta do your homework, gotta reach out, build a network. That's what I told him."

"You're part of Jack's network?"

"Happy to help. That's me. Yours truly. So when he called and asked me to check out that fella I said, 'no problemo, chico.' Well, not the 'chico' part. I only knew 'no problemo' at the time. Now I'm pretty much fluent."

Mrs. Plansky felt an urge to sweep the table clean, send the bacon, poached eggs, toasted muffins, coffee, silverware, all of it, flying through the air. "What fella are you talking about?"

"Kev Dinardo, of course. Try to keep up."

"You're saying that Jack first called you about Kev—called you from Arizona—and not the other way around?"

"Why not? I knew of the gentleman, of course, from your tennis escapades and such, but I didn't have much in the way of hard info. Business runs on hard info." All at once he looked anxious. "Or did that come later?"

"Did what come later, Dad?"

Mrs. Plansky waited. She took a sip of coffee, mostly just to see if she could do it without shaking, too late realizing—from the overpowering sweetness and milkiness—that she'd drunk from her father's cup. She put it down, pushed it away. He was concentrating on cutting off a mouthful of egg and muffin and hadn't noticed any of this.

"Dad? How did Jack know anything about Kev Dinardo?"

"Hells bells! He didn't. That's why he reached out. Reached out to me."

"But how had he heard about him in the first place? Where had he gotten the name?"

"Oh, that." Her dad chewed for what seemed like forever, then swallowed and got back to work with knife and fork.

"Dad?"

"Isn't it obvious? You meet a lot of well-off people in a job like his. Maybe you don't know this but our country—the US of A—is much smaller than it looks on the map."

"You're saying he met someone at the tennis center who . . ." She was having trouble keeping this straight, as though she was wandering around in his mind.

He shoved a big bite in his mouth and talked around it. "Exactly what I'm saying. This was back when I was still in that shithole."

"Arcadia Gardens?"

"What else?"

Arcadia Gardens, forty-five minutes away and one of the top-rated assisted livings in the state, had cost her—well, churlish to think this way. And there was no need for gratitude on his part or anything like that. But Arcadia Gardens was not a shithole. She considered making the point aloud, just for the record, and let it go.

"So Jack called you while you were still at Arcadia Gardens?"

"What I'm saying. He had a name for me to check out."

"Kev Dinardo?"

"That's the point, for chrissake. He heard of this guy—a mover and shaker, thumb in all sorts of pies—and wanted me to do some digging."

"But how, Dad? Did you know Kev? Had you even met him?"

"Hell, no. Aren't you listening? I knew someone who knew him. It's simple stuff."

"Someone at Arcadia Gardens?"

"Bingo!"

"Who, Dad?"

He swallowed the rest of his mouthful, leaned forward, and in a low voice, as though to avoid being overheard, said, "Polly."

"Polly? You mean the Polly that you—"

"Polly. I mean Polly."

"But weren't there two Pollys? Wasn't that part of all the trouble?"

"I don't remember any trouble. I'm trying to help you, Loretta, but you don't make it easy. You want to know about this Dinardo fellow?"

"Yes."

"And here I am telling you that Polly knows him. A source! Follow me so far?"

Mrs. Plansky didn't trust her voice not to release some of what she was feeling inside. She just nodded.

"Then there you go! We're on the same page." He raised his hand, palm facing her. It took her a few seconds to realize he wanted to high-five. She couldn't make herself do it.

"Who's the person who told Jack about Polly?" she said.

He slowly lowered his hand and slowly repeated the question to himself. Then his eyes brightened. "A gal from the tennis club! Where he teaches! Jack was teaching her tennis! It all makes sense!"

"And how does she know Polly?"

"The gal? How does the gal in Arizona know Polly?"

"Yes."

"Why, they're sisters, of course. Didn't I mention that already?"

Mrs. Plansky, although sitting down, felt dizzy. That was a first. She took a deep breath and said, "Maybe I missed it. What's her name?"

"Polly."

"I meant Polly's sister," Mrs. Plansky said, just about 100 percent sure of the answer.

"Can't help you there," her dad said.

"Lizette?"

His face screwed up in thought. At the same time, he began slicing off another forkful of his poached egg on toast. But he started having trouble with that. She took his knife and fork, gently and unobtrusively, and did it for him, handing back the silverware. The dizziness faded away.

"Thanks, Dad."

"For what?" he said, stabbing the piece she'd cut him.

Mrs. Plansky was on her way to the door, headed out to her car and the drive down to Arcadia Gardens when the landline phone rang. She picked up.

"Hello?"

"Loretta?"

A man. She recognized his voice but couldn't place it.

"Mitch, here," he said, and her hand, a bit ahead of her, tightened its grip on the phone. "We met awhile back. Insurance adjuster. Ring a bell?"

At first, she was too frightened—well, not frightened, more like caught off guard, no need to for all the emotion—to react. Then she realized that silence might be a good thing right now, a sort of weapon.

"Hello? Ma'am?"

She counted silently to ten. Actually only to seven, unable to bear the suspense she herself was creating. Then she said, "Mitch or Mr. Mitch?"

A pause followed by, "Ha!" But there was no amusement in it.

"Or neither," she said.

"It's Mitch," he said.

"Who do you work for, Mitch?" She put some spin on that "Mitch."

"I told you, ma'am. I'm an insurance adjuster."

"Employed by what company?"

"A reputable one. But this isn't about insurance. I'm calling on behalf of the homeowner, Mr. Dinardo. He's traveling and the cell service is just about nonexistent, but in making my report I happened to mention that you'd come calling. Mr. Dinardo wants me to tell you in the nicest way possible that you may have imagined feelings in him that frankly just aren't there, I'm sorry to say. He may not be back stateside for some time and he wants you to, well, feel free to get on with the rest of your life."

Had there been a chair in reach, Mrs. Plansky would have sat herself down. Instead she leaned against the wall, her legs unwilling to give full support.

"Ma'am? Did you get all that?"

She said the first thing that came into her head. "Where are you?"

"In my car," Mitch said. "But that's not relevant."

"Where is Kev?"

"See, that's not the mind-set he's looking for. Maybe you just need some time. To deal with the emotions and such."

Had she heard the rustle of paper, like Mitch had some sort of cheat sheet in hand? If so, what did that mean?

"Ma'am?"

"Yes?"

"I hope you got the message."

Click.

TWENTY-FOUR

Someone knocked on the front door. Mrs. Plansky opened it, expecting just about anything.

It was Hamish. The sun shone on his already sunny face. Behind him in the parking lot a rideshare car was idling, the driver staring at his phone.

"Good morning, Loretta! It looks like you slept well, I'm happy to see."

Had anyone ever said that to her? Not in so many words, not even Norm.

"Why, thank you," she said.

"I'm just swinging by to pick up Nina. Our flight's in a couple of hours. It's been a real pleasure to meet you. And I hope Val makes a quick recovery. I checked with my buddy over there. She was still stable at eight a.m., basically unchanged. Oh, and I picked this up, far from the latest model but maybe good enough for now." He produced a smart phone still in its box with what she took to be her new number written on the front in a clear hand, maybe the clearest she'd ever seen, outside of Miss Terrance's. *"Nina4me is the password. Password required to download a few apps, but of course you can change it to whatever you want."*

Mrs. Plansky, somewhat paralyzed by him, was a little slow to take the phone. She fought off an insane desire to squeeze his shoulder, just to make sure he was real. A man like this could do anything. She was thinking of dumping her whole problem—Kev,

Jack, all rest—on him, when she heard Nina coming down the hall, wheeling a carry-on.

Mrs. Plansky took the phone. "So thoughtful, Hamish. How much do I owe you?"

"Oh, let's settle up in future."

"But—"

Nina appeared. Her face lit up at the sight of him and his face lit up at the sight of her. A minute later they were gone. Mrs. Plansky watched the rideshare car until it was out of sight, and even after that didn't turn away for a minute or two. The concept of a heaven from which you could keep an eye on those you loved after you were gone had never been more appealing.

Mrs. Plansky drove into town, headed for the last traffic light, where Main Street split in two, right leading to the interstate and left to the state highway and Arcadia Gardens. She missed the green and sat waiting. The last building on her side was the Ponte d'Oro police station, a whitewashed stucco affair that from the outside could have been a home goods outlet except for the lack of picture windows. There was nothing intimidating or even official about it. Mrs. Plansky hit the turn signal and rolled into the parking lot.

She sat there for a bit, trying to rehearse her presentation and getting nowhere. Why? Because she had no script, that was why! Think, Loretta! She cudgeled her brain until it didn't want to be cudgeled for one more second and then got out of the car, entered the police station, and walked in a businesslike way to the front counter.

"Help you, ma'am?" said the uniformed duty officer, a tired-looking middle-aged man with one of those overgrown mustaches that hid his mouth and muffled his speech—an acoustic baffle that wasn't a good look in Mrs. Plansky's opinion, but commenting negatively about a person's appearance, even to herself, went against the grain.

She put a hand on the shoulder strap of her bag, ready to show ID if called on. "I want to report a missing person."

He gazed at her. Perhaps she misread the expression in his eyes, but she couldn't help thinking he'd been planning an easy, frictionless day, now under threat.

"Well, two," she added.

"Two missing persons?" he said.

"I believe so. Is there someone I can talk to? A detective, perhaps?"

He held out his hand. "ID."

She knew it, was all set.

He examined her license. "Loretta Plansky?"

"Correct."

"Preferred honorific?"

For a moment she had no idea what the hell he was talking about. When it hit her she smothered the temptation, maybe marmalade induced, to go with Your Royal Majesty and said, "Mrs."

He touched some button, not in view, and spoke into a mic, also not in view. "A Mrs. Plansky to see you. S-8."

A door opened in the background and a man who might have been the younger brother of the duty officer stuck his head out and waved her over. The duty officer opened a narrow door in the counter front and Mrs. Plansky went through.

"Mrs. Plansky?" said the younger man.

"Correct. Loretta Plansky."

"Detective Leffers," he said, his mustache not quite as overgrown as the duty officer's, making him easier to understand. "C'mon in; take a seat."

They sat in Detective Leffers's office, Mrs. Plansky on one side of the gray metal desk and Detective Leffers on the other. On the desk itself was a closed laptop, a phone, and nail clippers. On the walls hung framed photos, all having something to do with Gators football. Detective Leffers wore powder-blue slacks, a short-sleeve white shirt with black-and-brown stripes, and a green tie.

He took a yellow pad and pen from a drawer and got set in writing position. "So who's missing?"

"S-8 is for missing persons?" Mrs. Plansky said.

"Yes, ma'am." He shot her a quick second look.

"Kev Dinardo is the missing person."

"Can you spell that?"

She spelled the name. Detective Leffers wrote it down.

"His relationship to you?"

A tricky one. "We're tennis partners."

His pen began to move, then stopped. "Like operating a club or . . . ?"

"We're players. A team. A doubles team. Mixed."

"Mixed," he said.

"In doubles. When men and women play together."

He wrote something down, scratched it out, tried again.

"But friends as well."

He looked up. "Friends?"

Was this the right moment to go into that kiss on the dock, timing, unexpectedness, degree of passion, nuances of? It was not, and the right moment might never come along.

"We see each other socially. Not just on the court. But mostly on the court."

"The tennis court?"

She nodded. "At New Sunshine Golf and Tennis."

"The place with the big flamboyant tree out front?"

"That's Old Sunshine," she said. "New Sunshine has the arched bridge with the wishing well."

He wrote. Mrs. Plansky was good at reading upside down, a gift that had served her well in business once or twice. Detective Leffers was writing "wishing well." Mrs. Plansky was anxious to get to Arcadia Gardens. She searched her mind for ways to speed this up.

"How long has it been since you had contact with . . ." Detective Leffers checked his notes. ". . . Mr. Dinardo?"

She began counting on her fingers, backward to the kiss on the dock. But whatever number that was going to be wasn't necessarily right. What if Mitch's message from Kev was authentic? "Does hearing from him through a third party count?"

Detective Leffers put down his pen. The pinky finger on his writing hand was badly misshapen, sticking out sideways. Mrs. Plansky made a mental leap: he'd played for the Gators.

"Third party?" he said.

She made another mental leap. Mitch was a liar from start to finish. In fact, an enemy. She had enemies. Did Kev have enemies, too? Or was he the enemy? She just couldn't believe that, not emotionally. But rationally? Didn't it have to be on the table? The AC in Detective Leffers's office was feeble and the day was already heating up, but Mrs. Plansky felt suddenly cold.

"Forget that part," she said. "At least for now. It's possible Kev has enemies."

"Like who?"

"I don't know."

"Then what makes you say he has enemies?"

"Because they blew up his boat."

"When was this?"

"The last time I saw him. Do you have access to the Fire Department . . . log, is it? Records? Or the harbormaster's? You can look it up."

Detective Leffers looked it up, opening his laptop, tapping at the keys. His eyes moved, left to right, left to right—actually the opposite from her angle. She was on the point of finding some meaning in that, when he looked it up.

"Lightning strike. That's what it says here. Lightning strike."

She shook her head. "I heard an explosion just before. I'm almost close to sure."

"How close, ma'am?"

"How close? What do you—?"

"As a percentage, one hundred being the voice of God himself."

Mrs. Plansky realized she'd misjudged him. He was much smarter than his self-presentation. Hadn't she made the same mistake with someone else, and very recently? She told herself to sharpen up.

"Eighty percent," she said.

"That's a B minus where I come from."

"Agreed. But it goes up to a straight A in context."

"What context is that?"

"Well, there's a lot, and that's without even getting to the second S-8."

"Second S-8?"

"Wasn't that the missing person code?"

"Are you saying someone else is missing, too?"

"My son, Jack. Part of the context, but not as relevant to the explosion question as the goings-on at Kev's house. Ninety-two Seaside Way. Where the boat was docked. It's over by—"

"I know the house."

"You do? Has there been trouble before?"

He shook his head. "Knowing the town's my job."

"Ah." He was going to be very helpful, if only she could override some disconnection between them, its nature still unclear. She resolved to be totally honest with him. As totally honest as possible. "I have a confession to make."

He opened a desk drawer, took out a card, handed it to her, and then picked up his pen.

Mrs. Plansky checked the card. The heading: *Miranda Warning.* And then: *1. You have the right to remain silent. 2. Anything you say can and will . . ."*

"Oh, no," she said. "No, no, no, not that kind of confession. It's just that I broke in—not how to put it, the truth's just that I figured out the code. The digital code. There's no lock and key. Well, there is a lock of course but it's . . . keyless! That's what it is. But this isn't relevant, detective, so no need to write." He kept writing. "The point is everything was completely altered. I'm talking about the second time."

"The second time?" He stopped writing.

"The second time I broke in. Not broke in. Just . . . let myself in. As before."

He gazed at her. "How about we have ourselves a quick site visit?"

Detective Leffers rose and donned a suit jacket, powder blue like his slacks but not as faded. Because—Mrs. Plansky doing a little detective work of her own—the pants went to the cleaners more often than the jacket. She found herself liking his style.

They drove to 92 Seaside Way in two cars, Mrs. Plansky leading and Detective Leffers following in an unmarked sedan. No one was parked out front and dead palm leaves lay here and there on the pavers.

The house was quiet. They walked up to the door.

"Should I knock?" Mrs. Plansky said.

Detective Leffers made a be-my-guest gesture. Mrs. Plansky knocked on the door, not her usual polite knock but forceful, commanding, even menacing. She had the law on her side. But no one came to the door, no one called from within, and the silence didn't turn wary, just continued as regular no-one-home silence. Mrs. Plansky tried again, but just for the pleasure of hearing that militant knock.

"Okeydoke," said Detective Lefferts.

"Want to me to open up?"

"Why not?"

An odd question. She could think of some reasons herself, like it was against the law, for example. But now, for the first time in her life, she was the law! Or at least had the law by her side.

"It's 40–love," she said.

"Excuse me?"

"That's a tennis term. But it's also a beer—an IPA, the hazy kind—from his brewery. That's in Macdee. Familiar with Macdee?"

"No."

"Maybe we can get to that later. I'm just explaining why it makes perfect sense. Otherwise I'd never have been able to guess it."

"40-love is the key code?"

"Exactly! But in numeric form. Well, the '40' part is already numeric, but 'Love' has to be put in numbers, depending on where the letters are in the alphabet." She tried to remember the numbers but quickly realized she'd have to figure them out all over again. "Bear with me," she said, reaching for pen and paper.

"Four zero one two one five two two five," said Detective Leffers.

She turned to him, hoping this was not literally a jaw-dropping moment on her part, but afraid it was. He gestured toward the touch pad with his chin, a chin which she noticed for the first time, a much stronger chin than she might have imagined, her impression so skewed by that mustache. She pressed 4-0-1 on the touch pad and paused. He dictated the rest in a measured way. The light flashed red.

"Hmm," she said.

She tried again, this time with Detective Leffers dictating the whole thing, but now she was nervous and messed up twice before getting it right.

"It should be green," she said.

Red.

Detective Leffers stepped in and entered the code himself.

Red.

He gazed at her. She met his gaze.

"Someone must have changed it," she said.

"Uh-huh."

"Because it should be green. It was green the last time."

But Detective Leffers had already moved away, was walking under the house and onto the dock. Mrs. Plansky followed. He looked out to sea. She stood off to the side, a little behind him. A silence descended on them, grew oppressive, at least to her.

"The boat was tied up right there, with the bow facing south," she said. "I gave Kev—Mr. Dinardo—a lift back from the club because it was raining and he was on his bike. Also there was thunder, coming closer. We were standing where I am now when there was a boom of thunder. And just before that was a flash."

"Which you don't believe was lightning?"

"Correct. I shouldn't have said 'thunder.' A boom, that's all. And a flash. But not a lightning type flash. This one was redder."

"And then what?"

"The boat went up in flames. We tried to put it out—" She pointed to the hose, coiled on the dock. "—but it was no use." In fact, she was the one who'd worked the hose. What had Kev done? He'd watched that fire burn, his eyes unreadable, although maybe not completely. Hadn't they been heating up?

"After that?"

After that had come the kiss, this issue arising again. Mrs. Plansky sensed that the investigation was at a delicate stage, could be derailed by the sudden introduction of a dramatic but most likely immaterial fact.

"Well, the fire department arrived. And a patrol from the harbormaster. But by that time the boat had burned its lines, drifted off, and sunk. A Bertram 50S." She added that hard fact in case he was taking this down, which he was not.

"Did they salvage it?" he said.

"Yes."

"When?"

"I'm not exactly sure."

"That's all right." He took out his phone, walked to the other end of the dock, and made a call. Mrs. Plansky heard him talking but couldn't make out the words. She went to the edge of the dock and stared into the water. A fish rose up from underneath, almost to the surface. In fact, a hogfish, deep red with a stringy yellow dorsal fin. She remembered this hogfish, a buddy of sorts, from her snorkeling investigation, and took its appearance for a good sign.

Detective Leffers returned. The hogfish sank from sight.

"Spoke to the harbormaster himself. Salvage recovered zero evidence of any explosives. Cause was lightning strike, period. And nothing out of the ordinary was found."

He waited for her to say something, some sort of rearguard action beginning with *but* and which would turn out to be useless. Mrs. Plansky had a thought that didn't begin with *but*.

"There was one thing out of the ordinary," she said.

TWENTY-FIVE

They drove to Little Pine Lake, Mrs. Plansky leading, Detective Leffers right behind. She glanced in the rearview mirror. The detective was on his phone. She couldn't describe in words the expression on his face, but she didn't like it. It resembled how he'd looked when she'd started in on the Tee-Tee story—her dive, finding the figurine, her belief that it was pre-Columbian and valuable, the possible involvement of galleons and hurricanes—but he'd seemed less negative after she'd mentioned how she'd learned to free dive as a kid in Rhode Island. Now all she had to do to seal the deal was the "show" part of show-and-tell, and if not to quite seal it, at least to take some of the burden off her—well, no, not that. Just a little help would be fine.

"Nice place," he said, as they entered the condo and moved into the kitchen. "Me and my buddies fished this lake when we were kids, before all the development."

"Were there gators?"

"Oh, yeah."

"There just seems to be one now."

"A real big dude?"

"He looks big to me."

"That's what happens. An alpha comes along and the competition clears out."

Lucrecia had left a note on the fridge. "I dropped them off for an ice cream date. Back later."

"You live alone here?" said Detective Leffers.

Mrs. Plansky looked up from the note. She didn't like that question. How was it his business? "Any reason I shouldn't?"

"No, no, course not, sorry."

"As a matter of fact, my dad is living with me at the moment."

"Yeah? He must be pretty—" He seemed to change his mind about what was coming next. "—happy to be with family."

"Coffee?" she said.

"No, thanks."

"Wait here, if you don't mind. I'll go get her. Only be a moment."

"Her?" He smiled. "Not it?"

"You'll see."

Mrs. Plansky went into her bedroom, opened the desk drawer, and removed the padded envelope that was Tee-Tee's little home. She took the envelope into the kitchen.

"Meet Tee-Tee," she said, reaching into the envelope.

But Tee-Tee wasn't there. Mrs. Plansky felt around in the envelope, her motions increasingly frantic and there was nothing she could do about it. Meanwhile she felt Detective Leffers's eyes on her.

"I could swear . . ." She looked around the kitchen. Could she have . . . ? She had no memory of having left Tee-Tee in the kitchen. The last place she'd seen her was on her desk, not long after her meeting with Val at the gazebo overlooking the lake, and just before her second break-in, or perhaps incursion, at 92 Seaside Way, when she'd found all the mess cleaned up and everything hunky-dory. Had she put Tee-Tee somewhere else after that? Or was it simply that she'd slid Tee-Tee into the drawer without bothering with the envelope? Or left her in some other drawer? Or? Or?

"Be right back."

Mrs. Plansky hurried down the hall while doing her best not to appear hurried. She felt Detective Leffers's gaze between her shoulder blades.

Back in her bedroom she opened Tee-Tee's drawer and went through it, an easy task since there was hardly anything inside—a stapler, a box of pens, a package of Christmas cards she'd bought at a post-Christmas sale, a tangled nest of computer-type cables with no known use, at least to her. No Tee-Tee.

She went through the other drawers. She got down on the floor and peered under the desk. She pulled the desk away from the wall and checked the space back there. Then she made a general search of the whole room—the clothes closet, including the safe inside, the linen closet, the chest of drawers. She checked under the bed and even under the covers and under the pillows, like she was some dithering thing, capable of any haphazard mistake.

"Think!"

The makeup table! How obvious! It was standing in front of her face. She whipped open the drawer. On top lay the somewhat bloodied photo of Kev on board *Lizette*, his arm around that bombshell woman. Under that was the strange drawing of the triangle with the notch in one side and the *X*'s that she'd found in the mouth of the bronze fish. But no Tee-Tee.

Mrs. Plansky walked slowly back to the kitchen. Detective Leffers was looking out at the lake and just pocketing his phone. He slowly turned. She met his gaze. It wasn't easy, especially with his eyes now so guarded and distant.

"I'm afraid I can't find her. At the moment. I must have misplaced . . ."

He nodded. His expression changed. Was it now sympathetic? That should have been reassuring but it was not.

"Mrs. Plansky?" he said. "I hear you survived a plane crash the other day. Correct me if I'm wrong."

"You're not wrong."

"I did see something about it on the news but your name didn't come up."

Mrs. Plansky nodded.

"It must have been pretty damn scary."

She nodded again.

"I assume you got checked out at a hospital?"

"I'm fine."

"Did you go the hospital?"

"No. But there were medics."

"Medics?"

"On Jack O' Hearts Cay."

"That's in the Bahamas?"

"Yes."

"Don't know the place. Does it have a hospital?"

"It's just a speck on the ocean."

"Can I ask what you were doing there?"

"Well, it was about Tee-Tee, I guess you might say. The figurine. But it was mostly Val's idea."

"The pilot?"

"Correct."

"She's in a coma?"

Mrs. Plansky nodded.

Detective Leffers took a deep breath. "I played some football back in the day. So I know a bit about concussions. They can linger—take it from me—change your mind, if you see what I'm saying, get it out of whack. One other thing. They're not so easy to detect, concussions. Like by some medic out in the middle of nowhere."

"What are you saying?"

"I'm suggesting you go to the hospital and get yourself checked out."

"I don't need to be checked out! I'm perfectly fine!" Had there been some object at hand, a sugar bowl, for example, she would have hurled it across the room. A room that was oddly quiet, like the volume of her yelling had scared all other sounds away.

"Please take care of yourself, ma'am."

Detective Leffers turned and walked out of the house. Mrs. Plansky wanted to sit down and pound the table, or just lay her head on it and cry. Instead she did the dishes, methodically and extra-carefully, and gradually composed herself.

Mrs. Plansky walked up to the entrance to Arcadia Gardens, the rolled-up bombshell photo under her arm. The landscaping—

always impressive—was at its best this time of year, a riot of—well, no, not a riot, riots being out of control by definition, so this was more theatrical, a more-is-more scene of blossoms in all colors, special-order greenery, big shady trees, mostly cabbage palm but also some ancient bald cypress, the flower beds completely weedless, which took a lot of work in these parts, and lined with conch shells. The building itself could have been a well-preserved hotel from pre-war Florida days but was not yet ten years old. Julio, an attendant she'd gotten to know a bit, was just coming out.

"Loretta!"

He hurried down the steps. They shook hands.

"How's Dylan?" she said, Dylan being his first child, born toward the end of her dad's residency here, the Act-Two part.

"Doin' great! He loves the bath."

"Let's see."

Julio laughed and whipped out his phone. They watched a short video of a chubby infant splashing delightedly in a tub. Mrs. Plansky wouldn't have minded watching it again.

"He's lovely."

"Thanks. How's the big chief?"

"Unchanged."

"Ah. Don't tell me he's—I mean are we gonna have the pleasure of his company again? I didn't think we had any vacancies."

"Even if you did the answer's no. He's very contented these days."

"And you?"

"Ha!" said Mrs. Plansky. "Meanwhile I'm just trying to make sense of a few things." Which was true, if misleading. "Is Polly around?"

"Polly the older or Polly the younger?"

"I assume the younger."

"Right this way."

A resort-style pool deck stood behind Arcadia Gardens, with an Olympic-sized pool, cabanas, chaises longues, tables with umbrellas, a tiki-type bar. No one was in the pool and no one was on the deck, except for the bartender behind the tiki bar, polishing a martini glass in slow motion, and a woman on the far side of the pool, sitting in a wheelchair under an umbrella, smoking a cigarette, a champagne flute beside her.

Julio led Mrs. Plansky around the pool. The woman's head was turned in their direction but it was impossible to tell if she was watching them, because of her super-sized sunglasses.

"How should I introduce you?" Julio said in a low voice, his lips hardly moving.

"You should have been a diplomat."

"There's still time."

Mrs. Plansky laughed. The posture of the woman in the wheelchair changed. Now she was watching them for sure.

"Just Loretta, I think."

"À votre service," said Julio in what sounded like perfect French, the language of diplomacy.

"Good morning, Polly," Julio said. "How's your day going so far?"

"Don't ask," Polly said. She looked to be about Mrs. Plansky's age, although slimmer and perhaps better preserved. She wore a simple white silk top and sapphire-blue slacks, covered from the knees down by a very light throw. Mrs. Plansky was no fashionista but she knew these clothes had to come from Paris or Milan. Also whoever did her platinum blond hair was not someone Mrs. Plansky could afford.

"Meet Loretta," Julio said. "Polly, Loretta; Loretta, Polly."

"Nice to meet you," said Mrs. Plansky.

"You've joined our happy group?" Polly blew out a little smoke stream. "Or just sniffing around?"

"The second," said Mrs. Plansky.

Julio smiled an uneasy smile. "I'll leave you guys to it."

"Julio?" said Polly. "Be a doll." She tapped her glass.

"Of course. And for you Loretta?"

"Water would be great."

Julio looked over at the bartender. The bartender got busy.

"Water," said Polly, like the word was from a foreign language.

Julio withdrew. Mrs. Plansky waited for an invitation to sit, but gave up quickly and just sat. Polly's wheelchair had a small canvas bag hanging on one arm and poking out the top was some sort of metal and plastic contraption she couldn't identify. The bartender came with drinks—champagne for Polly, water with a twist for Mrs. Plansky. They clinked glasses.

"Cheers," said Mrs. Plansky.

"How old are you?" Polly said.

"Going on seventy-two."

Polly nodded like that was pretty much what she'd guessed. "Older than me," she said, "but you don't look like you need assistance. Yet."

"The truth is I wanted to talk to you."

"What about?"

Mrs. Plansky unrolled the photo and laid it on the table.

Polly gazed at it. She was a very good-looking woman but not in Lizette's class.

"What am I looking at?" Polly said.

Polly seemed to be looking at the picture but because of those sunglasses Mrs. Plansky couldn't be sure. Was there something wrong with Polly's eyesight? Mrs. Plansky pointed to Lizette, more accurately the woman who had to be Lizette. It was a certainty in her mind.

"Right," said Polly. "I see that. Two dreamers living the dream. So what?"

"But . . . but isn't that Lizette?"

"Who's Lizette?"

"Your sister? She's not your sister?"

Polly sat back. "Who are you?"

"Loretta," said Mrs. Plansky, a feeble reply if ever there was.

"For chrissake. Loretta what?"

"Plansky."

"God almighty. Related to that two-timing—make that three—son of a bitch?"

"That would be my dad."

"Figures." Polly stubbed out her cigarette, good and hard. "You've got the wrong Polly. Nice meeting you, indeed. You'll find the right Polly in the rooftop garden, acting out her delusions of grandeur." She turned to her champagne.

Walking away from the pool, her face feeling red, and not from the heat, Mrs. Plansky, way too late, of course, identified the object in Polly's canvas bag. It was an artificial foot, the high-tech bionic kind.

A woman wearing jeans, a denim shirt, and a red bandanna had the rooftop garden to herself. She sat sideways at a table with two glasses on it, filled with what looked like lemonade. She had a paintbrush in her hand and all her attention was on her easel, but Mrs. Plansky couldn't see the painting from her angle.

"Polly?" she said.

Polly nodded, a bit like a sleepwalker, and pointed her brush at the empty chair by one of the lemonades, the brush tipped in a shade of green that reminded Mrs. Plansky of Bahamian waters.

She gestured toward the glass. "Expecting someone?"

"You."

"The other Polly told you I was here?"

"Not directly. We don't speak."

Polly, this older Polly, didn't look nearly as old as Mrs. Plansky had been led to believe during the—what would you call it? Bimbo eruption? That was flat-out wrong given the three women involved, all of whom she had now met—Polly the Younger, Polly the Older, but not looking so old maybe due to bad information or good genes or first-rate cosmetic surgery or all three, and Clara. If there was a bimbo in the mix, it was her dad.

"I see," she said. "Julio, then?"

"It doesn't matter. This place is a hive. With a hive mind. That's what Dante left out of purgatory. The hive mind part."

Mrs. Plansky sat down, out of her depth already. And wouldn't her dad also have been out of his depth? Or were there scraps of his long-ago Princeton education still drifting through his mind?

Their eyes met. Polly II's were Bahamian green, tonally almost identical to the paint on her brush. That wasn't all. Mrs. Plansky could now see the painting, a partially finished small canvas of a nude woman looking right back at you. The body was young; the eyes were Polly II's eyes; the face was Polly II's face as it was today. The effect was . . . Mrs. Plansky searched for the word. Disconcerting? Arresting? Powerful? It was all those things and more. Mrs. Plansky had no expertise when it came to art. But art—first Tee-Tee, now this—had come knocking.

"Wow," she said.

"Wow," said Polly II, completely toneless yet contemptuous for sure.

"I'm just saying I like it."

"Gee whiz. Wanna buy it? You're the moneybags."

Mrs. Plansky folded her arms across her chest. "Where'd you hear that?"

"The hive? Remember? But it doesn't matter. I had no interest in Chandler's money, whether it was his or not. I have enough to keep me comfortably in the hive until death, as long as it's not too distant. My namesake's motivation was quite different. Money, money, money. Sex was what I wanted. What else is there?"

"Is that a serious question?"

Polly II turned to the canvas and started giving the subject's toenails a hint of green. "I keep forgetting how shockingly various people are."

"I'm just having trouble picturing my father as a sex object, even in his younger days."

"You'd be the last one. But let me assure you—if you didn't already know—that he's had wide-ranging experience with women, amateur and professional." She shot Mrs. Plansky a quick green glance. "It's a different world when the lights go down. As you may or may not know. But certain Cuban ladies do know. You can bet the goddam ranch."

For the first time in her life, Mrs. Plansky realized how bourgeois she was, pretty much completely. She unrolled the photo and laid it flat on the table. Polly II's gaze darted toward it at once.

"Where'd you get this?" she said.

Mrs. Plansky ignored that question. She pointed to Lizette. "Is that your sister?"

"Same father, different mother."

"And Lizette's her name?"

Polly II shrugged. "Could be improved upon—her mother was French or French Canadian or something of that nature—but what can you do? Meanwhile I asked you a question. Where did you get it?"

Mrs. Plansky sidestepped again. She pointed. "Do you know him?"

"Of course. Kev Dinardo."

"He and I are friends."

"Obviously. Did you think you could keep it secret from Chandler?"

"Why would I even want to do that?"

Polly II bit her lip, not at all subtly, but almost chewing. She came close to looking ugly for a moment. There was a lot of seething going on under all that grandness.

"Are you suggesting Kev gave you the photo?" she said.

"In a manner of speaking."

Polly II nodded to herself. "I didn't realize he hated her so much."

"Hated who?" Mrs. Plansky said.

"Lizette. Who else?"

"But hated her so much? What makes you say that?"

Polly II waved backhanded at the photo. "He obviously tried to deface it. Then he thought better and presented it to the new girl. The new girl now in possession of the old, if you follow."

"I'm not the new girl."

"No? You're quite presentable, really. Nothing like Lizette but who is? She had so many screen tests back in the day! They just couldn't believe she had no acting ability whatsoever!" Polly II laughed happily.

"When was the last time you saw him?" Mrs. Plansky said.

"Kev? It's been awhile. But we talk from time to time. Why? You're after something. Cough it up."

"How come they broke up, Kev and Lizette?"

"He didn't say? But that's men for you, every time. They think they're being clever, over and over and over. But they're not. Clever is us, not them. But the answer is Lizette wants money. Not like my namesake. I'm talking the big blockbuster bucks."

"But isn't Kev rich by any standard?"

"Not by Lizette's standard. Few can meet that. But she found one out in Phoenix. He owns—what? Most of downtown? I forget. That kind of thing. Found him and landed him. He's perfect. No kids, can you believe it? There were two and they died in an avalanche in Argentina. And only one wife for decades, and then boom! Ovarian. Lizette brought him back to life. There isn't even a prenup."

Polly II took a sip of lemonade. "Drink," she said, nodding to Mrs. Plansky's glass with her chin. "Take care of your skin."

"My skin?"

"Hydrate, hydrate, hydrate. Don't you know the female basics?"

Mrs. Plansky smiled, a smile that felt uncomplicated and comfortable. How crazy was that? But it just happened, all by itself. She took a big drink of lemonade. Delicious. "What do you know about my son, Jack?" she said.

"Chandler adores him."

That was a shock. Mrs. Plansky came close to saying, "He hardly knows him." And went with, "Why do you say that?"

Polly II shrugged. "He looks out for him. Chandler wants to help the boy make it big in the business world."

"Jack's forty-two."

"Just getting started, as you must know."

Mrs. Plansky did not know that.

"And furthermore he is by all accounts a handsome and charming fellow."

"Whose accounts are those?"

"Chandler's, for one, and Lizette's, for two. Would I be surprised to learn that she has—oh, so discreetly—gotten to know him quite well? She cares about him. Let's leave it at that. She thought Kev might be a useful contact, but given the state of things it would be best for me to run the idea by him. Me knowing the boy's grand-father, and all, and Lizette's relationship with Kev being how it is. So I called Kev, he said sure, and I looped in Chandler."

"And he told Jack about Kev?"

"As far as I know. This is all news to you?"

"Mostly."

"Maybe they're planning some sort of surprise. When's Mother's Day?"

"Second Sunday in May."

"Not so far away then." Polly II dipped her brush in Bahamian green. "Anything else I can help you with?"

"Do you know Ray and Rudy?"

"A vaudeville team? The names mean nothing to me."

"Maybe they mean something to Lizette."

"Then why don't you ask her?"

"Good idea."

"Presto!" Polly II took her phone from the pocket of her denim shirt, tapped at it. "Hi, it's me. Guess who's sitting right here." There was a slight pause. "Ha! Not funny. It's Loretta Plansky. She's got all sort of questions."

Polly II had smeared a tiny streak of Bahamian green on her phone. She wiped it off with her thumb and handed it to Mrs. Plansky. "She wants to talk to you."

Twenty-Six

"Hello?" Mrs. Plansky said. "Lizette?"

"Yup," said Lizette. "What's on your mind?"

There was so much. But the connection wasn't good. And it would have been nice if Lizette's voice, very self-assured, was a bit friendlier. Mrs. Plansky tried to boil things down to the essentials.

"Have you seen Jack—my son—recently?"

"I know he's your son. And what do you mean by recently?"

"When was the last time you saw him?"

"I'd have to think. A few weeks ago maybe?"

"Have you heard from him in that time?"

"No. Is something wrong?"

"That's what I'm trying to find out. What about Kev? Have you seen or heard from him?"

"Why would I? Didn't Polly bring you up to speed?"

Mrs. Plansky glanced across the table. Polly II had turned her attention to the painting and was greening in those toenails one by one, the strokes decisive. She seemed to be in another world.

"Do the names Ray and Rudy mean anything to you?" Mrs. Plansky said.

There was a pause. "Why do you ask that?"

"It's hard to explain."

"Are you saying they're out there? In Florida?"

"Rudy is, for sure. I don't know about Ray. He could be a man named Mitch. Or Mr. Mitch. But what's going on?"

"Mitch?" said Lizette. "I don't know any Mitches. You're not making much sense."

"That's not my fault!"

Polly's paintbrush went still. Right away Mrs. Plansky regretted snapping at Lizette. How would that kind of thing get her anywhere?

Silence on the other end. Then Lizette said, "I'm putting you on hold."

"But—"

Polly glanced over at her, smiled a little smile that seemed knowing.

"I'm on hold," Mrs. Plansky said.

"Of course you are," said Polly.

Lizette came back on the line. "Loretta?"

"Yes?"

"Interesting that both our names start with *L,* by the way."

"Interesting how?" At that moment she remembered the boat painter in white overalls who'd appeared at 92 Seaside to white out Lizette. Had there been some talk of Kev making a joke about leaving the *L* in place?

"It doesn't matter," Lizette said. "I just tried Jack."

"And?"

"No go. His voicemail's full. I hate the phone. I don't think I've had one good phone call in my whole life. You can't put heads together on the phone. Ever notice that? So why don't you come out here? As soon as you can. I'll pick you up at the airport. And why not bring your racket?"

"My racket?"

"Tennis racket. Jack says you're pretty good."

And then she was gone.

Polly's attention was back on the painting. "Lizette always gets her way," she said, not looking at Mrs. Plansky.

"But—"

"But what?"

But Mrs. Plansky was in no mood to board a plane, might never be in that kind of mood again. That was what. She kept it to herself.

*   *   *

Mrs. Plansky caught a flight to Phoenix, leaving Lucrecia in charge at the condo. She always flew coach, paying extra if necessary for a window seat. That way she could gaze into the sky the whole time and forget that she was locked in a tube designed to induce claustrophobia and panic, both much closer to getting loose on this particular flight. Her mind was in turmoil until they reached cruising altitude. Cruising altitude soothed her. She fell right to sleep and slept the rest of the way.

A dignified-looking man was holding a card with her name on it. She hesitated. He smiled. She went over to him.

"Welcome, Mrs. Plansky."

He tipped his cap—a chauffeur-type cap—and reached for her tennis bag, the only luggage she'd brought. Her instinct was to do for herself, but Norm always said it was insulting not to let people do their jobs. She handed it over.

"Lizette's outside. I'm Monty."

"Loretta," said Mrs. Plansky. They shook hands.

Monty led her outside. A sky-blue Rolls Royce stood at the curb, motor humming in a soft but powerful way, like a very big apex cat at rest. Mrs. Plansky had never been in a Rolls Royce. Monty opened the rear door. Mrs. Plansky stepped in.

Inside was a sort of parlor, the furnishings in high-end Scandinavian style. Lizette sat at a semicircular indigo banquette, with a fruit bowl and Baccarat pitcher of ice water on the table, Mrs. Plansky recognizing the design from catalogs she'd seen during her career in the kitchen business.

Lizette patted the seat. "Flight okay?"

"Better than my last one," said Mrs. Plansky, sitting down.

"Oh?" Lizette said.

Mrs. Plansky took that for a sign that Lizette knew nothing of Val or the plane wreck in the Jarndyces. She didn't reply, instead adopting an expression she thought was inscrutable. She really could be out of her mind sometimes. There had to be a screw loose somewhere inside her, had probably been that way her whole life.

"You must be dehydrated," Lizette said, filling a glass, also Baccarat.

Ah, an interest in hydration, just like her half sister Polly, although physically there wasn't much resemblance. Lizette was younger of course, at first glance looking much the same as she did in the photo with Kev, meaning still a bombshell. But Kev now looked older than in the photo, possibly six or seven years older or even more. As Lizette concentrated on pouring the water, Mrs. Plansky stole a close, unguarded look at her. She spotted very fine lines that she hadn't noticed at first, here and there on Lizette's face, plus the faintest of two vertical notches between her eyes. Mrs. Plansky had two similar notches, further along in their development. She decided that Lizette was not much younger that she was, maybe two or three years. But she didn't kid herself about the headline: Lizette was a bombshell, perhaps a late-stage bombshell but still a bombshell, while she, Mrs. Plansky, was what she was, not an unpleasant sight, especially on her good days.

Lizette raised her glass. "What should we toast?"

Mrs. Plansky glanced out the window and noticed they were on the move. There'd been no sensation that movement had started up, and there was no feeling of movement now.

"How about survival?" Lizette said.

"Survival?"

"In the face of everything life throws at us."

"Okay," said Mrs. Plansky. Lizette seemed to be surviving quite well.

They clinked glasses, Mrs. Plansky clinking carefully, mindful of whatever the replacement costs of those glasses might be. She took a sip. This was the best water she'd ever tasted, even better than the artisanal champ. She came close to asking the brand. Maybe she could afford a bottle now and then.

"And congratulations," Lizette said.

"On what?"

"Jack. He really is a sweetheart. And you're the mom, so credit is due."

What exactly was Lizette's relationship with Jack? Polly had hinted, but Mrs. Plansky wanted more than hints. She couldn't think of a good approach, or any, really. Meanwhile Lizette's eyes were on her, waiting and maybe even amused. Lizette's eyes weren't green like her sister's, but there was something Bahamian about them, not the translucent green of the shallows, instead the deep indigo of the waters over the continental shelf. All at once Mrs. Plansky found herself close to tears. Oh, how humiliating that would be! She mastered herself. Throughout this little internal drama the expression in those indigo eyes didn't change. Was it a step too far to assume that Lizette's interest in the inner workings of others was not strong in general, or if not that, then at least highly selective?

"Some very strange things are going on," she said.

Lizette pressed a button on her armrest. A tinted privacy window slid down, separating them from Monty. "Tell me more," said Lizette.

Did she have to trust Lizette? Was there any choice? Norm always said you had to give in order to get. It sounded shrewd but Norm was not shrewd. Instead he was a natural giver, so had just added the "getting" part to make himself sound like a tough guy to other tough guys in the business world, who probably saw through him. Norm actually was a tough guy, way down deep, starting with being tough on himself, the one place most of the tough guys she'd come across turned out to be soft.

"You said you hadn't heard from Jack," Mrs. Plansky said. "What about Kev? When's the last time you heard from him?"

"Oh, months and months. We're not on the best terms. My fault, I suppose. But what are you getting at?"

"I think they're both missing, not just Jack."

"Why?"

"A lot of reasons. I can't reach either of them, for one thing."

"Have you gone to the police?"

"I contacted a detective."

"And?"

"He wasn't convinced."

Lizette nodded. "Got it."

"What do you mean?"

"Guys. That's what I mean. A guy dealing with a situation featuring a woman and two quote 'missing other guys,' one her son, the other her . . . whatever. Do I need to explain? They pick on the messenger. You know how their minds work."

"I know how Jack's mind works," Mrs. Plansky said, with much more confidence than she felt.

"What about Kev's?"

Before Mrs. Plansky could answer, Lizette's phone flashed. It lay by the water pitcher, in easy reach. She glanced at it but didn't pick it up.

"That's a film director, very famous. An arrogant son of a bitch with bad breath. Did Polly mention I was starting a movie production company?"

"No."

"It's something I've wanted to do for a long time. But I was never in position to. Now I am. Dinardo Productions. I've kept the name. I'm tired of changing surnames and I like the sound of this one. Kev didn't understand why I wanted what I wanted, not that he could have done anything about it. But no harm done. In the end I wasn't his type. I'm sure he'll realize that eventually, if he hasn't already."

"How long were you married?"

"Eight years and a bit? Was it really that long? We must have been having fun." She slapped herself on the cheek, very lightly. "Oh, I'm so bad. Hush my mouth. We did have fun, of course. Kev's a fun guy. He has a sense of humor, lots of physical energy, and well, you know. Or don't you?"

"We're friends, mostly tennis friends."

Lizette smiled at her. Was there such a thing as a smile of disbelief? There was now. "I wish I'd known about you before I set Jack up with Kev. It was kind of roundabout, what with Kev's state of mind re yours truly, but I would have handled it very differently now that we've met, you and I."

"I don't understand what you mean about setting Jack up with Kev," Mrs. Plansky said.

"Really? You didn't know that Jack was dissatisfied? He's an excellent tennis pro, but do you think he'd be happy doing that in twenty years?"

"No."

"Then there you go. Kev's a very active investor—on the scale where he operates, anyway—with lots of contacts. And I was pretty sure they'd hit it off. Kev loves tennis, of course, and also scuba diving, and it turns out that Jack's got a background in that, too. So those were the happy reasons for what I did."

"There were unhappy ones?"

Lizette glanced out the window. Mrs. Plansky saw they were no longer moving, but were now parked by a marble pavilion. Beyond it lay a tennis court, a citrus grove all in flower, and past that rose an enormous house backed into a red rock slope.

"Home sweet home," Lizette said. "Let's hit for twenty minutes."

"You want to play tennis?" Mrs. Plansky certainly did not.

"Just to clear our heads."

Mrs. Plansky was about to say her head was perfectly clear when she realized that would have been a lie.

Mrs. Plansky changed in a cabana by the court, a green clay court, rare in Arizona because of all the water required to maintain it. She wore a blue skirt and a white tee. Lizette was in shorts and a crop top. Her abdomen was a workout or two from being one of those perfect six-packs. It almost looked Photoshopped.

They warmed up. Mrs. Plansky was at her very worst, legs heavy, eyes refusing to watch the ball. Lizette turned out to be light on her feet and very quick, with compact strokes from both sides. Mrs. Plansky couldn't keep the ball in the court. Lizette couldn't miss.

"Love your one-handed backhand," Lizette said. "Want to play a set?"

Mrs. Plansky did not, but refusing an invitation like that was unacceptable in tennis. Lizette served first, an ace down the middle, meaning an attack on that supposedly lovely one-handed backhand from the get-go. Then came an ace on the forehand side, both returnable by the lighter-legged version of Mrs. Plansky. She sank into a thick fog. The next thing she knew she was down four love and Lizette was looking bored. The sight of that woke something in Mrs. Plansky and her inner fog began to lift. Her legs stopped feeling heavy, her feet began taking those extra tiny steps that made all the difference, and soon she was doing the hitting and Lizette was doing the running. Mrs. Plansky didn't move like Lizette, she wasn't nearly as fit, her form was nowhere near as nice, but she hit harder and could pin Lizette in the corners and keep her there. Lizette's face grew redder and redder. She even came close to not looking like a bombshell.

Serving for the set at 6–5, 40–love, and now sailing along in one of those tennis zones where she could do no wrong, Mrs. Plansky suddenly realized that in the big world off the court she needed Lizette, so wouldn't it be better to lose the set? Of course it would! She could be so slow sometimes. Thank God there was still time. Mrs. Plansky double-faulted on the next serve, netted an easy volley on the point after that, and was preparing to double fault again when she happened to glance at the enormous house on the red rock slope. The house had a number of terraces, and on the topmost one an old man sitting in a wheelchair seemed to be watching, a male attendant in white standing nearby. The attendant leaned closer and held what looked like an oversized sippy cup to the old man's lips. Mrs. Plansky tossed the ball into the blue sky and whacked it with something close to fury, her hardest serve of the match by far. Lizette mis-hit the return off the frame, driving the ball into the citrus grove. Seven-five, Loretta.

They walked to the net. Mrs. Plansky held out her hand. There was a pause and then Lizette gave her a quick hug instead.

"For a moment there I thought you were about to let me back in," Lizette said.

"It's a funny game," said Mrs. Plansky.

Lizette stepped back slightly, as though taking in Mrs. Plansky from a fresh perspective. "Whatever it is that Jack's missing, you've got," she said.

"What are you talking about?"

"He's traveled all over the world, met all sorts of people, but there's still something innocent about him. I'm sure you're aware of that. So besides the opportunity with Kev and all that, it's another reason I wanted to get him out of here. The unhappy reason. You said you'd seen Ray and Rudy?"

"Rudy for sure. Ray maybe, if he's calling himself Mitch. A big guy, somewhere between forty-five and fifty, shaved head, mustache."

"Cauliflower ear?"

How could she have forgotten that? It should have been the lead. "Yes."

"That's Ray," Lizette said. "I don't want to say he's the brawn and Rudy's the brain. They're both the brawn and the brains. Their ambition is to be Kevs of the world, but they're nothing like him. Kev's decent. They're grifters. Rudy did something with oil wells in Guyana. Ray's ex-Special Forces, blew up the wrong building in Africa somewhere, told Jack a funny story about it. Meaning Jack found it funny. I did not. They had a scheme about cold storage something-or-other. Jack came close to asking me to invest but before he could get there the feds went after Ray and Rudy on some earlier thing that ended up getting dropped. I don't know the details but it spared Jack having to ask and me having to say no."

"Same," said Mrs. Plansky.

Lizette laughed, led Mrs. Plansky into the pavilion, took cold drinks from a fridge. They sat facing the house. The old man and his attendant were still on the topmost terrace. Lizette didn't look that way once.

"The cold storage idea survived in a shrunken down way and

ended up as a brew pub in Mesa, near the campus," Lizette said. "The idea was to expand across the country. That's around when I got Jack and Kev connected, before Jack could get swept up in the beer thing."

Lizette gave Mrs. Plansky a close look. She could feel her face being read.

"I was too late?" Lizette said.

Mrs. Plansky nodded. "Drop Shot Brewing. It seems to be the three of them—Kev, Rudy, and Ray. I don't know about Jack."

"Drop Shot?" said Lizette.

"And the IPA is 40–Love."

"There's Kev's sense of humor again." Lizette smiled to herself. "I thought I'd miss it, but I don't."

"The brewery's in a little town called Macdee—ever heard of it?"

"Sure have! Been there, in fact. Kev wanted me to see the place. It's where he grew up."

"I didn't know that."

"Did you know he grew up rough?"

Mrs. Plansky shook her head.

"No father. Alcoholic mother. Stepdads and boyfriends, every new one worse than the one before. Did he tell you about his bicycle?"

"No."

"Kev wanted a bike. He picked strawberries for a local grower, saved his pay packets, bought himself a used bike, fixed it up. One day he left it lying in the driveway and stepdad number whatever drove over it on purpose. To teach him a lesson. The lesson Kev learned was he'd wouldn't spend another night in that house. He carried what was left of his bike all the way to his cousin Huey's place, a shack in a swamp outside of town. Cousin Huey took Kev in and he never went back. Kev did well in high school, was good at baseball, got a scholarship to Rollins. Any of this familiar to you?"

"No."

"I met Cousin Huey. He lives on the same spot, by one of those Florida rivers that looks more like a stream to me, but the shack was replaced by a nice little bungalow, thanks to Kev. Cousin Huey's a character. Catches bass with his bare hands, that kind of thing."

"Is he still there?" Mrs. Plansky said.

"Couldn't tell you. This was three or four years ago."

"But he was living in Macdee?"

"Maybe not in Macdee proper. It's off the grid."

"What's the river called?"

"It's one of those Confederate names."

"Robert E. Lee?"

"Maybe. The bugs were terrible."

"Did Kev ever mention *Nuestra Señora de las Aguas*?"

"What is it?"

"An old Spanish galleon."

"Nope. New one to me. Does it have anything to do with pirates?"

"Why do you ask that?"

"*Treasure Island* was Kev's favorite book as a kid. It was the only book Cousin Huey had. Kev read it over and over. He can recite whole passages, pages and pages."

These new sides to Kev: Mrs. Plansky liked them all. But how did they fit in with—

"What was that thought?" Lizette said. "The one you just had."

Mrs. Plansky took in the sight of those indigo eyes, the eyes of a creature she probably could never understand, but with whom she was—for a very short time and only because she'd overpowered her on that green clay court—on an equal footing. She decided to tell her the whole New Sunshine/Old Sunshine story, starting with the tennis match and ending with what the authorities called a lightning strike but which she thought was an explosion. She left out the kiss, couldn't quite make herself go there.

Lizette leaned forward. "Of course it was an explosion, Loretta!"

"How can you be sure?"

"Simple. He blew it up."

"Kev blew up his own boat?"

"He said he would. That was just about the last thing he ever told me before I left."

"But wasn't that two years ago?"

"Almost three. He must have felt the time was right." Lizette flashed her a knowing grin that, for some reason, made Mrs. Plansky think of Delilah. The kiss on the dock and the fire in Kev's eyes took on new meaning.

"But what's going on now?" Mrs. Plansky said. "With him? With Jack?

Lizette shrugged. "Some sort of male boondoggle. It'll sort itself out." She took out her phone, did some scrolling, turned it Mrs. Plansky's way, displaying a photo of one of those mega yachts with a helipad and all the rest, berthed somewhere that looked like the Riviera.

"What's that?" she said.

"The new *Lizette*," said Lizette. "I thought *Lizette II* would be more fun, but my husband preferred simply *Lizette* and I didn't make a fuss. I can always change it . . . later. It's just paint, after all."

"You're right about that," said Mrs. Plansky.

The topmost terrace was now deserted.

TWENTY-SEVEN

The sun was setting when Mrs. Plansky parked in front of the Little Pine Lake condos. A text came dinging in from Hamish before she could get out of the car.

Just spoke to my buddy at UF Health. MRI, CT, PET all negative— neg. being good as I'm sure yk. Patient stable, no change. Any questions just ask!

Her question was: then why is Val still in a coma? She reread the text carefully, word by word, searching for a hint, and soon stumbling on *yk*. Was that a medical condition? Kidneys started with *K* but . . . then it hit her. *Yk = you know*! Ha! She got it, was up-to-date and in the mix. Mrs. Plansky had been a lone operator since Norm's death and that was all right, not the death but the lone-operator part. And she didn't expect to ever have another co-operator in life. But how about an occasional on-call backup operator whom she could consult once in a while? So far no candidate was on the scene. Until now. She could envision a future where Hamish . . . but pointless to think about that so soon, and also opening the door to some sort of jinx. She shut that whole line of thinking down and went inside.

"I'm home!"

No one heard her. It wouldn't have been possible, not over the volume of the music coming from the living room. She knew at once it was not a recording but live music: a guitar, bass, conga drums, a sax, plus two singers, male and female.

She peeked in, saw at once she'd missed the second guitar, the trumpet, and the backup singers. Her dad and Clara sat on a couch, holding hands, but all the others—Lucrecia and her husband, Joe, and several other couples she didn't know—were dancing. Was this salsa music? Whatever it was it sounded great. On the other hand all she wanted to do was go to bed this very minute. Lucrecia, incorporating a sinuous raising-the-roof gesture into her routine, spotted Mrs. Plansky. She made a chopping motion, like a bandleader cutting off the music. It stopped at once.

Lucrecia hurried over. Mrs. Plansky seemed to have turned up unexpected in her own home. She tried to remember what she'd told Lucrecia about her return plans.

"Loretta! I'm so sorry. This was the only chance for the band rehearsal."

"Rehearsal for what?"

"The wedding. It's next Saturday. Didn't your dad tell you? And of course I told him no way to tonight, knowing you were coming home. But this morning he said you'd called to say it would be tomorrow instead. Except, um, you didn't?"

They both turned to her dad. He was still with Clara on the couch but now engaged in conversation with the conga drummer, calling out what sounded like "andale, arriba!" That seemed to amuse the conga drummer and it delighted Clara, who clapped her bejeweled hands rapidly, like sparklers on the Fourth of July.

"How about just a few more numbers?" Mrs. Plansky said.

"On, no," said Lucrecia. "These girls and boys are done for the night."

Mrs. Plansky went into her room and lay down on the bed, just for a few moments and only to rest her feet. Going to bed was out of the question. There were so many reasons—it was too early, she hadn't brushed her teeth, and after a long airplane flight you took a shower. That was practically a law of the land, or at least her corner of it. The house grew quiet. A salsa rhythm, very soft, got going in the back of her mind. Norm said that during the day centrifugal force takes over your life and at night your gravity reels all the parts back in. Her nighttime gravity had been so strong when Norm lay beside her, like the gravity of the sun! Now it was more like the gravity of some flaky asteroid in an iffy orbit. The salsa rhythm died down.

Her phone was buzzing. Mrs. Plansky opened her eyes. Her room was dark and the buzzing phone was somewhere beneath her. She wasn't lying in her twisted K but in some other position, cramped and uncomfortable. She got herself sitting upright, not easily, and realized the buzzing phone was in her skirt pocket. This was why you changed out of your clothes and into a nightie before bed every night without fail.

She freed the phone, turned it right side up, which made the image on the screen turn upside down.

"Hell on earth!" said Mrs. Plansky, but quietly. She didn't want to wake her dad, or Clara, if they were having a sleepover. Was Clara a light sleeper? At that moment, she had the strangest thought. What if she, Loretta, caught the bouquet? How ridiculous that would be! She made a mental note to let any bouquets fly right on by, and fumbled the phone into place.

There was no name on the screen and no number. Hope, way ahead of her rational mind, bloomed inside her, and she answered the call.

"Hello?"

"Are you listening?" said the man on the other end, not Jack, not Kev. It was Mitch, or Mr. Mitch, whose real name, almost certainly, was Ray. His voice still bore traces of the southwest, but the friendly veneer was gone. There would be no more ma'aming.

"Yes," she said.

"Carefully?"

Mrs. Plansky was beginning to feel frightened inside. But she did not like being browbeaten, had bridled against it all her life. "Go on, Ray."

He paused. When he spoke again, his tone had changed, and now there was something violent flowing just under the surface.

"I don't like your attitude."

Mrs. Plansky said nothing.

"Weren't you in business? I thought you'd know something about negotiation."

"I wasn't aware we were negotiating."

"Oh, we are. We are for sure. Fact is, this has got to be the most important negotiation of your life. Care to take a stab at why?"

Mrs. Plansky had a horrible notion or two. She refused to voice them.

"Cat got your tongue?" He grunted, one of those grunts that erupts from an inner thought. "I actually saw that once," he said. "The cat thing."

This casual reminiscence, if that was what it was, terrified her. She sat perched on the edge of her bed, shaking.

"What you're negotiating for," he said, "is the life of your son." Then he added "ma'am"—the ma'aming not quite done with after all—as if he somehow knew that would destabilize her even more.

"What do you want?" she said.

"Now we're talkin'," he said. "Talkin' and cookin' with gas. What I want—what I have to have or else, just to be clear—is the map."

Map? What did he mean? She had no—And then she realized what she probably should have realized much earlier. She did indeed have a map: the strange drawing of a palm tree and a notched triangle that she'd found hidden down the throat of the bronze fish in the fountain at 92 Seaside Way. A map! What else could it possibly be? Well, a child's doodle, for one thing, and there were probably other possibilities that might come to her later. But she was way off track. A map of what? That was the question. And there were more. Hidden by whom? Kev? Jack? Someone else? But hadn't whoever wrecked the place—almost certainly Ray, possibly with Rudy's help—been searching for something? And now they'd figured out she had it? Or were they only guessing? They couldn't know she'd broken in, could they? But they must have known someone had been inside, someone who might inform the police about the trashing of the place, which explained why it got all fixed up again. But did any of that matter now? All that mattered was that they had Jack and she had the map.

"I have it," she said.

"Who knows that, besides you?"

"Nobody."

"Okay. Here are the rules. You tell no one about this, not before we do the deal and not after. You and me, that's our little circle, that's who's in the know. Got it?"

But what about Jack? Wouldn't he have to be in the little circle? Mrs. Plansky came close to mentioning that, but something inside her—not cleverness or shrewdness, neither of which she had much of—closed the door on that urge.

"Yes," she said.

"Meaning you got it?"

"Correct."

"Just you and me?"

"How many times do you want me to say it?"

"There you go with the attitude again. Do you want this to work out or not?"

"I want my son back, safe and sound."

"Then shape up. How long will it take you to get the map?"

"Not long."

"Fifteen minutes? Ten? Five? Less?"

"Less."

"Here's what's next. Go get the map. Talk to nobody. Including the cops. Do I even need to say that? You'd regret it till your dying day. Don't bring your phone. And no weapons. I'll be patting you down first thing. A flashlight's okay but don't even dream of signaling with it. I'll be watching."

"From where?"

"Our meeting place—the nice little gazebo on the south side of your nice little lake. I'll give you fifteen minutes. Any later than that and we'll be gone. Questions?"

"No."

"Then move." The line went dead.

Mrs. Plansky got off the bed in her dark room. He'd be patting her down first thing? She came close to vomiting. But this was about Jack, not her, and he'd said "we'll be gone," not "I'll be gone." She straightened her skirt and blouse—still the same outfit she'd worn on the plane, an almost unbelievable reality—then opened her closet and found sneakers without turning on any lights. The whole condo was well organized but her closet was the organizational champ. She put on the sneakers, went to the makeup table, removed the map, folded it in half, and tucked it in her skirt pocket. Then she took her flashlight from the bedside table, moved across the room to the slider, and started to open it.

Mrs. Plansky paused. She turned back and left the room, walking quietly down the hall, past her father's room and into her small open-space office at the end of the hall. A bookshelf stood against the far wall, and on the top shelf lay a copier. It communicated with her laptop, supposedly, by Wi-Fi, and crammed behind it was a sort of tumbleweed ball of cables that had connected it to the old laptop and were now obsolete, the new laptop being somewhat miserly when it came to outlets or porticals or whatever those tiny slots were called. But none of that was relevant now. All Mrs. Plansky wanted to do was copy, and the printer could do that all on its own. You just raised the cover like so, laid in the document upside down, pressed power, and touched Copy on the little screen. If you wanted more than one copy then further moves were necessary, but the default was one. Mrs. Plansky touched Copy. At first nothing happened, but that wasn't uncommon, the innards of modern technology being complicated, with lots of invisible back-and-forthing. She waited patiently. Then the power light went off.

She went through the same steps, repeating them exactly. This time the power light stayed on but no copying happened. Could it be a toner problem? Mrs. Plansky had a hazy recollection that this copier was tonerless. She could even see the face of the clerk at Staples as he explained the process, a chubby, gap-toothed face. But she was blanking on what he'd actually said. She bent down, fumbled around, unplugged the printer, plugged it back in. The power light, normally blue, turned red. Mrs. Plansky hissed at the machine.

She ended up making a quick pencil copy of the map on the back of an envelope by the faint light coming off the red power button, a copy she tucked inside the closest book on the next shelf down. Then, instead of sliding the original map back into her skirt pocket she tucked it in her bra. That seemed like the right move, although she couldn't have explained why. She put the flashlight in her skirt pocket, then returned to her room, pausing at her father's door and hearing nothing. She went outside, closed the slider, then headed past the boat rack, along the hard-packed dirt path to the trail that led to the pond cypress grove and the gazebo beyond. No lights shone in that direction, the trees all merging in one shadowy form. Also no moon or stars, but it was one of those strange overcast nights when the sky was somewhat reddish, maybe reflecting the goings-on below. Mrs. Plansky thought she could manage without the flashlight. To her right, the lake reflected the redness of the sky, very faintly. She felt oddly naked, as though she was covered only with what was hidden, namely the flashlight and the map. For some reason she thought of Washington crossing the Delaware. How nice if he could be with her now.

The first thing that went wrong was walking right into the rotting tree trunk that lay across the trail, the tree trunk she and Val had stepped around, which had now slipped her mind. It didn't hurt much, her right shin taking most of the blow, but in her surprise and fear she let out a cry. Maybe not loud, but now the element of surprise was surely gone. Where the hell was her self-control? She was almost seventy-two. The window for self-improvement was closing fast. But was this the time for self-beration? That could wait for later. She mounted the low rise out of the pond cypress grove, and through the silhouetted screen of the myrtle the lake appeared, dark and faintly reddish, more like a low mist than a body of water.

What was that sound? Mrs. Plansky paused to listen, one of her feet not quite touching down, hunting dog style. She heard nothing.

She moved on, up the slope to the top. To one side stood the gazebo, so tranquil by day but now an unsettling filigree of shadows. She could make out the simple bench inside. No one was sitting on it; no one was in the gazebo. Mrs. Plansky stood where she was, waiting for . . . well, she didn't know what. Jack to appear, take the map, hand it to Ray, somewhere nearby, and then walk with her side by side to the condo, where the second-floor guest bedroom awaited him? That would be nice. But it didn't happen. Nothing happened. Mrs. Plansky stepped into the gazebo.

"Sit down."

Ray's voice came from the darkness, somewhere behind the gazebo. The tone wasn't emotional, more matter-of-fact than anything, which was maybe why it terrified her all the more.

She sat down on the bench.

"Raise your hands."

She raised them.

There was a moment or two of silence. "Okay, put 'em down. Just a precaution—lots of little old ladies are packin' these days."

Mrs. Plansky, still scared, was now a bit miffed as well. She came close to pointing out that she was not little.

"Got the map?"

"Yes."

"Let's see."

She rose and turned to the darkness behind the gazebo, where Ray's voice was coming from. At first she could make out nothing, but then—maybe thanks to the deftness of Dr. Eileen Chang, the ophthalmologist who'd done her cataract surgery, giving back her teenage eyesight, or close—she distinguished one shadow that didn't belong with the rest, a man-shaped shadow. But just the one.

"Where's Jack?" she said.

"Now, now," he said. "One thing at a time."

"We have a deal."

Then the man-sized shadow was on the move, very fast, and Ray stepped over the waist-high gazebo railing like it wasn't there and stood before her at arm's length. Mrs. Plansky had forgotten how big he was, how powerfully built, how much space he took up. But on account of Lizette, the cauliflower ear was fresh in her mind. By some trick of the night that cauliflower ear was faintly red while his face and shaved head were a pale off-white. The mustache, too, was faintly red. Mrs. Plansky wanted so badly to turn and bolt away like a wild animal. She stayed where she was.

"Where's Jack?" she said again.

"First the map."

He looked down at her. She met his gaze. His eyes were intelligent, no doubt about that. Intelligent in all the wrong ways.

"What's it a map of?" she said.

His head went back slightly. How strange! Like he was offended. "What the hell are you talking about?"

Mrs. Plansky was starting to get annoyed, just couldn't help herself. Annoyance on top of terror: she'd never felt like this in her life. If she had a gun at that moment—well, best not to think thoughts like that.

"It must be an important map," she said, "if it's worth the life of a man."

Without moving, Ray somehow shrank the space between them. "Just stay in your goddam lane." He held out his hand, oversized even for a big man. "The map."

She shook her head. "First Jack."

His eyes narrowed. A storm was rising inside him. Mrs. Plansky could feel it. She made her second mistake, this one knowingly, cupping her hands to her mouth and shouting from the bottom of her lungs. "JACK! JACK, JACK!"

That huge hand shot out and plunged into the pocket of her skirt. That was disgusting. The map wasn't there, of course, so Ray ended up with possession of the flashlight. He drew it back like a club, but Mrs. Plansky had already pivoted away and was now on the run.

Out of the gazebo, onto the top of the slope, down the trail to— but no. Somehow he was already ahead of her, and not only that, but facing her, crouching, the flashlight oscillating slightly like the bat in the hands of a slugger coming to the plate. She whirled around and—but no. Her whirling days had passed. Mrs. Plansky stumbled, fell, tried to rise, slipped, fell again, rolled down and down between the myrtles, and splashed into the lake.

She looked up at Ray, striding down the slope like it was level ground. She began sculling with her hands, backing farther into the water. Ray swore at her and threw the flashlight. It hit her in the shoulder, plenty hard to hurt. He strode right into the water and kept coming.

Mrs. Plansky flipped over and started swimming. She was still a pretty good swimmer and now swam with all her strength, giving every stroke the maximum she had. She bore slightly to the right, with the idea of getting to the condo and—

That huge hand grabbed her ankle and jerked her to a sudden stop. Ray yanked her around and then they were face to face, the night reddening his eyes. He grabbed her around the neck.

"This'll work, you stupid bitch. But first the map."

And then you'll let me go? A pathetic response, and there was no way she could say it, not with him choking her like this, so she was spared the humiliation. Not the main point. He was going to drown her. That was the main point. What could be more obvious?

"The map!" he said, and then thrust his free hand down her front, like he knew the map was there, which he probably did by now. The intrusion of his hand where it did not belong was intolerable. Mrs. Plansky raised her own hand to smack him, at the same time feeling the brush of something hard, heavy, and rubbery against her leg. Ray's eyes opened wide. There was a moment of stillness out there in the lake when nothing happened, a moment like after the conductor has tapped the baton but before the orchestra starts up.

Then Ray screamed a wild, ragged scream that would have frightened her to death even all by itself, with nothing else going on. But things were going on, all right. There was surging and thrashing down below, like a gathering of a kind of power that was way beyond. Ray got whisked below the surface in mid-scream, blood spurting from his mouth, and something reptilian whacked her in the side, thrusting her away from the scene.

Mrs. Plansky swam toward shore. She wanted to swim fast—it was clearly the prudent choice—but there was no speed in her.

TWENTY-EIGHT

"What kind of map are we talking about?" said Detective Leffers. He had dark circles under his eyes and his hair was rumpled. He looked sullen and sleepy.

"I don't know, exactly," Mrs. Plansky said. "That's what he called it."

"This Ray person?"

"Correct. Supposedly he wanted it as ransom for my son, Jack. Maybe I didn't make that clear. It's what makes this so urgent."

"Have we got a last name?"

"Plansky, of course!"

Detective Leffers exhaled slowly, his lips a tight round O. "I'm talking about Ray."

Ah. A good question. Mrs. Plansky knew that Rudy's last name was Mesa, although that might have been suspect since he came from Mesa and was definitely not a man of trustworthy character. But had she ever heard Ray's last name? If so, it wasn't coming to her. Then she had a minor brain wave: Lizette would know!

"I'll do some checking," she said.

Detective Leffers gazed at her. They sat at the kitchen table, the sky just starting to look milky outside the east-facing window. Through the slider she could make out a couple of uniformed cops standing on the patio, their attention on the lake, where a Zodiac with a searchlight in the bow was motoring slowly back and forth in a grid pattern, the motor barely audible. Several neighbors were on their patios watching what was going on, but somehow none of this had awakened her dad. If there were sleeping contests for the very old he'd have a shelfful of trophies. He'd like that. Perhaps at Christmas she'd give him a shelfful of trophies for no reason.

"When would you be doing that?" Detective Leffers said.

For a moment Mrs. Plansky was lost. The night's events had revved her way up. Now she was revving down and down, sinking into exhaustion, physical and mental. Plus she had pains here and there, nothing serious but she could feel them, sapping what strength she had left. If this was what methamphetamines were like she wanted no part of them. She'd never wanted any part of methamphetamines in any case. Was that a failing? Was she lacking on the Dionysian side of life? She thought of that kiss on the dock. Was that memory going to follow her around forever?

Meanwhile she felt Detective Leffers's gaze, right between her eyes. The subject was what again? "Um," she said. She felt her face reddening. But how crazy to feel embarrassment about anything after what she'd just been through. "Later!" she snapped at him. "It's a different time zone."

"Where your contact is?"

"Correct."

"Okay," he said, "just Ray for now. Do you think he ended up with this map of yours? Or did it get loose from . . . from your clothing?"

"Does it make a difference?"

"Might help narrow down the search."

"It'll be pretty soggy, in fact almost certainly destroyed."

"Maybe."

"But," said Mrs. Plansky. "I made a copy."

"Yeah?"

"Just a sketch."

"Not on a copier?"

She shook her head. "A toner problem or something similar. But do you want to see it?"

"Sounds good," said Detective Leffers, not as enthusiastically as she might have wished.

Mrs. Plansky went down the hall and into the office. She raised the lid of the copier. She remembered leaving her sketch there, a sketch made on the back of an envelope. The image of the front of the envelope, with its logo from her bank, Palm Coast Bank and Trust, was clear in her mind. But there was nothing under the copier lid.

She gazed down at the empty space. Why on earth would the sketch have been in the copier? The sketch was the copy, for heaven's sake! That struck her as a rather sharp observation but otherwise Mrs. Plansky was at a loss. She looked all around, somewhat like a child who doesn't know how to search, just hoping the lost object would pop into view. Her glance fell on the bookshelf.

Ah-ha! She'd tucked her copy in one of the books, and not just any book but the closest book on the next shelf down. She grabbed it—*To Engineer is Human*, one of Norm's favorites, although she herself had bogged down in the middle—and checked inside the covers, front and back. No copy. She leafed through the pages. And there it was! The envelope with the copy she'd made on the back!

But no. It was an envelope, all right, but addressed to Norm from an accountant they'd used. On the back was a shopping list, written in his neat hand, beginning with *onions, red* and ending with *flowers for L, tulips if nice.* She tried not to pause over that but couldn't help herself. Early in their relationship he'd somehow gotten it into his head that tulips were her favorite. Tulips were not her favorite, not even close, but she hadn't disabused him of the notion. How many tulips had he given her over the years, sometimes to mark an occasion, more often just because? Dozens and dozens of dozens. Tulips were her favorite now, by far. When she was dead and gone she wanted a tulip or two laid on her grave from time to time. Perhaps she'd even think of some way to see that it happened. She slipped the envelope carefully back into *To Engineer is Human* and moved on to the next book.

And the next and the next and the next. And then all the books on the next shelf down, and the next and the next. Things started getting messy in her little office. Mrs. Plansky didn't find her copy of the map.

She went back to the kitchen, testing various phrases in her mind. Detective Leffers wasn't there. Also daylight now shone through the windows. She spotted him outside, down by the lake on his phone, his back to her. He'd left the slider slightly open. She took that— completely unreasonably but nevertheless—as a sign that he was not a good detective. Mrs. Plansky went outside, closed the slider firmly behind her, and walked down to the shore.

There were more Zodiacs on the water now, some describing more grids, some with scuba divers aboard, some with trailing lines, one with a crewman heaving a heavy dragnet off the stern. A breeze came off the lake. It carried Detective Leffers's voice.

". . . nope, and like I said don't hold your breath. She's—what can I tell ya—not a hundred percent with—" He stiffened, cut himself off, sensing her presence, maybe a better detective than she'd thought. "Call ya back."

He slipped the phone in his pocket and turned to her, eyebrows rising.

"You're dragging the lake?" she said.

"Already done the whole area where the suppo—where the incident took place. Nothing so far. No body. No gator sighting. How are we coming along with that map you referenced?"

"A copy," Mrs. Plansky said. "I—I seem to have misplaced it, but—"

He smiled a smile she didn't like at all—the self-satisfied smile of a good guesser—and made a sweeping motion with his hand. "Don't worry too much. Maybe the boys will turn up the original."

"But didn't I mention how soggy it would be?"

"I wouldn't worry too much."

"Okay, except—" She gazed out at the lake. A diver was surfacing and shaking his head no. "Isn't it true that alligators conceal their . . . their kill under a sunken trunk or something like that? For later?"

"I've heard that," said Detective Leffers.

"And isn't it possible that Fairbanks has moved on to some other lake?"

"Who's Fairbanks?"

"The name of the gator."

"It has a name?"

"Well, not officially. In my mind."

"In your mind."

"Not that he resembles Douglas Fairbanks," she said, thinking maybe she should justify the name. "It was more that he has a certain star power."

"The gator?"

"Yes."

Detective Leffers smiled. "You have quite the imagination."

It took her a moment or two to start getting the implications of that. The silo within, where she stored her rarely used heavy artillery, began to open. What was wrong with this man? Jack was somewhere out there and in bad trouble. Why couldn't he grasp that? It was the whole point. It was everything! But before any outburst got started, Mrs. Plansky saw a woman approaching from the side of the condo. She wore a lime-colored pantsuit, carried a shoulder bag of briefcase design, and had her hair pulled so tightly back in a ponytail that it had to hurt.

"Mrs. Plansky?" Detective Leffers said. "Meet Dr. Elspeth Prindle from Human Services. She runs the Seniors Department, best in the state."

"Hello?" said Mrs. Plansky. She didn't mean for that to sound like a question but that was how it ended up.

"Pleased to meet you," said Dr. Prindle. "I'm so sorry for this ordeal of yours. Is there someplace we can talk?"

Detective Leffers moved discreetly away. What was there to be discreet about? He knew the whole story. She'd been assaulted by a horrible kidnapper or extortionist or whatever Ray was, almost drowned in an alligator attack, and her son was some sort of hostage. Weren't these bald-faced realities that should be treated in a bald-faced manner?

"About what?" she said.

"This really would be better in a more appropriate setting," said Dr. Prindle.

Mrs. Plansky raised her hands, palms up. "What's inappropriate about this?"

"Somewhere calmer would be better, don't you think?"

"What are you talking about? I'm perfectly calm." Not true, of course, and the sudden rise in volume had made that apparent to Dr. Prindle. Mrs. Plansky could see that in her eyes.

"That does raise the issue of why I've been called in," Dr. Prindle said.

"What do you mean?"

"It's just that sometimes, especially as we experience the changes that come with growing into our later selves, the mind can become over-stimulated in certain ways while under-stimulated in others. Does that make sense?"

Oh, it sure did, and in the most infuriating, most alarming and even menacing way possible. "You don't believe me?" She pointed at Detective Leffers, some distance away. "He doesn't believe me?"

"I wouldn't put it that way, Mrs. Plansky. It's more a matter of interpretation."

"What are you talking about?"

"No offense," Dr. Prindle said. "But just because someone isn't returning your calls doesn't mean he's missing."

"We have nothing more to discuss." Mrs. Plansky turned on her heel. "Fairbanks is smarter than all of you put together."

An insane remark, exactly wrong for the occasion, but there was no taking it back. Mrs. Plansky marched across the patio, went inside, pulled the slider closed with plenty of extra force, and locked it.

Mrs. Plansky fumed, watched the futility out on the lake, fumed some more.

"Fairbanks, appear, for God's sake! Pop up!"

Fairbanks did not pop up. A plan began sketching itself out in a corner of her mind. But first came her responsibilities. She knocked on her dad's door.

"Entrado!"

She went in. He was alone and sitting up in bed, reading a book. That was a first in a lifetime of experience with him.

"Good morning, Dad. What are you reading?"

He held up the book: *Death in the Afternoon*. "It's about the sport of bullfighting. I'm brushing up on all things Spanish."

"Do they have bullfighting in Cuba?"

He shrugged. "Haven't gotten to that part. But it stands to reason. They speak Spanish." His attention returned to the book.

"Dad? Did you have any plans for the—"

Her dad's bed—a king—had two bedside tables, one on his side, the other on the other. And on that second table, half-hidden by the lamp, stood Tee-Tee. Mrs. Plansky walked over and picked her up.

"Dad? What's this doing here?"

His eyes shifted toward her. An impatient frown was taking possession of his face. She knew that frown. He was past ready for her to be gone.

"Oh, that," he said. "Clara likes it. It helps her sleep. Have you heard of santeria? It's like voodoo except more normal. Little statues are part of it. Also seashells, but we don't have any, not the right kind."

"But where did you find it?"

"Find what?"

"This, Dad." She held it up.

"Somewhere for sure. Your room, maybe? Mi casa and all that."

"Mi casa?"

"My house. My house is your house. It's an old Cuban saying. Meaning you're welcome here. But what I'm saying is the thing was around. Don't you remember me explaining it's spray-painted? Worth, I don't know, ten bucks? Clara doesn't mind. It's the symbolism. That's important to her. Do you know what I symbolize?"

Mrs. Plansky didn't know and didn't want to know. "I hear the phone," she said, an outright lie. She backed out of the room and closed the door, Tee-Tee safely in her grip. Tee-Tee had been in the house the whole time, not truly missing at all. This was the first thing that had made sense since Lizette had gone up in flames. If Mrs. Plansky had been a superstitious person she'd have taken it for a good sign, but she was not a superstitious person.

Out on the lake, the search team seemed to be packing it in. There were no dead bodies lying on the decks of any of the Zodiacs, not Ray, not Fairbanks. On shore Detective Leffers and Dr. Prindle were having some sort of conversation. Mrs. Plansky did not wish she could hear what they were saying, far from it, wanted nothing to do with them. She took the fact that Tee-Tee hadn't left the house as a good sign after all.

Twenty-Nine

Kev had never talked about his childhood in Macdee, never mentioned Cousin Huey, the most important figure in it, according to Lizette. What else had she said? Something about Cousin Huey living in a shack, maybe not in Macdee proper but somewhere nearby? That sounded right. Nearby, in a shack on a river where the bugs were terrible. But now a bungalow, not a shack, paid for by the grown-up Kev many years later. The name of the river? Wasn't it Robert E. Lee?

Mrs. Plansky, at the wheel of her car but still in the driveway, pulled up a map of Macdee on her phone. Lucrecia was driving away, still in sight, with her dad and Clara in the backseat, like Lucrecia was a chauffeur. Clara seemed to lick her finger and dab at something on her dad's face just as the car disappeared around the bend onto the highway. Meanwhile there were several rivers and streams in and around Macdee, none of them named Robert E. Lee. But one of the streams, rather minor although it seemed to connect to the Intracoastal and eventually the sea, was called Stonewall Creek.

"Let us cross over the river and rest under the shade of the trees," she said, his last words being pretty much all she could remember about Stonewall Jackson, other than the fact that he was a great fighter. Putting aside for the moment what he'd been fighting for, Mrs. Plansky knew that a great fighter was now what she had to be, a sort of Stonewall Plansky. She smiled a certain little smile she had, a smile of self-amusement, seen during her whole lifetime by no one, not even Norm—although right now she did have the feeling of being watched. She glanced over at the passenger seat where Tee-Tee lay, and yes, Tee-Tee's golden eyes seemed pointed in her direction. That was fine. Mrs. Plansky was not letting Tee-Tee out of her sight, and maybe Tee-Tee was having similar thoughts about her. Tee-Tee was some sort of god, of course, which she'd known the moment she saw her.

A dirt road ran between a golf course, abandoned and overgrown, and Stonewall Creek. After the golf course came a trailer park, an enormous cement slab that might have once been a warehouse floor but which now was cracked and weedy, and a stand of oak trees, many showing hurricane damage. On her right, the south side, Stonewall Creek flowed on unchanged, murky blue and slow. After a mile or two the road narrowed, grew ruttier, and came to an end by a dead palm tree, its one remaining leaf brown and dried out. She hadn't passed anything that could be called a bungalow.

A Ford pickup, many decades old and faded colorless by the sun, stood under the tree. Mrs. Plansky parked beside it and got out of the car. A mosquito bit the back of her neck. She opened the trunk, found a can of bug spray, and sprayed herself. A mosquito bit the back of her neck.

She examined the pickup. It was very clean, inside and out. Nothing on the seats, front or back, and the bed was empty. It smelled of fish.

A narrow path led onward, meaning east, from the palm tree. It was flanked on both sides by hardwoods, their trunks scarred in places and their branches sometimes meeting overhead to form a canopy and make things shadowy down below. Mrs. Plansky locked her car. Then, with Tee-Tee in her bag and the bug spray in her hand, she started along the path.

The population of the whole state was what? Closing in on thirty million? But after only a few steps Mrs. Plansky felt alone in the world, and not in a bad way at all. So many problems sprouted from inside the human heart, individually and en masse. Take away humans and presto! This lone human trod on, stumbling once or twice on tree roots crossing the path, which swung away from Stonewall Creek for half a mile or so and then curved back to the creek, or more accurately, she saw, the creek curved back to her. These woods, this creek, were beautiful in a shady, buggy way, but without humans to share them with what was the point? On the other hand—

Mrs. Plansky stopped short. Up ahead lay a clearing and in that clearing stood a small single-story house, light blue with dark blue shutters and a dark blue door. In fact, a bungalow. A small front lawn that needed mowing led down to a pier extending thirty or forty feet into the creek. Tied to the pier, bow facing the creek bank, was a yacht with a tall tuna tower. She began moving toward it, but as though under a spell. This was not a generic yacht with a tall tuna tower. It was, quite specifically, a Bertram 50S. And not just that, but white with crimson trim. White with crimson trim? Her heart was pounding. *Lizette*? Yes, *Lizette* in every single way. She began to run, losing her grip on the bug spray in her haste. *Lizette*, somehow not exploded but . . . but . . . but were they right, Detective Leffers and Dr. Prindle? Was she a madwoman after all?

Mrs. Plansky ran onto the pier, a clumsy, panting run, bow to stern alongside the yacht, which close up was still *Lizette* in every way she remembered. She reached the stern, whipped around to see the name.

Not *Lizette*. The name on the boat, painted not in gold, as *Lizette* had been, but in light blue with dark blue outlines, was *Somethin' Fishy*.

She stood there, staring at that name, hands on hips, her breathing refusing to get back to normal. Sounds came from inside the boat cabin. Someone was moving in there. Was it Kev? Didn't it have to be? Kev would now appear and make sense of everything.

The cabin door opened and a man stepped out. Not Kev. This man was somewhat older and also weather-beaten, which Kev was not. He was lean, leathery, bald with a white ponytail, wore cutoff khaki shorts, a plaid flannel shirt that looked much too warm for a day like this, and nothing on his feet. In one hand he held a cigarette—actually, as she smelled right away, a joint. In the other hand was a big bloody knife.

He looked her up and down, quite brazenly. But she must have been imagining that. Mrs. Plansky hadn't been looked at up and down in some time. If ever.

"Hey, there," he said.

"Hello," said Mrs. Plansky. "I didn't mean to disturb you."

"No disturbance." He dismissed that idea with a wave of the knife.

"I'm looking for Kev Dinardo's cousin Huey. Kev's a friend of mine."

"Yeah?" He looked her up and down again, for sure and perhaps with more interest this time.

"A tennis friend," Mrs. Plansky said.

"Then you must be pretty damn good. Kev's pretty damn good." He crossed the deck, leaned way over the side, swished the knife in the water, and wiped the blade on his shorts. "I'm Huey," he said. "Who do I have the pleasure?"

"My name's Loretta. Loretta Plansky."

"Well, I'll be damned."

"Excuse me?"

"Wanna see something?"

"I don't really—"

"Hang on to this."

He laid the knife on the gunwale and handed her the joint. Mrs. Plansky held it carefully, like it was dangerous. How ridiculous! She was quite familiar with joints, had smoked more than one, some decades ago.

"Welcome to take a hit offa it," Huey said. "I got no diseases. Not the kind you can catch, anyways. That I know of."

Meanwhile he was removing his flannel shirt. He hung it on the rail and turned sideways, with surprising, even artistic grace, a bit like a runway model on display. On his arm—a muscular arm for a man his age—was a series of tattoos, from shoulder to wrist. They were pretty much the same: plump red hearts, the color more vibrant as she scrolled down. The only difference was in the names inked in black across each heart. For example, the one closest to the shoulder, which Mrs. Plansky took to be the first, was Dollie. He pointed to the third one down, on the meatiest curve of his biceps, and said, "Feast your eyes."

The name was Loretta.

"Love of my frickin' life," Huey said. "She even looked like you. Younger, o' course, considerable. And not so . . ."

He made a motion with his hands suggesting . . . surely not heftiness? Really? Who would do a thing like that?

"We was what?" Huey went on. "Twenty-nine? And the whole issue of being somewhat related. There's that. But I still think of her. Ain't that how it goes?"

He held out his hand. Mrs. Plansky had no idea why. Then it struck her. The joint. She gave it back. Huey demolished most of what was left in one mighty inhale and spun the butt into the water. He glanced around. "What a day, huh?"

"Yes," said Mrs. Plansky, "but—"

"But you're here on business, looking for Kev."

"That's right."

"Well, I ain't seen him, not in months." He looked into her eyes. His were faded blue, like old denim. "Is something wrong?"

"I think so."

"Come aboard, Loretta." He reached out to help her. Huey turned out to be enormously strong, practically lifting her over the rail with just that one hand.

"Coffee?" Huey said. "Also there's doughnuts. Pretty much what we got."

"Coffee would be nice," said Mrs. Plansky.

They were in the galley of *Somethin' Fishy*. On the counter lay the remains of a grouper, the largest she'd ever seen, decapitated and partially filleted. Huey flipped it over and sliced the fillet off the other side with one very quick motion of his big knife.

"Cream and sugar?"

"Black's fine."

"Yeah? Never met a woman who took her coffee black." He filled two mugs. "There a Mr. Plansky?"

"Not anymore."

He clinked the mugs together and gave her one. "Sorry for your loss."

"Thank you."

He took a sip, stealing a quick glance at her over the rim of his mug. "You and Kev an item?"

"We're friends. I'm very worried about him."

"How come? Is he sick?"

"No, nothing like that. And my son's caught up in it, too." Mrs. Plansky started in on her story, leaving out that kiss on the dock, which exerted a powerful force on her that she was reluctant to explain to herself, to say nothing of Huey. Mrs. Plansky did her best to keep things coherent, but soon he was slumping and taking some rather lengthy blinks. She hurried along, skipping the tennis match with Lizette and ending with Ray and kidnapping and Fairbanks and how no one in authority believed her.

After that there was silence, Huey sitting trancelike and a few drops of grouper blood dripping off the counter and falling to the deck. Without looking he reached into a paper bag, grabbed a doughnut—chocolate with sprinkles—and chomped off half of it. He seemed to come back to life.

"Any questions?" Mrs. Plansky said. "Do you know any of these people—Ray, Rudy, Ducky, my son?"

"Nope," he said. "Just Kev. 'Cept there is a Ducky in these parts, come to think. What'd he look like?"

"An older fellow, very skinny."

"Look you in the eye?"

"No."

Huey nodded. "Ducky Macdee. Didn't know he was out of the can."

"Macdee?" she said.

"Last in the line that founded the town. What's that thing where it all runs out of energy and goes to crap?"

"Entropy?"

"Sounds right. That's Ducky. We had a little set-to once." Huey's faded old eyes brightened.

"What was he in prison for?"

"This time? Couldn't tell you. You name it. But go back to the statue thing. Can you draw me a picture?"

"I can do better than that." She took Tee-Tee from her bag and set her on the counter, well clear of the grouper remains.

"Well, well, you don't say." Huey picked up Tee-Tee and kissed the top of her head. "Long time no see."

"Meaning . . . ?"

"Hell, was me who found her. Gave it to Kev as a gift. The least I could do." He made a motion taking in the surroundings. "Look what he done for me."

"I gather you did a lot for him," Mrs. Plansky said. "When he was young."

"He tell you that?"

"No. It was Lizette."

"Lizette. Man oh man. I only met her a couple times, but jeez." He gave Tee-Tee a gentle pat on the butt. "I took Kev in, you might say. I was still practically a youngster myself, but self-supporting. Anyways, he took off in life. I'm proud of that. Don't even understand what he does." He held up index finger and thumb, with just a little space between them. "Tiny numbers, tiny, tiny, multiplied by who knows what. And then—blast off." He put Tee-Tee on the counter, not quite where Mrs. Plansky had placed her but instead on a blood smear. "Wanna know the story? About me finding her, I'm talkin' about."

"That was my next question."

"Remember that map? In your story?"

"Yes."

He laughed. "Loved that part—the door code, the fish. Mind me askin' how old you are?"

"Going on seventy-two."

He studied her face then nodded, making no remark about how she looked much younger, not a day over sixty-five, that kind of thing.

"First you gotta know that I fished all over. Not just Florida waters, but the Bahamas, Turks and Caicos, Puerto Rico, on down. Then there's the fact how much Kev loved pirate stories way back when. So one day, this was a few years ago, after he gave me this, the boat, I was down in the Jarndyces, where you had that crash. A hurricane blew through the week before, trashed the whole chain, waves washing right over some of them cays. I had me a little problem with the electronics, needed a safe anchorage for a couple of days, a hurricane hole. To fix the damn thing, see what I mean? And there's only one good anchorage in the Jarndyces."

He opened a drawer and took out a notepad and a pen. "That map of yours—look something like this?"

Huey, in a firm quick hand, drew a triangle with a notch in one side.

"Yes," Mrs. Plansky said. "Is that one of the Jarndyces?"

"Lady Cay. That there notch is the hurricane hole."

"Lady Cay? Next to No-Name?"

"You got it."

"I didn't see that notch."

"Can't. Not from No-Name. It's on the other side. Follow me so far?"

"I think so."

Huey nodded. "You got brains. Some guys like women with brains, some don't. Ever notice that?"

"I have."

"Whaddya think it means?"

"The heart has its reasons."

His head went back. "Wow. There's the proof." His attention returned to the sketch of Lady Cay. "Meanwhile I got my engines in pieces—goddam alternator problem in both of them, but different if you can believe it—but I'm also exploring the place. All kind of shells washed up from the storm, and I got me a collection over at the house. Anyways, it was on one of those little explorings where she turned up." He pointed to Tee-Tee.

"So you drew the map and marked the spot?"

"Exactly right! Are you somethin' else or what?" Consciously or unconsciously, Huey scratched his Loretta tattoo. "It was near a big ol' palm tree. The storm ripped away this bejeezus hunk of coral and there she was down the hole, stickin' up from the mud, upside down."

"Was there anything else in the hole?"

"Just what Kev said! The very words! Nope, and I dug around some. But he got into doin' research and found a story about this Spanish treasure ship, *Nuestra* somethin', somethin', going down in a storm. No proof it was ever near Lady Cay, but you know Kev."

Mrs. Plansky was pretty sure she did not know Kev, but she left that to one side and pointed to Tee-Tee. "Maybe not proof but she comes from Peru."

"Yeah? News to me. I was thinkin' Mexico all the way. Anyways Kev jumped on this buried treasure idea. It's in his psychology from when he was a boy. But that's me just blowin' smoke on what I know nothin' about. My opinion on wrecks around Lady Cay— there I know a little bit and I can tell you they all gonna get sucked out to deep water. I'm talkin' deep. Did you know the continental shelf's practically walking distance from the east side?"

"I did."

His eyebrows, mangy and white as ivory, rose. "What other surprises you got in store?"

"Absolutely none."

Huey tilted his head to one side, maybe trying for a new angle on her. "Boilin' it down—wrecks? Sure thing. This little lady washed up from one. But nobody buried her. She was all alone in that hole and I dug deep. We're not talkin' buried treasure."

"But Kev didn't believe you?"

"Nope, not about there bein' nothing else. He's makin' plans for full-scale buried treasure. I'm talkin' archaeology."

"Making plans?"

"Rome wasn't built in whatever it was. Gonna take time. Gov'ment bureaucrats!" He slid open a galley window and spat through the opening. "Bahamian gov'ment bureaucrats, to boot!"

"Kev's coordinating with the Bahamian government?"

"What I just said."

So many moving parts and now they were speeding up. For a moment or two, maybe more, Mrs. Plansky got lost in their mechanism. Then she felt Huey's gaze.

"You're sayin' Kev's missing?" he said.

She nodded. "And Jack. Missing and in trouble."

"How about we swing over to that beer place? See who's kickin' around."

Mrs. Plansky didn't think anyone would be kicking around. She couldn't have explained why, except it had something to do with what had happened to Ray, and the different ways the word might spread. But as for the next step, she had no ideas.

"Okay," she said.

"Hang tight," Huey said, leaving the galley and disappearing in the cabin. She assumed he was getting his shoes, but when he returned he was still barefoot, but now carrying a rifle.

"What's that?" she said.

"Henry lever action twenty-two."

"I meant is it really necessary?"

"Huh? Din't you tell me gators was in the mix?"

"Yes, but . . ."

"And maybe kidnappers?"

"Bring it," Mrs. Plansky said.

A few minutes later they were on the path that led back to Huey's old pickup, walking side by side, Huey shoeless and with the rifle on a strap over his shoulder. At one point the path narrowed and they proceeded single file, Mrs. Plansky in the lead.

"Some guys," he said, "don't mind a lady with a . . . what would you call it? A considerable back end? I'm in that camp."

"We all have our little peccadillos," Mrs. Plansky said without turning, perhaps putting too much emphasis on "little."

THIRTY

The white gravel lot in front of Drop Shot Brewers was empty. Mrs. Plansky and Huey climbed the stairs to the porch. The old farmhouse was silent. A sign on the door read: CLOSED FOR RENOVATIONS.

Huey banged on the door. "Hey! Open up!"

Nothing happened. But then? A footstep? Very faint. She glanced at Huey.

"You hear somethin'?" he said.

"I'm not—"

Then came a sound like the closing of a door, distant and furtive.

"Son of a bitch!" said Huey. "Makin' a run for it out the back way."

He hurried down the stairs and headed around the building. Huey's hurrying speed turned out to be not very fast and Mrs. Plansky caught up almost right away. She reached the back of Drop Shot Brewers first, in time to see Ducky running across a weedy field, a waddly run perhaps only slightly faster than Huey's. At the end of the field stood what looked like an equipment shed, backing onto a dirt road. Beside the shed sat a battered old van. Ducky already had the keys out. Mrs. Plansky saw them glittering in his hand.

Behind her, Huey called out, "Stop, you dumb asshole, else I'll blow your head off."

Ducky did not stop. If anything he ran faster, or at least put more energy into it.

"Had your warning," Huey said.

Mrs. Plansky turned to him. He was already taking aim. "Please don't shoot."

"Want him to get clean away?"

She didn't want that. "Aim for the legs," she said.

"Do I look like Annie Oakley?"

Huey pulled the trigger. There was a bang, not very loud, and Ducky cried out and crumpled a step or two from the old van.

Ducky lay moaning on the ground, writhing a bit from time to time. When Mrs. Plansky managed to get the left pant leg of his overalls rolled up, they all saw that the bullet had made a shallow groove alongside the calf, taking out some skin and flesh, but not actually penetrating.

"Jesus H," Huey said. "Almost missed. Got a mind to walk back there and give it another whirl."

"Perhaps some other time," said Mrs. Plansky.

"Almost missed?" Ducky said. "Then how come I'm bleeding to death?"

"Get up," said Huey.

Ducky just moaned and writhed some more. There was some blood, true, like from a shaving cut. Huey had an emergency medical kit in the old Ford. Mrs. Plansky fetched it and dabbed hydrogen peroxide on the wound. Ducky cried out and twisted around to look.

"I'm still bleeding! Bleeding like a stuck pig."

Mrs. Plansky cut off a length of bandage but before she could apply it, Huey said, "Don't you have some questions? First, if you see what I mean?"

"Good idea," said Mrs. Plansky.

"Oh my God!" Ducky said. "Withholding medical treatment? That's a direct whatchamacallit of the Geneva thing!"

"Question one," Mrs. Plansky said. "Where are they?"

"You won't get a peep out of me," Ducky said.

"If we had us some salt we could rub it in the wound," said Huey.

"But you don't."

"I could get a stick," Huey said. "Poke around in there."

"Where's who?" said Ducky real quick.

"Kev Dinardo and my son."

"Who's your son?"

"Jack Plansky."

"It's all his fault."

"How so?" said Mrs. Plansky.

Ducky gazed at her, blinked a few times, and tried again. "Whoa! What the hell are you doing here anyways?"

"Where should I be?"

Ducky clamped his mouth shut. Mrs. Plansky slipped her bag off her shoulder and started rummaging around. "Where is that saltshaker?" she said.

"Very funny. Who has a saltshaker in her bag?"

"Restaurant souvenir collectors." Mrs. Plansky rummaged some more. "I know it's in here somewhere."

"You'd really do that?" Ducky said. "Pour salt in my wound?"

"She's lookin' forward to it," said Huey. "You don't know this gal."

Ducky shrank back, arms rising in terror. "No, no, anything but that. I'll talk, I'll talk. Word of honor."

"So talk," Huey said.

"She should be, well, maybe passed away, Huey. This here gal of yours. DOA if she didn't give up the map. Or maybe even if she did. She's not too popular around these parts, what with all her meddling. Ray's the type who blows his lid sometimes. But Rudy's more dangerous. More the type who enjoys dishing out pain."

"You've seen him do that?" Mrs. Plansky said.

Ducky nodded but did not meet her gaze.

"To whom?" she said.

"He was kinda pissed when you turned up. Following him, like."

"Kev was here?" Mrs. Plansky said, her voice rising on its own.

"Not just him."

"Jack, too?"

Ducky stared at the ground, answer enough.

"How come you've always been a douche, Ducky?" Huey said.

Ducky shrugged one of those hey-what-can-you-do shrugs.

"And how did you even get involved with these guys?"

"Ray and Rudy? Give me a tough one! They needed somewheres to set up the brewery. All this here, land and buildings, was mine. I sold it to them."

"No way you still owned this spread."

"Did, too. Well, the bank, plus all this foreclosure issue. But Mr. Dinardo straightened it all out."

"Kev wrote the check to the bank?" Huey said.

"Pretty much. This was all about the beer business. Ray and Rudy were the experts, Mr. D was interested in getting into it, Jack put them together, and you're lookin' at employee number one. But there was a side deal, just between Mr. D and Jack. Seems like Mr. D wanted to give Jack—a real nice guy, miss, but not the type for gettin' tied to the Rudys and Rays of this here world—a, um . . . where was I?"

"Kev wanted to give Jack something," Mrs. Plansky said.

"Right, read my mind. He wanted to give Jack a leg up, or a fresh start, somethin' of that nature. Not that he wasn't a success. Tennis equipment? Was that it? But Jack was broke. Mr. D had this plan for just two of them, the side deal. It was all about some hidden treasure down in the Bahamas. Top secret, meaning Rudy and Ray were supposed to be in the dark. But Rudy has these feelers in his brain, and one night over drinks with Jack, man-to-man, like, he got the story out of him. Rudy holds his liquor real well. Jack's the other kind. That's how it's all Jack's fault, where we started. So there you go. How about bandaging me up and we'll be on our merry separate ways, no charges pressed?"

"Charges?" said Huey.

"You did shoot me, Huey. Still against the law in this county, last I heard."

Huey was holding the rifle muzzle down and didn't change that position at all, but he did seem to tighten his grip on it.

"But let's not get ahead of ourselves," Ducky said. "What else do you need to know? Ask me anything."

"What happened after Rudy found out about the treasure?" Mrs. Plansky said.

"They told Mr. D they wanted in, Rudy and Ray, I'm talkin' about. Wanted all the details, especially about the map part. Mr. D said no. That's when the rough stuff started. Ray's your guy when it comes to explosives, learned in the service."

"He blew up Kev's boat?" Mrs. Plansky said.

"Just to get his attention, like. And maybe there was some other explosion. By then I was mostly on my lonesome around here. But before that, Rudy and Ray grabbed Jack as a sort of hostage, and told Mr. D to come up here and bail him out. Tell a soul and Jack was a goner, kind of thing. Then they grabbed him, too, locked 'em both in the shed."

He gestured with his thumb at the toolshed behind him. She'd been so close! Mrs. Plansky felt faint, wanted something to hold on to. There was nothing. She steadied herself.

"It got a might physical, like I mentioned," Ducky was saying, "not that I witnessed any of that personal. Mr. D ended up sayin' where to find the map, a fountain in his house, if I remember. They'd already been to the house, trashed it, but they missed the fountain. When they tried again, it wasn't there. Ray went kind of bananas on Mr. D after that, but Rudy got the idea someone else took the map. If so, cops might be in the picture PDQ, so Rudy had this idea of making it all nice again at Mr. D's place. Then there's the airplane angle. This reporter working on the treasure thing tried to get in touch with Mr. D. Rudy took the call on Mr. D's phone, like he was Mr. D, and got this invite on some plane trip to the Bahamas. Well, you can guess what Ray did after that. Then when you ended up still alive, Mrs., um, Plansky, they got to thinkin' you had the map. Somehow, in spite of being an old lady such as . . ." He caught a look on Huey's face. "A mature female such as yourself, and all. So the plan was for Ray to handle the map department while Rudy took Mr. D and Jack and got started. Corporate type division of labor, if you follow."

"Got started on what?" said Mrs. Plansky.

"Why, the digging," Ducky said. "Mr. D knew the general area. Time waits for no man."

Mrs. Plansky and Huey exchanged a glance, then nodded at each other at the same instant. Were they some kind of team, even a dangerous one? If so, how timely!

She knelt. "Let's get you bandaged up," she told Ducky. "Then you're coming with us."

"Huh? You can't make me."

"It's your one and only chance to stay out of the can," Huey said.

"What the hell? You're not even the law."

"Say hello to how things work," said Huey.

Huey steered *Somethin' Fishy* down Stonewall Creek to a river and then to the Intracoastal, stopping to fuel up at a marina with ocean access on the east side. Mrs. Plansky offered to pay for the fill-up, of course, the amount turning out to be rather shocking.

"Nice calm day," Huey said, as they hit open water. "Be there in eight hours, tops."

"My goodness," said Mrs. Plansky, who'd been expecting maybe half that, although clearly for no good reason. "Should we call in the authorities?"

"How are they doing so far?" Huey laughed and patted the console. "This baby's got the V-12's. Maybe you didn't cotton onto that."

"I did not."

"Care to take a guess at the cruising speed?"

"I'm sure it's remarkable."

"Forty knots!"

"Wow!"

"Heh heh. Maybe take it down a notch or two over the Gulf Stream. Might get a little snappy. Care to put your feet up for a spell? Master stateroom's all made up."

"I'd like to put my feet up, too," Ducky said.

"You're first mate," said Huey. "First mate stays here in the cockpit with me."

"I can't swim," Ducky said. "I get seasick."

"Whaddya know! The exact qualifications."

Mrs. Plansky went into the master stateroom up in the bow, sat on the bed, gazed through the porthole at the sea unreeling by. She worried about all the obvious possibilities, then moved on to the more obscure ones. After a while she lay down. The bedding was clean and the pillows smelled of aftershave, the same aftershave that Norm had used. It came in a green bottle with a silver cap but she couldn't remember the name. She closed her eyes. How tired she was, through and through! Sleep was what she needed. It wouldn't come. The light through the porthole changed from blue to orange. After quite a long time she realized her hands were balled into fists, squeezed tight. She opened them. The ocean, with a combination of rocking and bouncing—like one of those high-tech swaddling cradles for infants, with the personalized aftershave add-on—put her to sleep.

The motion changed, all its components ramping way down. Mrs. Plansky opened her eyes. It was dark in Huey's master stateroom. She sat up, then crept forward on her hands and knees to the porthole. Nighttime with a bright moon high above reflected thousands and thousands of times on the waves below. In the middle distance, meaning just two or three miles away, rose a low dark shape with others like it strung out on either side. She thought she could make out something tall and narrow rising on the nearest low dark shape. Would that be the lone palm tree on Lady Cay? Her pulse sped up at once.

She walked out of the cabin and into the cockpit. Huey was at the wheel and Ducky was in the fetal position, sleeping on the deck. Huey smiled at her, his remaining teeth the color of moonlight. There were dark patches under his eyes and his face looked drawn and pale.

"Get some shut-eye?" he said, his voice low.

"Yes, thank you," she told him, almost in a whisper. *Somethin'*
Fishy was keeping its voice low as well, just a soft rumble. Their speed
was nothing like forty knots, maybe no more than five or six. "Are
you all right?"

"No complaints." He gestured with his chin. "See what's up
ahead?"

"I do."

"Caught a light flash a couple times."

"Is it late?"

"Three forty-two."

"What are they doing up at this hour?"

"We'll know soon enough," Huey said.

Lady Cay came closer and closer. A light flashed near the palm
tree. Huey throttled back and back, finally into neutral.

"Take the wheel," he said. "I'm going forward to drop the anchor."

"What do you want me to do?"

"Fish me out, case I fall in."

Huey moved onto the foredeck, not like a young man, but at least
like the kind of old man who knew what he was doing. He opened
the anchor locker, dropped the anchor almost splashlessly off the bow,
returned, and shut down the engines. Then he went over to Ducky
and gave him a kick, none too gentle.

Ducky sat up and began a complaint.

"Zip it. What happens now is I lower the dingy and we take it
real quiet into shore. After that it's single file, Mrs. P, you, me. No
noise, no talking. Got it?"

"I need to pee," Ducky said.

"Hold it till we're on the beach."

"I can't."

"No talking."

Huey lowered the dive platform off the stern, then got the dinghy
over the side and tugged it back with the bowline. Mrs. Plansky

climbed in first, then Ducky, Huey last, the Henry .22 now strapped to his shoulder. He handed the dinghy paddle to Ducky.

"Take us in."

"I don't know how."

"No talking."

Ducky paddled them into the beach, a distance of only thirty yards or so, although it seemed to take a long time. The beach looked bright white in the moonlight. Mrs. Plansky felt exposed.

"Drag 'er up," Huey said.

Ducky dragged the dinghy free of the water.

"Take your piss," said Huey.

Ducky took the longest piss Mrs. Plansky had ever witnessed, and as a wife, mother, and grandmother she'd witnessed many.

"Let's go," Huey said. He pointed to a path Mrs. Plansky hadn't seen, leading inland off the beach. She went first.

The path, sandy with lots of crushed shells, led past some spiny bushes and up a low rise. The whole cay was visible. To the right she could see the notch, an incut from the ocean where another boat, smaller than *Somethin' Fishy*, lay at anchor. Far to the left was the channel with its rip current, and No-Name Cay on the other side. Straight ahead rose the lone palm tree. Something flashed from over there, a very brief and strange flash as though from below. In that split second of light, Mrs. Plansky made out a dark form at the base of the palm tree.

She glanced back. Ducky's eyes were open too wide, like he was close to full panic. Huey's eyes were narrowed and he now had the rifle in his hand. He gave her a curt nod, just part of their teamwork. Mrs. Plansky moved on.

Closer and closer, now at the top of the rise and descending. They came to a thicket of sea grapes off to one side. Mrs. Plansky moved behind it. The others followed. They gazed down the little hill.

The palm tree stood in a small clearing. Nearby was a dark round hole in the ground. A light flashed from down in there. And then a voice from the same place.

"Did I say it was break time? I don't remember that."

Then came a thump. The voice was Rudy's. The thump was something bad.

"I don't like this," Ducky whispered.

"Shut your goddam mouth," Huey whispered right back.

The dark form at the base of the palm tree shifted, now more in the moonlight. The dark form was in fact a man, sitting on the ground, tied to a tree. He turned his head in their direction. Kev. His nearest eye, the left, was swollen fully shut.

"Ducky," Huey said, mouthing his speech more than just whispering. "Go."

"What do I say again?" Ducky's voice was pretty much at normal volume.

"'Ray got the map but he's in bad shape. Follow me.' It's simple. What's wrong with you?" He gave Ducky a push. Now Kev was looking their way, beyond doubt. Mrs. Plansky and Huey crouched behind the sea grape bushes. Ducky tottered on down the path. Huey raised the rifle to firing position. Was he panting a little bit? She wasn't sure.

Ducky drew even with the palm tree. He glanced Kev's way and said, "Evening, Mr. D."

Mrs. Plansky refused to believe she'd heard that. Ducky reached the hole in the ground, leaned over it, and spoke, his words not clear to her. Nothing happened after that for maybe a whole minute. Then Rudy appeared in a sort of stop-motion way, like he was climbing a ladder, which turned out to be the case. He stepped out of the hole, a flashlight sticking out of the back pocket of his chinos, pulled up the ladder, and took a careful scan all around, his gaze passing over the sea-grape screen and moving on. Rudy looked immaculate, like a trim county-clubber about to play eighteen, except for how the moonlight shone in his eyes, ice-cold and intense.

He followed Ducky across the clearing and onto the path but passed him almost right away. Ducky began lagging farther and farther behind, which wasn't in the plan. Rudy came striding up the path, closer and closer. Huey knelt in firing position right next to her. Any moment now he would say "Freeze," and stand up, the rifle pointed at Rudy, unmissable at that range. Rudy kept coming. The expression on his face was a combination of negatives: aggression, confusion, anger, suspicion.

Now, thought Mrs. Plansky. Now! She glanced over at Huey, who according to the plan should have been rising. Instead his eyes had gone blank. He sagged over and lay on his side, letting go of the rifle and clutching his chest with both hands. Rudy hurried right on by, revealing a gun in the waistband of his pants. Ducky stopped where he was, ten or fifteen yards behind. He peered at the sea-grape screen, slowly backed away, then started running off deeper into the interior of Lady Cay.

Mrs. Plansky knelt by Huey, put her hand on his shoulder. He was trembling. "Huey. What's wrong?"

"Goddam ticker." His voice was high and feathery. "Take the rifle. Go."

"But—"

"Go."

Was there even a choice? Mrs. Plansky took the rifle. She'd never fired a gun of any kind but like all moviegoers had seen plenty of gunplay. How hard could it be? With the rifle strapped over one shoulder, muzzle down, and her bag on the other, she walked quickly down the path to the clearing. An idea hit her at once: Kev would know all about rifles. She hurried over to him.

"Loretta? My God, what's going on?"

Without thinking, she kissed his forehead and said, "Do you know how to handle a rifle?"

Kev blinked a few times, like he was trying to get up to speed. "Yes, but . . ."

Right, of course. He was chained to the tree, arms tight to his sides, a padlock fastening the ends of the chain together. "Where's the key?"

"He's got it."

"So, um . . ."

"Get Jack! Go!"

Mrs. Plansky rose and ran to the hole in the ground. She looked down. The depth surprised her, seven feet, maybe more. Down at the bottom was a steeply sloping pile of freshly dug sand, a pool of briny-smelling water, and Jack, wearing only shorts and gazing at nothing. He looked up.

"Mom? Mom!"

He rose, not easily. Normal Jack would have been able to rise with ease, but normal Jack was not so skinny, and didn't have a big purple bruise on his belly and a swollen jaw. Mrs. Plansky put down the rifle and lowered the ladder into the hole.

"Climb up, Jack. Can you do it?"

Normal Jack could have climbed a ladder, especially one leaning like this, with no hands, but this Jack could get up only one rung before falling back. Mrs. Plansky placed the rifle on the edge of the hole and made her way down the ladder. At the bottom, the briny smell was now much stronger—reminding her of a sinkhole that had opened up on a playground not far from Little Pine Lake—and the wet sand she stood on was somehow sucking at her feet. "Darling," she said, and hugged him for a second or two, before giving him a gentle tug toward the ladder.

"Up we go."

Jack stepped onto the first rung. She steadied him and pushed him up at the same time. Rung by rung they mounted the ladder, Jack seeming to gather strength toward the end. He reached the top, fell forward onto the ground. Mrs. Plansky was two rungs away from the top herself, her head and shoulders above ground level, when she heard someone fast on the move, and Rudy appeared at the top of the rise. He paused, took in everything, his eyes like two miniature moons, stony white, then drew his gun and kept coming, now at a full sprint. He fired a shot. It pinged off a rock, somewhere in the bushes.

Mrs. Plansky picked up the rifle. She held it the way she'd seen people hold rifles, aimed it at Rudy, coming right at them, and pulled the trigger. It wouldn't pull. She recalled there was something called a safety but couldn't find anything that fit the bill. And now Rudy was almost on top of them, trying to keep his gun aimed at Jack, counting this time on a point-blank shot. That was unthinkable. What if she simply levered this lever thing and tried again? Like so.

BAM!

The earth seemed to tremble beneath her. Rudy cried out—his gun pinwheeling into the night—and lost his balance. So did Mrs. Plansky, as the recoil, which she hadn't taken into account, knocked her off the ladder. The rifle flew out of her hands and she fell to the bottom of the hole, landing on the slope of freshly dug sand, the breath knocked out of her. From above came thumping and grunting, the sounds of a struggle, maybe with a kick involved at the end, and a man came tumbling down, landing on his back with a splash in the water.

It was Rudy. One of his arms was bleeding slightly but otherwise he looked unharmed, if no longer presentable at the first tee. He got to his feet, his gaze never leaving her. The look was elemental, as though civilization hadn't happened. He raised his hands, curled for grappling, and stepped forward. He was going to strangle her. Mrs. Plansky tried to rise, tried to get into some sort of defensive position, but, oh, how slow she was, slow and weak! Rudy's lips turned up in a smile that scared her more than anything else that was happening. He took another step. All at once the bottom fell out. Not the whole bottom, maybe, but certainly the briny pool part. It emptied right out, all the water sucked away, and Rudy got sucked away with it, vanishing straight down into the earth in a flash, with just time for the beginnings of a nightmarish expression to twist his face.

Then the hole began to collapse on itself, a cave-in from all sides. Mrs. Plansky glanced down and saw she'd dropped her bag. It fell into blackness and disappeared.

"Mom! Mom! The ladder!"

Mrs. Plansky turned to the ladder, now on the move itself, got a hand on it, got a foot on it, tried to go up. Tee-Tee was in that bag. Tears welled up in her eyes. What would she do without Tee-Tee? Life was for the living, of course, as everyone knew. But still.

Mrs. Plansky heard water, now surging up from underneath. At the same time the earth around her seemed to be vanishing. Not so much that the hole was gone, more that everything was a hole, tilting her this way and that. Jack reached down and with all the strength left in him pulled her out of that geologic chaos. She crawled away, tears streaming down her face, tears she wiped away before anyone could see.

THIRTY-ONE

Mrs. Plansky took Jack in her arms. At first he was trembling, but it stopped after a minute or two. He squeezed her tight, although not very, on account of his weakened state.

"Oh, Mom." His heart beat against her chest like a hummingbird.

Huey appeared in the clearing, announced he'd found a forgotten nitro pill in his pocket, and was back to shipshape. He fetched bolt cutters off *Somethin' Fishy* and went to work on freeing Kev—Rudy turning out to have worked Jack and Kev one at a time, chaining the other between shifts. They shouted for Ducky but got no response and no one went to search for him. From time to time, Jack or Kev gave Mrs. Plansky gentle little pats on the arm or shoulder.

"Enough," she said.

Rescue showed up shortly after dawn: a Coast Guard helicopter, a Coast Guard cutter, and a Bahamian patrol boat. They asked lots of questions, first of everyone, meaning Jack, Kev, Huey, and Mrs. Plansky, but they ended up talking mostly to her. They examined the site of the cave-in, now filled with briny water almost to the top, took pictures, surrounded this and that with yellow tape. A Bahamian sailor found Ducky hiding in some bushes near the cut between Lady Cay and No-Name.

"What's the story with this fellow?" the sailor said.

There was a silence. A decision had to be made and Mrs. Plansky made it. "He's with us," she said. "He had a bit of a breakdown."

"The day he was born," Huey muttered, but no one heard him.

The medic helped Huey onto the helicopter, and also Jack because the medic suspected his jaw was broken. Ducky was assigned to the cutter. Kev, even though one of his eyes was still swollen shut, was going to take *Somethin' Fishy* back to Huey's place. He and Mrs. Plansky had a private conversation down on the beach.

"Coming with me?" he said.

Mrs. Plansky gazed into his eyes. Well, just the one. He really was a handsome man. She liked almost everything about him.

"I wanted it to be a surprise," he said. "Getting Jack involved in the *Nuestra Señora* business."

"Of course," said Mrs. Plansky. "But there's room on the helicopter and I think I've had enough boating for now."

He smiled that small, quickly vanishing smile of his, the one that flashed when he was struck by an unexpected insight. "Did our ship already sail, Loretta?"

She smiled back and gave him a peck on the cheek.

"You again?" said a Coast Guard officer as she boarded the helicopter.

The wedding of Chandler Wills Banning and Clara Dominguez de Soto y Camondo, held at the New Sunshine Golf and Tennis Club, was spectacular, if not very big. The Cuban musicians were fabulous and Hamish joined in, somehow getting a salsa sound out of his bagpipes. Mrs. Plansky danced, slowly with Huey, who still looked rather pale, and faster with Jack.

"Mom, I just don't know how I'll ever be able to thank—"

"Shut up and dance," said Mrs. Plansky.

Basil Nottage and his wife were among the invitees. Mrs. Plansky danced with him as well.

"Lady Cay's now an archaeology site, closed to all visitors," he said.

"But they're not going to find anything?"

Basil shook his head. "They just don't know it yet. Except for the one body—that might wash up somewheres."

Clara was the star of the show. Her wedding dress, custom made by a famous designer in Little Havana, was magnificent, and Mrs. Plansky understood why when she found out the cost. "Oh, and there's this," her dad had said, handing her the invoice. She herself had toyed with the idea of wearing her tropical blues, but had ended up in the silk floral dress she always wore on formal summer occasions, made for her years ago by a seamstress in Cranston, Rhode Island she'd known from childhood.

After it was over and most everyone had left, Mrs. Plansky and Lucrecia put their feet up and shared a bottle of champagne.

"We're making progress," Mrs. Plansky said.

"Oh?"

"About getting them into one of those assisted livings that take couples," Mrs. Plansky reminded her. What was this? Lucrecia, maybe the most straightforward person she knew, now not meeting her gaze? "The whole purpose of the wedding? Remember?"

Lucrecia took a big swig. "It turns out she loves your place."

"Well, it's much too small, so that's that."

"There is this one possibility of an addition."

"It's a condo, Lucrecia. I can't just put on an addition."

"Oh, for sure, for sure. But the board likes the plans. The fact that it's an end unit really inspired him."

"Who? And what board?"

"The architect. He's in Barcelona so it's all been remote, so far. And it's the condo board. If you ask me, I'd say they're eager to get involved with someone of his prestige."

Mrs. Plansky took a big swig herself and got to work on killing the bottle. The next day—with the condo all to herself, the happy couple on their honeymoon—she was shelving *Death in the Afternoon* when her copy of the treasure map fell out and drifted down to the floor.

*　*　*

Mrs. Plansky visited Val in the hospital. It was just the two of them. Val looked not too bad, maybe a little thinner. She lay in bed, eyes still closed but breathing on her own, and on an IV for her nutrition. Mrs. Plansky sat in a chair and took her hand. Val's pulse felt strong. The worry, Hamish had said, was on the mental side, not the physical.

"You're the one who should write this up," Mrs. Plansky said after ten minutes or so. She began filling Val in on everything. Even though she'd witnessed much of it and participated in some, it turned out to be hard! What a jumble! On and on she went, fumbling, backtracking, maybe even misremembering in a few places. She got so involved that she didn't notice right away that Val's eyes were open.

"Oh, my! Val?"

"Water," Val said.

Mrs. Plansky rushed over to the sink, filled a Dixie cup with water, started to prop Val's head gently up. Val raised her head by herself. Mrs. Plansky put the cup to her lips. Val took a small sip and then a big one. Mrs. Plansky sensed some change flowing through her.

Water. This whole story was mostly about water. What a thought!

"There's your lead," Mrs. Plansky said. "Water."

Val looked up. "Nice," she said. She turned her head, seemed to take in the surroundings. "Yes."

"Hello. Loretta?"

"Yes?"

"My name's Guillermo Something-or-Other." Of course he didn't say *Something-or-Other* instead spoke his real surname, a complicated one Mrs. Plansky didn't quite catch. "Melanie's an old friend and she's sponsoring my application to New Sunshine. She thinks our games—yours and mine—would be complementary."

"Does she?"

He laughed. "The truth is I saw you over on Court Four the other day and made the observation myself. But Melanie agreed. There's an eight o'clock mixed doubles round-robin tomorrow if you're interested. Be done by nine thirty before it gets too hot."

Mrs. Plansky tried to think of a reason to say no and failed. "Okay," she said.

"Great. I was thinking we could arrive a little early, say seven forty-five, and loosen up a bit. I'll bring the coffee."

"Okay."

"I take mine black. How about you?"

"Same," said Mrs. Plansky.

"Perfect. See you there."

"Thanks, Guillermo."

"Everyone calls me Bill."

"Bill," she said.

Fairbanks disappeared for days. Mrs. Plansky was thinking he'd taken over some other watery realm when she spotted him one morning. He was sunning himself on the muddy strip of shoreline bordering the myrtles that grew in front of the gazebo. How relaxed he looked! Yes, even regal, in a reptilian way. But wasn't there something reptilian about some kings? Take Henry VIII, for example.

Speaking of Henry VIII, Fairbanks's appearance had changed somewhat, like he'd grown, although not in length. It was more around the middle. He'd plumped up considerably, now seemed to be more than a little on the portly side. Like Santa. Well, not like Santa. That was ridiculous.

All at once he shifted a bit and seemed to be gazing her way. In fact, directly at her. Mrs. Plansky gave him a companionable little wave and went inside.

ACKNOWLEDGMENTS

I'm so happy to have such a superb team at Forge. Many thanks to Kristin Sevick, Troix Jackson, Libby Collins, Jennifer McClelland, Anthony Parisi, Linda Quinton, and Michael Segretto.

ABOUT THE AUTHOR

Diana Gray

SPENCER QUINN is the pen name of Peter Abrahams, the Edgar Award–winning author of many novels, including the *New York Times* and *USA Today* bestselling Chet and Bernie mystery series, *Mrs. Plansky's Revenge, The Right Side,* and *Oblivion,* as well as the *New York Times* bestselling Bowser and Birdie series for younger readers. He lives on Cape Cod with his wife, Diana, and his dog, Dottie.